PRAISE FOR

ENDANGERED

"White-kn... ...to read this
book if yo... ...selling author

"A terrific... ...fan of wild-
life descriptions, a spunky main character, and a great plot,
grab a copy of *Endangered* . . . Sam is the kind of outdoor
adventurer you love to root for and her budding relationship with FBI Special Agent Chase Perez is both realistic
and tension filled. As the clues to who done it pile up and
time runs out on a planned hunt to take out Sam's beloved
cougars, the pace quickens, the danger escalates, and the
suspense mounts . . . Well written and terrifically paced,
Endangered is a great read set in beautiful country with
characters readers will find fascinating."   —AnnArbor.com

"The first Summer Westin Mystery is a terrific wildlife
investigation in which the biologist and the Fed know time
is running out on the toddler and, perhaps, the cougars.
Their inquiry is filled with stunning twists while readers
will believe they are trekking the wild high country alongside the lead duo. With a nod to Anna Pigeon, readers will
enjoy going outdoors with Sam as their guide."
                                        —*Genre Go Round Reviews*

"Spellbinding . . . [With] old-fashioned nail-biting, stay-up-
late-to-see-what-happens suspense."
                                        —*Once Upon a Romance*

Berkley Prime Crime titles by Pamela Beason

ENDANGERED
BEAR BAIT
UNDERCURRENTS

UNDERCURRENTS

PAMELA BEASON

BERKLEY PRIME CRIME, NEW YORK

THE BERKLEY PUBLISHING GROUP
Published by the Penguin Group
Penguin Group (USA) Inc.
375 Hudson Street, New York, New York 10014, USA

USA / Canada / UK / Ireland / Australia / New Zealand / India / South Africa / China

Penguin Books Ltd., Registered Offices: 80 Strand, London WC2R 0RL, England
For more information about the Penguin Group, visit penguin.com.

UNDERCURRENTS

A Berkley Prime Crime Book / published by arrangement with the author

Berkley Prime Crime Books are published by The Berkley Publishing Group,
BERKLEY® PRIME CRIME and the PRIME CRIME logo are
trademarks of Penguin Group (USA) Inc.

For information, address: The Berkley Publishing Group,
a division of Penguin Group (USA) Inc.,
375 Hudson Street, New York, New York 10014.

ISBN: 978-0-425-25205-5

PUBLISHING HISTORY
Berkley Prime Crime mass-market edition / April 2013

PRINTED IN THE UNITED STATES OF AMERICA

10 9 8 7 6 5 4 3 2 1

Cover photos: *Pinnacle Rock* and *Galapagos Islands*
© Andrew Holt/Photographer's Choice/Getty Images; *Galapagos Shark*
© Scott Sansenbach/Flicker/Getty Images.
Cover design by Judith Lagerman.
Interior text design by Laura K. Corless.

ALWAYS LEARNING   **PEARSON**

To my sister Jeanine,
who can always find the silver lining.

ACKNOWLEDGMENTS

I'd like to thank my team at Berkley Prime Crime—Tom Colgan, Amanda Ng, Kayleigh Clark, and the many others whose names I do not know—for their work on my mystery series. My agent, Curtis Russell, always deserves a special acknowledgment for all his efforts on my behalf and for maintaining his enthusiasm about my writing. I also owe a special thank-you to my critique partner Christine Myers, for her help in making this a better book. And I want to salute all the conservation groups out there for their courageous efforts to preserve the wild places on our beautiful planet.

PROLOGUE

SAM Westin stared out her back window at the endless cold rain drizzling through the shaggy limbs of the Douglas firs. According to the calendar, the shortest day of the year had passed a week ago, but she couldn't discern any increase in daylight. Her tiny home office always felt like a dark, damp cave in December. And somehow, although she always swore not to let it happen, the holiday season had ambushed her again with its constant reminders of what she was missing. Family. Company parties. Year-end bonus pay. She envied her housemate Blake, who had happily blown his bonus on Christmas presents for his thirteen-year-old daughter and a rental tux for the fancy New Year's party he was attending at his company.

Most of the time Sam was content to be independent and self-employed. December was just a quiet boring period when she could do extra work. But this year, the economic recession had tag-teamed with her seasonal frustrations to make the days even more dismal. She had very little work lined up; and even less company to brighten the days. A week ago, on Christmas Eve, her FBI lover Chase had stayed overnight. Now he was off doing extended training in an undisclosed location. She wasn't sure they had parted on the best of terms, and she wouldn't have a chance to set things right until their next rendezvous in late February. So, here she was again on New Year's Eve without a man to kiss at midnight.

Sam turned back to her computer. On the screen was the terrible novel she was editing for her mechanic, Ralph, in exchange for replacing the brake pads on her Civic. It was a truly awful Army story, with too many bullets and too little plot. Ralph had hinted that he wanted to self-publish it. She had a feeling that his story was part memoir, so she needed to tread carefully. What the hell was she going to tell him? Why had she put herself in this position?

The answer was desperation. She had only three short articles on her work calendar for January. She'd volunteered to write articles for local nonprofits in the hope that making new contacts would lead to future pay, but volunteer work didn't pay the bills, which were rapidly stacking up. Laid-off employees got unemployment compensation; the out-of-work self-employed weren't even counted.

When her land line rang, she answered without looking at the caller ID. Any interruption was welcome at this point. "Westin."

"This is Tad Wyatt calling from Key Corporation."

Key Corporation? That was unexpected. A decade ago she had worked briefly for Key on an encyclopedia project that got axed after only a few months. The company hadn't called her since. She had never heard of Tad Wyatt.

"Summer," he began, revealing how little he knew about her by using her given name instead of her nickname. "We admired that speech you did for *The Edge* last year. That was amazing."

"It wasn't *for* them, they just sponsored me at the wildlife conference." Was that damn video of her still playing on YouTube?

"Whatever," Wyatt said. "That cougar thing you did before that was sweet, too. We really respect your work.

We'd like you to join our expedition to the Galápagos Islands."

The rain-soaked forest view outside her window was instantly replaced by a vision of a tropical beach. White sand. Turquoise water. Palm trees. Dolphins. The farthest south she had ever been was Puerto Vallarta. This guy wanted her to go to Ecuador? She fought to keep her voice calm and professional. "That sounds intriguing."

In recent years, she'd accidentally developed a reputation for death-defying stunts. No way was she adding serving as shark bait or bungee jumping into volcanoes to her list of credits. "What sort of project is this?"

Her cat Simon scratched on the doormat in front of the patio door. Holding the phone to her ear, she walked over and slid open the door. Simon stared at the pouring rain and twitched his tail, no doubt hoping for something better.

"You may know that recently, Key received some unjustified negative publicity about our charitable donations."

"I read about that." Key raked in billions in profits, but their only donations had been computers loaded with their own products, which served to extend Key's software domination around the globe. That history made the company CEO, Scott F. Key, seem especially gluttonous now that it had become trendy for the superrich to publicize their selfless gifts to charities.

"We want to show the world where our hearts really are, so we're supporting various worthy causes and featuring their projects on *Out There*."

Sam knew that *Out There* was Key's glitzy site featuring high-drama stories and peppered with links to other sites selling products that also profited Key in some way. It was about time *Out There* featured worthwhile content.

"Sounds like a good plan," she said, nudging Simon's backside with her foot. The cat dug his claws into the doormat. She closed the door, barely missing his whiskers. He glared, his green eyes full of resentment. Sam scooped him up and lifted him to the windowsill, where he had a good view of the chickadees gobbling seeds from the birdfeeder.

He twitched his tail and made chirping noises, sounding like a bird himself.

"We've got health projects in India and cooperative farming projects in Africa," Wyatt told her. "In the Galápagos, we're teaming up with the Natural Planet Foundation."

Yes! She pumped a fist in the air. The Natural Planet Foundation was not a showboat group looking to grab headlines. The organization conducted research studies on the health of ecosystems around the world. She often used their data in her environmental articles. "I'd be proud to work with NPF."

"I should explain that *half* our team in the Galápagos will work with a Ph.D. biologist from NPF to do a marine survey."

Even better. She was tired of being a solo act; human partners were a definite plus. Her mind conjured up a gray-bearded Ph.D. type. Bifocals. In her imagination, he had a kind smile. She'd won the Lotto! "How many people will be on the Galápagos team?"

"The marine biologist will work for NPF. You'll be *Out There*'s intrepid reporter in the field."

"What? *I* will be the whole team?" Maybe it wasn't a Lotto win after all. Why couldn't she ever land reasonable jobs?

"The NPF biologist will be there, and *Out There*'s readers will *think* we have two reporters in the islands. We're doing this with all our reporters now. We want you to write posts each day under two different names."

She should have known there'd be some sort of crazy catch to such a dream assignment. "Two posts every day?"

"Short posts—five hundred to seven hundred words each. With pictures or video. We'll supply you with state-of-the-art camera equipment, so it'll be easy to deliver the visuals. You excel at producing short, exciting articles, as we both know."

Wyatt was right. She did know how to do precisely

what he described. She'd done it plenty of times. He was promising a trip to Darwin's enchanted islands, land of giant tortoises and flightless cormorants. Marine iguanas. Penguins!

Remember the bills, her conscience nagged. "The pay?" she asked.

"A thousand dollars a day, plus expenses. The expedition begins February twelfth."

She moved back to her desk to grab her Nature Conservancy calendar. The February page featured a photo of a frozen waterfall. February twenty-second through the end of the month had a big red line through it under the words *Ski Trip with Chase*. She couldn't miss that. No matter what, they'd pledged to meet up then. "I have another assignment that begins February twenty-second. Will that work?"

"Of course," he said. "We're allotting a week for the project and travel time. It'll be like a vacation."

Sam didn't have to weigh the proposition long. On the minus side: schlepping around camera and computer equipment, meeting daily deadlines with punchy stories. On the plus side: the tropics, a like-minded teammate, exotic animals, and more money than she'd earned in the past three months. She could almost feel the sun on her skin now.

"So, a post every day about the islands by Wilderness Westin, expert hiker and kayaker," Wyatt prompted.

"No problem." The pseudonym still felt silly, but she'd used it off and on for a couple of years now. She *was* an experienced hiker and kayaker.

"And another by a new character that we'll create for the underwater adventures. You *are* a diver, right?"

"Ah." It was all she could get out. She quickly paged backward though the calendar, through the frost-covered ferns of January to the current date, December 31. A frozen waterfall suspended from a snow-topped cliff.

Almost six weeks before the expedition. She was a good

swimmer. She was an excellent photographer. She was used to working under difficult conditions.

"Summer? You still there? I asked if you're a certified diver."

How hard could it be to do her job underwater?

"Of course," she lied.

1

BY the time Sam finally stepped into the brilliant sunshine of the Galápagos Islands, she felt like she'd toured the entire Western Hemisphere in one day. She'd driven to Seattle in the wee hours of the morning, boarded a plane for Houston, then another for Guayaquil, and then another for Puerto Ayora. She'd barely had time to introduce herself over dinner to Dr. Daniel Kazaki before she'd fallen asleep. Now, only sixteen hours after touching down, she was preparing to jump into the Pacific Ocean with him.

She had looked forward to sun, but she wasn't quite prepared for the contrast between the Pacific Northwest and the equator. Daylight in the Galápagos was blinding, even from behind the polarized screen of her sunglasses. She blinked at the surroundings, feeling like a mole that had been suddenly unearthed. She hoped she wouldn't feel similarly exposed in the water. She'd passed her dive certification course with flying colors and done well in the underwater photography class. But today was the real test.

Her first posts at *Out There* were due tomorrow. She had this one day to pass herself off as an underwater pro. Or at least not reveal herself as an inept pretender. Last night at dinner, when she told Dan that all her dives had been in the Pacific Northwest, he said ominously, "Good, then you'll have no problem with the currents here."

She studied the water around their boat. Unlike the Pacific Northwest, there were no fields of bull kelp here to indicate the water's flow. "Have you explored this location before?" she asked Dan.

"Several times." Clad in a wetsuit unzipped to the navel, neoprene sleeves tied around his waist, he leaned against the side of the cabin cruiser. He nibbled the end of a pen, his brow wrinkled in concentration as he studied the clipboard he held. "It's easy; great for gear checkout."

Easy. Halleluiah! She picked up her digital camera and zoomed in on him. While he did have a kind smile and a few shallow wrinkles around his almond-shaped hazel eyes, Dr. Daniel Kazaki was in no way the gray-bearded academic she'd imagined. In fact, he was a few years younger than she was, and his muscles would have been the envy of many a high school gym class. Sam prayed she'd be able to keep up with him.

She pressed the shutter button. Dan looked up. He pulled the pen from his mouth and frowned at the tooth marks that dented the plastic. "Bad habit. You're not putting that on the front page?"

"It's a blog. It's up to the editors where the photos go. I'm just a peon."

"Impossible. I refuse to have a peon for a partner." He grinned. "Ready to go in?"

"Almost." She checked her regulator and buoyancy control device vest—BCD for short—for the tenth time, twisted the valves on her main cylinder and her emergency pony tank to be sure they were fully open, studied the readout on her dive computer, breathed from her safe-second mouthpiece again to assure herself that she could use it in the event her primary mouthpiece failed. It was like preparing for a space walk.

She straightened and studied the surroundings, trying to

postpone the dive a few minutes longer. A short distance to the east, a spear of rock broke the mirror glare of the Pacific. To the north and west lay Santa Cruz Island and the town of Puerto Ayora, where they had slept last night.

"Zip up," Dan told her, shrugging into the sleeves of his wetsuit.

Key Corporation had supplied her with a sleek black wetsuit that featured neon green and yellow insets and GET OUT THERE in fluorescent yellow script across her breasts. It made her look quite the dive diva, even if she did say so herself. It was a custom order, designed to hug her muscular five-foot-two-inch frame. For a woman resigned to spending her life rolling up cuffs, the perfect fit was a rare luxury.

The air temperature had to be over ninety degrees Fahrenheit and she was not eager to enclose herself in thick neoprene. "Do we really need these wetsuits?"

"You'll see." Reaching behind his back, Dan pulled up the cord attached to his zipper, stretching his wetsuit tight across his upper torso. Centered in the middle of his chest was a rectangle of gray duct tape, peeling at the edges. Curious. The rest of his gear looked to be in excellent shape.

Dan tugged up his hood, buckled on his fins, and then reached for his tank. As he hefted the strap of his BCD over his right shoulder, she snapped another photo. "Marine biologist at work," she named it aloud.

"Save the film for the sharks."

"There's no film." She snapped the camera into its waterproof housing and mounted the lights she would need below the surface. Then she caught up with the end of his sentence. "Sharks?"

"If we're lucky, we'll see a nice big hammerhead."

Nice big hammerhead? Perched on the starboard side next to Dan, Sam reluctantly harnessed herself into her equipment and tugged on her fins. She pushed her regulator into her mouth and took a quick suck of metallic-tasting air.

Dan tethered a small handheld computer to his left wrist

with a black cord, and then patted himself down, checking equipment. "Time to blast off." He looked toward the boat cabin. "Ricardo?"

A dark-skinned man in khaki shorts and green shirt emerged. A red can of cola sweated between his callused fingers, and a pair of sunglasses perched on top of his head.

"We're going in now."

Ricardo's gaze focused on the patch on Dan's wetsuit. "You have a rip? I have glue; I can fix." He stepped forward and pulled at a loose corner, exposing part of a circular NPF logo beneath the tape.

"It's no big deal." Dan quickly smoothed the tape back down.

"N-P-F?" Ricardo pronounced it with Spanish letters, *Ennay-Pay-Effay.*

Dan shrugged. "They gave me the wetsuit. I'm a university professor."

Ricardo frowned. *"Pero . . .* but NPF—"

"Could you hand Sam her camera?" Dan interrupted. "We should be down less than an hour. No need to move the boat; we'll circle and come back here."

Ricardo nodded. Then he pulled his sunglasses over his eyes, cloaking his gaze. Sam recognized the mirrored lenses as a brand that gang members were killing each other for in U.S. cities—PCBs. PCB was a hip designer, not the toxic compound found in EPA cleanup sites, but the idea of poisons apparently also appealed to the gangsta crowd. The glasses seemed out of place here.

It was too risky to jump into the water holding the expensive camera, and on this small boat, there was no platform to gently step off from. Sam folded the attached lights against the camera and handed it to Ricardo.

"Let's go." Dan shoved his mouthpiece into place, pulled down his mask, and backflipped headfirst into the water.

After a last longing look at the sunny surroundings, Sam stretched her mask strap over her French braid, then held her face mask and regulator with one hand and followed Dan's lead. The jade green water closed above her. She rolled to the surface to take the camera from Ricardo's outstretched hands, then exhaled and sank into the foreign world.

A school of silver fingerlings, scattered by her splashdown, regrouped in a swirl around her. Sunlight stabbed the water in bright beams that reflected from the pearlescent scales of the tiny fish. *Beautiful.*

She took a breath. The canned air didn't taste bad, although it was dry as the desert. It was the sound of her breath that rattled her nerves, amplifying the intake and outflow of her own lungs like a ventilator. A vision from her childhood welled up in her imagination. *Tubes and wires and pump, breathing for a woman who was more machine than mother.* Sam willed the dreaded hospital memory away. She was not her mother, or the nine-year-old girl watching her die. She was thirty-seven now, a strong woman on an adventure.

First rule of scuba: breathe slowly and continuously. She tried to relax and do exactly that. The glittering surface receded as she descended, pinching her nose and puffing air into her sinuses to equalize pressure in her ears. Her computer readout marked fifty feet below the surface. So far, so good. She'd been down to seventy on her training dives. Rolling to a horizontal position, she spotted Dan twenty feet below her, gliding over the coral-encrusted seafloor. She sank down to join him, remembering at the last second to add air to her BCD to prevent a crash landing.

Dan plucked a tube-shaped creature from the rock and held it out. She nodded to show she recognized the sea cucumber, one of the overfished organisms NPF was especially interested in counting.

Dan gently repositioned the animal on the rock. Another of the orange-and-white species crawled a short distance away, side by side with a pale yellow one. She watched Dan tap the count into his handheld computer.

A school of bullet-shaped silver fish, each at least a foot long, swam just ahead of them. Big-eye jacks? She'd have to look them up later in her Galápagos wildlife encyclopedia CD. Dan held up ten fingers three times, then two fingers on his left hand.

Crap. She forgot she was supposed to be helping. Taking a quick glance at the gray blurs disappearing into the blue, she nodded, agreeing with the count. The look in Dan's eyes told her that he knew she was faking.

He pointed into the murk. Sighting along his finger, Sam spotted a dark shadow headed their direction. *No.* She wasn't ready for a shark. As the creature approached, she concentrated on breathing slowly.

The shadow transformed into a spherical beast with wings. A turtle, flying underwater. *Whoa.* The sight was amazing. Dan returned to his examination of the ocean floor—he'd probably seen hundreds of sea turtles. Sam swam closer to the marine reptile. Its dark eyes were huge and soft, almost spaniel-like. Black spots freckled its pale green beak and neck. The turtle ignored her, gliding past with powerful thrusts of its long flippers. She took a photo with the turtle in the foreground and Dan hovering over a cluster of starfish in the background.

She finned back to Dan, who obligingly plucked a mottled red-and-white lobster from among the starfish and held it out toward the camera. As she centered his figure in the frame, his head jerked and a cloud of bubbles burst from his regulator. Alarmed, she curled the fingers of her right hand into an "okay?" sign. Another burst of air bubbled from his regulator, then he quickly jabbed a finger at his throat, and returned the okay sign. Just coughing.

It was understandable. The compressed air was dry; her own throat felt tight and scratchy. As she reframed man and lobster in the viewfinder, she noticed a torpedo shape in the blue gloom beyond him. *Uh-oh.* She took a breath and pressed the shutter button, exhaled, and then pointed.

After a quick glance, Dan thrust his fingers into a vertical fin on top of his neoprene hood. Scuba sign language for shark. There was no mistaking the dorsal fin on its back, the flattened profile. It was indeed a shark. Sam hovered uncertainly in place. What was a diver supposed to do to look avoid looking like food?

Dan held his hands out, two feet apart. A little shark? As it swam closer, she saw that he was correct. It was bigger than two feet, but probably no longer than three. Its sleek hide was an intricate mosaic of shaded patches. A leopard shark. Harmless, gorgeous, and best of all, alone. As the shark swam upward, she followed with the camera, capturing a shot of the shark suspended beneath the triangular shape of their boat. Even as she snapped the photo, Sam knew she shouldn't have glanced up. She had a perfect view of the bubbles streaming upward from both regulators. There was fifty feet of water between her and normal air.

Her breathing sounded mechanical and forced now. *Calm down,* she told herself. In—hiss. Out—bubble, bubble, bubble. *You signed up for this.*

She looked down. Below, Dan stared at her and coughed again. The display on her computer was flashing, the technological equivalent of a stern teacher shaking a warning finger. She'd been down with Dan, up after the turtle, down with Dan again, and then up after the shark. Yo-yoing. A definite no-no. Letting air out of her buoyancy vest, she slowly sank again, holding out her arms in an underwater shrug, then pointing to her camera, hoping he'd read that as being an overly enthusiastic photographer. If her fingers trembled, maybe he'd attribute it to the water's chill. He had definitely been right about the wetsuit. Her computer registered seventy-two degrees Fahrenheit, which was surprisingly cold when you'd been suspended in liquid for thirty minutes.

With another burst of bubbles, Dan turned away, circling over the algae-mottled seabed, searching for more marine life. She followed, gliding a yard above the rough black lava, delighting in the marvels of a red-and-white cushion star and a psychedelic display of orange cup coral.

Suddenly the rock floor beneath her fell away, and she found herself suspended above a deep chasm. Dan was below her, his form made hazy by a shoal of tiny blue fish between them. His bubbles streamed up between the darting shapes. One air globule hit her mask squarely in front of her right eye, and clung there like a droplet of mercury until she turned her head and it rolled away to continue its journey to the surface.

She was suspended in blue-green space. It felt marvelous and frightening and astounding, all at the same time. Her air gauge showed almost 1000 PSI left; she was breathing well, not too fast. She was gliding through the liquid womb of Mother Earth with fish and reptiles and—what *was* the proper classification for sea cucumbers, anyway? Echinoderms? Her wildlife biology studies had focused on mammals; she needed to brush up on the cold-blooded classifications.

She came face to face with an exquisite purple lace fan. On land, she would have said it was part of the fern family. Down here, coral? She wasn't sure. According to her books, corals came in many shapes, sizes, and colors. So did sponges. To make identification even more confusing, other creatures mimicked plants. Bryozoans? She didn't yet know which name applied to which creature. Or even if it was one creature she was staring at. Some marine organisms were actually groups of animals. *Mind-blowing.*

They'd been down for nearly forty minutes. Hadn't Dan told the boat pilot they would circle? They hadn't. Unless her underwater navigation skills were seriously flawed, they hadn't traveled very far at all. Shouldn't they be swimming more, counting more? Beneath her, Dan listed slightly to starboard. His computer dangled on its wrist cord in the slight current. He floated facedown, barely moving. Sam joined him to see what was so mesmerizing. Unable to detect much of interest within his range of vision, she tapped him on the shoulder. When he didn't react, she tugged at his arm.

His body rolled toward her like a mannequin. Behind the face mask, his eyes were dull, his eyelids at half-mast. She flashed the "okay?" question at him.

Dan floated listlessly, unresponsive.

2

DAN seemed only semiconscious, barely breathing. Sam grabbed his air gauge. He had 800 PSI, plenty of air left. What the hell was wrong? She jerked a thumb toward the surface, asking if he wanted to go up. His half-closed eyes stared blankly. She reached out and tapped his face mask directly in front of his eyes. He blinked and a bubble of air burst from his regulator.

At least he was alive. Maybe his regulator wasn't working right? She frantically ran her gaze over Dan's equipment. He had an octopus, which involved more hoses than her safe-second mouthpiece built into the inflator hose on her BCD. What could be wrong? She had rehearsed only one rescue scenario, the out-of-air drill. She let her camera dangle from its safety strap, reached down, put her alternative regulator into her own mouth, and then thrust her primary mouthpiece toward him. With the same motion that she used to entice her cat Simon into playing with a feather, she waggled the mouthpiece in front of Dan's face.

No response.

Desperate, she yanked his mouthpiece out and jammed

hers between his jaws before he could inhale, then tapped hard on the regulator, forcing a burst of air into his mouth. That woke him up. He kicked, his right heel connecting hard with her shin. The regulator hose jerked taut between them, and she grabbed the strap of his BCD and pulled him close to keep him from ripping the mouthpiece out.

She watched as he took a deep breath. Were his eyes a fraction more focused now, or was that just wishful thinking? She again jerked a thumb toward the surface, followed by the "okay?" sign. He coughed, nodded slowly, and clasped his fingers around her shoulder strap. They finned slowly upward. Her camera and his computer dangled beside them on their tethers, gently bumping their thighs as they ascended.

When her computer dinged at eighteen feet, they hovered for the recommended three-minute safety stop. Clinging together like mating dolphins, staring into each other's eyes and breathing the same air, was almost unbearably intimate, and Sam was relieved when they finally broke the surface. She waited until Dan spit out the mouthpiece and pressed the inflator button on his BCD, then she pushed him away from her. At the sight of him floating, conscious and breathing between hacking coughs, her galloping pulse finally slowed.

After the turquoise world below, the glare of sunshine was downright painful. Sam squinted as she sucked in huge lungfuls of real air. When she could talk again, she yelped, "What the hell happened down there?"

"Damned if I know." Dan coughed once more and then leaned back into the water with his eyes closed.

They'd surfaced a good thirty yards from the boat, but it motored in their direction and then slipped into place beside them. Sam handed up the camera to Ricardo. She and Dan removed their fins and tossed them on board. She followed him up the ladder into the boat.

Aboard, she unbuckled her belt and dumped her tanks and gear into the cockpit. She pulled her legs up onto the seat and wrapped her arms around her knees in an attempt to control her trembling.

Dan's hand grasped her shoulder. "Thank you. Please tell me *that's* not going in your post."

"It can't," she muttered. "No pictures." Not to mention that she was too confused about what happened to tell any coherent story.

"Good. I'd never live it down." He seemed recovered now, although his movements were sluggish and his face was the purple-red of a sliced beet. Turning away from her, he dug through his gear bag.

How could he be so calm? If becoming catatonic was a routine scuba event, she was giving up the sport right now.

Unfolding herself, Sam reached for her computer console. The needle on her air gauge was in the red zone. Two hundred PSI. Or maybe less. Her instructor had told her never to surface with less than five hundred.

She picked up Dan's gauge. Stretching the hose to which it was attached, she held it out toward him. "You had plenty of air."

He pulled some sort of electronic gizmo out of his bag, disconnected his regulator hose from his BCD, and then applied the gizmo to the end of the air hose. After a few seconds, he held the device up for her to read. "Seventeen ppm carbon monoxide."

"What?" Air, healthy air, the air that all life on earth depended on, contained less than five parts per million of carbon monoxide. Her tremors came back with a vengeance. "How can that be?" She took the meter from him and snapped it onto the end of her own regulator hose.

Ricardo emerged from the cabin, holding an orange in each hand. He stood a foot away, staring at them. *"Un problema?"*

"Everything's okay now," Dan told him. Turning to Sam, he said in a low voice, "We'll discuss this when we get back."

The meter reported that Sam's tank contained 2.9 ppm,

acceptable for normal compressed air. She disconnected the device and passed it back to Dan.

"Interesting fishes down there?" Ricardo handed each of them an orange. Sam accepted hers gratefully, glad to have something to dig her shaky fingers into.

"Just like we expected," Dan told the boat pilot. "This area is pretty devoid of sea life."

"Devoid?" Her jaw dropped. "All those fish. Sea cucumbers. Starfish. A turtle. A shark."

Dan turned his gaze on her. "A fraction of what was here ten years ago. Especially the sea cucumbers."

A scowl darkened Ricardo's face.

"Of course, we're close to town and outside the reserve, so I'd expect it to be more or less fished out." Dan slicked back his hair with his hands and looked up at the boat pilot. "We'll have better luck tomorrow when we're inside the marine sanctuary. Right, Ricardo?"

The Ecuadorian did not return Dan's smile. "Tomorrow . . . is no longer possible," he answered. "This boat, she is busy."

Dan's eyes narrowed, and the two men assessed each other for a tense moment. Finally Dan said, "Then we'll find another boat, *amigo*. You can take us in now."

As Ricardo turned away toward the cabin, Sam noticed the distinctive outline of a cell phone in his back pocket. They seemed as common here as in the States.

Beneath their feet, the engine rumbled to life. Dan rubbed his temples with his fingertips, wincing.

"You okay?" Sam asked.

"My head aches. But I'll be fine."

She jerked a shoulder toward the boat cabin. "What's up with Ricardo?"

"Mea culpa. The NPF logo—I should have been more careful." He wiped a drip from the end of his nose.

"Should have been more careful about what?"

His gaze shifted toward the boat cabin and back to her. "Later."

She concentrated on peeling her orange. "How can you get carbon monoxide in a tank of air?"

"Most likely exhaust of some sort near the compressor intake."

Dan casually tossed out the words, but they made Sam's breath stop halfway up her windpipe.

He shrugged. "It might have been accidental."

3

ALARM bells clanged in Sam's head all the way back to Puerto Ayora. The combination of adrenaline and jet lag made her nauseous and she had to keep her gaze on the horizon, but she couldn't stop thinking about the incident. Contaminating Dan's tank with carbon monoxide *might* have been accidental? She couldn't wait to hear his explanation. But after they hopped off at the dock in Puerto Ayora and the boat had pulled away, he said only, "I'll return the tanks. You take the rest of our gear back to the hotel."

She frowned. "Are you nuts? I'm not letting you out of my sight. Especially after what just happened."

He studied her face for a few seconds. "I know what you're thinking, but seriously, don't sweat it. That tank thing was probably an accident."

Tank thing? Probably an accident? Her mind was swirling and his words weren't helping. "I'll be a couple of hours, no more." Dan beckoned to a wizened man leaning against an equally ancient car with a TAXI sign on the roof. The fellow trotted in their direction.

"José will take good care of you." He lightly slapped the taxi driver on the back. "Right, José?"

The driver turned to her. "You got the money, honey, I got the time." He looked at least ninety years old. But he loaded the two heavy gear bags into the trunk of his decrepit Ford with surprising agility, and opened a back door, gesturing her in.

She resisted Dan's gentle hand on her back. "We shouldn't separate."

"Look," Dan said, "I need to sort out alternative arrangements. I know the terrain and the language. You don't. Plus, I can see you're jet-lagged and you've probably got business stuff to do."

All good points. "But—"

"I'll be fine. Really." He pressed his hand against her back again, and Sam climbed into the backseat.

José recklessly sped through the streets of the small town, trailing a wake of windblown trash. The amount of litter in the town surprised her. She'd read that recycling was mandatory here. Bins for paper, glass, and plastic were stacked alongside each pastel-colored building. Yet the back alleys and drainage ditches were filled with discarded plastic bags and Popsicle sticks and foam egg cartons.

There were no cruise ships in the harbor, and the school-children had already gone home, so the roadways weren't crowded in the late afternoon heat. That was a good thing, because José had little regard for driving on any particular side of the street. Sam saw only a few pedestrians, including a black woman with intricately braided hair, whom José seemed to aim directly for. The woman leapt from the street into the doorway of a store, shaking her fist. Her angry figure was swallowed up in the ensuing cloud of dust.

After depositing their dive gear on the doorstep of the six-room Hotel Aurora, José grasped Sam's fingers along with the folded dollars she thrust at him. "A-OK, babycake. Come up and see me sometime. Got a rocket in my pocket." A lecherous wink creased his face like a fold of fruit leather. He drove off in a belch of black exhaust.

Sam stepped into the hotel lobby and pushed her sunglasses to the top of her head. It looked like the place would be full tonight. A quartet of pale-skinned, long-haired young women—two blondes, a brunette, and a ponytailed redhead—stood before the hotel's reception desk, conversing in what sounded like a Scandinavian language. The three tables that made up the lounge/breakfast area were occupied, one by a couple in matching Hawaiian shirts who hovered earnestly over a guidebook, another by an elderly woman with a suitcase by her side, and the other by a short-bearded man with sunglasses hanging from the V of his shirt and a folded newspaper before him.

Struggling with a bag of heavy dive gear hanging from each shoulder, Sam headed for the stairs, determined to get a shower before all the hot water was gone. As she staggered across the lobby, Mrs. Vintner, the tiny Swiss proprietress, stepped out from behind the desk.

"Mizz Vestin." Mrs. Vintner wiped her hands on the hips of her skirt. Sam had liked her at first sight, because the top of the woman's head reached only to Sam's eyebrows, making five-foot-two seem statuesque for a change. "Ve have problem."

Sam shifted a bag strap on her shoulder. "Oh?"

The woman shot a quick glance toward the lounge area. "Your room. And Mr. Kaza-ki? I say before you can have rooms for five days, but is not so. After tonight, no rooms are free. You must leave. You understand?"

What? After the "tank thing" and then Ricardo refusing to take them out again, this was too much. Sam dropped the heavy gear bags to the floor and angrily crossed her arms. "No, I don't understand. Explain it to me."

"Is my mistake. In the reservations. I am sorry. Is best, I think, you go to Baquerizo Moreno." Her gray eyes connected with Sam's gaze for only a few seconds before flitting away. "You tell Mr. Kazaki?"

"I most definitely will," Sam said. The town of Puerto Baquerizo Moreno was not remotely close; it was on a completely different island.

Dan had reserved these rooms. Maybe he could work out the problem. "I'm sure Dr. Kazaki will want to talk to you about this."

Mrs. Vintner lowered her gaze to the blue tile floor. "Sorry." After a last glance toward the lounge, she scurried back to her post at the reception desk.

Sam turned to survey the lounge tables. The Hawaiian-shirted couple was still head to head over their guidebook. The elderly woman was gone, along with her suitcase. At the other table, the bearded man was now invisible behind his newspaper.

As she bent over to grab the gear bag straps, her sunglasses fell off her head and skittered across the floor. The redheaded tourist scooped them up, inspected them for a second, and then held them out. "Here. Is not broken." Her words had a foreign lilt.

"Thank you." Sam smiled. "Where are you from?"

"Norway. You are American?"

"Yes," Sam said. "Welcome to the Galápagos."

The tourist returned to her friends. After pushing the glasses back onto her head, Sam hefted the heavy gear bags again and lugged them to her room. On previous field assignments, her accommodations had been tiny tents in rocky canyons or dense forests. The small hotel was quirky but charming: the entrance was hidden down a side street, but a few of the rooms peeked out over the roof of a restaurant below, revealing a view of Academy Bay. The coral-painted walls, white lace curtains, and heavily lacquered wooden furniture seemed like a luxury. Her laptop looked at home on the little table under the window, which overlooked the curve of the waterfront. Damn it! Who knew what sort of accommodations they'd find in Puerto Baquerizo Moreno?

She headed for the shower. When she emerged from the tepid water, her body felt refreshed and her brain felt slightly less foggy. She pulled on shorts and a T-shirt, and sat down at her computer. After connecting to the hotel's wireless network, she downloaded her e-mail, then checked the current page at *Out There*.

The featured stories on *Out There*'s home page were an immunization project in India funded by Key Corporation, and an article about skiing in Kashmir, which was conveniently linked to bargain ski vacations available on Key's travel site and skis and snowboards for sale on Key's catalog site. The byline for the immunization story belonged to Kat Monroe, a tall slender woman dressed in a sari, while the skiing article was attributed to Bomber Bryant. According to the accompanying photo, he seemed to be a downhiller built like The Incredible Hulk, who tackled monster moguls without the least concern for the precarious shelf of snow hanging above him. Given that she was now *Out There*'s dynamic duo in the Galápagos, Sam suspected that Kat Monroe was also Bomber Bryant.

Assuming a different online personality made Sam feel like a character in a video game. It didn't seem quite kosher to pretend to be someone else. *It's just another pseudonym,* Wyatt argued. So here she was, sworn to nondisclosure about her split personality.

In a corner of the home page, a video window showed an aerial view of the Galápagos. She watched as that photo transitioned into another, a group of marine iguanas silhouetted against the sunset, then to an orange background with the words *Launching Tomorrow! Our intrepid women reporters—Wilderness Westin and Zing—team with the Natural Planet Foundation for Galápagos adventure!*

Her new alter-ego was *Zing*? Sounded like a name for mouthwash. What would her cybercharacter look like? *Out There* was so influenced by young focus groups, Zing would probably have spiked black hair and pouty lips and a bustline as impressive as the Rocky Mountains. *Intrepid women reporters?* Sam picked up her hairbrush. "Day One, Galápagos adventure," she murmured breathily into the bristles. "Our intrepid team barely survives their first dive, and then finds themselves homeless."

She was still in the Galápagos, and she was still earning a thousand dollars a day, she reminded herself. All expenses paid. She was wearing shorts and sandals in February.

Already she'd seen an amazing collection of undersea creatures. She still had the famous island fauna to look forward to.

She threw the hairbrush onto the bed and checked her watch. Fifty minutes had passed. Shouldn't Dan be back by now? She paced across the room to look out the window. Same bay and hills, a few different people on the street. She couldn't even call Dan; he said his cell phone had been stolen in Guayaquil. She should never have let them get separated like this.

She chewed her thumbnail as she watched boats jockey for position in the bay. *Don't sweat it,* Dan had said. The town wasn't big; he couldn't have gone far. She could find the dive shop if she needed to. He was probably making other boat arrangements. She decided not to panic for another half hour, and went back to the computer to download her e-mail.

Five minutes later, Dan knocked at the door, a bottle of dark beer clutched in each hand. She gestured him in. He perched on the edge of her bed and then held out one bottle to her.

"Don't look so happy." She took the bottle from him. "We've just been thrown out of the hotel."

He nodded. "I thought that might happen."

"You did? What the hell is going on, Dan?"

He cocked his head the same way Simon did when the cat was trying to telecommunicate his feline exasperation. "They told you about the political situation down here, right?"

"They who? Key Corporation?"

He rolled his eyes toward the ceiling and sighed. "I forgot you're not working for NPF."

NPF will handle the research, she remembered Wyatt explaining. *Your job is entertainment.*

"I like to think I'm working *with* NPF," she told Dan. "I have worked for conservation organizations in the past." She fingered the three parallel scars on her thigh that were a constant reminder.

His hazel eyes lingered on the faint pink cougar scratches on her leg. "Mementos from a previous assignment?"

"Yes." An unwelcome blush flooded her face. It seemed an eternity since a man had gazed at her body like that. She and Chase had left messages for each other, but she hadn't actually talked to him since Christmas. She called him her lover, but they were not exactly having a torrid love affair. She wasn't quite sure *what* they were having. Or where it would go.

Meanwhile, Dr. Daniel Kazaki was sitting on her bed. He was a handsome man. An interesting man. Tanned, fit, muscular. Japanese-Irish-American. Intellectual and athletic. Her brain rested there a long minute before it added *"and married."* She gave herself a mental slap.

Dan's gaze returned to her face, and she prayed her thoughts didn't show on the surface. He took a sip of his beer before saying, "You know about the conflict between the conservation community and the fishermen."

"Of course." The information she could find in English about the conflict had been scarce, but she'd gleaned a few interesting facts. More than 90 percent of the Galápagos Islands were within the National Park boundaries. International conservationists were determined to keep the Galápagos park waters pristine, while fishermen naturally wanted to exploit them. "I know that Sea Shepherd has chased down illegal fishing boats, and I read about a couple of ugly incidents with the fishermen's union, one in the nineties and another in 2004, when they took the scientists hostage at Darwin Station. And I saw another article about an illegal shark catching incident."

"You found reports of only a few incidents?" He rolled his eyes again.

She bristled at his tone. She'd done her research before leaving Bellingham. "I read the Darwin Foundation's latest strategy document," she told him. "It's all about cooperation between the local population and the scientists. And the new Constitution of Ecuador states that nature has the legal right to be protected, doesn't it?"

His gaze bored into hers. After a few seconds, he raised one eyebrow.

"Rose-colored glasses?" she guessed.

"It's not your fault. The tourism industry, not to mention the local government, is skilled at burying these incidents under an avalanche of hopeful-sounding news." He took a swallow of beer before continuing. "Here's the truth as I know it: In 2007 alone, outside environmental groups uncovered over ninety thousand illegal shark fins here. And twenty thousand illegal sea cucumbers. Nobody was punished. A boat with almost four hundred shark carcasses on board was caught in 2011. The case has never gone to trial. And the poaching is still going on."

Sam's brain had gotten stuck on Dan's first fact. *Ninety thousand shark fins?* Did that mean ninety thousand sharks? Even counting multiple fins per shark . . . Yeesh, how many sharks were left? Her head filled with frightening visions of dense hordes of sharp-toothed predators even as her heart sank at the thought of so many wild creatures killed here. *Twenty thousand illegal sea cucumbers?*

Her imagination couldn't even envision such huge numbers of any sort of creatures. And nobody was punished? She took another sip of beer. The muscles between her shoulder blades tightened as her brain fit the pieces together. Commercial fishing was illegal within the park and marine reserve. Dan was here to do a survey of marine life. He'd be documenting the effects of activities that the locals wanted to keep secret. "So it's no surprise to you that we've been tossed out of the hotel."

"I couldn't reserve another boat, either. Nobody will take us out diving."

Damnation! *Day One, Galápagos adventure. Our intrepid team is homeless* and *out of business.* How could her dream assignment go bust before it even got started? She hadn't even had the chance to see Charles Darwin Research Station or any of the islands. "And now you're telling me that we can't charter a boat because the boat owners are in sympathy with the fishermen?"

Dan snorted. "Most boat owners *are* fishermen."

She frowned. Damn Key Corporation, anyway. According to her contract, half of her assignment was "to accompany NPF personnel on dives and report on their activities." But odds were that Wyatt was even more clueless than she had been. It wasn't as if the decision makers at Key kept their fingers on the pulse of the worldwide conservation movement.

"Key told me this was going to be a vacation." Her voice sounded whiny, even to her. She took another swallow of beer. "Shit."

"Treat it like a vacation, then." Dan drained his beer, set the bottle on the floor beside his feet, and then raised both arms over his head, stretching. "Man, it feels so good to be doing something important again." As he lowered his arms to his lap again, he noticed her expression. "Don't look so worried. Nothing will happen; the last thing the locals want is bad press. We'll lay low, we'll do our jobs. We'll be gone in a week."

Easy enough for him maybe, but she wasn't getting paid to be invisible. Could she write mainly touristy stuff? And he wasn't being completely honest. Something already *had* happened. "What did you find out about your air fill? Did somebody sabotage your tank?"

He shrugged. "I just can't be sure. Maybe a car's exhaust pipe was too close to the compressor intake when the tank was filled."

She gave him a skeptical look.

"Seriously, it can happen in careless shops anywhere," he said. "That compressor was pretty much held together with baling wire and duct tape. The windows and doors are always open, so whatever's in the parking lot ends up inside the shop, too. Was the contamination intentional?" He shrugged again. "I doubt it. After all, your tank was okay."

Good point. But all her gear was labeled *Out There* and she'd never set foot in Ecuador before, so they—whoever "they" were—might not have known who she was, whereas

Dan had conducted surveys here in the past. The dive shop workers might have known he worked for NPF.

"We'll check the CO content on every fill from here on, just in case," he concluded.

Great. Maybe the locals were out to kill them; maybe not. Paranoia in paradise.

Dan smiled and pushed himself to his feet.

"Why are you smiling?" Did he have some macho warrior fixation? Was he looking forward to butting heads with the enemy? "We don't have a boat. We can't do all the diving from shore, can we?"

He shook his head. "We've got a huge area to cover."

"So what do we do now? We're not stopping the survey, are we?" That was the last thing she wanted to do; she'd never bailed on an assignment before.

"No way. We can't put it off. We shift to Plan B." He walked to the lace-curtained window. "I looked up an old buddy of mine—Eduardo Duarte. He's a naturalist guide with the park system. The tour boat he's assigned to this week has empty cabins, so he arranged for us to join them for a six-day tour of the islands. They're Americans; we're Americans—we'll blend in. The captain is a diver, too; he carries a small compressor onboard. He agreed to refill our tanks, and Eduardo will take us to our dive sites."

Sam's fog of discouragement lifted. Subterfuge. With allies. Definitely more her style than hand-to-hand combat. Obviously, Dan did know his way around down here.

He tapped a finger on the windowpane, pointing to a large, sleek fiberglass vessel that rocked gently among smaller craft in the harbor. "That's our yacht, *Papagayo.* See—they're already tying up your kayak. Okay with you, partner?"

So she'd lost the coral-colored walls, the patchwork quilt, her little computer table. So there might be a little animosity in this town. They'd be away from the locals on the tour boat. Key Corporation had supplied a satellite phone; she could send her posts from anywhere.

Her assignment still included exotic wildlife, tropical islands, and a real live partner on the right side of the fight. "Plan B it is, then. Early dinner?" she asked. "I'm about ready to collapse from hunger."

"About that." Dan stood up, hefted his gear bag from the floor, and headed for the door. "There's just one little catch in this deal. *Papagayo*'s leaving at six thirty."

"Tonight?" Sam checked her watch. It was nearly five forty-five now.

"Meet me at the back door in half an hour." He closed the door behind him.

Her stomach growled, and she put a hand on her belly. She checked the window again. *Papagayo* looked like a decent place to bunk for a week. She'd be on a luxury cruise instead of taking daily boat trips out from the islands. So they had to check their air fills. A little paranoia was probably a good thing in a diver.

4

SAM envied Dan's calm confidence. Actually, now that she thought about it, she envied Dan's life. He had a good job and a loving wife waiting for him, while she had only her usual uncertain employment, her housemate Blake, and her cat Simon at home. Chase was—well, who knew where Chase was at any given time? He was a hard man to track down.

She pulled out the satellite phone Key had loaned her, called the FBI office in Salt Lake City, and asked for Agent Perez. Not there, even though it wasn't quite 3 P.M. in that time zone. Typical. She declined to leave voice mail. Next, she tapped in Chase Perez's home number. At least she could leave him another message to let him know she was thinking of him. She was trying to convince herself that this new awkwardness between them was all in her imagination.

"Speak!" a deep voice barked.

She was startled to hear the actual man instead of his voice mail recording. "Chase?"

"Summer!" His tone softened. She heard sizzling in the

background. "Sorry, I'm just . . . um . . . in the middle of doing a stir-fry for a late lunch, and you know how that goes."

"Um-hmmm." Microwaved lasagna was about as involved as she got in the kitchen. One of Blake's best qualities as a housemate was his love of cooking.

"You know how you've got about five seconds between *al dente* and *al disposal*?" There was a clatter, a muttered "Damn it," a louder crash, then he was shouting in a far-away voice.

"Chase? Chase?" Had he been attacked?

"Still there? Sorry about dropping you on the floor like that, but the wok was doing this Vesuvius thing."

"Vesuvius?" She pictured shooting flames.

"It's under control now. And this"—she could hear him chewing—"is delicious. I've discovered a new Korean recipe. I'll make it for you when we get together next week. It's an excellent antidote for dreary winter weather."

She inhaled the tropical night air seeping in through her open window, redolent of salt water and grilled fish close up, with a slight tinge of burning garbage somewhere in the distance. Winter and her promised ski trip with Chase seemed a world away.

"When did you get back?" she asked. She put him on speakerphone while she folded her laptop and stowed it in its padded case.

"This is just a temporary layover. I called you this morning but all I got was voice mail. Whose phone are you using now?"

"A client's. You'll never guess where I am." She'd been waiting to surprise him with this.

"You do sound a little distant. The summit of Mount Rainier?"

She snorted. "Hardly. Two hints—it's seventy-five degrees outside right now and the national language is Spanish."

"Miami?"

"Funny." She moved to the bathroom and collected

her sunscreen, moisturizer, and toothbrush. "I'm in the Galápagos."

"Ecuador?" He groaned loudly. "Oh, Summer. Why don't you ask me before you do these things?"

What? She'd expected an "I'm envious" or maybe a "Lucky you!" She returned to her bedside and tossed the items into her duffel bag. "Why *should* I ask you?"

"Because I have insights into matters that you are not privy to," he said. "I'm almost afraid to ask—what are you doing down there?"

She told him.

He groaned again. "Since when are you a diver?"

She'd wanted to surprise him with that, too. His disparaging tone grated on her. "Chase, there are lots of things you don't know about me. My life cannot be so easily condensed into a convenient FBI background report." At least she liked to think that was true. Nowadays she wasn't so sure.

"Mi corazón, let me assure you that you are frequently a mystery to me."

She punched the speakerphone key off and put the phone back to her ear. "Chase, about what I said at Christmas—"

"Let's have that discussion face to face. You *are* still going to show up for our ski trip, right?"

"Of course." *No matter what,* they'd promised. If only she could get rid of the fear that their upcoming vacation would be a test she couldn't pass.

"How's the Galápagos gig going so far?" he asked.

"We've had a little trouble—"

He was quick to interrupt again. "What kind of trouble?"

She wanted to discuss Dan's air-fill problem with someone, but Chase would have a million questions she couldn't answer. "Maybe *trouble*'s too strong a word. Just sort of . . . noncooperation. Some of the locals don't seem too happy that we're working for the Natural Planet Foundation."

He mumbled something in Spanish that sounded like a

swear word. "Watch your back, Summer. Better yet, pack it in and come home."

Just who did he think he was talking to? He knew that she wasn't a delicate debutante. "It's under control, Chase. Dan—that's my expedition partner, Dr. Daniel Kazaki— he speaks Spanish and he knows how everything works down here. He's done surveys for NPF before. And the islands are wonderful," she hastened to add.

"I wish I were in the tropics. The high here is supposed to be twenty-six today. I could have used crampons just to walk to the barbershop."

She loved his shining wings of thick black hair, the polar opposite of her own fine platinum blond. "I hope you didn't get too much cut off."

"Is all of it too much?"

"What? Why would you do that?" Was he kidding? His lack of response told her he wasn't. "Never mind, you don't need to answer. It's for a job." She tried to picture him without his full head of blue-black hair, his part as straight as a knife slash on the right side.

"Yeah, I'm on assignment. I actually shaved it a couple weeks ago, but Nicole said she wasn't touching it again, and do you know how hard it is to shave your whole head?"

"Uh, no," she said, still stunned at the mental image of a bald Chase.

"I have an American flag, the 'Don't Tread on Me' version, tattooed on my right bicep. The snake opens its mouth and hisses when I flex."

She laughed. "Now I know you're putting me on."

There was a clink of tableware before he asked, "Did I mention the silver skull dangling from my earlobe?"

"Oh, no. Does this have anything to do with those crimes in the Southwest? Don't tell me you're going to hang out with those nut—"

"Don't be dissin' my buds."

Fire bombings of Latino-owned businesses, thought to be the work of anti-immigration groups, had recently erupted across Nevada and Arizona. Hate crimes fell under the FBI's mandate. Hadn't there been a story about bodies found in the desert, too? Illegal immigrants from Mexico, if she remembered right. How could Chase Perez work undercover on that case?

"You have olive skin," she said.

Fortunately, the man had so far proved adept at following her zigzags of thought. "A deep tan, especially after all the sun lamps my head has been under lately." he said. "I'm a sun-loving skinhead."

"You have dark eyes." A deep earthy brown, to be exact. Latino eyes, Native American eyes—his father was Mexican-American, his mother was full-blood Lakota. Starchaser Perez's eyes were as far from blue eyes as anyone could get. "Doesn't the Bureau keep a blond surfer type for this sort of thing?"

"I volunteered him for a security detail in Anchorage. I think he was pleased."

"Right." She looked around the room to see if she'd missed any items. There, her sleep shirt lying half under the pillow.

"I'm not joining the Aryan Nation, sweetheart. FYI, I am third-generation Italian-American and my mama makes the best gnocchi you ever tasted."

Sam wasn't sure what gnocchi was, let alone what it tasted like. She sighed. "At least Nicole will be with you, right?"

"Of course. She's dolled up like a TV evangelist, bleached blond big hair and all."

It was hard to picture Chase's sophisticated auburn-haired partner transformed in such a manner. "I wish I could see that."

"I've got pictures. For future blackmail. You never know when you're going to need extra money."

She laughed out loud. This was what she most loved about him—he could always lighten her mood.

"I can't wait to spend a whole week with you, Summer."

"You'll be back in time?" *No matter what.* He'd said it, too.

"No sweat. I can see it now, us zooming downhill at breakneck speed, you wearing one of those stretchy jump-suit things."

"Cross-country skiing," she corrected. She was the sturdy athletic type, not a sleek snow bunny. "Rain pants and gaiters and wool sweaters. I don't have one of those 'jumpsuit things.'"

"I'll buy you one. Hot pink. What in the hell are gaiters?"

"Have I ever told you what I did to the last person who gave me something pink?"

"Turquoise, then. Do they make them in turquoise?"

"I wouldn't know; I don't wear jumpsuit things. I'm sup-posed to ski in public with a skinhead?"

"I'll wear a hat."

"Will you still have the tattoo?" Damn; the thirty min-utes she had to pack were nearly up. "Chase, I've gotta go now. I'll call you tomorrow."

"You can't; I'm heading out soon. But Happy Valen-tine's Day *mañana*."

So it was; she'd completely forgotten. "You, too, *mi amor*." Why was it easier to say she loved him in Spanish than in English?

"Ciao for now, mi colibrí."

"What'd you call me?"

"C-O-L-I-B-R and I with an accent. Look it up, *querida*." He ended the call.

Slipping in mystery words here and there was Chase's way of teaching her Spanish. She hadn't yet decided whether the habit was endearing or annoying. She grabbed her sleep shirt from the bed, zipped it into her duffel, and loaded herself up like a pack mule for the trip down the stairs.

5

AT six fifteen, Sam and Dan skulked down to the harbor. At least it felt like skulking to her. She hoped everyone in town was slugging down mojitos in the bars or had their eyes focused on the horizon and not on the two overly burdened tourists waddling down the dock. The sunset was certainly worthy of attention. She found it hard to divert her own gaze from the stunning sight of Academy Bay transitioning from molten gold to violet silk.

It didn't seem fair to fly so far south in February and get no more hours of daylight than she had at her northern home latitude. But Ecuador was named for its position on the equator, and that zero-degree latitude meant the hours of daylight and darkness didn't vary much, all year round.

Her sunglasses slid down her nose as she thumped her bags on the dock next to the four air cylinders Dan had rented. She pushed the glasses to the top of her head. "I feel like an outlaw slinking out of town before I get caught."

Dan waggled from side to side to let a duffel drop heavily from each shoulder, and then ducked his head to lift the strap of a third from around his neck, leaving only his binoculars dangling against his chest. "We've already been caught. Or at least discovered."

"So we really are in hiding?"

"It's usually wise to remain incognito when among the locals," he answered vaguely.

"But the Internet coverage . . ." She'd been hired to broadcast their presence, after all. To the entire world, no less. "Why would the Natural Planet Foundation ever agree to this deal with *Out There*?"

"What do you think?" Dan rubbed the thumb and the first two fingers of his right hand together in the universal sign for money. "NPF is hard up for donations, like all non-profits these days. Key Corporation is funding this survey. Plus, international support is always the best defense; and we want the survey results to become public as soon as possible. You can write about the Galápagos in general, can't you? You won't pinpoint *exactly* where we are?"

"I won't use your name. And I definitely won't say we're on a tour boat," she told him. *Out There* wouldn't want the public to think their intrepid women reporters lounged around on yachts. "And I won't be specific about locations."

"That's the trooper." He slapped her gently on the shoulder. "This is my fault; I should have glued a real patch over that emblem on my wetsuit before I left home. I expected the local politics would have simmered down by now; it's been years since the *pepino* war."

"Pepino?" She was feeling more clueless by the minute.

"Sea cucumber."

"Ah." She moved on to the next worrisome word, *war*. "I read there was trouble about overfishing sea cucumbers, but I never heard it called a war."

Dan's gaze met hers. "Maybe *war*'s too strong a word. Nearly wiped out the *pepinos*, but no people were killed. Now the poachers have moved on to new species."

"So you'll document what's going on and I'll broadcast it." She chewed her lower lip for a minute; remembering Wyatt's admonition that NPF was responsible for research and she was responsible for *entertainment*. Illegal fishing might be news, but it did not sound particularly entertaining. She set that worrisome thought aside for a moment as she remembered that Chase had called her a Spanish word. "Dan, what does *colibrí* mean?"

He considered for a moment. "Hmm. I'm trying to remember. *Col* is cabbage, so maybe *colibrí* is something made with cabbage? Coleslaw?"

That wasn't very flattering. Why would Chase call her coleslaw?

An inflatable dinghy neared their position, and Dan raised his hand in greeting. When its rubber fender bumped the dock, a short, stocky man in matching khaki shorts and shirt leapt from the bow and tied the craft to a metal cleat. His thick black curls were salted with gray, and his weathered face was heavily lined; clearly he'd spent years in the sun. Sam guessed his age to be late fifties or early sixties.

"Amigo!" Dan and the man embraced each other, and then Dan turned to Sam. "This is Eduardo Duarte, the most senior naturalist guide here in the Galápagos. We've worked together several times. Eduardo knows more than most scientists at Darwin Station."

The guide beamed. "They come for a few years. I work here for almos' thirty."

"I'm honored to meet you." Sam held out her hand, and Eduardo shook it.

Dan slapped Eduardo on the back. "I hear they're planning a parade for you, man."

The older man blushed. "Not a parade. *Una fiesta*, nothing more. And not for a month." Turning to Sam, he explained, "I am the first naturalist guide to achieve thirty years, so I am the first to retire with a pension."

"Congratulations," she said. "Eduardo, what does *colibrí* mean?"

"Hummingbird." He wrinkled his brow in confusion at the sudden change of topics.

Dan chuckled. "Obviously my translation skills are rusty. I guessed it meant *coleslaw*."

Eduardo laughed. Sam smiled. She liked the idea of being a hummingbird in Chase's eyes. She adored the tiny resilient Anna's hummingbirds who visited her feeder, even in the midst of blizzards. If only she were half as tough as they were.

Eduardo tilted his head in the direction of the dark-skinned helmsman, who had stepped out of the boat and was busy loading their gear. "This is Tony, first mate of *Papagayo*. He has no English."

"*Mucho gusto*, Tony." Chase had taught her the polite response for meeting someone.

Tony extended his hand to help her over the rubber bumper. His square jaw and brown eyes looked vaguely familiar. Had she seen him around town? She didn't really think so; she'd only been here twenty-four hours. "Nice dinghy," she mumbled to cover her confusion.

"*Panga*," Eduardo said. "Rubber, wood, fibe-glass, no matter—here we call all little boats *pangas*."

As they motored out to the yacht, their wake rocked half a dozen gaily painted wooden fishing boats, rigged with winches and nets. Small skiffs—*pangas*, Sam reminded herself—bobbed at their sterns like children clinging to their mothers' skirts. The fleet made a colorful collage, lit by the last rays of the sunset. She scanned her pile of luggage for one of the digital cameras Key had loaned her. Out of the corner of her eye, she saw a huge black shadow flash through the water beneath the boat. She jerked upright and squinted at the shining pane of the water's surface, trying to make out the shape as it sped away.

"Beachmaster," Eduardo said.

She followed his pointing finger. A huge bull sea lion hauled himself out of the water onto a yellow skiff tied behind a fishing boat. Already listing low in the water under the weight of two smaller female sea lions, the panga sank a few more inches, nearing the waterline. The females bleated their annoyance and slid off into the water, tipping the craft, which then slipped silently beneath the surface.

The beachmaster vanished as well, again becoming an underwater shadow.

The space the yellow skiff had occupied was now only flat water. Sam imagined the owner emerging from the cabin in the morning, ready to step into his dinghy, and finding only a line disappearing into the aquamarine depths. *Creepy.*

Eduardo broke into her thoughts. "This happen all the time. Inflatable"—he patted the rubber bumper on which he sat—"is best."

She pressed her lips together to stop her internal editor from mouthing corrections to Eduardo's English: *an* inflatable, happen*s*, fib*er*glass. The man spoke at least one language more than she did.

He smiled. "You will find sea lions are rulers of the Galápagos. Here we call them *lobos del mar*, wolves of the sea."

Actually, that made more sense. With their pointed snouts and long necks, the pinnipeds looked a lot more like canines than felines.

Beside her, Dan raised his binoculars to focus on a gray blip on the southern horizon. She squinted again. It was a large ship of some kind.

"Supply ship," Eduardo guessed.

"I can't make out the name, but it looks like it's written in Japanese or Chinese characters." Dan lowered the binoculars, letting them hang on their strap against his chest again. His posture was rigid.

Eduardo studied Dan for a minute, and then he looked away toward the shore. Sam glanced at Tony. The first mate's gaze was fixed on the water ahead.

An Asian supply ship? That seemed odd. Wasn't the Galápagos colony too small a market for deliveries from other countries? Then she clued in on the reason behind Dan's tense attitude—a large ship like that probably would not have cause to *deliver* to the Galápagos, but one might want to *pick up* a load from another boat in the area. There was only one thing these islands had that Asia would want:

seafood. Had it been caught legally outside of the marine reserve or poached from within?

Tony abruptly killed the engine as the inflatable nudged up against a small platform at *Papagayo*'s blue-and-white stern. A crewman, his shirt the same blue and white as Tony's, secured the panga's bowline and then offered Sam a hand. She stood up a little unsteadily, then picked up her laptop case and duffel.

Tony pulled the duffel strap from Sam's shoulder and slung it over his own. "We bring."

So Tony did know some English. "I'll carry my computer," she told him. Clutching the laptop protectively with one hand and the crewman's hand with the other, she stepped out onto the landing platform.

Eduardo pointed up a set of stairs to the main deck. "You go up the stairs to the lounge. The others have already eat—early dinner tonight. But Constantino will see that you receive sandwiches."

Dan scrambled over the heap of gear to join Sam. "No more bucking our own bags. We're traveling first class now."

She followed him up the stairs.

The lounge turned out to be an enclosed communal area on the main deck, divided into halves by a center stairwell. Stationary teak tables and padded blue benches marked the rear half of the room as a dining area. The forward half of the lounge was filled wall to wall with plump beige vinyl couches. On these, six passengers reclined—four senior citizens, obviously seated in pairs, and two much younger and slightly scruffy men, all with white name tags pinned to their chests. Their faces were turned attentively toward a young man standing before them. His guide uniform was identical to Eduardo's. He stood next to a map on a stand and was orienting the group, using a pen as a pointer.

Constantino, a large man who also wore a crew shirt and a name tag, emerged from behind a small wet bar nestled next to the stairwell. He motioned Sam and Dan to a dining booth still damp from a recent cleaning. Ceramic plates laden with sandwiches and fruit appeared in front of them, served by a dark man in a sweat-stained undershirt with soapsuds on his forearms. Sam felt a twinge of guilt at adding to the guy's normal workload.

Tony and two other crewmen in blue T-shirts shuffled into the room, hunched under Sam and Dan's gear. The trio disappeared noisily down the central staircase into the nether regions of the boat.

"Vino?" Constantino stood beside them, now with a white towel over one arm and a bottle of wine in each hand, his ample belly brushing the edge of their table. "From Chile," he added, as if this was important information.

"Tinto," Dan responded. Constantino splashed red wine into his glass.

Sam pointed to the white wine, and he filled her glass to the brim. The flavor was dry and crisp. "Good stuff." She took another swallow.

"Chilean wine is usually good," Dan agreed. "Don't take Ecuadorian, no matter how pretty the bottle is."

The sandwiches—chicken, bacon, and avocado—were delicious. As they turned their attention to plates of sliced cantaloupe and pineapple, Eduardo joined them, sliding onto the vinyl seat beside Dan, a stack of printed material in one hand. A glass of red wine appeared instantly at Eduardo's elbow, delivered by Constantino.

The baggage handlers, now empty-handed, silently passed the table on their way back outside. Sam studied their profiles as they passed. "Dan," Sam said in a low voice, "does Tony seem familiar to you?"

Dan watched the crew members as they slipped through the doorway and then disappeared toward the stern of the ship. "He looks a little like Ricardo."

"Ricardo?"

"Our boat pilot this morning."

Had that actually been this morning? This was starting to feel like the longest day in history. "Maybe they're related. Did you get Ricardo's last name?"

Dan shook his head and then speared a piece of pineapple with his fork.

Eduardo shrugged. "There are many Ricardos. And many relations in the Galápagos." He slid a blue-and-white booklet across the table toward Sam and another toward Dan, and then opened his own matching booklet to a page featuring a map of islands linked by dotted lines. "The itinerary of this boat. You see"—he unfolded another map, which Sam recognized as the one Dan had shown her last night—"we pass very close to all your inspection points. No problem, except for Wolf." Eduardo tapped his finger on a spot near the top of the booklet page.

She opened her own booklet. Eduardo's finger was on an island far to the north. On her page, the island dot was labeled *Wenman*. "You mean Wenman?"

Eduardo shrugged. "Wenman, Teodoro Wolf—same island."

Squinting, she saw that the tiny print in parentheses beneath the larger label did say *Teodoro Wolf*.

"You must make special arrangements to go there," Eduardo told them. "It is far to the north."

Sam studied the map. Due to a long history of use by both British and Spanish plunderers, all the Galápagos Islands had both English and Spanish names. The native Galapagüeños seemed to use whichever name they liked best. What was she supposed to call the various islands in her posts? Maybe she should have Wilderness use one set of names and Zing use the other? Would that be entertaining, educational, or just confusing?

"You have arrive just in time," Eduardo continued. "Tonight we motor all the way to Isabela and Fernandina, the far west and newest islands. Your cabins are four"—he nodded toward Dan—"and yours, three, Sam, down below. *Bienvenido*—welcome!" He hoisted his wineglass.

Sam raised her glass to clink against Eduardo's. His warm greeting was such a relief after the brush-off they'd received on the dive boat and at the hotel.

The knot of tourists edged past their table toward the outer deck. Eduardo smiled and nodded at them as they

passed. To Sam and Dan, he murmured softly, "I will introduce you tomorrow at breakfast, when all are present."

Sam suddenly felt crowded. What was safe to tell the tourists? She'd put her foot in her mouth for sure. She wasn't used
to interacting with a group. Some of her extrovert friends had
even accused her of being socially retarded. She pulled her
laptop case upright. "There's an upper deck, right?"

Eduardo nodded. "Stairs at the back."

She turned to Dan. "I'm going up top for a bit."

"I'll meet you there in a few minutes."

She slid from the booth. It was fully dark now, with
both sky and sea a midnight blue. The moon had not yet
made an appearance: the horizon was a strip of black velvet
that swallowed the stars. Water lapped softly around the
yacht. An unseen marine creature, probably another sea
lion, splashed near the port side. She slung the strap of her
laptop case over her shoulder and walked to the stern, passing a cabin labeled 2 with white curtains discreetly pulled.
There was no doubt a mirror-image cabin on the other side.
On the main deck, these were probably the most expensive
cabins. She climbed the metal stairs to the upper deck.

At the top of the stairs was an open-air deck bordered by
a waist-high double rail. The upraised structure of the
bridge loomed behind her, accessible by a couple of short
steps on either side. Inside, a light on a side wall illuminated
a white-uniformed man working at a desk in the corner.

The brochure called *Papagayo* a yacht, not a cruise
ship. She wondered where the dividing line was. Not that it
really mattered; she couldn't mention their accommodations in her posts. She wasn't sure she should even tell Tad
Wyatt about the change in plans. Key had given NPF a
huge budget to take care of all expenses; there would probably be no questions.

She pulled out her cell phone and called her voice mail
at home. Only Chase's message awaited her there. *Where
are you, querida?* She'd been gone for two days and she
had only one call? That was depressing.

Dan appeared out of the dark. He wistfully eyed the instrument in her hand. "Is that a satellite phone?"

"Yep. Courtesy of Key's equipment department." The phone was a little bigger and heavier than the average cellular model. A nub of antenna extended from its top. She extended it toward him. "Be my guest."

He took it and punched in a number, then murmured, "Hi, honey." Turning his back to her, he hunched over the railing.

Would a man someday talk to her with that well-worn warmth in his voice? She stared out at the dark horizon, remembering the last moments she had spent with Chase.

They had been perched on a cliff on the small rocky peninsula known as Teddy Bear Cove, watching the sun set to the west behind Lummi Island. The waning light painted the water of Chuckanut Bay in broad strokes of lilac and silver. The rounded head of a harbor seal plowed a V in the water briefly near Dot Island, and then sank out of sight again beneath the silky surface of the bay.

It was Christmas Eve. They were encased in fleece and Gor-Tex, and cozily cuddled together on the rock, Sam sitting between Chase's outstretched legs, with his arms wrapped around her. She felt blessed by the natural beauty of the place she chose to call home, the mild coastal weather, and the closeness of the man she was growing to love. It was one of those rare perfect moments.

And then Chase leaned close and murmured in her ear, "Come live with me."

Her brain screamed, "What?!" but she managed to keep her lips still while a million thoughts careened through her head. Did he mean for her to give up her cabin in the woods and move into his condo in the heart of Salt Lake City? Give up the woods outside her door with the pileated woodpeckers and great horned owls and the trails threading through the Chuckanut Mountains? Give up the saltwater bays, the forested islands and the porpoises, jellyfish, and kingfishers? There were mountains and forests close to Salt Lake City, but there would certainly be no harbor seals. Where would she kayak?

But she ached for more time with him. People thought that she had chosen a solitary life, but she always hoped for a partner. The trouble was that the men she knew always ended up wanting her to become someone else. Even though she'd remained friends with Adam Steele after their shared escapade in the media spotlight, she didn't trust any man to care about her as much as he did about himself.

But Chase's words proved he loved her and wanted to stay with her, didn't they? He was asking her to share his home. Then again, Chase was rarely *at* home, at least as far as she knew. Bellingham was full of college students and old hippies and environmentalist types; she'd finally landed in a place where she felt like one of the crowd. Salt Lake City meant religion and conservative politics. And he lived in a third-floor condo. What would she do with her cabin, her cat, and Blake?

Chase's sigh was so deep that she felt his chest expand against her back. His exhaled breath gusted warmly across her neck and cheek.

Oh God, she'd waited too long to respond. "Chase, I—"

"Never mind." He wrapped his arms around her more tightly. "I should have known better."

"Chase, it's just—"

"It's okay." He paused, swallowed, and then said, "We'll talk more on our ski vacation in February. We're getting together then, no matter what. Agreed?"

"Agreed," she murmured. She turned in his arms and kissed him.

Then the sun winked out behind the islands to the west and they walked back to the car as the early winter darkness fell around them. Their dinner at Boundary Bay Brewpub felt strained to her.

For Christmas, Chase gave her an exquisite painting of a mountain lion silhouetted against a sunset, a beautiful reminder of their past shared adventure. She gave him a new backpack, which now seemed impersonal in comparison to his gift. Despite all their loving words, their parting kiss on Christmas Day lacked its usual heat.

Had she blown it? Was Chase insulted by her response, or lack of it? If so, he hid it well. Then again, the man was nothing if not enigmatic.

But she shouldn't be thinking about her personal life now. She had a job to do. She powered up her laptop and checked the e-mail she'd downloaded earlier. A message from Wyatt at *Out There* reminded her that tomorrow was her and Zing's debut, so she'd better come up with an exciting!! leadoff for both of them. The deal, he reiterated, was a story per character per day, with Wilderness Westin doing general ecology and travel issues and Zing doing adventure dive stories and explaining what NPF was doing in the islands. Was Dan's near death exciting enough for him? No, probably not—she had no visuals, Dan was still functioning, and he insisted it was probably an accident.

Sam was surprised to find a message from Maya, the teenage delinquent she'd befriended on a trail crew last summer, where the kid was doing public service work in lieu of jail time. *Former* delinquent, she reminded herself. They'd kept in touch. Sam was teaching Maya embroidery and, she hoped, some basic ethics and life skills.

Gt addr fr Blk; swt dl 4 u; c u 3-12!

It took Sam a couple of read-throughs to decipher the girl's code. Why was she texting? Maya was a foster kid; she didn't have the money for a cell phone of any kind. Sam frowned. Just because Maya couldn't *pay* for one didn't mean she didn't *have* a cell. The girl was still on probation for a string of burglary charges.

Finally, Sam's brain translated the message: *Got address from Blake; sweet deal for you; see you March 12.* What the heck was March 12? She tried to envision the calendar on her wall at home. Oh jeez, was that spring break? She'd promised that Maya could spend the school vacation with her and Blake to get a break from her foster home. They were going to design some quilt squares to represent Maya's life and ambitions. Sam could hardly wait to see what ideas the girl came up with. In July, Maya would turn eighteen and be ejected from the foster care system. Sam was more than a little worried about what would happen after that. The kid had already suggested that she might live in a tent in Sam's backyard.

The hum of a boat motor approached and then abruptly stopped at the stern of the ship. Sam stood up, leaving the laptop on a deck chair, and walked to the railing. A small boat with TAXI spelled out in lights above the cabin unloaded a tall silver-haired man, a dark-haired woman, and a pile of bags onto *Papagayo*'s stern platform. Tony rushed to greet them.

"She's right here." Dan nudged her with an elbow, saying, "No, not like her photo at all—in person, she's a real dog." He clamped his thumb over the microphone and held out the phone. "She wants to talk to you. Not one word about the dive today, okay?"

"Hello?" Sam said uncertainly.

"Summer? This is Elizabeth Kazaki. I just wanted to tell you how glad I am that you're with Dan on this trip. I know he gets a little down sometimes when he's away from home."

A little *down*? *That's nothing; he nearly died today, Elizabeth.* "He's fine," she said aloud.

In front of her, Dan pressed his hands together in a thank-you gesture.

"I'm relieved to know he's got a dependable dive buddy, Summer. I get so worried when he goes solo."

"Solo is never a good idea," Sam said. She sure wouldn't want to be a lone human eighty feet below the surface. Especially after today. "And call me Sam."

"Really? Summer's such a nice name. Well, Sam, I hope you both enjoy yourselves down there. Don't let Dan do anything crazy. Take care of my husband."

"I'll do my best, Elizabeth." She handed Dan the phone.

He listened for a moment, said, "Love you, too," then ended the call and handed the phone to her.

"Dan, we need to talk. What's the deal here? Obviously,

Eduardo knows who we are, but is it okay to tell the others? Or are we supposed to—"

A clatter of footsteps rattled down the steps from the bridge and then down the stairs to the main deck. The man in white uniform—the captain, judging by the epaulets on his shoulders—met the silver-haired man at the top of the stairs and shook his hand. Then the captain gallantly kissed the hand of the dark-haired woman. She followed two blue-shirted crew members carrying their luggage into Cabin 1. The captain disappeared into the galley area.

A whiff of tobacco smoke preceded the silver-haired gentleman as he climbed up to the top deck. He wore a light blue running suit, and as he strolled toward them, his cigarette gave off a red glow in the darkness. "Evening," he murmured as he passed to the railing farthest from them.

"Evening." Sam nodded at him. Turning back to Dan, she changed tack. "Elizabeth says I'm supposed to take care of you."

"Of course." He grinned. "Isn't there an ancient Asian saying to that effect? You saved my life; now you're responsible for me."

"That can't be right. What kind of reward is that?" Sam shook her head. "Must be a bad translation." She slipped her laptop back into its case, then slung the phone in with it.

The new arrival approached again, waving his smoked-down cigarette and glancing about uncertainly. Finally spotting an aluminum trash container, he crushed the cigarette out on the metal skin, and then flicked the butt inside. "Sorry," he said, turning to Sam and Dan. "Nasty habit." He held out his hand. "Jonathan Sanders." His nails were as carefully buffed and manicured as his hairstyle. "My wife Paige and I have Cabin one."

Sanders exuded wealth and confidence. An aging Hollywood star, perhaps? "I'm Sam, and this is Dan."

"Call me Jon," Sanders said. "I hear that you two are marine scientists. Working with Darwin Station?"

How had he heard about her and Dan? Would he consider working with Darwin Station to be a point in their favor or a strike against them?

"We're not attached to that organization, although of course we know them," Dan hedged. "Sam here's a writer as well as a biologist."

So at least she knew it was okay to say that much.

"Interesting," Sanders said. "I've done a bit of diving in my time. I didn't know it was possible on this boat."

His words sounded like a challenge. Sam looked at Dan.

"We have a special permit," Dan told Sanders.

"I see." Sanders abruptly turned to the east, studying the rising moon. "Lovely night, isn't it?"

The forward lights came on in the bridge room behind them, casting their shadows onto the deck. Beneath their feet, *Papagayo*'s engine throbbed to life. Muted shouts in Spanish and loud clanks attested to the raising of anchors at stern and bow.

The yacht swung westward, putting the lights of Puerto Baquerizo Moreno behind them. The wind lifted Jonathan Sanders's silver hair. He turned into the breeze, smiling. "Our adventure begins."

Sam's adventure had begun two days ago. Her body was not coping well with the time change and the relocation and the near-death experience, even if it hadn't been her own. She yawned as she picked up her laptop case. "You'll have to excuse me. I know it's early, but I'm bound for bed."

"Me, too." Dan turned toward the stairs. "Good night, Jon."

As they made their way through the empty lounge, Dan touched her hand. "Sam, about the dive tomorrow. This checkpoint we'll be going to—there's nothing around for miles but a seamount and a buoy chain."

Endless blue-green dapples dotted with unidentifiable swarms of shadowy creatures washed across her imagination. An infinity of water. She swallowed, her throat suddenly dry. "Okay."

"The bottom's over three hundred feet deep."

"But we don't have to go that deep, right?" she asked.

His brow wrinkled. "Three hundred feet?"

She'd slipped up. Anything over one hundred was a danger zone, she remembered. She couldn't even imagine what three hundred feet of water would look like below her. She forced a laugh. "I'm *kidding*. Yeesh!"

He studied her face. "Just how many dives have you logged?"

No way was she going to confess to the actual puny number. "Not that many," she admitted. "But enough."

"You won't be scared?"

"Me, scared?" She tried for a chuckle of bravado. It came out a little strangled. "I'm not letting you dive alone, if that's what you're suggesting." She shook her head. "No way. Especially after—" Had the bad-air incident really happened only hours ago? Seemed like days had passed since then.

"Sam, this time I watched them fill our tanks at the shop, and then I tested for carbon monoxide just to be sure. If you're nervous—"

She cocked an eyebrow at him. "Why do you think I'd be nervous? Who rescued whom today?"

He stared her down. Her gaze broke away first. "Look, Dan, I admit it, I *am* a little nervous; after all, I've never been in the Galápagos before. I'm not always quite sure what's going on." *Always?* Heck, she hadn't been sure what was going on since the moment she'd stepped off the plane.

He shrugged. "Only the usual. It's the Galápagos."

Was she supposed to know what that meant? "Are we safe now?"

"As safe as we can be."

Did he mean that to be reassuring? He put a hand on her forearm. "I'll understand if you don't want to dive the seamount tomorrow. There's usually a strong current in that channel."

A strong current? *Crap.* On her fourth open water dive in the San Juan Islands back home, there'd been a brisk current. The students had practiced going up and down a buoy chain, so she'd passed that hurdle, sort of, but she hadn't found the experience exactly pleasant. The bottom there had leveled off at only seventy feet.

This is the assignment you accepted, she reminded herself. The one you lied to get. *Suck it up.*

"This is what I signed up to do," she told Dan. "I have to be there to write the story. I have to be there to take the photos and video. I'm your dive buddy. No matter what happens, I have to be there. Got it?"

He held up both hands in surrender. "Got it, buddy."

They made their way down the last set of stairs. Below the water line, a harsh pine scent failed to disguise the faint odor of mildew. The narrow hallway held a strip of dark blue carpet between cheaply paneled walls. Four numbered doors. She stopped in front of Cabin 3 and turned to Dan. "Did Eduardo give you our cabin keys?"

"No key," he intoned, doing a near-perfect imitation of Eduardo's accent. "You will find no lock on your cabin doors." He turned the knob on Cabin 4 to demonstrate. "We are all friend here."

"I sure hope so." She pushed open her own door. That pile of equipment on the upper bunk represented a lot of money.

The door to 6, the cabin next to Dan's, opened. One of the tourists they'd seen earlier, a young man with ragged hair and mustache, emerged. "Speaking of friends," he said.

Chagrin washed over Dan's face. "Sorry to be loud."

"It's not you," the stranger assured him, smoothing his mustache with a finger. "The walls are made of recycled newsprint." He thrust out a hand. "Brandon Venning. Welcome to steerage." He pulled another young man out to meet them.

Mustachioed Brandon Venning and red-haired Ken Pruitt shared Cabin 6. Grad students from Columbus, Ohio. It seemed odd to Sam that graduate students were vacationing in February, but it was none of her business, and she didn't have the energy to care at the moment. Barely managing to stifle a yawn, she told them, "If I don't remember your names tomorrow, just slap me around."

"No problem," Brandon said. "You two want a beer? We've got a case." He inclined his head toward Cabin 6.

"Thanks, but I can barely stand up now. See you in the morning." She stepped into her cabin and closed the door behind her, leaving the three men in the hallway.

Cabin 3 was tidy in a military sort of way, although as she emptied her bags, she realized that not everything would easily fit into the drawers and the tiny closet. Good thing she had no roommate. She dumped the extras onto the lower bunk, changed to an oversize T-shirt, and brushed her teeth in the tiny bathroom—or was it called a head, even on a yacht?

Papagayo's engine, muffled by the rush of ocean alongside, throbbed like a heartbeat. She attached the satellite phone to its charger and plugged it into the lone electrical connection in the bathroom, then plugged the laptop into the only outlet in the bedroom. Clearly this floating hotel was not designed for the electronic age.

She wasn't used to sleeping in a basement closet of a room. She needed to at least *see* outdoors, even if there was only a sliver of moon to enjoy tonight. She climbed onto the upper bunk, where a small porthole framed the evening sky between slaps of gray water.

Turning her head, she stared at the door for a full minute. Dan didn't seem to mind the lack of a lock. He seemed to take all their setbacks in stride, which was unnerving in itself. Was getting bad air and being tossed out of your hotel the usual routine here? Was she naïve to expect a pleasant trip in a Third World country? Alone in the dark, she felt paranoia creeping back in.

We are all friend here. Was it true? The crew seemed friendly enough, including Tony. She really shouldn't condemn the man just because he looked a little like the hostile boat pilot. But had someone in town told Sanders that she and Dan were marine scientists? She hadn't gotten a look at the driver of the taxi boat. She climbed down from her bunk and jammed the lone chair beneath the knob of the unlocked cabin door.

The yacht bucked over a wave, and she thought about the beachmaster sinking that panga in Academy Bay. Both of *Papagayo*'s skiffs were winched out of the water and securely tied up, along with her kayak—she checked before descending the stairs. She'd never slept on a boat before. A boat as big as *Papagayo* would be difficult to sink, wouldn't it? She took the life vest from the tiny closet and slung it across the foot of her bunk, where she could reach it easily.

As she pulled herself back onto the upper bunk, a fin slid past just below the porthole. She pressed her face close to the Plexiglas. A shark alongside the ship? A bad omen. The fin surfaced again, keeping pace with *Papagayo*. Sam held her breath. The creature rolled, its gray skin gleaming in the dim light. Its head turned in her direction. She expected jagged teeth and a flat cold gaze, but instead the creature exposed a rounded snout and regarded her with a huge intelligent eye.

A dolphin! The best of all possible omens. Sam chuckled softly to herself. As if in response, she heard hoots of male laughter from the other side of the hall. Brandon and his roommate Ken seemed nice. Eduardo certainly was. Even Jon Sanders had acted friendly.

Maybe the bad air *was* accidental. And the hotel, just sloppy record-keeping. Dan seemed to know what he was doing. And Eduardo was looking out for them now. She was being paid to report on nature in the Galápagos, every environmentalist's dream. She was cruising the islands on a luxury yacht, for heaven's sake. This *was* going to be the tropical adventure she'd envisioned when she took the job, no matter what Chase might think. Her dreams alternated between attending a strangely pleasant skinhead party and staring down a big hammerhead to get a really exciting!! photo.

CHASE Perez put his toothbrush back into its holder and ran a hand over his shaved scalp. Did he look too Indian? Too Mexican? Nah, he could pass; he'd already passed for a couple of weeks. Charlie Perini. Italian-American father and mother, emphasis on the American. All-American skinhead.

"Yo, Charlie," he said to his image. He flicked his earring with his fingernail, set it swinging on his lobe. Weird feeling; lopsided. Maybe it felt different if you had both ears pierced, like Summer did.

What an ass he'd been. It was way too soon to ask her to move in with him. He was just so damn frustrated. They hadn't spent more than two solid days together, even counting the crazy backwoods race through Utah when they'd first met. What she was thinking now? Maybe she'd never considered a long-term relationship with him? At Christmas he'd seen a package on her bookshelf, addressed to her from Adam Steele. Why did she still keep in touch with the slimeball who used her to further his own career? He knew the diamond earrings she wore on special occasions had been a gift from the newscaster. But diamonds did not seem Summer's type, and neither did Adam.

Now she'd flown off to the Galápagos to swim with iguanas and count fish with another man. A marine biologist, who would be exactly her type. Damn. Chase could envision her reclining on a beach in a bikini, her gleaming silver-blond hair shimmering in the sun over nearly naked breasts.

"In your dreams, bro," he snorted. The Summer Westin he knew was unlikely to wear a bikini, especially one that left her breasts nearly naked. Summer's dresser drawers more likely held two identical blue Speedos designed for swimming laps. Maybe he'd surprise her with one of those one-piece-but-deadly-sexy numbers, black Lycra slit down to her navel, barely held together with laces.

"In February, Charlie?" he chided himself. He'd have to settle for seeing her in stretchy skiwear.

No matter what, they'd pledged each other. Now he had to make sure their rendezvous happened; Nicole had already promised she would help. He'd pulled off a few meetings in disguise before, but this was his first extended undercover job, and it was taking forever. They were close to making the right contacts; he could feel it. They'd heard about Dread several times now. It was best to make the target come to you. With luck, that would happen tomorrow. He and Nicole had already spent a couple of weeks laying the groundwork.

He was always canceling out on Summer; it was hard to kick their affair into high gear when they met up only every couple of months. But on the ski vacation, they'd finally share a string of days. And nights. He pictured Summer in lacy black lingerie.

How had he developed this desire for a woman he rarely saw? He never lacked for willing women. Carlotta, a friend of his cousin's, made it clear she was waiting for his call. And Maureen, the evidence clerk at the office, touched her fingertips to his hand this morning and gave him a smoldering look. Maureen would wear black lingerie, he was sure. Or maybe even red.

Did Summer own lacy lingerie of any color? He'd never seen any on his visits. But then, she was full of surprises. Scuba diving, for chrissake. The Galápagos. He tried to reassure himself that she was safe. Attacks by locals on the international conservation community there had settled down in recent years, hadn't they? The islands were too remote to be a major conduit for drug runners. These days, there was only the occasional run-in between illegal fishing boats and radical environmental groups.

Environmental groups. Like the Natural Planet Foundation. *Illegal fishing.* Summer was doing an underwater survey. Shit. His imagination filled with James Bond scenes of underwater harpoon-gun shootouts and above-water boat chases and explosions. He headed for his computer to check the latest briefings from the State Department.

Summer Westin was definitely not boring. Neither was she exactly normal. The woman had a propensity for diving headfirst into hot water.

6

"HELLO, Zing." Sam stared at her alter ego on the laptop screen. The muscular young woman wore a sleek black-and-white swimsuit that mimicked the gleaming skin of an orca. Although the front zipped most of the way up to a modest mock turtleneck neckline, the effect was one of barely contained sexual energy. The tattoo of a leaping dolphin graced Zing's right shoulder, framed by curtains of undulating auburn hair. She looked like she could kayak through a typhoon and then wrestle a shark onto her plate for dinner. It was no wonder the gal was intrepid.

Sam pulled up her own photo on *Out There*'s website. Wilderness Westin was a platinum blond pixie. Okay, there was a certain brazenness to the image: she did have a rainbow boa constrictor draped around her neck, and a pixel-poker in Seattle had erased her tank top straps so she appeared to be wearing nothing but the snake and a strategically placed drape of jungle vines and blossoms. But next to Zing, Westin looked a definite wuss.

A quiet tap on her door interrupted her thoughts. Dan

stuck his head in. "Ready, partner?" His voice was barely above a whisper. "Eduardo's loading up to take us out."

It was only six thirty, not quite daylight. She wanted to dive into coffee and scrambled eggs, not into a liquid abyss. She forced a smile. "Coming."

"Meet you on the stern platform." The door closed softly behind him.

She turned off the computer, rose from the chair, and slid it under the desk to make enough space in the tiny cabin to pull on her wetsuit. In the bathroom, she scraped her hair back into a bun, fastening it in place with hairpins. Flexing her neoprene-covered arms, she said forcefully to the mirror, "I am Zing."

It didn't make her feel any more intrepid.

She dropped the pose and slung her camera strap over her neck. Pre-coffee, it took all her focus not to bang her gear against the walls as she trudged up the narrow stairway.

Eduardo had thoughtfully packed sweet rolls and coffee. Twenty minutes later, as they crossed open water, the sugar and caffeine had improved both her mood and energy level. The sea was almost flat, the quiet water reflecting the silvery pink of the sunrise. She tried to absorb the serenity of the surroundings but found it difficult to drown out the buzzing anxiety in the back of her mind.

Three hundred feet of water. Anything could be down there. Woman-eating monsters. Dolphins could be down there, too, she argued with her fears. That would be wonderful, to swim with dolphins. Another sea turtle would be welcome. According to her guidebook, whale sharks frequented the Galápagos, and she'd dearly love to see one of those harmless giants. Nudibranchs—she wanted to see the flamboyant sea slugs featured on her identification CD.

Dan applied the CO analyzer to both their cylinders, taking care to show her the reading. It showed 2.6 ppm, an acceptable level. Eduardo watched from his position at the rudder. If he thought it was odd that they were checking the air, he didn't show it. She assembled her gear,

listening carefully for air leaks, breathed twice from both
her mouthpieces, double-checked the protective housing
surrounding her camera to make sure it was sealed. She
finished just as they arrived at Buoy 3492, a black-and-red-
striped structure topped by two balls, in the midst of endless water. As Eduardo cut the panga motor and they
drifted close, the buoy tilted slightly. When Eduardo
snagged the buoy with his hook, a bell clanged loudly, but
he tied the panga off to the structure nonetheless, and
turned around to help Sam with her camera.

Now there was no choice but to do her job.

"Bit of a current here," Dan told her. "Stay close to the
seamount."

As soon as she was in the water, the reason for the
buoy's location became evident: the marker was anchored
to a pillar of lava that leveled off less than fifteen feet below
the surface. Buoy 3492 was a warning to keep large ships
from colliding with the obstacle. For most boats the seamount wouldn't be a problem, except perhaps in rolling
waves. She was relieved to see that the seamount was not a
thin needle of volcanic rock, but at least a couple dozen
feet across at its coral-encrusted summit. Lower down, it
became even more substantial, its jagged plateaus alternat-
ing with steep drop-offs, like a volcanic wedding cake rising from the cobalt depths.

Dan quickly dropped into the lee of the rock formation.
Sam descended more slowly, cradling her camera in one
arm and sliding her free hand down the buoy chain. Saying
there was a "bit of a current" was an understatement. The
force of the moving water stretched her body horizontally
like a flag snapping in the wind. But at least the water flowing past was lukewarm here, not ice cold like some of the
other currents in the Galápagos. And the rock below beckoned with clusters of corals, sponges, and rainbow-colored
fish.

A cluster of yellow groupers dispersed from the base of
the anchor chain on her arrival, leaving behind confetti-
like shreds of the unfortunate creature they had been

feeding on. After the current blew her across the summit like a tumbleweed, the large fish regrouped behind her. She fought her way downward, and was relieved when she reached the protection of the broader rocky flank. After she got her breathing under control, she located Dan some thirty to forty feet below her. He was largely obscured by schools of darting fish above him, but his bubbles rose in measured, steady bursts, which was reassuring. They had agreed that he would work on his counts alone today; he knew that she had to gather material for her first blog post.

Determined to relax, she turned her attention to the rock shelf in front of her. Among the ragged protrusions of lava lay several pieces of boating debris. Many items were made unidentifiable by splotches of pink or lavender—new patches of corals and sponges—but she could make out the shapes of an old anchor and a length of chain. She spied a wicked-looking fish gaff that had been lost recently enough to have only a few spots of growth beginning on it; she could even make out a few letters on a small metal plate that clung to it, held in place by a screw on one end. The fish zipped around over the debris field, feasting on pinkish masses there, zooming into tight clusters to snatch bites and then darting out to swallow them at a safe distance from their fellows.

A barracuda hovered not far from her left elbow. The toothy predator was no longer than three feet, but its flat black gaze and its total lack of motion were eerie. She eyed it warily. It seemed focused on the cloud of bright blue fish in front of her, but she couldn't be sure it wasn't eyeing her appendages or the silver hoop earrings she now realized she'd forgotten to remove. The barracuda suddenly darted forward. She backpedaled with a little squeak of alarm, and the blue fish exploded outward in all directions, abandoning their meal. The barracuda flashed in a tight circle through the suddenly empty space, snapped up a large chunk of flesh it located between sponges, and then hovered above the remains of a gray corpse wedged among spiky orange corals.

Sam made herself breathe out slowly as she brought up her camera. With the premises momentarily absent of fishy forms except for the 'cuda, the little plateau was a grisly scene. The carcasses of at least half a dozen sharks lay scattered over the lava landscape. On two corpses that had not yet been chewed to shreds, she saw that steaks had been hacked from their sides. The fins were missing from their backs, sides, and tails.

She snapped a couple of close-up stills of the carnage, then switched to video and filmed the scene. Farther below she could see other bits and pieces of flesh snagged on rock shelves, attended by darting shapes. Curious, she released some air from her buoyancy vest and sank.

The current sucked her away from the pillar. Her pulse leaped into overdrive. She kicked hard to move back into the protection of the rock face and made herself inhale slowly and take stock of her surroundings. As she glanced upward, she was startled to see a hammerhead glide only a few feet over her head. The shark was not more than five feet long. But still, a hammerhead!

After she remembered to breathe again, she realized she was still sinking, and added air to her BCD to level off at seventy feet. Tearing her focus away from the hammerhead, she looked below for Dan, and spotted another hammerhead, this one at least a seven-footer, only a few yards below her fins. Sweet Jesus! She had a sudden urge to streak for the surface, but she forced herself to take a deep breath and stay in place. *I am Zing,* she told herself. She focused the camera on the shark below.

The hammerhead spiraled in on a large chunk of carcass snagged on a ragged lava outcropping. Waggling its stalk-eyed head, the shark raised a flurry of small crabs before it managed to rip off a satisfactory bite. Very impressive, in a weird alien cannibal sort of way. She was amazed that the shark didn't whack an eyeball in the process of eating. The hammerhead backed away and swam in a tight circle, shadowed by a fleet of fish snapping up the scraps that drifted from its mouth. Then the shark returned for more of its cousin's flesh.

Zing really should dive down there for a closer shot. *Right.* Wilderness Westin wasn't buying it for a minute. She settled for switching to still photos at maximum zoom.

Sam backed farther away from the seamount, keeping one eye on the hammerhead as she searched the dark blue water below for Dan. Her heartbeat tripled as she spotted a huge mass rising from the depths. Gray-blue, it moved unnaturally, seeming to writhe as it rose from the shadows. Giant squid? Octopus? Great white? She glanced quickly back at the large hammerhead, which remained intent on its meal. Turning her back on the shark, she focused the camera on the creature from the abyss. In a startling movement, a piece of it broke away, swimming upward with wobbly motions, and then she saw that it was not one monster, but three hammerheads moving like a pack of wolves, dogging another type of shark. Their prey could barely swim, she saw now, because its dorsal and pectoral fins had been sliced off. The poor creature didn't have a prayer of escape. It was dragged in one direction then another by the attacking sharks. A remora detached itself from the dying shark and circled uncertainly, searching for a new ride. She filmed in fascinated horror as two of the hammerheads ripped chunks from their live victim.

A sudden pressure on her forearm made her jerk her head up, expecting a carnivore at her elbow. Dan hovered beside her. He raised a thumb toward the surface, signaling that he was ready to go up. She nodded. Their bubble streams cleared the space overhead of fish as they slowly rose, dumping air from their BCDs as the vests expanded with the decreasing pressure. Sam kept a wary eye on the sharks below.

At thirty-five feet she spotted a crimson-and-white spotted lobster peeking from a hole, and stopped to take a last photo. She needed at least one reminder of the incredible beauty existing side by side with the brutality down here. A low hum throbbed through the water, a different frequency from their panga motor. When she raised her head, she saw the red-and-yellow-striped hull of a small boat slicing through the water, moving away.

On rising from the lee of the seamount, she missed the buoy chain and was immediately dragged several yards away by the current. Then she had to focus on keeping hold of her camera and kicking hard to rejoin Dan beneath their panga. By the time she surfaced, she was puffing like she'd run a marathon, and the other boat was turning in the distance, though she couldn't see clearly through her mask in the blinding morning sun. Judging by its speed, it had a powerful motor.

Eduardo took their tanks and helped them belly flop into the inflatable. As soon as Dan was settled, he asked Eduardo, "Why did you wave that fisherman off?"

The guide shrugged. "For safety. He could not know there was divers here."

Interesting. Eduardo hadn't denied that the other boat belonged to a fisherman. "You know the owner of that boat?" she asked him.

Eduardo glanced at her and then at Dan, then seemed to realize that he'd said something he shouldn't have. "Galápagos is a small community. He is a cousin."

Dan's gaze met hers, and she knew he was thinking the same thing she was. Eduardo's cousin may have been illegally fishing for sharks here.

IN spite of the gruesome start to the day, Sam felt ebullient during breakfast back on *Papagayo*. She and Dan had collected valuable data for the NPF survey and surfaced in good shape. She'd not only faced down sharks, she'd gotten decent video footage of them. She was a pro. Heck, she *was* Zing.

"And you're a marine biologist, too?"

Sam looked up from her empty plate to the silver-haired woman across from her. Gail? No. Abigail, Abigail Birsky.

Wife of Ronald Birsky, the bald gentleman seated next to her. From Nashville.

"Not marine," Sam corrected. "By training, I'm a wild-life biologist—mostly land-based critters, like wolves and elk and cougars and such. But there are darn few jobs for us, so these days I'm mostly a freelance writer. I try to focus on nature whenever I can. That's why this trip is so perfect—the Galápagos Islands are a nature lover's dream."

When Constantino asked if anyone wanted more of the Spanish omelet, both Sam and Dan eagerly handed their plates in his direction. Abigail and Ronald exchanged an amused glance over their still-half-filled plates, and Sam suddenly remembered her manners. "And you two? Do you spend your time touring the world?"

"I'm a retired minister," Ronald drawled. The tall man's neck and shoulders curved into a perpetual stoop. Probably from bending to hear shorter parishioners. Or maybe from accommodating his wife, whose silver head reached only to his shoulder. He leaned toward her now. "Abigail's my better half."

Abigail's pale blue eyes twinkled as she patted Sam's hand. "I look forward to getting to know you."

Outwardly, Sam smiled; inwardly, she groaned. She'd grown up with constant *tsk-tsk-tsk*s from her minister father and an ever-present circle of church ladies. Dan had already shown the Birskys photos of his pretty wife and precious child. And then Sam had noticed Abigail Birsky's glance toward her empty left ring finger.

Hey, I'm in a relationship with a hunky dangerous Latino-Lakota skinhead, she wanted to say, but that would probably not impress the Birskys. Not to mention that she wasn't sure what the "relationship" part was. Maybe she'd finally have a chance to sort that out in the coming week.

Constantino plunked down her second serving in front of her and Sam gratefully applied herself to eggs and toast instead of blurting out something she'd regret later.

Abigail smiled at the server and said sweetly, "Thank you, Tony."

Her husband laid his hand atop hers. "His name is Constantino, dear."

Abigail's cheeks pinked. She squinted in Constantino's direction, saying, "Oh dear, I'm so sorry," but the server was already halfway back to the kitchen.

Ronald reassured his wife. "All these foreign names are confusing, aren't they? I wouldn't worry; I don't think he even heard you."

Sam's gaze flitted around the dining area as she tried to recall the names of all these people she and Dan had met on board *Papagayo*. Maxim, Eduardo's clean-cut dark-skinned young colleague, was easy to remember. Dressed in the khaki shirt and shorts of the Galápagos Park naturalist guide uniform, he and Eduardo stood out from the tourists and ship's crew. Jonathan Sanders, she remembered from last night. In daylight, she could see that his pretty wife Paige was much younger than he. Brandon and Ken, the grad students from the lower deck.

In the booth ahead were the—Robinsons? No, Robersons. From Cabin 5. Jerry was a muscular man with a steel gray crew cut and a disapproving glare, who looked exactly like the retired policeman he was. He was either a naturally grumpy old guy or he'd taken an instant dislike to half the people on board, Sam and Dan included. He was counterbalanced by his wife, Sandy, a middle-aged bottle blonde with huge parrot earrings and an infectious smile.

Abigail patted Sam's hand again. "I can't wait to go snorkeling this afternoon. Did you see wonderful fish on your dive this morning?"

"There are always amazing things to see in Galápagos waters," Dan quickly interjected.

Sam shot him a glance. Did he think she wasn't smart enough to keep her mouth shut about the shark poaching?

"Are you joining us for our hike on Isabela this morning?" Ronald asked.

Sam shook her head. "Unfortunately, no. Dan and I have work to do." Today she was on a schedule that was the reverse of the tour group; she'd gone diving at dawn and now would work while they hiked on Isabela near Tagus Cove. Then this afternoon, as they snorkeled, she'd explore the route they had hiked in the morning.

After shoveling the last bite of eggs into her mouth, she slid to the edge of the seat. "Speaking of work, I'd better get to it."

Dan nodded. "Sam's right. I'd better write my report before I forget what I saw this morning." He rose from the booth and preceded her down the stairs.

SAM carried her laptop and satellite phone to the upper deck. She had the place completely to herself. The crew members were all busy in the kitchen, cleaning cabins, or off shepherding the small tour group on Isabela with Maxim and Eduardo.

The only drawback to working outdoors was that the sun was intense. She had to tilt the laptop screen forward to see the images. The shark videos and still photos looked damn good, if she did say so herself. She selected the most dramatic ones and zipped them into a compressed file.

Between *Papagayo* and Isabela's shore, gulls wheeled and shrieked, arguing with larger black-winged birds. Boobies? Frigate birds? She couldn't tell from here. A sea lion briefly surfaced next to the ship, exhaled loudly, slapped the water with a flipper, and then disappeared again.

Had Charles Darwin enjoyed this exact view from the HMS *Beagle* in 1835? She could hardly believe that she was here, in the cradle of the theory of evolution, in the famous naturalist's playground, six hundred miles from anywhere. It felt almost sacrilegious to use a computer in this historic place, to rely on satellite phones and Internet service. Even in the remotest places, people moved closer to machines and farther from the natural world every day. It was kind of sad.

But she was not a historian. It was her job to tell the world what the islands were like now, not in Darwin's time.

She stared at the blank word processing screen for a minute. Where to start?

She reminded herself that she was supposed to provide entertainment and it needed to be Exciting!! She typed *Sharks!* Then it all came easily. She wrote about the beautiful leopard shark yesterday and the ghastly scene this morning, segueing briefly to the lobsters and sea cucumbers and then bringing the story back to poaching and the fact that humans were obviously the predators to be most feared in the Galápagos. Dan found her as she'd just finished editing it down to the 700-word-maximum her contract stipulated.

"Joining us for lunch?" he asked.

Surprised, she checked her watch. It was nearly one o'clock. The tour group had come back without her even registering their return. And she *was* hungry again. "I'll be there in a minute."

She quickly uploaded Zing's first post and the shark images and then took her laptop back to her cabin.

A small heart-shaped box of Valentine's chocolates rested on her pillow. Chase? No, that was crazy; he didn't even know where she was staying. Then she remembered that crew members could enter her cabin at any time. Actually, anyone on board could. She took a quick peek into Dan's room. A box of candy rested on his pillow, too. It felt like they shared a stalker.

She arrived late to the dining area. Dan had joined the grad students and Eduardo. She ended up seated with the captain and the Robersons. Sandy was enthusiastic about the Valentine gift. "Aren't the chocolates yummy, Sam? Such a lovely touch."

"Nice idea," Sam agreed, nodding at the captain, embarrassed that she had been suspicious instead of grateful.

Jerry said little and glowered at her throughout the meal. Sandy chirped about how wonderful their lives were. "We have so much time, now that we're retired." She beamed. "We're going to travel all over the world." She beamed in the captain's direction. "Have you traveled far, Captain Quiroga?"

Quiroga ate European style, with a knife in one hand and a fork in the other. He waved his knife in the air as he told them that although he worked in the islands, his family owned a small company on the mainland. "I hope to return to Guayaquil in five years to take over the business from my father."

Sam had switched planes in Guayaquil. From the airport tarmac, the west coast city seemed like a steamy swamp. "You wouldn't choose to stay in the Galápagos?" she asked.

"The Galápagos is good for making money; but not for home. The problem is the world."

"The world?"

"Because of Darwin, the whole world believe Galápagos belongs to them."

In the last few weeks, Sam had researched the history of the islands. A grandiose statement from the World Heritage Centre website leapt into her mind: *World Heritage sites belong to all the peoples of the world, irrespective of the territory on which they are located.*

She forked up the last of the delicious flounder. "What sort of business is your company in Guayaquil?"

"You like that fish?" The captain pointed his knife at her plate.

She nodded.

"*Fábrica Quiroga* is what you call a cannery." He smiled, showing startling large white teeth under his thick black mustache. "We preserve the best of Ecuadorian fishes so all can enjoy them."

She smiled back uncertainly. Captain Quiroga was in the fishing business? Did he know who she and Dan worked for? Was he trying to tell her something?

7

"SOUTH of the border, down Mexico way!" Nicole sang off-key at Chase Perez's side. He swayed with the raucous crowd in time to the music, but his mind was elsewhere.

"That's where you be-long, that's where you should *stay*!" Protestors around him raised their voices on the last word. Nicole jabbed her elbow into his ribs to remind him he was supposed to be participating.

The crowd on this side of the street was only half as large as the pro-Latino gathering on the other side. So far the Tucson cops in between had managed to keep the two separate. Raising his "American Wages for American Jobs!" placard, Chase shouted, "Take your tortillas and go home, goddamn wetbacks!"

A television camera swung in his direction. *Damn.* If his parents or siblings saw this footage in Boise, he'd never live it down. But maybe they wouldn't recognize him in his hairless, tattooed, and pierced state.

"Yeah, baby, you tell 'em," Nicole crooned, clasping her hands around his arm. How she managed not to break one of those fancy inch-long lacquered nails was a mystery to him.

Chase's scalp felt hot. Had he slathered on enough sunscreen up there? What a peculiar way to spend Valentine's Day. If he'd stayed an accountant, he'd be planning a night of hot sex with his girlfriend instead of waving signs with his married FBI partner at a protest march.

The news he'd uncovered about the Galápagos gave him heartburn. There had been several violent encounters between poachers and the Galápagos park patrol in the last six months. Worse, he'd found references in Ecuadorian newspapers to a Shark Fin Mafia.

The pro-Latino crowd on the other side of the street began to chant, and the people around Chase heckled them back. This protest could flash from boring to ugly any second now. Maybe that's what needed to happen to move this job forward. According to the FBI Internet trollers, the man they were searching for, a leader named Dread, was likely to be at this rally.

Dread was a name that repeatedly cropped up on websites that celebrated crimes against immigrants in southern Arizona. Dread harped a lot about lost construction jobs and how illegal aliens were drug runners and thieves. He preached that decent Americans needed to take back the country, with bullets if necessary. And plenty of bullets had been found in the four bodies discovered a week ago in the Arizona desert.

The corpses were those of a teenage girl, two young men sporting gang tattoos, and Liam Cisneros, an undercover DEA agent. If they'd been carrying drugs or weapons, the evidence was long gone by the time their bodies had been reported. All had been shot multiple times. Cisneros had last reported to his superiors that he was traveling with NUC, a gang feared by Homeland Security to have infiltrated the U.S. Border Patrol.

So many questions surrounded Cisneros's death that it was hard to know where to start. Were the young people he died with NUC members? Had they been killed by vigilantes who shot all illegals they encountered crossing the border? Was a rival drug cartel picking off the competition?

Was the Border Patrol involved in the murders? Evidence of the involvement of Border Patrol officers in both human smuggling and drug smuggling had recently been uncovered, but the identities of the criminals were still unknown. Everything about the Cisneros case was disturbingly nebulous. It was hard to clean up a problem when you had no idea who had caused it or how big it was.

"This is pure bullshit," the man to Chase's right side growled.

"Amen to that." Chase turned to look at him. He was African-American and built like a linebacker.

"Like your shirt." The guy pointed at the letters CWU printed on Chase's sleeveless tee. He turned to display the lettering on the back of his own T-shirt. CONSTRUCTION WORKERS UNITED.

Chase grinned. Their advisors had scored on that detail. "Erection Perfection," he said, reciting the CWU slogan. Behind him, Nicole snickered.

The guy turned back and thrust out a fist. Chase tapped knuckles with him.

"Dave Redding," the black man said. "They call me Dread."

At last. "Let me guess." Chase studied the guy's bulging biceps. "Roofer?"

"Stonemason," Dread spat. "Or at least I used to be, before the goddamn spics took all the jobs at half the wages."

"Charlie Perini." Chase shook Dread's hand, gripping hard so the other man wouldn't detect the lack of calluses on his fingers. "Finish carpenter, when I can find it."

Dread crooked an eyebrow. "Haven't seen you around."

"Only been in Arizona two weeks," Chase said, wading into the getting-to-know-you stage. "Just blew in from Florida. You'd think there'd be tons of work down there after the hurricanes, but no." He jerked a shoulder at the gathering across the street. "Two guesses why, and the first one doesn't count. I read about some new retirement communities going up here; figured they could use carpenters. But shit, I was wrong again."

Dread made a face. "Yeah, shit."

"Hey, is there even a CWU hall in this burg?" Chase pronounced it "see-woo" like he'd been instructed.

The black man shook his head. "Not anymore. They pretty much busted us up about six years ago. Can't find a union job anywhere in this state anymore."

"Hiya, I'm Charlie's wife, Nikki," Nicole broke in. She brushed a strand of curly blond hair from her brow and looked up at Dread. "This is just so much pointless crap." She waved a hand to indicate the crowd around them. "Don't ya think? There's gotta be a better way to get the *real* message across. You know, stop dancin' around and cut to the chase?"

Dread studied her for a long moment, like a rattlesnake evaluating a gopher as potential lunch. Finally he said, "There might be a way. If you want to get in on some *real* action."

Nicole grinned. "If we can't do *con*-struction, maybe we should try *de*-struction."

Dread glanced at Chase. He shrugged, trying to look nonchalant. "I've always enjoyed demolition work."

Dread leaned close. "Tomorrow night, there's a meeting at seven o'clock at the Horseshoe Tavern on Second Avenue. Then we're gonna take a little ride over to the barrio, if you know what I mean."

Nicole raised her face toward Chase. "We can make that, can't we, sugar?"

He turned to Dread. "Never been there, but we'll find it. Should we bring anything?"

"Everything you got." He held Chase's gaze for a minute to be sure his message got across.

A male blue-footed booby marched in place on the basalt shelf of Isabela's shoreline, oblivious to Sam kneeling less than a yard away. The bird raised one webbed foot and displayed it, toes outstretched, for a long moment before lowering it to the ground. He presented the other in a similar fashion, as if to show that they were a perfectly matched pair, the brightest blue feet on the island.

The observing female booby wore a weary expression. She'd probably seen this performance a thousand times. She'd probably seen brighter cerulean toes. In fact, her own webbed feet were every bit as blue as his. Sensing her waning attention, the male thrust a tiny twig toward her with his beak. No response. He discarded the twig and picked up a water-rounded stone and goose-stepped with renewed fervor, then wrapped up his performance with a loud honk and skypoint, raising his black-tipped beak and wingtips in rigid salute to the blazing sun overhead.

The female shook out her wings and fluttered off into the waves a few yards beyond the shoreline. The male's military bearing collapsed in a ruffle of feathers. A tiny squeak of exasperation escaped his sharp beak.

"What can I say, buddy?" Sam lowered the video camera. "You gave it your all. But it looks like a buyer's market." Scattered over a wide area, hundreds of blue-footed birds danced for prospective mates, guarded eggs ringed with guano, or fed huge fluffy white chicks. Sharing the boobies' nesting range were magnificent frigates. The black birds were not nearly as majestic on land as they were in flight, except when the males inflated their scarlet chest pouches into valentine balloons during mating displays.

Sam had been on Isabela now for nearly three hours. She'd beached her kayak in the cove and examined the centuries-old graffiti carved into the cliffs by whalers and pirates. Then she climbed the steps from Tagus Cove to Lake Darwin, an almost perfectly round pond that was obviously an extinct volcanic crater. From there she climbed to another promontory, from which she could see five of the island's volcanoes, as well as the bay from which she'd come and Fernandina to the west. She enjoyed exploring the trails alone, snapping photos of the views at leisure.

The island's animals were so unafraid of her that they didn't even scuttle away. She'd spotted two flightless cormorants along the shore, and startled several herons closer to the lake. She had to watch where she placed her feet so as not to step on a nesting booby or the tail of an iguana sunning itself on the rocks. For years she'd been accustomed to deducing the presence of wildlife from scat and paw prints. Here, she was in constant danger of tripping over the actual beasts.

Strictly speaking, tourists were not allowed to explore without a naturalist guide in Galápagos National Park, but Eduardo had told the tourists that Sam had special permission to kayak over and conduct a scientific wildlife census. The first part was true; Key Corporation had made a huge donation to the park in exchange for permission for her to wander on her own, but she couldn't tell anyone that.

She pushed herself to her feet. The bird activity was remarkable, but there was nothing going on that hadn't already aired dozens of times on PBS nature programs. Too bad *Out There* had chosen February for their Galápagos adventure: the avian giants of the islands—the waved albatrosses—wouldn't return from their yearly travels for at least another month. According to Eduardo, only a few of them remained here in the islands during the winter. She hadn't spotted one yet.

Wilderness Westin would do a humorous post tonight. Her video clips of dancing boobies, head-bobbing iguanas, and male frigate birds puffing up their scarlet chest balloons certainly lent themselves to comedy. That would strike a good balance after Zing's downer report of mutilated sharks.

She headed for the bay along one of the paths lined with white rocks. The guides and tourists were snorkeling farther south. Now and then she could hear a shout or the hum of an outboard amid the barks of the local sea lion colony. She had left Dan with her satellite phone on the upper deck, preparing to upload his data to NPF. She'd also shared her videos and photos from this morning, in case NPF could make use of those, too. The world needed to know that although the Galápagos might still appear pristine from the surface, violent crimes were taking place here in the marine reserve.

Juvenile sea lions basked in the sun on the white sand. One had curled up on the back hatch of her kayak, another snoozed in the cockpit, and a third had draped itself across the kayak bow. She took a photo. The closest pup opened one eye at her approach, but it didn't move until she nudged its tail with her sandal. The three bundles of brown fur grudgingly abandoned her boat and flippered off into the surf.

Sam felt a twinge of guilt. It was against the rules to molest any creature in the park, and tourists were not supposed to even touch them.

She still had a bit of time before sundown, so after stowing her cameras in the kayak's watertight compartments, she pulled out her snorkel gear and waded into the cool water up to her knees. The bite of the vinyl mask skirt on her temples told her that she should have applied more sunscreen hours ago.

The temperature dipped as she finned farther out, floating over stark hills and valleys of lava. Schools of jacks angled in and out of the black canyons below, flashing silver in the shafts of sunlight that striped the water. A wave bounced her sideways, and she tasted brackish water in her snorkel. Too close to the rocks. *Pay attention, WildWest,* she chided herself, *or you'll have lava rash on top of that sunburn.*

She watched seaweed undulate through streams of bubbles as the waves lapped against the chain of boulders. A dark shape materialized below her, against the undersea lava cliff. A long scaly tail wagged in time with the surf. A marine iguana, mottled black and red. Long claws held it in place as the creature cropped algae from the rock. A

miniature dragon. The Galápagos waters were a cornucopia
of marine life, filled not just with fish and the usual squishy
things one would expect, but also with lizards and turtles
and birds. *A little world within itself,* Charles Darwin had
written.

A torpedo whizzed by her head. She flinched automati-
cally, then turned her head to look. She wanted the projec-
tile to be black and white, a Galápagos penguin, but the
silhouette was dark brown. A sea lion pup. The youngster
made a neat pirouette and set a new trajectory, zooming
toward her. Letting her body sink until only the top of her
head and the tip of her snorkel protruded from the water,
she held her ground, slowly paddling in place. With his
black eyes locked on hers, the pup rocketed toward her,
bubbles streaming from his pointed snout, aiming directly
for her mask. What in the hell—Sam thrashed, nearly
swallowing her snorkel. At the last second, the pup veered
off and vanished into the darker blue beyond. Sam surfaced to spit out salt water.

Eduardo was right—the sea lions were the rulers of the
Galápagos. They were everywhere. The beachmasters
patrolled their areas, barking constantly, on high alert for
intruders trying to make time with their harems. According to Maxim, a big bull ripped a ham-size chunk out of a
snorkeler's thigh only last year. Sounded like these sharp-
toothed mammals were greater threats than the local
sharks. But she'd also learned from her online research that
the bull seals here were prey as often as predators, because
a beachmaster penis was considered a valuable aphrodisiac
in Asian markets. Could she use the word *penis* in a post on
Out There?

Finally cool again, she swam back to the beach, peeled
another sea lion pup off her kayak, and paddled to *Papagayo*. After dinner, she made plans with Dan and Eduardo.
Tonight, the boat was moving south to anchor near Fernandina Island. Eduardo would be tied up with the tour group
the next morning; he wouldn't be able to take them diving

until late afternoon. Dan seemed disappointed, but Sam looked forward to spending hours climbing Alcedo, one of Isabela's many volcanoes.

IN her cabin after dinner, she edited her film, stringing the short video clips together, and wrote a short text accompaniment for Wilderness Westin's post.

> Imagine wandering among animals that have no fear of humans. In the Galápagos, people are the oddball species, and at times it seems like the birds and lizards and sea lions are making fun of me. On Isabela, the animals didn't even move out of my way. It's almost insulting. I get no respect!

She sent a note to the editors, suggesting they add a rap music background to the video. She hoped *Out There* readers would appreciate the variety. Finishing her first posts felt good. She was getting into the rhythm of her tropical assignment: dive and write as Zing, then kayak and hike and write as Wilderness Westin. Zing's posts would be all exciting!! drama that should please NPF; Wilderness's would be pretty travel stories that would please the tourists. Entertainment for everyone. Piece of cake. This week was going to be a blast.

After she sent her files and received the notice of receipt, her laptop chimed to signal arriving e-mail. As well as several business reminders from Key Corporation, there was a message from Chase, sent at 3 A.M. this morning.

The subject line was, "Hi Babe!" *Babe?* Adam used to call her that, and the word had always irritated her. How like Chase to start off with a salutation he knew would rankle her. She could picture his sly grin now.

> Happy Valentine's Day, mi salsa picante! We're hitting the trail again in the wee hours this morning—wish us luck. I'm ready for the Arizona desert: the sleet is rattling the windows in my

condo. Have your colleagues take a picture of you in a bikini:
all I've got is you with that damn cougar. Can't wait till we
meet again. Feb 22, no matter what.
  P.S. I translated the attached for you. Be careful.

Attached to Chase's e-mail were two newspaper stories,
one an editorial from a Quito daily; the other a factual article from Lima, Peru, about the Asian market for seafood
delicacies. After a quick skim, she closed them. She
already knew about the fishing problems here; she was in a
good mood at the moment and she didn't want any bad
news to muck up her day.

There was another friendly note, from her housemate
Blake. It started off with, *Are you getting this?*

She read on to learn the small news of her household
back in Bellingham. Simon stashed a dead mouse in one of
Blake's running shoes. Since she had left town, it had
snowed and melted. The rain gutter over the back deck was
plugged again. And Blake hoped to find romance with a
Canadian from British Columbia named Jacques, whom
he'd just met in person after they'd found each other on the
Internet. *You might be okay with a long-distance relationship,* he wrote, *but I'm ready for an everyday companion.*

Would Blake move out? Or maybe she'd get a second
housemate? That might be a little weird. Nothing like
being the third wheel in your own home.

Was she okay with having a lover who was so rarely
present? She couldn't even reach Chase 90 percent of the
time. Would their week together bring them closer? He'd
find out that she truly didn't cook and wasn't interested in
learning how to. Would she find out that he never read
books or was addicted to television sports? Their conversation usually revolved around what each of them had done
since they'd last seen each other. What the heck would they
talk about when they woke up with each other day after
day? How could he have asked her to move in with him?

A knock sounded at her door. "Wine, top deck, five
minutes," said Dan.

"Or beer," added one of the grad students. "Be there."

"Or be sorry," chimed the other.

Sam shut down her computer and climbed to the top deck behind them. She lounged on a deck chair in the warm night air and marveled at the unfamiliar scatter chart of southern stars overhead. Her damp home near the Canadian border seemed delightfully far away.

8

BEFORE breakfast the next morning, Sam checked her posts at *Out There*. The editors had done a good job with Wilderness Westin's videos, using a bouncy instrumental background that made the prancing birds and nodding iguanas and annoyed seal pups seem like they were participants in a dance competition. There were less than a dozen comments, mainly a few fans saying hi and hoping she wouldn't get attacked by wild beasts or whackos on this assignment.

I'll bet, she thought. Through no fault of her own, events had given her a daredevil reputation. Now she fretted that if something horrendous didn't happen, her bosses would think she wasn't sufficiently entertaining.

SanDman wrote, *I can tell you're going to get into trouble again.* Who the hell was he? Two readers asked what it was like to work with Zing. She wrote a general reply saying that it was awesome to wake up to dawn in the tropics and she couldn't wait to see more of the islands. Then she added, *Zing is a real pro.*

She switched to Zing's post. The editors had set the

shark video to appropriately ominous-sounding music. The
page background was an underwater shot blown up from
one of her photos. There were more than fifty comments.
Most expressed horror about the shark finning, and a few
asked if she had been terrified while filming those scenes.
But three were downright hostile.

> It is not ur country! Go back to ur fucking
> country!—Payor155
>   Our fish, our business. You watch us, we watch you.
> You hurt us, maybe . . .—DomiMan
>   Puta americana! No sabes nada de eso!
> Imbecil!—MarB9844

Yikes. She was surprised the monitor let the first two
through. She could use her dictionary or an online translator to decipher the last one, but she wasn't sure she wanted
to. The exclamation points made the message pretty clear
and the word *imbecil* was readable even in Spanish. Key
Corporation had inadvertently done her a favor by making
her write under a secret pseudonym. She typed a short
reply to everyone: *Thanks for all your comments. Diving in
the Galápagos is exciting. I'm proud to help NPF do their
vital research here.*

She switched to her personal e-mail. Only one message,
from Tad Wyatt.

> Zing—fantastic post! Obviously controversial. Excellent job.
>   Westin—cute, but try for something more exciting next
> time.

Exasperated, she chose not to answer him. There was
nothing more from Chase, but she knew that he could not
communicate often when he was "on assignment." She
turned off the computer.

After breakfast, Dan retired to his cabin to work. Sam
launched her kayak at the same time the tour group and
guides departed in the two pangas for Fernandina, the

newest island of the Galápagos, still shiny with black lava that had erupted only a few years ago. Instead of following the group, Sam paddled north and east and landed a few miles up the shoreline on Isabela. After hauling her kayak up the rocky shore out of the reach of waves, she headed for a rough path Eduardo had shown her on a map. The trail climbed steeply up the slopes of the cone-shaped Alcedo volcano. Alcedo was home to the largest colony of *galápagos*, the giant tortoises for which the islands were named. She wouldn't have time to reach the summit and descend into the crater where most of the tortoises lived, but with luck, she'd encounter at least one of the giants before she had to turn back.

Near the shoreline, vegetation was almost nonexistent, consisting only of a few prickly pears and scrubby, nearly leafless bushes. Heat radiated up from the swirling patterns of black lava underfoot: pahoehoe and ropy aa forms that looked as if they had been free-flowing only yesterday. The barren lava was a stark reminder of how young these islands were: geologically speaking, the Galápagos were still forming. She took several photos of the lava field, although she suspected that the dark rock would look even less interesting on a computer screen than it did through her camera lens.

It felt good to be in motion and on foot again. Traveling via yacht was relaxing, but not good for staying in shape. The slope she was climbing belonged to one of the five active volcanoes on the island. The two volcanoes on southwest Isabela—Cerro Azul and Sierra Negra—had erupted several times in the last decade. She had been surprised to learn that such a volcanically active island hosted a small town: Puerto Villamil. According to Dan, the community was mostly made up of local fishermen and their families, who had a history of building in forbidden areas, among other illegal activities. A string of environmental crimes had been documented in Villamil but never prosecuted.

After learning that, she was glad the town was not on

Papagayo's itinerary. Maybe one day Villamil would disappear under an avalanche of lava and nature would take back the whole island for revenge.

It was possible. Less than five years ago, on Fernandina, the La Cumbre volcano had erupted, spilling lava into the sea and parboiling sea lions and fish.

As she trotted up the steep path, she started to feel parboiled herself. Sweat soaked her T-shirt and hiking shorts and the swimsuit she wore underneath. The density of vegetation increased with the altitude. She stopped periodically to take photos of the tall bushes and small trees, hoping to identify them later. A few birds that might have been some of Darwin's famous finches twittered among the branches, but only a hawk stayed in position long enough for her to snap a still shot. Alongside the trail she spotted only a few small, black, uninteresting lizards.

At noon she paused to rest on a rock and consume the sandwich and fruit juice the *Papagayo* galley staff had packed for her. There was more breeze at the higher elevation, but it couldn't dry the volume of sweat pouring from her skin.

This arid, volcanic landscape was not how she'd visualized the Galápagos. When she dreamed of Pacific Islands, she imagined palm trees and white sand beaches. The view of the ocean was nice, but the lava reminded her of Craters of the Moon monument in Idaho, and the cactus and scrub bushes reminded her of the high desert in Arizona.

The thought of Arizona brought Chase to mind. She could not envision him with a shaved head. Would she still feel lust for a man with no hair? It gave her the willies to think about running her fingers over a shiny bald head, and that realization bothered her. Was she really so superficial? No, she decided. Her previous lover, Adam Steele, had been movie star handsome and *she* had ditched him. He'd moved to San Diego to take a television anchor position, but they remained friends from a distance. She checked in on Adam occasionally on the Internet. He called once in a while to find out what she was up to. He'd even sent her a

Christmas gift. She knew that annoyed Chase, but she
didn't have so many friends that she was ready to give any
of them up. Besides, it was kind of nice to think Chase
could be jealous of another male, even if the emotion was
totally unwarranted.

A scratching sound caught her attention. Off to her left,
off the trail. She heard a solid thump, as if someone
dropped a bowling ball. Whatever was over there, it
sounded big. There were no large terrestrial predators in
the Galápagos. She bushwhacked toward the noise, brushing through a clump of stinging nettles that set her calves
on fire. Moving more carefully after that, she skirted the
worst plant offenders until she came to a series of shallow
impressions dug into the dirt. Weird.

A loud hiss came from the bushes behind her. Startled,
she whirled. And there was one of the prehistoric beasts
she was seeking. A galápago stood on its tiptoes, stretching
its neck in her direction as it regarded her with hooded
eyes. It wasn't one of the true giants she had hoped for, but
its head came up to her thigh, and it was easily twenty
times the size of the biggest tortoise she'd ever encountered
before. She focused her camera. The high, thick shell didn't
look much to her like the saddle for which it was named.
Then again, she wasn't all that knowledgeable about
ancient Spanish saddles.

After a moment of mutual staring, the tortoise decided
Sam wasn't worth getting excited about. It turned its attention to cropping the grayish leaves from the bush it was
burrowed halfway into. Near the claws of its right foot
rested the sun-bleached skull of a long-nosed creature. In
the United States, she would have guessed the skull
belonged to a deer, but here, it was probably the remains of
a feral goat. Before a government killing campaign, invading goats had numbered in the hundreds, eating everything in sight, threatening the native ecosystem and nearly
starving the tortoises to death.

She switched her camera to video mode and filmed the
tortoise eating. She could see how these mellow giants

were easy prey. In past centuries, sailors had simply carried them off to ships to store for later meals; eventually the practice made the giant tortoises nearly extinct. She knew that poachers still killed a few now and then. One blow from a machete to its outstretched neck and the placid reptile in front of her would be history. She wondered how old this particular tortoise was; how many times over a mother or grandmother or even great-grandmother. Or maybe it was a grandpa? Determining tortoise gender usually meant checking the lower shell or examining the tail area, and she wasn't about to attempt either of those with this enormous beast.

Near the top of the bush, a bee buzzed around a few yellow flowers, the only blooms Sam had seen in miles. Apparently the flowers looked pretty good to the galápago, too; because it pushed itself as high as it could, standing with one foot on the goat skull, and finally managed to reach one of the lower blooms, which quickly vanished into its jaws. Sam was sorry to see the flower disappear, but then, soft cool petals probably tasted pretty good after munching through a bale of leathery leaves.

Communing with a creature whose relatives had been around since dinosaur times proved to be less interesting than she'd expected. After a half hour, the tortoise's total concentration on chomping and swallowing became monotonous. She stood up. "Well, buddy, I'm glad we met, but I can't say you're the most scintillating company. I need to be getting back."

The tortoise belched, and then farted for good measure. Sam was reminded of flatulent cows in rural Kansas, where she grew up.

"Same to you," she told the tortoise. "Have a good life, my friend."

She hiked back down the mountain, taking photos of the distant water and islands as she descended. One hawk and one giant tortoise were pretty slim pickings for Wilderness Westin's post today. There was no way these images would achieve the entertainment level that Wyatt wanted. Maybe she could combine them with archived photos of one of the Galápagos volcanoes erupting in recent years and write about the harsh environment of the islands. That felt more like the right track, though still seemed too dry. But maybe that was just because she personally felt dehydrated at the moment. Diving was hard work, but it was easier to write interesting posts as Zing. Dan said the dive this afternoon would be an easy one. She looked forward to that experience.

As she neared the beach where she'd left her kayak, she spotted a dozen male marine iguanas, resplendent in their red-and-green mating colors, vying for position on the highest lump of lava. Two of the large lizards still glistened from a recent expedition into the surf. She put the camera on video mode and framed them in the viewfinder. Remarkably, instead of moving away, three iguanas waggled a few inches in her direction, their long curved toenails scratching against the rock. She dropped to her knees and leaned close. The central subject of her composition chose that moment to eject twin streams of salt water from his scaly nostrils.

"Thanks." She wiped the lens with the hem of her T-shirt. "I don't mean personally; I really didn't need a shower of snotty salt water, but it will make good video."

The iguanas regarded her with humorless black eyes. The nearest one bobbed its head, hissing loudly.

"The rock is yours," she assured him, retreating. "As a matter of fact, you can have the whole island."

If she didn't hurry, she was going to be late for her dive with Dan. She would have the current with her on the way back, but several miles farther to go, because the boat had moved to a new location farther south in her absence. She hustled down the path between the white-painted rocks that marked the official park trail, taking care not to tread on the red-and-yellow Sally Lightfoot crabs that scuttled in and out of crevices in the lava.

This time there were no sea lions on or in her kayak, but a small female had stretched out alongside, dozing in the narrow strip of shade the boat cast on its eastward side. Sam nudged her with a toe, and the sea lion reluctantly rose and lumbered out into the water.

After stowing her camera and hiking boots in the rear hatch, Sam strapped on her sandals, and carried the kayak to the waterline. In the bay, more sea lions barked and splashed near a cluster of rocks. She paddled that way, hoping to catch at least a glimpse of a penguin—her guidebook said they were sometimes found in this area.

Shadows moved beneath the water's surface, but none were black-and-white birds. As she paddled closer to the lava outcropping, she counted at least a dozen juvenile sea lions as they surfaced with excited barks, then ducked back beneath the waves.

The clarity of the water here was astounding. Beneath her, the pups rocketed in and out of underwater canyons like missiles whose guidance systems had run amok. What poor creature were they terrorizing now? Somewhere at the base of this rock formation was a long tube cave, Eduardo had told her—a common sleeping area for sharks and a favorite exploration sight for divers. To her surprise, between the cavorting sea lions, she saw a diver there now. Neoprene-covered calves and black swim fins extended from beneath a rock ledge. How odd. She looked back toward the shore. No boat anywhere. Did he swim out from the beach?

Focusing on the water again, she watched the sea lion pups swirl around the figure, darting in to nip at the long swim fins. The largest pup grabbed the diver's right fin in its teeth and tugged. The fin popped off, and the sea lion streaked away with its treasure, its companions racing to catch up, like dogs competing for a bone.

Sam's breath stopped in her throat. Why hadn't the diver kicked the sea lion away? She stared through the clear water at the nearly motionless pale blur a foot below, feeling a sudden chill.

No bubbles. There were *no bubbles* streaming up from the diver's regulator.

No. This couldn't be happening. She jammed her paddle beneath the bungee web on the kayak deck, then jerked the coiled bowline from beneath the web and tied the nylon cord around her wrist. Face mask—had she brought it? Yes. She found it in the pouch behind her seat and jammed it onto her face. Where was her snorkel? Oh hell, she didn't need it. She pushed herself out of the kayak, and then, after taking several quick breaths, she jackknifed beneath the surface, propelling herself downward with strong breast-strokes and straight-legged kicks.

The scene swam into sharper focus. A crescent rip in the leg of the diver's wetsuit revealed torn white flesh. There was a current flowing at this depth, and the diver's legs fluttered as she moved closer. The diver was a man. He was not in the tube cave but caught by one arm wedged into a crevice in the lava pillar.

Her lungs ached. The kayak line yanked at her wrist. She yanked back and kicked and breaststroked hard to stay in place against the current. She maneuvered partway into the lee of the rock pillar and grasped the bare ankle with both hands. No response. She pulled. The diver floated backward, his tank scraping the rocks with a sound she felt more than heard. He rotated toward her. He rolled face up, revealing a deep gash that began at his neck and crossed over his jaw to run up the side of his face. He'd lost his regulator mouthpiece. *Sweet Jesus.*

Her lungs were bursting. Her head felt like it might explode. The current was pushing her away from the rocks, and the kayak tether jerked her wrist upward. Even as she was pulled away, she forced herself to look at the diver's face. Strands of dark hair floated above the puffy, bruised skin of his forehead. Blue-purple lips. His mask was filled with water, but through it she saw lifeless hazel eyes. *No. No. This couldn't be.*

She kicked her way to the surface and burst through into the sunlight, gasping and floundering in the waves. *Papagayo* was anchored out of sight behind a rocky peninsula. Too far away; it would do no good to yell for help. *Sharks,* she reminded herself. *Stop thrashing.* The diver was beyond saving. She counted down from ten, sucking in air and willing her pulse to slow. After a moment, when she could breathe again, she reeled in her kayak and climbed aboard, bellyflopping onto the stern, then lying facedown and straddling the boat and inching forward until she could swing her legs into the cockpit.

All the way back to the yacht, her brain chanted, *Oh God no, oh God no, oh God no*, in rhythm to her strokes. She had seen a corpse before. She'd prepared herself to find the diver was dead, at least as much as anyone could prepare herself to look into the eyes of death. But she hadn't been prepared to see the face of Daniel Kazaki.

9

SAM slid her kayak into place alongside one of *Papagayo*'s pangas at the stern, climbed out onto the landing platform, and tied off the bowline to a cleat. The world felt off-kilter; the sky and sea undulated in ripples around her. She pressed her back against the square stern and closed her eyes for a moment against the bright dizziness, relieved to feel the yacht's solidity supporting her spine, its fiberglass smooth and substantial under her fingertips.

Dan couldn't be dead. Their dive wasn't even scheduled to start until more than an hour from now. An easy dive. She could hear his voice in her head as he told her about it. Their next dive destination was nowhere near the path to Alcedo and those rocks.

Maybe what she'd seen wasn't real; maybe she was hallucinating from too much sun and exercise. The current and the bowline had pulled her away from the diver; she couldn't have focused clearly on his face. Her intestines were doing gymnastics. Maybe she had food poisoning. Or this was a nightmare, and she was going to wake up any second.

She climbed to the main deck and then headed down the interior stairs toward her cabin. Muffled voices and the sound of running water emanated from Cabins 5 and 6. The tour group had come back from their expedition. Maybe Dan was in his cabin, too, typing at his computer.

She turned the knob and pushed open his door. Dan's clothes were strewn across the lower bunk; his notebook computer sat closed on the tiny desk.

This nightmare was real.

Dan was dead.

Oh God. Her heart dropped to the floor and felt as if it bounced off the hard cold steel and then lay there, bruised. She stepped into the room and closed the door behind her. A photo was taped to the wall above the desk. In the picture, Elizabeth held Sean's hand up in a mutual wave to the camera. Sam pressed a hand over her mouth as her memory replayed Elizabeth's words from their phone conversation: *Take care of my husband.*

"Oh, Dan." She turned away from the photo and surveyed the room. "What the hell happened? Why did you go diving without me?"

She pushed aside his clothes and sat down heavily on his bunk, resting her head in her hands, pressing her hands over her eyes. *Think.* What should she do now? There was no 911 service here, and even if there had been, Dan was beyond saving.

Why had Dan been diving at all? There was no way he could drift from here to those rocks; the current was flowing in the opposite direction. He might have jumped off *Papagayo* this morning before the ship moved, but why would he do that? How did he lose his regulator mouthpiece? Was the hose cut, along with his neck and face? Burned into her memory, his body looked as if someone had swum up behind him and attacked him with a knife. Which implied that there were divers nearby who were willing to commit murder. Were the fishermen that violent?

Dan had been sure they'd be safe on the tour boat. She

thought of Ricardo, the boat pilot who first discovered they were working with NPF. Had he learned their new location? But why would Ricardo travel all the way to Isabela Island to murder Dan now? He could have killed them both by simply abandoning them while they were underwater.

Someone in the Hotel Aurora had frightened Mrs. Vintner into throwing them out. Someone in the lobby; someone Ricardo had called?

The dive shop had given Dan a tank full of carbon monoxide.

Was there more going on here that Dan hadn't told her? She took her hands away from her eyes, sat up, and looked at the room. Bunks, desk, computer. Would there be a clue in Dan's data or e-mail? In the United States, the police would seize his computer right away.

She slid into his chair. Dan had left his notebook in sleep mode, and when she pulled the clamshell open, the screen lit up, displaying a portion of a photo she'd taken yesterday. Dan had zoomed in on the debris field, filled with chunks of dead sharks and pieces of metal. Without the feathery corals and colorful fish, the image was a hideous close-up of rotting garbage. Had he been trying to identify the species of the carcasses, or perhaps trying to determine how many shark corpses lay there?

She closed the photo window and opened the file manager to display the computer's contents. Inside the desk drawer beneath the computer, she found a few paper receipts, a thumb-size flash drive, the CO analyzer Dan used to test their tanks, and Dan's handheld computer—the one he used to keep counts and make notes while diving. Her brain filled with the image of him tapping its keys, looking up at her, his eyes crinkled in a smile behind his mask.

Tears blurred her vision. Oh God, there had to be an explanation. She had to figure this out.

She wiped the wetness away with the back of her hand, snapped the flash drive into the USB port, and quickly copied his e-mail message folder, as well as every folder that looked like it had anything to do with marine biology or the Galápagos. Footsteps creaked across the floor overhead. After turning off the laptop and pocketing the tiny drive, she shoved the CO tester, Dan's handheld computer, and the paper receipts into her shorts pocket. She checked the hallway to be sure it was empty, and then crossed over to her own room.

If an enemy had come after Dan on *Papagayo*, she could be the next target. She slid the CO tester into her own desk drawer, but hesitated to leave the USB drive there. And it might not be safe to load that information on her computer. The tiny room didn't hold many good hiding spots. Finally, she slit open the paper cover on a tampon in her travel container, and shoved the flash drive inside the cardboard tube. Next she opened one of her fish ID books, pulled the paper receipts out of her pockets, smoothed out the crinkles to make them lie down smoothly between the pages. One receipt was from the dive shop for the rentals of their four air cylinders. The other was written in Spanish, but she recognized *Coqueta*, the name of the boat they'd hired on the first day. The receipt was signed by Ricardo Diaz. She slapped the book closed around the receipts and then thrust it back between two other books she'd brought.

If Dan had been killed because of his work with NPF, his handheld computer might hold the data the killer wanted to squelch. Where could she stash the handheld? She dumped the tiny bottles of shampoo and conditioner and sunscreen and bug spray from her kit bag, pushed in the handheld, covered it with a few tissues, and then reloaded the travel bottles on top.

In the bathroom mirror, she caught a glimpse of herself: a red-eyed, red-faced woman. Flyaway blond wisps of hair stuck out from her French braid like pieces of straw. She wore only one silver hoop earring. She fingered her bare earlobe, which was puffy and a little sore. Where had she ripped out her earring? She pulled off the remaining hoop, splashed water on her face, and smoothed down her hair.

Grabbing her satellite phone, she exited the claustrophobic cabin.

Could Dan have had another bad air fill or equipment failure? Returning to the ship's stern, she opened the door to the engine room, where she and Dan stowed their scuba gear. She knew it was unreasonable, but still she found herself expecting to see his tank secured in the elastic loops against the wall, his BCD and regulator dangling from the hooks above. Instead, there was an empty space between her gear and Captain Quiroga's. A lump formed in her throat as she touched the naked hook that should have held Dan's buoyancy vest.

She inspected the air compressor. The intake was mounted high on the exterior wall. She didn't see how carbon monoxide could be sucked in off the ocean breeze.

The engine itself occupied only a portion of the room, and the exhaust vented to a different wall than the compressor's intake. Besides, surely Dan would have tested the air fill before going into the water.

Could someone have tampered with Dan's equipment in some way? The far wall held three doors, all closed. Crew quarters. And the naturalist guides—Eduardo and Maxim—must sleep down here as well. It would be easy for any of them to exit through this room to the stern platform of the yacht without being noticed by anyone on the upper decks.

A dark-skinned crew member entered the engine room through the door behind her and stopped in his tracks, startled to find her there. She'd seen him before, but she had no idea what his name was. She opened her mouth to explain her presence, but when he mumbled, *"Buenas tardes,"* she remembered that he probably didn't speak English. After checking a gauge on a pipe, he slipped out again.

She stood for a minute, staring at the exit door, chewing her thumbnail. Her head throbbed; her eyes burned with unshed tears. What the hell was she supposed to do now? What she wouldn't give to have Chase here. Or her father.

Or her housemate Blake. Any of her park ranger friends.
Maya. Any friendly face. Anyone she could trust.

She heard the second panga motor up outside, then
heard Eduardo's voice, along with another man's. She
pushed open the engine room door and stepped out into the
bright sunshine of the platform. Maxim's dark head and
Eduardo's graying one were bent over the stern cleats as
they secured the inflatable.

Eduardo looked up. His dark eyes immediately filled
with concern. "Sam—"

Eduardo Duarte was a fellow conservationist. A friend.
A coconspirator. He knew about the trouble she and Dan
had run into on their first day together. She blurted out her
horrible news: "Dan is dead."

Maxim's mouth fell open. "What?"

An agonized expression took possession of Eduardo's
weathered face. "But how—" He held his hands out, his
fingers open as if he might be able to catch a reason. She
burst into tears and fell into his arms.

THREE hours later, Sam sat cross-legged on the cold steel
of the top deck, talking into her phone. "Call me as soon as
you can," she said for the tenth time on Chase's voice mail.
"I really need to talk to you."

She pressed End, pocketed the phone, and turned to
concentrate on the fiery sphere of the sun sinking into the
bronze waters of the Pacific. She was not yet drunk enough;
she badly needed a distraction. She desperately hoped to
see the green flash, that legendary instant when the sun
shot out startling green rays in the last second before it disappeared below the waterline.

The boat rocked in the slight swell. A metal cable
clanged somewhere up near the bow. The pelican perched
on the radar fixture overhead took off in a noisy whir of
wings. Footsteps approached, and she reluctantly pulled
her focus back to the horror of the day. She turned to face
three somber men.

"We can find no body," Captain Quiroga told her. He explained that Tony, using Quiroga's scuba gear, had gone under while other crew members snorkeled, but they'd found nothing. She stared at them, unbelieving, moving her gaze from Eduardo's teary visage to Tony's unreadable expression to Quiroga's sympathetic eyes.

Her mouth was dry; her tongue felt swollen. It was difficult to form words. "But I saw him. I touched him." Oh God, she was going to have to go back to that bay and retrieve Dan's corpse. She stood up unsteadily. "I'll take you there; I'll show you."

The captain nodded, and for a horrible second Sam thought he was agreeing, telling her to don her wetsuit and go in search of Dan's body. But then he said, "Perhaps the current. Or animals."

She took two steps toward the stairs.

Eduardo grabbed her arm, stopping her. "No." His dark-eyed gaze held hers. "We search. We are careful. True, Sam, he is not there."

What did it mean? Had the current or the sea lions carried Dan's body away? Oh Lord—sharks? She shouldn't have moved him; she should have wedged his body back into that crevice. But she'd been out of air. The current and the kayak had been tugging her away. And how could anyone be expected to grasp the corpse of a friend and jam it . . . Her hands trembled as if they were creatures separate from her body.

Again, she searched the faces of the men before her, letting her eyes linger on Tony's features. Did he know what happened to Dan? He hadn't said a word in Spanish or English. Were the three men telling the truth? Did they believe that *she* was telling the truth? She couldn't read anything beyond weariness and concern in their expressions.

Captain Quiroga cleared his throat. "It is obvious, Dr. Kazaki is not on board. His dive equipment is gone also. For now, he is officially missing. We must wait for the police." After a quick pat on her shoulder, he turned away and the other two followed, leaving her alone again with the sunset.

The sun winked out, but Sam could still see an image of the last bright sliver burned into her retinas. No green flash. On the backs of her eyelids, the warm blurry horizon jelled into a cold, still face. Staring hazel eyes. Blue-tinged lips. She hurriedly opened her eyes.

The first stars glinted against the darkening sky. The shrill cries of the gulls had died away, replaced by lapping water and the incessant barking of sea lions near shore, and the rumble of a distant motor purring across the waves. From the dining room below, she caught an occasional phrase of conversation, a clink of silverware or thump of a glass against the wooden tables. How could the tour group eat? What had they been told?

A strand of hair blew across her cheek. She brushed it away from her face, felt for the bottle at her side, and raised it to her lips. As Dan had warned, the Ecuadorian red wine had a harsh bite, but it seemed more appropriate for this occasion than the Chilean Chardonnay that Constantino had offered.

Someone laughed below, a hearty guffaw. Jerry Roberson or Jon Sanders, she couldn't tell which. How could they enjoy themselves? Of course, to them Dan was a stranger: the marine biologist with an Asian face, one of the two mysterious divers who were not part of their tour group.

She stared at the black liquid expanse of sea between the ship and the island. If Dan had slipped into the water from the stern platform of *Papagayo*, someone on board had to have seen him, hadn't they? Maybe not, if he'd suited up in the engine room and simply stepped outside. But a rocky peninsula divided the ocean between the bay she'd found him in and the last position of *Papagayo*; how could he have swum around that? It had taken her fifty minutes to paddle that distance; it was a lot farther than a diver would swim on one tank of air. But then, he hadn't had air, at least not at the last. A sea lion or a shark might have carried him to those rocks. But then there was the missing regulator mouthpiece and the cut on his neck

and face; that hadn't looked like the work of sea lion teeth.
And if it had been a shark . . . She shook her head, unwill-
ing to let her imagination visualize the results of a shark
attack.

The bad air. The boat pilot. The hotel owner. All warn-
ings? What the hell had she stumbled into? She crossed her
arms and leaned forward, trying to loosen the knot of muscles constricting her shoulder blades. Had she and Dan
traded the nebulous dangers of Puerto Ayora to move onto
a boat where their enemies could spy on them at every
moment? Tony looked like Ricardo, the hostile boat owner.
Was Tony an enemy? Captain Quiroga owned fish canner-
ies. Would he want to kill a scientist who was trying to stop
illegal fishing?

Would she be next? A hard crack on the head and a
quick toss over the railing were all it would take for her to
join Dan in the depths. She could almost feel the rush of
cool water against her face. At the moment, it didn't seem
like such a bad fate.

She thought about phoning her father in Kansas, but
then remembered that he was in Europe on a long-awaited
honeymoon with his old-friend-now-new-bride Zola. Sam
rarely called him anyway, and certainly never when someone died, because she knew that if he said one word about
God's will or being at peace in heaven, she'd start yelling at
him about his religion being all BS. They'd both end up
miserable. Her father believed that she lived a dangerous
crazy life, and if this wasn't perfect proof of that, what
was? She set the phone down beside her on the deck,
reached for the railing, and pulled herself toward the dark
sea. Thrusting her feet out over the deck edge, she let them
dangle into space and rested her throbbing forehead against
the cool metal railing.

Soft footsteps approached. A gentle hand settled on the
top of her head, light as a bird. Abigail Birsky, the preach-
er's wife. The lecture was coming, any second now. *Mysterious ways of the Almighty, angels singing, gone to a better
place.*

"The captain just told us. I'm here, dear," the soft Southern voice murmured. "If you want to talk. Or for any way I could help."

"Me, too."

Sam looked up, startled at the male voice. Ken swiped nervously at his mustache, then said, "You okay?" He seemed to be evaluating her position at the deck edge. Behind them hovered Jon Sanders, holding hands with his wife Paige.

"I'm not jumping," Sam reassured them. She had no urge to die. "I just need to be alone."

"Sure you don't want company?" Ken asked.

"I'm sure." She wanted to get the hell off this ship, fly back to her home in the woods, sit in front of her fireplace with her cat Simon purring in her lap. She'd make a reservation first thing tomorrow.

They left, but she didn't feel alone. Looking up at the bridge above her, she spotted the crew member she'd met in the engine room this afternoon. The poor guy was probably assigned to keep an eye on her. She returned her gaze to the dark mass of the island in the distance and the surrounding black water. The muffled voices of passengers and mechanical clanks and clinks gradually gave way to the lapping of waves and the occasional wail of a gull. All she could think of was Dan floating, endlessly floating, through all that dark water.

The throb of a powerful engine finally broke her trance, and a deep voice pierced the darkness. "*Oye,* Papagayo!" A splash signaled the departure of the sea lion resting on the rear platform. Then a thump shuddered throughout the ship as another boat joined them.

Male voices, speaking Spanish, rose from the stern. Sam caught the words *desaparecido* and *muerto.* Disappeared, perhaps? And *muerto*—dead, she knew that word. Heavy footsteps clanged up the metal steps onto the main deck below her, and then faded away on entering the lounge.

Thanks to the bottle of wine Constantino had given her,

she was working her way toward numbness, but right now her entire body still ached. Headache. Backache. Heartache. In their three-day acquaintance, Daniel Kazaki had become a friend. Kindred spirits didn't show up often in her life. During their first dinner together in the Galápagos, she and Dan had discussed the wonder of reef creatures extracting minerals from seawater to build their intricate shells.

"Imagine," he'd said, his eyes shining, "if people could synthesize building materials out of air and soil with their own bodies, everyone could have their own shell."

"The big shells would shove the little shells off their reef." She was more than a little cynical about the human species.

He chuckled. "Or society would be divided by different colors of shells." Yep, definitely a kindred spirit. The conversations she shared with Dan were the same ones that made her relatives question her sanity.

The conversations she *had* shared. Dan was past tense now. She raised the wine bottle to her lips again.

Thudding footsteps on the metal stairs preceded the two men. Captain Quiroga now wore dress whites, no doubt in deference to the men who stood to his right, a tall thin blond and a fat balding officer in khaki uniforms and caps with official-looking tricolor insignias on them. The blond crooked a long index finger in a come-here gesture. *"Señorita. Por favor."*

Instead of *policía*, the captain introduced the officers as *fiscalia*, which seemed to be the Ecuadorian word for "police." This was not an interrogation, they told her. Just a few questions. It sure felt like an interrogation, as she sat in the captain's office in a molded plastic chair that dated from the sixties. Her head throbbed from the rumble of the generator and the diesel fumes. Drinking so much cheap red wine probably didn't help.

"He was Japanese?" The question came from Eduardo, who was serving as interpreter.

Sam glared at him. He knew the answer to that question. Eduardo shrugged and tilted his head toward the two officers. *Just translating.* They'd been over this ground before. Were the officers hoping to trip her up a second time around? She knew no lies to trip over. "I said Irish-Japanese-American. Daniel Kazaki was American. You have his passport." She inclined her head toward the captain's desk, where her passport lay alongside Dan's.

The potbellied cop—Aguirre, according to his nameplate—put his fingers to the corners of his eyes and pulled his eyelids into slits. The blond officer laughed. Eduardo's cheeks turned scarlet.

Sam wondered if many cops were so mean-spirited. Chase was a cop of sorts; she didn't want to believe he'd laugh at a victim. She wished he were here to make sense of the situation. She sure could use a Spanish-speaking FBI agent now. Why couldn't the men she hooked up with ever be supportive? Or even available?

Aguirre spoke to her. "What was Kazaki doing here in the Galápagos?" Eduardo repeated in English. His expression remained disinterested, as though he had never met Dan, had never shared a glass of wine with him.

One more time. "Dr. Kazaki was conducting a marine survey. A count." She found herself speaking loudly, slowly enunciating every word as though that would make the two officers suddenly comprehend English.

"Counting what?"

She shrugged. "Fish. And everything else."

"Sea cucumbers?" Eduardo pronounced the word *ko-kombers*.

Dan had filled in her sketchy knowledge of the sea cucumber—*pepino*—"war" that had erupted more than a decade ago. Lured by fantastic prices paid by Japan and Hong Kong, local fishermen had risked the bends and even death to collect the slug-like creatures. For years, the corpses of drying *pepinos* hung from every roof in the Galápagos towns. Then the real battle started: international conservation groups versus local fishermen, with the Ecuadorian government alternately enforcing or ignoring quotas, depending on who wielded the most power at the time.

Where did the poachers hang the *pepino* corpses to dry now? The new constitution promised protection, but those were only words on paper. She couldn't get yesterday's vision of mangled sharks out of her head. "Dan was counting cucumbers, fish, turtles, sharks, rays—everything," she said.

"The porpoise?"

She remembered the porpoise surfacing outside her cabin porthole the night before last. When this still seemed like her dream assignment. "Of course," she told them. "He would include porpoises, too."

Eduardo shook his head. "No, the porpoise of the count! They want to know the why."

She took a breath. Surely they knew why an organization would want a fish count. Was it dangerous to say it? "He was hired to make a report to the Natural Planet Foundation."

The two officers exchanged a scowl. What was going through their heads? If the report showed a continuing loss of sea life inside the marine sanctuary, would that provide the *fiscalia* with evidence they needed to pursue poachers? Or would they worry the report would make local law enforcement look inept?

"Why are you on this boat?" Aguirre asked. "You are not among the list of passengers."

She told them about the bad air fill in Puerto Ayora, about how Dan had nearly died on their first dive. She choked and her vision blurred as the reality hit her again. Dan *had* died in the water today.

The officers listened to Eduardo's translation, their faces impassive. When she could continue, she explained how she and Dan had abruptly been forced to leave the hotel, and how they'd moved to *Papagayo*. At that point Eduardo stumbled in his translation and seemed to search for words. A rapid exchange ensued between him and the officers. Eduardo appeared increasingly uncomfortable. Was the back-and-forth about the arrangement that Eduardo had made with Dan to get them onto the boat? But why would that would be an issue? She and Dan had occupied empty cabins.

Abruptly the conversation ceased. She waited for a translation from Eduardo, but he studied the floor while the police studied her.

"Who will call Dr. Kazaki's wife?" she finally asked. *Please don't tell me it's my job.*

The blond policeman rose. His uniform nameplate identified him as Schwartz. Sam half expected German to come out of his mouth each time he opened it. But of course he spoke in Spanish, and Eduardo translated. "For now, Dr. Kazaki is officially missing. We will inform the American Consulate. They will deal with his family and with NPF."

Had Schwartz sounded hostile when he mentioned NPF? To her ears, everything the officers said sounded harsh. With a sweep of his hand, Schwartz gathered Dan's passport as well as her own from the desktop in front of him. He tapped them into a neat packet and buttoned them into his shirt pocket.

"Hey!" She jumped up from her seat. The room briefly wavered around her, and she grabbed the back of the chair to steady herself. How much wine had she swallowed?

Schwartz rattled off a long string of words in Spanish.

"They will keep your papers for a few days," Eduardo explained.

"Until when?" She intended to catch the first plane back to the States. She glared at the officers. "I'm a U.S. citizen!"

Officer Aguirre snorted and crossed his arms over his wide chest. He'd probably heard that line more than once.

Eduardo shook his head, a barely perceptible motion. His eyes begged her not to make a scene.

"Can I go?" she asked.

"You are dismissed," Eduardo confirmed.

Officer Schwartz added a few more words.

"For now," Eduardo translated, his eyes somber with warning.

10

SAM stood on the stained carpet of the narrow hallway, staring at the door to 4, Dan's cabin, as she clenched and unclenched her fists.

Just a plain wooden door set into the metal frame. The door was not even fully closed; the police had neglected to latch it. What had she expected? Yellow crime scene tape? She pushed the cabin door open.

Dan's porthole was shadowed now by the dark gray hull of the official boat, which bore an emblem that read, ARMADA DE ECUADOR. The police had arrived on a military boat. According to Eduardo, that was the norm down here.

Whoever had retrieved Dan's passport had not disturbed anything else that she could see. She closed his door and opened her own. Everything in Cabin 3 looked the same as when she'd left it.

She drank two glasses of water, hoping to dilute the wine in her system. She booted up her computer and found a listing online, tapped in the number of the U.S. Embassy in Quito, and waited breathlessly for a friendly voice. Instead, she got a recording. In Spanish.

"Unbelievable!" The Spanish recording was followed by one in English. The Embassy was closed; hours were nine to five on weekdays; appointments with the office must be arranged in advance; call the local police for emergencies. Goddamn it! What if dealing with the local police *was* the emergency? The recording ended in a loud beep. Did that mean that she could leave a message? She summarized the situation, left her cell number, and then ended the call, unsure if she'd been whining to dead air or to voice mail.

She searched further on the Internet, came up with the name and number of a U.S. Consulate in Guayaquil. She called that and got the same recording as she had at the Embassy, left the same message to the same silent line.

Then, as she scrolled through the information on the consular website, she found a note stating that Americans in emergency situations in the Galápagos should call the U.S. Consular Agent for the Galápagos on Santa Cruz Island. Finally! She sat on her lower bunk and twitched a foot as she punched the number in. Another message in Spanish. Then it switched to English: "John Parker, Consular Agent for the Galápagos, will be unavailable until March tenth. If you have a problem, please contact the American Consulate office in Guayaquil."

Damn it! Her colleague had been killed, she might be next, and the police had effectively prevented her from leaving. She jumped up, anxiously strode the five steps to the bathroom and back, banged her knee against the desk chair, turned toward the bathroom again, whacked her shoulder on the partially open closet door. This was not a room designed for pacing, especially when the pacer had consumed half a bottle of wine.

Her cell phone chimed. She snatched it up eagerly.

"Sam?" A male voice. American.

"Chase?" It didn't sound like him, but oh God, she wanted—

"Where the *hell* are your files? You gonna keep us up all night? It's nearly nine P.M."

Mike Whitney, the managing editor of *Out There*.

A wave of guilt, immediately followed by one of annoyance and then another of grief, washed over her.

"There's been—" Her throat tightened. She swallowed quickly and forced herself to continue. "There was . . . an accident here, Mike. It's nearly midnight. I don't think I'll make it tonight."

"You don't think you'll make it tonight? This better be one hell of an accident. What happened?"

Dan Kazaki died today. The sentence was on her lips, but she hesitated. Officially, Dan was only missing. Who knew when the American Embassy would notify Elizabeth Kazaki? If she told Whitney that Dan had died, *Out There* would splash the news across the Internet in a matter of minutes.

"What's wrong, WildWest?"

"Don't call me that." She hated the way the Seattle team talked about her as though she were a virtual character like Zing.

"It's only a few hundred words. They told me you were a pro. Did you take *any* film or photos today?"

"Uh . . . yeah." She could see only two choices: explain what was going on here or send him enough to get him off her back for now. The photos and video from her hike up Alcedo were still in her camera.

"Well, then, if you value your contract and you don't want to cost me *my* job, you sure as shit *better* send us some posts. If those files don't hit the server in less than an hour, Wyatt will have both our heads."

For a long moment, she heard only a loud buzzing on the line, or maybe it was the roar of rage building inside her head. But none of this was Whitney's fault. "They'll be rough," she muttered. "But you'll have them in half an hour."

Her anger cooled as she connected her camera and downloaded her media files. It was a relief to focus on her job. For Wilderness Westin, she packaged her video clips of the giant tortoise and the iguanas and quickly crafted a post about how the reptiles had adapted to life on the islands, the tortoises living at elevations where more plants grew, and the iguanas adapting to a life in the sea, eating seaweed instead of the leaves and fruit they would have subsisted on in lusher areas.

For Zing, she pulled up the visuals she hadn't yet sent— the photo of the barracuda hovering over the debris field, the video of the hammerhead showering crabs as it bit into the carcasses. She wrote about how the marine sanctuary was not a safe place for these creatures. She threw in a few photos of the sea cucumbers from her first dive with Dan. As she was sorting through those, she found the first photo she'd taken, of Dan with his pen in his mouth, looking in her direction. It hurt to look at that smile.

Just as she prepared to send Zing's post to Seattle, a knock sounded at her door, and the two uniformed men opened her door and stepped in, filling her tiny cabin.

She stood up and slid the chair under the desk to make room, uncomfortably aware of the heavy odor of sweat and cigarettes emanating from Officer Aguirre just inches away. He carried Dan's notebook computer under one arm.

Schwartz thrust a photo toward her. Elizabeth and Sean. She averted her eyes from those happy faces. *"Familia* Kazaki," she croaked. The officer nodded, tucked the photo into his shirt pocket.

Aguirre explored her cabin, pawed through her clothes and books in the closet, while Schwartz kept his gaze on her. Her breath stopped as Aguirre's hand passed over her tampons. She turned back toward her computer. Would they confiscate her laptop? She quickly pressed the key combination to send the files to Seattle.

Schwartz's hand shot out to grab her arm. *"Qué hace usted?"*

"What?" Where was Eduardo? She needed a translator. Schwartz placed a hand on the corner of the laptop screen as if to fold it shut. She grabbed the opposing corner, holding the laptop open. "No."

What the hell was the word for *work*? Something weird,

something like travail. *"Travalo,"* she tried, gesturing toward herself. "My *travalo."*

"Trabajo," he corrected. *"Usted es cientista también?"*

She knew the words for "you"—*usted*—and "too"—*también*. Sounded like he was asking if she was a scientist, too. "I am a writer." She held her hands above the keyboard and made motions of typing. "Writer."

"Escritor. Autor," Schwartz guessed.

The last word sounded like "author." Close enough. She nodded.

"Pero ustedes trabajaban juntos." His blue eyes searched hers for agreement. There were a lot of syllables in there she didn't recognize.

"Trabajaban juntos." He held two fingers up together.

She and Dan worked together? Why did he keep asking? "Yes."

A look passed between the two officers. A trill of fear zipped through Sam's body. What had she just agreed to? Had she given them good reason to clap her in the local jail? But then, Schwartz straightened and said something to Aguirre, who nodded and exited into the hallway. As she watched the door close behind them, she heaved a sigh of relief, and folding the laptop screen down, she leaned forward and rested her forearms and head on top of it. After a moment, she heard the fan shut off and the laptop go into sleep mode.

Would *Out There* expect her to complete this assignment by herself? She didn't need to ponder that question for more than a few seconds: of course they would. That was her claim to fame, after all; she was a one-woman team: writer, photographer, videographer. Hiker, kayaker, climber. *Diver.* She had asked for this, hadn't she?

No, she argued with herself. She'd signed up to dive and photograph and write. She hadn't signed up to watch a friend die, to get tangled up in a murder investigation. What the hell was she supposed to do now?

A few minutes after 1 A.M., she heard the rumble of the Navy boat's engines as it pulled away. The reverberation was replaced by the repetitive barking of a patrolling sea lion bull outside and heavy steps overhead in the ship's lounge area. Maybe now that the authorities had gone, Constantino and the captain were helping themselves to the bar.

She sat up and opened the laptop. Dan stared at her from the screen. *I refuse to have a peon for a partner.* She rubbed at the tears in her eyes. Sniveling wuss. Zing wouldn't sit around feeling sorry for herself if *her* friend had died. Zing would never sob alone, cowering in a dark cabin. Sam slid off the chair, stuck a small notebook and pen into the back pocket of her shorts, and slipped out of her room.

The walkway around the main deck was quiet. A gentle breeze tickled her nostrils with odors of the rocky shore a few hundred yards away: the sweat-like scent of seaweed decayed by a day of blistering sun, along with the acrid mix of bird guano.

She leaned for a minute on the deck rail, letting the night air cool her burning face and dry her wet cheeks. Among the dark triangles of lapping waves, large black discs bobbed just under the waterline. The swish of a flipper sparked a curlicue of luminescent algae. Sea turtles. Pacific greens, or maybe the subspecies they called black sea turtles down here. Just this morning she'd taken a photo of these marine reptiles, their speckled heads lifted out of the water as they begged for breakfast scraps at *Papagayo*'s stern like aquatic cocker spaniels.

The creatures of the Galápagos didn't flee from humans. Sometimes they didn't even give way to the two-legged intruders. This was still a magical place. But it was unlikely to stay that way.

The turtles bobbed on the surface, resting silently near the boat in the quiet water. Would these trusting animals be next on shopping lists in Taiwan and Tokyo? She had to at least try to prevent that.

Turning away from the water, she slid open the door to the lounge area and stepped inside. The lights were dimmed. Around the corner in the tiny alcove behind the bar, she heard deep voices murmuring softly, but a wall separated her from the speakers and she couldn't make out the words.

She moved toward the lecture area and turned on a lamp over the bookcase of reference books. Kneeling, she trailed her fingertips across encyclopedias of marine life, a few guidebooks on the Galápagos, and then finally found what she was searching for, a book of maps. Sitting close to the lamp on the nearby couch, she checked for maps of currents. She thumbed through the pages until she found Isabela Island.

The men emerged from the alcove and then stopped, startled by her presence. The top buttons of the captain's dress whites were undone, his tie loose around his neck, his hair rumpled as if he'd run his hands through it. She was surprised to see that his companion was Jonathan Sanders. Sanders downed the drink he held in one swallow, set the empty glass on the end table. Turning to Quiroga, he said, "Good night, Captain." He swiveled in her direction and inclined his head. "Good night, Miss Westin. Tomorrow will be a better day."

Sam doubted that. Sanders strode to the sliding door and exited quickly, headed for his cabin.

Captain Quiroga bent toward her. "Señorita Westin, the lounge is now closed. All passengers should be in bed."

"Are the police finished?" she asked.

He scratched at the shadow of whiskers on his cheek. "Tomorrow the *fiscalia* will return for questioning." He clasped his fingers around the book she was holding. "Please, good night."

He pulled the book from her grasp. It was okay; she'd found what she'd been looking for. According to the charts, the current that swept past them now was joined by two others that swirled around the islands. The arrows were bold, indicating strong currents. If he swam out—or was dropped off a boat—past the rocky peninsula that guarded their previous anchorage, Dan could have drifted to the bay where she'd found him.

Quiroga slid open the door to go outside, letting the fresh breeze fill the lounge. Then he paused, waiting for her to descend the interior stairs to her cabin. She felt his gaze on her back as she headed for her airless subterranean quarters. Would anyone protest if she carried her bedding up to the top deck and slept under the stars? Maybe if they all went—if she suggested it to the rest of the bottom dwellers: Sandy and Jerry, the Cabin 6 students, Dan . . .

Shit. How often would such a thought ambush her in the days to come?

CHASE and Nicole—now known locally as Charlie and Nikki—sat in the Horseshoe Tavern, sharing beer and their fake sob stories of lost jobs and home with Dread and three other protesters. Chase sipped his beer slowly, memorizing details to communicate later. Randy Dakin was a brown-haired twenty-something hulk, whose hair and beard were exactly the same quarter-inch length, giving him a concentration camp look. He wore a muscle shirt, exposing a shield design tattooed on his bicep. His thin wife Joanne looked to be a few years older than Randy. She didn't say much, and her jawline held the yellowish stain of an old bruise.

Completing their band of six was Alvin Marshall, who understandably used only his last name. He was a slight, mean-looking man with a scar that bisected his left eyebrow, the kind of man who wouldn't carry a gun in plain sight but would have a switchblade in his back pocket. After they'd all had a couple of rounds and eyed one another for a suitable amount of time, Dread handed out the address of "the action" for the evening. They all left in their own vehicles.

Nicole drove their dented pickup truck out of the suburbs while Chase's thoughts traveled out of the country, thousands of miles to the Galápagos Islands. This morning, *Out There* had featured two posts from Ecuador: Summer's usual online persona, Wilderness Westin, and someone named Zing. While Westin's post was a lighthearted island tour with blue-footed birds strutting to rap music, Zing's post was all about illegal fishing, with some horrific footage of a finless shark being ripped to shreds while still alive. Westin's post received only a few bland comments, but Zing's post had garnered dozens of responses in both Spanish and English. The negative messages could be summarized as *This is none of your business; go home, bitch.* There was an implied *Or else.*

Summer hadn't mentioned Zing; only a partner named Dr. Kazaki. Chase had the sickening suspicion that Wilderness and Zing were the same small blond woman. If she'd shot that underwater footage of circling sharks, she was taking a lot of risks down there. Why was she hell-bent on getting herself killed?

Who was he to talk? she'd argue. Yes, his job was risky, but Nicole had his back and he had the full force of the FBI behind him. Summer had what—a handful of do-gooder conservation types? Like that would protect her from violence.

Nicole switched on the radio, tuning it to a talk radio station renowned for lambasting both local and national government. *No better than Nazis,* the host said now. *They should all be taken out and shot.* It was a frequent refrain from him; the guy could have been talking about the Arizona state representatives, the national government, or gays or any other minorities. Chase grimaced. Only two days into this gig and he was already sick of sticking to his low-brow character, but the dirt brown Suburban he saw in the rearview mirror was a reminder they were constantly under observation. Supper last night was scorched ribs and corn and Coors at a greasy barbeque joint. Then he and Nicole had spent a restless night in a local campground, trying not to bump backsides while sharing an air mattress in the pickup bed.

He rubbed at the coating of grit on the back of his neck. He hoped his next undercover gig would be playing a high roller in some luxury hotel in Vegas or Miami. Summer's blog posts hadn't mentioned where she was staying. Were there upscale hotels in the Galápagos? He thought of the islands as a thatched hut kind of place, all wooden boats and lizards and mosquito nets.

Nicole parked in the far corner of a gravel parking lot and pulled on the brake. "Ready, Charlie?" She poked him in the shoulder with a long nail decorated with a miniature American flag. "Are you in there, hon?"

Summer was tough, he reminded himself. She was with Kazaki, an experienced diver and scientist who understood Spanish and the local political situation. Chase briefly stuck his tongue out at Nicole. "Dyin' to see some action, sweetbuns." That earned him a smoldering look. He turned to take his rifle out of the rack behind him. "Lock and load, Nikki darlin'."

The address belonged to an ancient one-story ramshackle motel hunkered down beside the former highway on the outskirts of Tucson. It was after midnight when they arrived. The place was dark except for a dim light that overhung a corner of the parking lot. A tire swing dangled from a leafless tree near one corner of the building, and a kid's tricycle was parked in front of door number 8. The vehicles in the gravel lot—mostly worn Ford pickups, old Nissans and Hondas—had license plates from Arizona, Nevada, and California. More than one had a child's car seat in the back.

"Shit, this one's got *two* baby carriers." Nicole rested her baseball bat on the ground to peer in a car window. As she bent over, her shirt rode up, revealing the Glock she wore in the small of her back.

"Don't go all soft on us," Chase/Charlie grumbled beside her.

"Restin' places for baby cockroaches," Randy's wife Joanne murmured, giving Nicole a curious look.

Nicole/Nikki persisted. "How do y'all know these folks

are all illegals?" Chase thought she was laying on the Southern accent a bit too heavily.

Joanne rested her right hand on the pistol she wore at her waist. "If they ain't cockroaches themselves, they're livin' with cockroaches."

"And there's only one way to get rid of cockroaches, right?" Randy held up a gasoline can in one hand and a cigarette lighter in the other.

"Amen," Chase said. He held the rifle in his right hand as he turned to address Dread. "So, what's the grand plan here?"

"We want 'em to run back to their hidey-holes and tell their friends there's not a welcome mat out for them anymore. We burn them out and trash their cars, strand 'em on foot like they were when they came here. If you got to hit a cockroach, get an arm or leg. We don't want to kill anyone tonight."

"Sounds good," Chase said. "You four want to take the front? Nikki and I'll cover the back." He and Nicole trotted into the shadows at the side of the old wooden building.

As he'd suspected, there were already several windows open along the back of the building. People in various stages of dress were escaping out the windows and dashing into the desert. Anyone desperate enough to live here would be watching for trouble.

He could easily envision his grandfather living in a place like this when he'd first come to the States. None of Chase's family ever talked about how *Abuelo Perez* had crossed the Rio Grande, just about how hard he'd worked his whole life—mechanic, logger, and finally, small store owner, proud to put Chase's father and uncle through college.

"Hey, *cucarachas*!" Marshall's voice roared out front. "Listen up! Go home!" His shout was followed by a huge whoosh of ignition. A fireball leapt over the flat tarred roof of the building.

Chase galloped up to a window from which a baby girl dangled, ripped the kid from the extended arms, and then dragged the woman over the windowsill to join her daughter outside. *"Váyense, rápido!"* he murmured softly, pressing the child into the mother's arms and urging her to run. Nicole made her way through the closest bushes, scattering the sniffling kids hiding there into the blackness of the desert beyond.

Along with the smoke, shouts drifted over from the front of the motel. "Go back to Mexico! Goddamn wetbacks!" Then, "Hell yes, you'd better run!" followed by a couple of shots.

Chase joined Nicole, crouching among the shrubs. "Damn," she said. "Hope we don't have to shoot anyone."

Chase wondered what unspeakable acts DEA agent Cisneros had committed to infiltrate the cartel. Had any of those led to his death in the desert?

A pudgy man dressed in T-shirt and undershorts fell out a window, scrambled to his feet, and dashed across the dusty yard.

"Cockroach!" Nicole shouted loudly. "Get him, Charlie!"

Chase fired two shots over the guy's head. Half the motel was on fire now. *Please God, let everyone be out.* He tried not to think about how the burning rooms likely contained everything these people owned. On the opposite side of the building, the other four attackers whooped like a group of drunk teenagers, their laughter and shouts punctuated by crashing noises.

He and Nicole headed back around front. Three of the numbered motel doors hung open, and Randy emerged from one, holding a bottle of tequila in one hand and waving a wad of cash in the other. "Look what I found!"

Dread scurried out of another, smoke trailing in his wake. He carried a backpack, and the pockets of his jacket looked suspiciously full.

In the parking lot, Joanne and Marshall smashed windshields and headlights with a bat and a tire iron. The tinkling of breaking glass sounded almost festive.

"Save some for me!" Nicole trotted toward a car with her baseball bat over her shoulder.

Chase joined Dread and Randy. He kicked in the door to Room 6 and stood in the doorway, the neck of his T-shirt pulled up over his nose to filter the worst of the smoke. Through the whitish haze he saw that the curtains were ablaze, showering black sparks over the bed and chair, which would burst into flames any minute. In the corner of the room several plastic-wrapped bundles were stacked into a small tower. The covering on the bundles sprouted holes as he watched. Black plastic dripped flames onto the floor as the smoldering contents gave off the distinctive sweet smell of burning marijuana.

A black-and-white with flashing lights zoomed over the hill. "Shit!" Dread yelled, dashing for his car.

Their group scattered as the cruiser slid to a stop in the gravel. Chase raced toward Nicole and dove to a hiding spot between cars, halfway to their truck. Two uniformed officers leapt out of the cruiser, guns drawn, crouching behind their open car doors. "Stop! Police! Stop or we'll shoot!"

Chase was painfully aware that neither he nor Nicole wore bulletproof vests, and that the local cops had no inkling that two FBI agents were on-scene. Crouching on one knee and doing his best to keep his head down, he took careful aim at the lone light in the parking lot. Nicole, lying on her stomach and sighting beneath a ruined station wagon, put a bullet into a front tire on the squad car a fraction of a second before Chase pulled the trigger on his rifle and blasted out the light. In the ensuing darkness and confusion, the vandals all managed to escape.

The six of them met up at 1:45 A.M. back in the Horseshoe Tavern.

Chase swept a hand over his sweat-slick scalp and clinked his beer glass against Dread's. "That was the most fun I've had in a long time. Thanks for lettin' Nikki and me join the party."

Marshall stood and shucked his denim jacket, revealing a shield tattoo on his upper arm identical to Randy's. Sitting again, he drained his glass and thumped it down on the scarred table in front of him. He stared first at Chase, and then at Nicole. "That was some shooting you guys did. You sure you're not ex-military?" He held out a clenched fist toward Randy, who joined him with a fist bump and a chorused "Hooah."

That explained the camaraderie of those two. "Military? Not us," Chase snorted. "We're a little too old to volunteer to get shot at by ragheads."

Dread turned his cold gaze on Chase. "*I'd* say it was almost like you were law enforcement."

Chase tensed and narrowed his eyes to slits. He sat back in his chair, crossed his arms, and studied Dread, debating the best comeback.

Nicole patted Chase on the bicep. "Down, Charlie. I'm sure our new friend here didn't *mean* to insult us." Turning to Dread, she said, "For your information, we're a hell of a lot *better* than law enforcement. Charlie and I won a whole lot of shooting contests back in Florida. The Southern Sting Shootout was our favorite."

The ATF owned the www.southernstingshootout.org website. In the archives was a supposedly thirteen-month-old article about Charlie and Nikki Perini, husband and wife sharpshooters who won the club championship three years in a row.

"Felt good to shoot again," Chase contributed in a gruff voice. He fingered his skull earring.

Dread's dark eyes moved from Nicole to him. "You still compete?"

"Hardly ever," Chase told him. "Entry fees are steep, and then you gotta pay for all that ammunition. Unemployment ran out over a year ago, and there's been nothin' but shit work ever since, you know?"

"I know how that goes." Dread's shoulders relaxed and he took a swallow of his beer.

"We get by." Nicole laid her hand on top of Chase's in a show of wifely support.

Chase noticed a fleck of blood on her cheek, probably from flying glass. He pulled a paper napkin out of the holder on the table, dampened it in the sweat on the outside of his beer glass, and then wiped the blood from her face. She gave him a curious look and he showed her the red smear on the napkin.

"Thanks, hon," she drawled.

"We know exactly what you're going through," Joanne said. She looked at Marshall. "That's why we're here, to help get the jobs back and stop all these criminals coming in. There's no place safe anymore. Drug runners everywhere."

Randy gestured for the waitress to come over. "Somebody's got to take action. The government can't handle the job."

"Let me buy you both a cold one," Dread offered Chase and Nicole. He shot a look at Marshall, who reached into his jacket pocket, pulled out a wad of bills, and then tossed them on the table in front of Chase.

The top bill was a worn fifty with stains and tattered edges. The stack was at least a quarter-inch thick, held together with a rubber band. "What's this?" he asked.

Dread leaned forward, his elbows on the table, and said in a low voice, "Your cut from tonight."

Chase studied the money but didn't touch it. Nicole's lips twitched in a slight smile. It was the second big test tonight. He asked, "Two cuts?"

Dread nodded. "Course."

Chase folded the stack of bills and stuffed them in the front pocket of his jeans.

Marshall grinned at him. "There's a bottle of tequila with your name on it, too."

"I adore tequila," Nicole said.

Dread remained silent as the waitress delivered another pitcher of beer to the table. As soon as the woman was out of hearing range, he hefted the pitcher and filled Chase and Nikki's mugs. "You don't need to be broke anymore."

"That right?"

"I'd like to talk to you about a show our group's runnin'

down south by the border. We could use some talents like yours."

Chase raised an eyebrow in Nicole's direction. "Sounds intriguing," she said.

"The ammunition's on us," Dread said. "All you can use." A dark smudge on Dread's thick neck might have been part of an old tattoo.

The rest was hidden by his shirt, but what Chase could see looked like the amateur inkings that prisoners often bestowed on each other. "What kind of contest is it?" he asked.

Marshall snickered. "Shooting rats in the dump. Whoever takes them all out wins."

"Spic rats," Joanne clarified.

"What's the prize?"

"Whatever they're packing," Randy said.

Marshall added, "Plus, they learn turnabout's a bitch. They come here to steal from us, and—surprise! We take everything they got."

Chase turned to Dread. "What if they're carrying drugs?"

Dread folded his hands on top of the table and stared intently at Chase. "We sell 'em to fund the cause." The black man didn't look at his other comrades, but Chase could feel the tension humming between members of the group as they waited for his and Nicole's reaction.

The group was dealing drugs, too; or at least Dread was. This was going well. Chase glanced again at Nicole. Her gaze was cool and steady. Like him, she knew the real choice of the moment was between becoming an active participant or becoming the next corpse found in the desert. Turning back to the others, Chase said, "Count us in."

Dread grinned and held out a fist. "Welcome to the New American Citizen Army."

Chase bumped knuckles, then leaned back and took a swallow of his beer. So the group was looking for sharpshooters. Either these were the same scumbags who had gunned down Cisneros and the others last week, or there was a whole network of armed vigilantes out there ready to kill anyone crossing the Mexican border. Either way, he and Nicole had just joined the team.

11

THE next morning Sam awoke to shrill cries and the bottom view of a pelican squatting on the light stanchion directly above her head. She pushed herself up from the deck chair and ran her fingers through her hair. No sticky globs. A flash of white shirt above caught her eye. The captain waved a hand at her through the window of the bridge. Tony stood beside him.

Her head throbbed. She vaguely remembered thinking about sleeping up here. Apparently she'd done it. Thank God she was decently covered. She wore a green T-shirt dress that served dual duty as nightshirt. The sun was peeking over the black hump of a different island. Her pillow and blanket lay on the deck chair. How could she have snored through raising anchor, starting the engines, and anchoring again? The answer lay in the empty wine bottle rolled into the wadded towel beside her makeshift bed.

The dawn was painfully bright. The slanting rays glancing off the water made her teeth ache. She had a whale of a hangover.

She fumbled her way down the two flights of stairs to

her cabin. Under the shower, memory slowly returned. After dragging her pillow and blanket up to the top deck, she found her half-empty wine bottle right where she'd left it. Eduardo had been there, too, with another bottle of wine, which they'd shared, along with bittersweet memories of Dan. Sam was surprised to learn that the two had met nearly nine years earlier, when Dan was a doctoral student working at Darwin Station.

As she brushed her teeth, she frowned at herself in the mirror. What else had Eduardo told her? Had he said anything about Dan's whereabouts during the afternoon? Had she even asked?

Sam checked her printed itinerary. *16 Feb, Floreana (Charles) Island.* So that lump of lava out there was Floreana Island, or Charles, or whatever name they were calling it this week. Were the officials still searching for Dan's body to the west of Isabela?

17 Feb, Puerto Ayora and Darwin Station. Yes. She needed to revisit Puerto Ayora. She never had a chance to explore the town or see Darwin Station, which served as headquarters for Galápagos National Park and as a primary research station for scientists from around the world. Maybe she'd find someone there who knew Dan; someone not involved in the tourist trade, who could give her some honest information about who to trust and who to stay clear of. If she could get her passport back, maybe she could leave tomorrow.

She called the American Consulate in Guayaquil, and ended up explaining her situation to the consul's secretary, a woman with a heavy accent. She concluded her story with, "The authorities took my passport and visa." The following silence stretched out so long that she finally added, "Hello?"

"Yes," the woman said. "I listen to your message left on the machine."

And? Sam wanted to yell. *Why didn't you call me back?* Gritting her teeth, she said mildly, "So you understand why I need your help."

"What is your involvement in this?" the woman asked.

She felt like she was being questioned by the police again. This was the *American* Consulate, for chrissakes—shouldn't they help American citizens? She explained who she was working for; that she was posting reports about the NPF study in the Galápagos.

"And your purpose in doing this?"

That was the second time she'd been asked that. She hesitated, suddenly certain that there were definite right and wrong answers to that question. Earning her pay was probably not one of the acceptable responses. "Dr. Kazaki was hired to make a report of the environmental status in the marine sanctuary. I was hired to dive with him and write about the experience."

"Your intent was to criticize the government of Ecuador?"

"Of course not." At least not directly. But if the marine survey showed that the islands were not being protected, that would naturally reflect badly on Ecuadorian authorities in general. As it should.

"You know that you can be arrested in Ecuador for participating in a demonstration?"

What? First time she'd heard of *that*. "There was no demonstration."

"It was a protest?"

Sam gulped, thinking about the critical tone of Zing's article yesterday, not to mention the graphic shark video. "No. Dr. Kazaki was counting fish. I am writing articles." She was not about to identify herself as a blogger to this woman.

"On the worldwide Internet."

This conversation was not going well. "Look, Miss . . ."

"Campo."

"Miss Campo, writing articles for the Internet is my job. And now a man—my friend and expedition partner—is dead, under suspicious circumstances."

"The *fiscalia* say he is missing."

"Trust me, he's dead." Sam blinked away the image of

Dan's lifeless face behind his scuba mask. "Don't you think you should be investigating this?"

"We will monitor the situation," Miss Campo said. "Please do not hesitate to call again if your American consul can be of any further assistance to you." The phone went silent.

Sam wished she had an old-fashioned cradle to slam the phone receiver down onto, but had to settle instead for punching the End button as hard she could, which was not in the least satisfying.

So much for help from the authorities. She probably couldn't get on any plane without her passport. And even if she had it now, it didn't seem likely she'd be able to convince anyone to ferry her to the airport today.

Resigned, she sat down and checked the posts on *Out There*. Responses to Zing's new article numbered nearly one hundred. Quite a few were in Spanish. She scanned the English comments. The readers seemed to be arguing among themselves. One side took the point of view that here was yet another arrogant American tree hugger butting into a foreign country's affairs. The opposing side praised Zing as a champion for the environment.

She checked her personal e-mail. There was nothing new from Chase. She settled for reading his translated attachments from the day before. According to the Quito article, it was well known in the Latin American press that illegal fishing was taking place all along the western coast of South America, with the catch mostly destined for Asian markets. The other piece was an editorial from Puerto Baquerizo Moreno, about how citizens in the Galápagos had the right to fish and farm wherever they wanted.

Galápagos Should Benefit Ecuadorians

The islands belong to Ecuadorians; not to tourists and not to some mythical World Heritage Centre. Why does Quito allow other countries to exercise control over Ecuadorian territory? Citizens of Ecuador should have the right to fish and farm anywhere within our country. Abolish Darwin Station and remove the scientists and park police. Increased development will bring jobs and more tourists. If the current government cannot stand up to international pressure and defend the rights of its own citizens, then this government should be overthrown by any means necessary.

Consider the implications, Chase had written at the end. Sam felt a chill. This was a local editorial. *Papagayo*'s crew lived in these islands. Had Quiroga been hinting at his opinion when he mentioned his cannery and the problem with "the world"? Had Dan, a known conservationist and foreign scientist, been "removed" by someone on board?

Her satellite phone chirped. She picked it up. The tiny screen identified the caller: *Kazaki, Daniel.* She dropped the phone on the bed and stared at it in horror.

Of course it wasn't Dan. It had to be Elizabeth. Had she been told about Dan? Or was she trying to reach him? Either way, Sam wasn't ready to talk to her. She covered her ears with her hands until the phone's godawful bleating finally stopped. When she heard the other passengers leaving their cabins to go up to breakfast, she joined them.

After choking down coffee and toast and sympathetic murmurs from the others, she decided to go on the scheduled nature hike with the group. There was likely to be safety in numbers, and Wyatt and Whitney still expected her to write her posts today. Between the underwater footage she had shot on the first day and some terrestrial photos gleaned from a walking tour today, she could slap something together for both characters.

But cute videos and pleasant travelogues weren't what she wanted to produce. She wanted to write about Dan. Unfortunately, she didn't have enough information to write a coherent article. She was the only one who had seen his corpse. All she had was a mystery. And a throbbing headache.

In her cabin, she downed three aspirin and stuffed her camera gear in her backpack and walked to the stern to join the tour. One panga, riding low in the water, was already bearing the first group of tourists toward Floreana Island. Was Papagayo's second panga still somewhere near Isabela, trolling for Dan's corpse? She hadn't seen either the captain or Tony at breakfast.

Ken, Dan's drinking buddy, leaned next to her on the railing. Others waited below on the platform.

"How're you doing?" Ken asked.

"Fine," she choked out. *Please don't be kind right now, or I'll break down.*

"Did Kazaki drown?"

Dan's slack open mouth and slashed throat swam up in her memory. "I don't know."

"You weren't with him at the time of the accident?"

What? The captain told the passengers it was an accident? She had an abrupt sickening realization that all the passengers had been gone when she paddled away in her kayak. Nobody had witnessed her departure. Or Dan's, apparently. She turned to face the grad student.

"Ken, while you guys were off on your morning hike, I paddled my kayak further down the coast and went hiking alone on Isabela, up towards the Alcedo volcano. When I left at nine A.M., Dan was working in his cabin." At least she assumed he was; she hadn't actually checked before launching her kayak. "As I was coming back, I saw sea lions playing around some rocks, and I just happened to find Dan—"

The story sounded improbable, even to her ears. She took a shaky breath and continued, "His regulator mouthpiece was missing. He had a gash across his throat and face. His lips were blue." Her voice cracked as she relived the sight of her friend's vacant eyes behind his water-filled mask.

"Sorry." Ken shifted his gaze to the rocky shores a short distance away, giving her a chance to compose herself. "What do you think happened?"

"I have no idea." She swallowed painfully.

An awkward silence descended. Ken self-consciously ran his fingers through his hair. "Where the hell is Brandon? I better go get him." He escaped up the stairs.

Abigail Birsky, dressed in a long denim skirt and T-shirt and carrying a canvas tote over one arm, climbed carefully down the steps, clutching the railing tightly. Sam said hello, and then asked the older woman, "Abigail, was everyone with you when you went hiking on Fernandina yesterday?"

"Everyone?"

"The whole tour group? The crew? Both park guides?"

The wrinkles on Abigail's forehead came together in a V as she considered. After a few seconds, she said, "Jon Sanders didn't come." She lowered her voice and whispered with a smile, "Probably didn't want to disturb his coiffure." Then she continued in a normal tone, "Jerry Roberson stayed behind, too. Sandy said he had a headache." She brushed a thumb across her lower lip, considering. "Eduardo was there the whole time," Abigail said, "pointing out plants and animals for us. Such a sweet young man."

Sam smiled at her reference to Eduardo as a young man. But Abigail was probably twenty years older than Eduardo.

"And then, in the afternoon, Constantino and Maxim came in the dinghies, following us while we snorkeled." Abigail dipped her head once, as if punctuating the end of her account.

"How about the captain and the rest of the crew?" Sam asked.

The older woman shrugged. "They stayed on the boat, I suppose."

So Tony was not accounted for yesterday. But speak of the devil—he neared now, driving the inflatable, to take the second load to the island. As soon as he landed the dinghy and looped a rope around a cleat on the stern of *Papagayo*, he turned toward the gas tank and fiddled with a hose there.

Ken, Brandon, Maxim, and Ronald Birsky came down the steps to join Sam and Abigail. They all stepped into the inflatable and found seats on the wooden benches as Tony focused on switching the gas hose from one tank to another.

"Tony," she said.

He looked up.

"What is your last name?"

"*Tu apellido*," Maxim said, doing his guide duty as translator.

"Diaz," Tony murmured, his expression guarded.

Her suspicions were right on, then. "Do you have a brother named Ricardo Diaz, with a boat named *Coqueta*?"

Tony pursed his lips, wrinkled his brow, then began, "I have no Eng—"

Maxim quickly translated Sam's question. Tony stared at the water for a few seconds, clearly uncomfortable. Then he blurted out a few angry sentences in Spanish and abruptly put the engine in reverse, causing everyone to grab on to their seats. After he slammed the gearshift into forward, he turned the inflatable toward the island, his gaze focused on the shore ahead.

Maxim leaned close to Sam. "He says that Ricardo Diaz has the same father but they are not friends."

"I see," Sam said. "That explains the resemblance." Her powers of observation were still intact, then; she hadn't simply been paranoid about the similarity between Tony and Ricardo. Tony's gaze flicked her way, and she smiled at him in an attempt to prove she meant no harm, but he quickly looked back toward the island.

Maxim leaned close to murmur, "Diaz left the mother of Tony to marry the mother of Ricardo. It is a local scandal."

"Do the families live in the same town?"

Maxim shook his head. "Baquerizo Moreno"—he pointed with his chin toward Tony—"and Ricardo comes from Villamil."

Puerto Villamil, the fishermen's stronghold. She wanted

to ask Tony more questions about his half brother and the local fishermen, but the way the first mate's jaw was clenched did not suggest cooperation. Could she believe anything he said?

"Galápagos is a small community," Maxim said, repeating Eduardo's words from two days ago. "Many are related somehow."

Which reminded her that she shouldn't trust anyone who lived here.

The panga landed at Post Office Bay among sea lions sleeping in the sun. A few opened their eyes or shifted a flipper on the brown sand, but that was all the notice they took of the inflatable and people.

The tour group walked up the path to the wooden post office barrel. Maxim explained that mail had been deposited by sailors on the island for more than two centuries, in hopes that a passing ship would post the envelopes on returning home. These days it was obviously tourists who deposited the mail, judging by the number of colorful postcards Maxim pulled from the barrel, and when Maxim distributed one piece of mail to each of them, it was clear that other tourists were expected to get them to their final destination. The postcard she received was addressed to Calgary, Alberta. Good; postage to Canada was relatively cheap and easy to come by at home. Brandon and Ronald left postcards of their own for someone else to pick up.

Maxim pointed out the remains of a Norwegian fishing village that had gone bust, and then talked about the island's scandal in the 1930s. An Austrian baroness moved in with two lovers and plans to build a luxury hotel, managed to piss off other families already settled on Floreana, and then mysteriously "disappeared" along with one of her lovers. The baroness's other lover ended up dead under mysterious circumstances, along with a fisherman and another settler from Floreana. Maxim hinted that the remaining inhabitants of the island knew more than they would talk about.

With each mention of "missing" or "dead," someone in

the group glanced at Sam. Of course Dan was in her thoughts, but she had no tears left. The emotions running through her mind were guilt, because she felt so numb, and disgust at her own species. Human history was full of these stories: toss a handful of people together in a contained environment such as a small island, and sooner or later, some would kill others. Murderers got away with their crimes every day, all around the world. It would be so easy to make someone go "missing" forever among the bleak islands and swift currents here. Would Dr. Daniel Kazaki become just another mysterious missing person in the Galápagos?

They joined the other tour group for a box lunch at another landing site, Punta Cormorant. Eduardo explained that the green color of the beach was due to olivine crystals. Olivine, he added, was a cousin to a green gemstone called peridot. In Sam's current state of mind, all this information seemed so irrelevant. In her head, she could hear her father explaining, *Life goes on*. She needed a moment—or more accurately, a day—of time standing still to mark Dan's death.

They walked a short trail to a small lagoon, where pink flamingos were feeding in the brackish water. Sam took a photo that seemed more like Florida or Africa than her vision of an island in the middle of the Pacific. The long-legged pink birds were accompanied by a great blue heron sauntering slowly along the shoreline, searching for prey. Sam was accustomed to seeing the gray long-necked birds hunt along the fern-lined shores near the Canadian border. To her eyes, this one looked out of place among lizards and lava.

They ended at another small beach composed of white sand from coral. "A favorite nesting place for green sea turtles," Maxim added.

"Are they safe?" Sam asked. "Do the eggs and hatchlings survive?" Turtle eggs and meat were considered delicacies in most parts of the world.

Maxim frowned. "It is nature," he said, and then changed

the subject to talk about the plans for the rest of the day: snorkel at Devil's Crown and a trip to the highlands to see a handful of giant tortoises.

On the horizon, two boats were visible: a small sailboat less than a mile away, and another tourist yacht in the distance. Now that Sam thought about it, the only time she hadn't seen a boat of any kind was when she had kayaked by herself to the remote area of Isabela. Boats were everywhere.

Had Dan seen a suspicious boat near *Papagayo* and donned his dive gear to go check it out? She tried to picture the scenario. Dan, diving unseen below the surface. Two converging fishing boats: one low in the water, heavy with an illegal load of sharks—her imagination colored the boat red and yellow like the one driven by Eduardo's cousin—and the other a large, high-powered cruiser, a courier for an Asian ship that waited on the horizon.

She had a vision of swimming beneath the surface, amid bodies of still-wriggling sharks sinking through water red with blood. She shivered. The blood and wounded sharks would attract other sharks, just like the poor finless shark she'd seen the day before yesterday. What were the odds of a scuba diver surviving in the midst of a feeding frenzy?

But that scenario didn't make sense. If Dan had been attacked by sharks, his body would not have been whole. If she could trust her shaky memory of his corpse, all his limbs had been intact.

Scratch the shark feeding frenzy, then. Maybe the fishermen had just begun to de-fin the sharks or pass *pepinos* from one boat to another. Suddenly Dan popped up from below, and—she remembered the fishing gaff lying at Buoy 3942 amid the other debris lost from boats. And one of the men—he resembled boat driver Ricardo in her mind's eye—with gaff in hand, cracked Dan over the head. Plausible. She rubbed the back of her hand across her sweating forehead. All too plausible. Maybe the fishing gaff had ripped Dan's air hose. But why would any poacher operate within sight of *Papagayo*?

It occurred to her that just because Dan had been found dead in the water didn't mean that he was killed in the water. His death could have been made to look like a scuba accident. Which brought her back to someone on board *Papagayo*.

"Miss Westin?"

She jumped and nearly dropped her camera, banging it painfully against her hipbone. Maxim stood beside her, his boyish face wrinkled with concern. "You are okay?"

Jeez, she must look like an idiot, standing mesmerized on the sand long after her group had moved on.

"Yeah, I'm all right." She pushed her sunglasses back to the bridge of her nose. "And call me Sam."

Maxim smiled. "Okay, Sam. We are over here now. It's a good afternoon for a swim."

She allowed herself to be herded back to the group.

TWISTED in the sheets of his lumpy bed in the cut-rate South Tucson motel room, Chase Perez had a nightmare about shooting a group of criminals. A righteous shooting, self-defense. But as he turned over the bodies, they all appeared to be innocuous-looking strangers. The last one was Summer Westin.

He woke with a jerk. In the other bed, Nicole was snoring softly or, more accurately, making little moaning sounds with each breath. Those noises had probably inspired the damn dream.

The numbers on the bedside clock morphed from 5:59 to 6:00 A.M. Not quite sunup yet. Chase rolled onto his back and stared at the stained tile ceiling while his heart rate subsided. Nicole had sent their report last night via their secure e-mail address, so their SAC would know their status. There'd been no messages for either of them from the outside world, which meant no known problems with their families. But then, Summer wasn't on his family list and wouldn't know how to contact him through the Bureau.

He had to know she was safe. He slipped out of bed,

quietly dressed in running shorts, T-shirt, and worn jogging shoes, and locked the door behind him. Outside, the morning air was cold. Rosy streaks of dawn were just beginning to break over the gray-brown hills to the east. He did a few stretches and retied his shoelaces as he checked the parking lot and surrounding buildings for observers. Nobody else was up yet. Then he set off jogging down the alley behind the motel, staying alert, listening for footsteps or car engines behind him.

The birds scolded him from the trees as he ran slowly through the streets on the dusty outskirts of town. Each year it got harder to find public phones, and directly calling someone from home on a cell, even a throwaway, was too much of a risk while they were undercover. There. No, someone had ripped the receiver off, left the useless cord dangling from the machine. He jogged on, and six blocks later located an old-fashioned phone booth outside a twenty-four-hour Laundromat. Staring through the scratched plastic booth walls, he tapped in the number for his home voice mail. A delivery truck tossed newspapers into doorways across the street. Closer to him, a couple of stray dogs investigated odors deposited along the curbs. After sniffing around the base of the phone booth, they moved on down the street.

Eleven voice mail messages awaited him. First was a call from his sister Raven about their parents' upcoming fortieth anniversary in May—she wanted to throw a party for them and wondered if he'd be able to come to Boise then. He'd respond to that later; Raven was used to not hearing from him for weeks at a time.

The rest of the calls were from Summer. *Please call me when you get this. Call me as soon as you can. I really need to talk to you.* Was she sobbing? He'd seen her scared, he'd seen her mad, but he had never known her to cry. What the hell was going on down there in Ecuador? According to the time stamps, she'd left all the messages yesterday evening.

He deposited more money, then dialed her home

number and rousted her housemate Blake out of bed. The guy wasn't happy. "I haven't heard from Sam since she left for the Galápagos. Cripes, man, do you know it's not even six A.M. here?"

Chase apologized, but before he hung up, he got Summer's work number from Blake. When he called her satellite phone, he only got a cheery voice mail message: *Hi, you've reached Reporter Summer Westin at* Out There. *I'm doing exciting work in the field right now. Leave a message and I'll call when I can.* It wasn't even her voice; sounded more like a chirpy high school girl.

"Carajo," he muttered, punching the phone booth wall in frustration. Then he realized the voice mail system was recording. "Uh, this is Chase, *querida.* I'm so sorry I missed your calls. What's going on? Are you okay? And damn it, you can't even call me back. You know why. I'm at a public phone now. I'll call again when I can."

A pretty dark-haired young woman jogged down the other side of the street. Their eyes met briefly, and she smiled and waved as she ran past. Chase waved back, then continued with his phone message. "I wish you'd jump on the next plane out of there. But I know that's not likely to happen because you're, well . . . you. So for once, I'm glad you're with another man. Kazaki damn well better be protecting you." He and Nicole were hitting the road today with their New American Citizen Army buddies, destination unknown, but he couldn't tell Summer that. Instead, he said, "I *will* find a way to meet up with you on the twenty-second, no matter what. Stay safe, *mi corazón.*"

He cursed with each step as he jogged back to the motel. Had Summer really been crying? He ached to hold her, and they weren't even on the same continent.

Nicole was in the shower when he let himself into the room. He booted up Charlie's suitably ancient laptop, located the hotel's unsecured wireless network, and brought up *Out There*'s page. There were two new posts. Wilderness Westin's was all about giant turtles and lizards; its tone could best be described as educational. She had to have written it sometime yesterday—had it been before or after her phone calls?

Zing's post was critical of the situation there and featured a couple of gruesome video clips of sharks feasting on fish corpses. The negative comments in response to Zing's post, especially those in Spanish, had doubled since yesterday. Was this what Summer was upset about?

The posts sounded very different. According to the photos, Zing appeared to be a young athletic redhead. Maybe Summer wasn't the daredevil photographer shooting the shark videos after all. He hoped that was the case. Sea kayaking and climbing volcanoes were a lot safer than swimming with sharks and poachers.

In her photo, Wilderness Westin was smiling, as few people would be with giant snakes hanging around their necks. But that was his wild woman. He touched the tip of his index finger to his lips and then pressed it to the screen over her heart. *"Te quiero."*

Nicole emerged from the bathroom, her body wrapped in a robe and her hair wrapped in a towel. She took one look at his face and at the computer screen, rolled her eyes, and drawled, "I oughta shoot you right here, Charlie, lustin' after that reporter gal." Then she flashed him a stern look that reminded him he needed to stay in character at all times.

He shut down the laptop and stood up. "Ah, baby, you know the lust is only in my heart."

"Don't call me baby," she said. "Before you hit the shower and shave your head, hon, could you get me a cup of java from the lobby? They advertised free doughnuts and coffee for breakfast."

He closed the laptop. "Bad coffee comin' right up, sweet cheeks." He ducked out the door before she could throw something at him.

SAM waded along the shoreline to take an uncomfortable seat on a gnarled root next to Eduardo. At least her perch was in the shade. She sat morosely, watching the tour group snorkel in the bay over Devil's Crown, a sunken volcanic crater. Should she join them? She might be able to get another underwater photo for Zing's post today. Then she realized that she hadn't brought the waterproof housing for the camera. Or her snorkel gear. Given the amount of wine she'd consumed last night, she was a little surprised she could still walk and talk.

Eduardo's gaze was fixed on his Teva-shod feet resting on the sand beneath the water's surface. He looked wrung out, just like she felt. He probably had a hangover, too.

"I see Paige Sanders decided to join the group today," she remarked to him. "Jon doesn't seem like he wants to participate in the tour."

Eduardo shrugged. "The captain tells me that Mr. Sanders has been here before."

That seemed odd. "Then why would he go on a tour?"

Eduardo turned to face her. His eyes were streaked with red. "His wife Paige is new."

She thought about the deferential way that the captain and first mate had greeted the Sanderses, and about how Jon had been drinking late with the captain. "Sanders seems like an important man."

Eduardo nodded. "A rich man."

A rich man who seemed to be friendly with Captain Quiroga, although it was hard to imagine what the two might have in common. Sam resolved to look into Sanders's background later.

A shout from Maxim broke up her thoughts. He stood waist-deep in the middle of the lagoon with a face mask pushed onto his forehead. Sam caught only the name *Roberson*. Maxim held his hands out in a questioning gesture. He had to be looking for Jerry or Sandy.

Eduardo pointed to a cluster of rocks dotting the water's surface near the east side of the bay and yelled, *"Por las rocas!"*

Maxim nodded, then pulled his mask into place. Before his expression was concealed by mask and snorkel, Sam noted the look on the young guide's face. Dark squint, lips pressed into a grim line, rigid jaw. "Is Maxim mad at you, Eduardo?"

Eduardo fixed his gaze on his young colleague, who was now swimming toward the rocks. He sighed. "Somebody dies in your tour group, it might hurt your job, you know? I am only one month from retirement, the first Galápagos naturalist guide to work for a full thirty years, the first to get a pension." He paused to flick his foot at a small crab that was advancing underwater toward his toes. "Maxim, he is a guide for only two years; he is worried for his reputation."

After a minute, she asked, "Eduardo, do you think it's possible that someone here wanted to kill Dan?"

His head jerked back as if she'd slapped him. "Who wants to kill him?"

It was her turn to shrug. "Illegal fishermen? They might be worried about his reports." About the poaching that she, writing as Zing, had made public.

"They wouldn't *kill* him." Eduardo looked at his clasped hands for a long moment. "I tell the police . . . I stress . . . it must be an accident."

"I saw Daniel, Eduardo. His regulator mouthpiece was missing, his throat was slashed. Why would you say it was an accident?"

He replied without meeting her gaze. "Because it has to be." His voice broke on the last word. He reached up and pinched the bridge of his nose between his eyes. A tear slid down his weathered cheek.

She touched his arm. "We both lost a friend."

The way Eduardo emphasized the word *kill* made her wonder what they might do instead. She understood that she might be discussing local fishermen. They could be his friends, his neighbors, or his relatives. *Galápagos is a small community.* But she was getting fed up with this laissez-faire attitude of the locals. The world would be a terrible place if everyone simply looked the other way while their neighbors committed crimes. If Dan had died because of what he'd found, and she stopped the count and the Internet reports, then Dan would have died for nothing. And *they*, whoever the hell *they* were, would win. And thousands more animals would die in this place that was supposed to be a sanctuary. She couldn't let that happen.

It was just her and Zing now. She rubbed her forehead, trying to smooth away the ache that had settled there. "Eduardo, we are close to Ola Rock, the next site on Dan's list. I want you to take me there."

His chin jerked up. "Alone? I could not let you dive alone. Especially now."

"We missed the site we were supposed to survey yesterday. I have to do Ola Rock today if we're going to Puerto Ayora tomorrow."

Eduardo didn't respond.

"I'll ask the captain to dive with me," she said. "Or Tony." Although the thought of being alone underwater with either of those men gave her the chills.

Eduardo immediately shook his head. "No. The captain would not approve."

"Of what?" Continuing the fish count, or of himself or a crew member coming with her?

He turned his face back to the bay, watching the group. "Dan should not dive alone."

Eduardo's use of the present tense jarred her. She bit her lip, wanting to correct the sentence to *should not have been diving alone*. Was Eduardo implying that she had somehow let Dan down? Had she? Finally, she said, "But that's what he decided to do. And now I have no choice but to dive alone, too."

Eduardo's gaze flicked back to her. The creases across his forehead and around his eyes were deep. Had he slept at all? He pulled his mirrored sunglasses down over his eyes and shook his head. "No. We cannot. It is too dangerous."

"You made the deal, Eduardo," she said quietly. "You already took the money. Dan told me you were an honorable man. The captain took Dan's money, too." That last part was a guess on her part, but Eduardo did not deny it.

Who else had been in on the deal to bring them on board? And perhaps more important—who else knew about the deal, but had not profited?

Eduardo sighed heavily. Then he pointed out to the water. "Look."

A dark shape approached the beach, swimming just beneath the water's surface. Sam tensed, trying to identify it. Too narrow for a turtle. Didn't seem graceful enough for a ray or a dolphin. A beachmaster?

The creature erupted from the shallows in a flurry of black neoprene. Jerry Roberson spat out his snorkel and shouted to his wife, "Sandy! I saw a manta ray!"

As Roberson slipped back underwater, Sam slid off the mangrove root and stood knee-deep in the shallows, watching the man's rapid progress underwater. "Wow. Jerry can really swim. I can't hold my breath for even half that time."

"Oh yes," Eduardo responded. "He tells me he was a diver for the United States Army." He pursed his lips together for a moment, then corrected himself. "No, the Navy. Like heroes in the movies. He was a Navy Seal."

Sam stared at Roberson's shadow gliding beneath the dappled surface. She wrapped her arms around herself, thinking about Dan out there somewhere, drifting with the current. She wondered what else she didn't know about Jerry Roberson. And about everyone else on board *Papagayo*, for that matter.

A confusion of thoughts lapped at her brain like the aquamarine water swirling around her knees. What would happen if Dan's body was never found? What would happen if it was? How could she force the police to give her passport back? She hated this feeling of just . . . waiting.

Why in the hell did Chase have to go undercover, right when she needed his help more than ever? What good was having a lover if you couldn't even find him when you needed him? Was he in danger, or was he having the time of his life? She reached for her satellite phone, then realized she'd left it on the boat. Chase could be calling her right now. The aspirin had worn off, and her head throbbed again. She felt like an idiot. *Had* she been an idiot to take this assignment?

Eduardo, who was Dan's friend, too, sat only inches away. Nine other people were within shouting distance, and even more waited back on *Papagayo*. They might be sympathetic strangers, but they were strangers nonetheless. And there was a chance that one or more might be a killer. She'd never felt more lonely.

As if Eduardo had read her mind, he touched her shoulder lightly and said, "Sam, you are not alone. When the others go to the highlands this afternoon, I will take you to Ola Rock."

12

SAM was grateful to see there was almost no current flow-ing past Ola Rock, at least not one visible at the ocean sur-face. It was easy to understand why the formation had been given the Spanish name for "The Wave." The small islet was a thick gray upright fin that culminated in a curlicue approximately twenty feet above the water line, giving it the appearance of a wave frozen into stone. There was no beach. Eduardo shifted the motor to idle and the dinghy bumped against the intersection of rock and turquoise sea. The water-smoothed lava rock sloped steeply down and disappeared into the surrounding ocean. Sam hoped a sheer vertical wall did not await her below.

She backflipped off the dinghy, painfully aware that she was diving alone for the first time. She had checked the air in her tank before attaching the regulator, and now, as the face of her dive computer lit up in the water, she was relieved to see her equipment was functioning normally. She floated on the surface for a few minutes, checking the area below to make sure no sharks lurked close by. The water was a murky green; she couldn't see beyond a few

feet. She was in the midst of an algae bloom. *Wonderful.*
Anything could be down there. Her imagination instantly
conjured up a great white swimming toward her with open
jaws.

She reminded herself that she had been underwater in a
blackout before: her one night dive in the pitch-black, frigid
waters of Puget Sound. By comparison, this daylight dive
in warmer water should be a piece of cake. Of course,
she had been with four other divers then, and they had a
dive master to guide them. No matter, she tried to reassure
herself; bubbles always travel upward and she had a com-
pass and depth gauge built into her dive computer. She
couldn't really get too disoriented, could she? *Enough with
the dithering*, she chided herself. *Just do it, Zing.*

She rolled upright next to the dinghy's bumper and held
out her hands for the camera. Eduardo acted as anxious as
she felt, holding the camera a little out of her reach as he
said, "Please to be extra careful."

"That's my plan," she promised. "I'll count, I'll take a
few photos; I'll make this dive as short as I can."

He handed her the camera. She clipped the camera strap
to a ring on the front of her BCD, then let the last of the air
out of the vest and exhaled. As the water closed above her
head, she fought an urge to jet back up to the surface. *Never
dive alone.* How many times had she seen those words in
dive manuals? If she hadn't been along on their first dive
together, Dan would have died. If she'd been with him on
his last dive, would he have lived? Or would they both have
died?

She couldn't afford to think about any of that at the
moment. She had a job to do. Expert divers went out by
themselves all the time. Since she wasn't anything close to
an expert, she would be extra vigilant. The noise of the dinghy motor reverberated so loudly through the water that
she would have no difficulty locating it again. She took a
deep breath and pinched her nose to equalize pressure as
she slowly descended. Her mask fogged up. She tweaked it
to break the suction, let in a trickle of water to clear the fog

inside, then sealed it to her face again, exhaling through her nose to prevent mask squeeze.

The visibility remained poor for twenty feet below the surface. The late afternoon sun filled the water with light, but the layer of suspended algae was so thick that she couldn't clearly make out any objects beyond a couple of yards. It was like swimming through lime gelatin, but a whole lot creepier. She could squint into the green distance all day and still not be able to distinguish any creature, large or small, harmless or ferocious, that might be waiting for her. Fish could detect movement with their electrical sensors. All she had was her eyes and ears, and both were almost useless in this environment. *You still have your brain. Stay calm, do your best. Do it for Dan.* After filling her lungs with air, she blew it out slowly, streaming loud bubbles up through the algae fog. *Go, Zing.*

Turning facedown and hovering two feet above the bottom, she followed the sloping rock face downward, stopping at a depth of sixty feet. At least the visibility was slightly better at this depth; she could see fish twenty feet away. She had decided the way to survey a tiny islet like Ola Rock was to circumnavigate it at one depth, then rise to another level and repeat the process, slowly spiraling up toward the surface.

According to Dan's notes, Ola Rock should be a prime feeding area for sea cucumbers and shellfish. She swam slowly, counting and identifying as best she could while she circled the small island. Carrying both Dan's handheld computer and her camera would have been next to impossible. Instead, she'd strapped a small slate and attached pencil to her left wrist. She scribbled on the slate periodically, letting her camera dangle down from the strap attached to her vest. The arrangement was awkward, but it was the best she'd come up with.

After the first ten anxious minutes, she started to find the experience of diving solo rather tranquil. No one was watching and judging her skills. She exhaled and sank a few inches, inhaled and rose. The more she relaxed, the easier she could hover motionless in the water. She was finally getting the hang of neutral buoyancy.

The black volcanic rock floor transitioned to a Kelly green plane of slick algae, interrupted periodically by olive-colored seaweed streamers and yellow and orange sponges. She took photos to send to NPF. The area looked like it should be an ideal grazing ground. Hundreds of starfish of various colors crawled among the algae, along with clusters of black-spined urchins, but she counted only four sea cucumbers, three lobsters, and nine crabs. A small school—she counted eight—of yellowtailed surgeonfish grazed on the algae, moving ahead each time she swam forward. She stopped to capture an image of a spiraled fuchsia ribbon anchored to a rock. She knew the neon pink coil was the egg mass of some creature, but she'd have to match it with one of her reference books.

Although it made for boring composition, she snapped a couple of pictures of the nearly empty green plane stretching away from her. Was this barrenness the result of poaching? Having never been here before, she had no way to tell. It would be up to the scientists at NPF to make a comparison.

She'd always imagined that the underwater world would be absolutely silent. Instead, she heard not only the sounds of her own breathing, but a melody of clicks and gurgles and metallic pings as the water moved against various surfaces and marine creatures signaled to each other. These noises overlaid the background rumble of the idling panga motor.

On the windward side of the islet, the rock was more rippled, and the algae had been mostly swept away. She found a few more crabs and lobsters and fish among the rock formations. A giant fish ball comprised of hundreds of small silver fish, swimming so close together that she couldn't see through them, hung in the water like a solid sphere. Wow. She'd seen this on television, but it was amazing to see up close. Did the fish naturally travel in a ball formation, or were they swarming to protect themselves against a predator she hadn't yet spotted? The last thought was unsettling.

She abruptly realized she could no longer hear the sound of the motor, and felt a swell of panic. Had Eduardo left? No, he wouldn't, she reassured herself. Maybe he had turned off the motor to save fuel. She checked her computer readout. She had slightly more than 1000 PSI left—plenty of air and therefore plenty of time. Channeling Zing again, she continued on course and picked up the rumble of the motor again after a few more yards.

The fish ball did not move away as she approached. The swirl of fish was so extensive she had little choice but to swim through it. The fish flitted out of her way as she finned through their midst, then closed ranks behind her, and fortunately, no sharks or other monsters appeared in the midst of the silver cloud. *Amazing.* On the other side, she snapped a few photos of the living sphere, made up of at least five hundred fish. She'd identify the species later.

She was on her second circumnavigation at forty feet and 700 PSI when she found a fishing line snagged on a ragged lump of lava. The nylon cord streamed off in a horizontal line, vanishing into the distant gloom. It was disturbing to think that if she had been swimming only a foot lower in the water, she might have become entangled without ever noticing the line floating above her.

She released air from her BCD and knelt on the rocky bottom, letting the camera dangle from its strap. Gingerly taking hold of the line, she reeled it in, wrapping it around her left hand. Her dive gloves were fingerless so she could work the camera buttons, but she was glad to have the protection of the thin neoprene between the line and her hands. The first hook, strung on a secondary line that dangled off the main, was wickedly sharp but blessedly empty. Just as she feared, she was pulling in a section of a longline, an illegal fishing device within the marine sanctuary.

As far as she was concerned, longlines should be illegal everywhere. Longlines, attached to floats at the surface, typically stretched for a mile or more, dangling hundreds of hooks. In her home area of the north Pacific, longlines were usually set by commercial halibut fishing boats. But too often boats that deployed them failed to recover the whole line, leaving sections to float and "fish" on their own. They weren't as destructive to the ecosystem as bottom trawling with nets, but longlines senselessly killed all kinds of creatures attracted to the bait. As she continued to reel in this line, she felt something heavy but as yet invisible in the pea-soup distance. The weight didn't pull back, so odds were that it wasn't alive. She couldn't help recalling the horrific vision of Dan's corpse. When a large mass surged toward her out of the murk, two long black limbs trailing behind, she held her breath.

Slowly the corpse came into focus. *Damn*. She could tell by the exquisite undulating patterns on its feathers that it was a waved albatross, the first one she'd ever seen. Each wing, as long as she was tall, fluttered in the current as if the magnificent bird was still trying to fly. The hook was lodged in its throat. *Double damn*. She took a second to check her computer—she was down to less than 600 PSI. Time was running out. Holding down the coil of longline under a knee, she took a sad photo of the drowned albatross. Waved albatrosses mated for life. Was the mate of this one soaring somewhere above the islands, endlessly waiting for him to return?

Letting the camera dangle again, she reached for the dive knife she kept in a sheath attached to the bottom of her BCD. She cut the line that led to the hook in the bird's throat. Then she sheathed her dive knife again, shoved the corpse away, and reeled in the rest of the longline.

There was one more hook, dangling a chunk of decayed fish. When she touched it, the glutinous mass slipped off the metal barb. Then the line ended. She was at 500 PSI and had been underwater nearly an hour, longer than she'd ever stayed before. She tucked the coil of line and hooks inside her largest BCD pocket, wrapping the hooks with the line so they wouldn't puncture the vest's air bladder. The zipper wouldn't close over the bulky bundle, so she held a hand over the pocket opening as she finned her way back toward the boat, rising slowly as she moved up the flank of Ola Rock, holding her camera in the crook of her arm and watching her computer count down the recommended time to decompress.

The engine noise increased and the visibility decreased as she got closer to the surface. She nearly collided with the panga, its gray rubbery skin abruptly appearing only inches in front of her mask. Surfacing, she inflated her BCD and spat out her mouthpiece. It was good to see blue sky, breathe endless air, and hear earthly sounds again.

Eduardo was clearly happy to see her return, too. "I worry," he said, taking the camera from her.

"Sorry, the dive took longer than I thought. I found a piece of longline, so I had to retrieve it."

He frowned. "This line could drift from a long way, even from outside the reserve."

Or not, she thought to herself. Eduardo, like everyone else in the Galápagos, seemed eager to put the best spin on everything. "A waved albatross was impaled on one of the hooks."

"Very bad." He made a face. "The bird see the bait fish from above, he dives, and then he swallow the hook." He made a twirling gesture above her head with his hand, and she turned around to let him take hold of her tank valve. She unbuckled her BCD and shrugged out of it. Eduardo hauled the tank and her attached BCD over the dinghy bumper. Then she bellyflopped into the boat, sliding onto the floor like a beached mackerel. She righted herself and checked the slate on her wrist. Nobody else would be able to interpret her chicken scratches there, but she would remember well enough to make sense of the letters and numbers. She ripped apart the Velcro straps and set the slate carefully aside, then popped off her fins and face mask, pulled herself up onto one of the benches, and reached for a bottle of water.

Eduardo shoved the panga away from the shore with an oar, and then pushed the throttle forward. Sam turned to face the bow. She couldn't wait to post her last photo. The image might be gruesome, but the longlined albatross was a perfect example of what was at stake here.

"Dan," she murmured, raising her water bottle into the wind, "I did it for you."

She combed out her French braid with her fingers and let the breeze dry her hair as they sped back to *Papagayo*. She not only had survived diving alone, but had recorded the counts, taken her photos, and documented more evidence of illegal fishing. Hot damn, she *was* intrepid; she *was* Zing. But sadly, she was also a solo act again.

Her schedule for *Out There* required not only the usual two posts today, but also two half-hour chat sessions that night. After reading Zing's hate mail for the last two days, she worried about who might show up to debate with her alter ego. Until she could write about what happened to Dan, she'd have to pretend this trip was business as usual.

As they neared *Papagayo*, Sam noticed the military boat anchored alongside. At the tiller, Eduardo tensed at this reminder of Dan's death. Tony and another crew member were handing dive gear up to a uniformed sailor on deck. The two *fiscalia* officers, Schwartz and Aguirre, stood officiously at the bow, watching Sam and Eduardo as the inflatable bumped up against *Papagayo*'s stern. Nobody said a word. Tony disappeared through the engine room door. The other crew member helped Eduardo tie up the panga and then carried Sam's dive gear and tanks into the engine room. As she and Eduardo climbed the stairs to the main deck, Tony emerged, now dressed in a wetsuit. He untied the Navy boat, and then leapt aboard as the boat pulled away. Obviously the search for Dan's body was still in progress.

As soon as she got back to her cabin, Sam checked her cell phone, scrolling back through received calls. The last was an unidentified number—Chase's frustrating message from this morning. Earlier was the call from her editor in Seattle and still earlier, the jarring listing of *Kazaki, Dan-*

iel. Elizabeth had left no message. Had she been informed that Dan was missing and was mostly likely dead?

Nobody had called since Chase's message this morning. *You can't call me.* That was so typical. Why didn't she ever have normal relationships? The only men she attracted were those who used her to further their own careers— okay, to be fair, that was only one man, Seattle television reporter–now–San Diego anchorman Adam Steele—or men who were simply not there when she needed them. Okay, the latter category was only one man, too. And it *was* Chase's job to disappear on FBI assignments. She was always traipsing off somewhere on jobs, too; so she really couldn't justify feeling too sorry for herself. She hated it when her interior conversations ended in self-recrimination like this.

She focused on putting together her blog posts. Writing for Wilderness Westin was easy enough with photos of flamingos and the post office barrel and the twisted history of Floreana.

Creating Zing's story was more of a challenge today. The pictures from Ola Rock were nearly as murky as the water had been there; she had to supplement with stock photos to show readers what a waved albatross and sea cucumbers actually looked like. She identified the pink ribbon of eggs as those of a nudibranch, or sea slug. She was starving and late for dinner, so she left Zing's post in rough draft form and raced to slide into her seat with Brandon and Ken in the middle of the evening meal. As soon as she stepped into the dining area, the conversation died.

"Ignore them," Ken murmured. Brandon nodded his agreement. Constantino kindly brought her a salad and an extra large glass of wine in addition to the main course.

As Constantino delivered the dessert course to the other tables, Captain Quiroga entered the dining area, wearing his white dress uniform. He cleared his throat. "Officers Schwartz and Aguirre of the *fiscalia* are here to question all passengers about Dr. Kazaki's disappearance."

The cluster of tourists looked at each other. Most expressions were perplexed; a few people looked worried. Jerry Roberson's face, as usual, wore a glower.

"It is the normal routine," the captain assured them. "They will question the crew, too. We will begin after dinner."

After they'd finished dessert, the tour group was shepherded to the lounge for the customary evening lecture by Maxim. A few minutes after they had left the dining area, Officer Aguirre signaled Jerry and Sandy Roberson that they should follow him to the upper deck. Sam finished her meal alone in the dining area. Although she could see the other tourists and they could see her, for the moment everyone seemed to be pretending that she was invisible. After swallowing her last spoonful of passion fruit mousse, she slipped out through the doors onto the walkway, and then climbed the stairs to the captain's office, where the interviews were taking place. Flattening her back against the outside wall near the open porthole, she listened as the officers questioned the Robersons.

"How would I know what he was up to?" Jerry Roberson said angrily. "All I know was that it had something to do with fish, and that he was a Jap."

"Jerry!" His wife admonished.

Sam heard a brief exchange in Spanish between Eduardo and one of the officers. Then Eduardo quietly asked, "You mean he was Japanese?"

"That's what I said, a Jap."

Sandy again yelped, "Jerry!"

Roberson then said, "Well, *excuse* me. These guys know what I mean. I served in Vietnam. My father and my uncle died on Okinawa in World War Two. Japs, Chinese, Koreans, Vietnamese—those slant-eyed bastards are all the same; they don't give a shit about anyone except themselves. You guys know that. They're the ones who are poaching all your fish, right? We always got problems with them off the U.S. coastlines, too."

No wonder Jerry Roberson had glared at her and Dan.

To him, Irish-Japanese-American Daniel Kazaki was simply a Jap, and she was clearly allied with the enemy.

Did Roberson, an ex–Navy Seal, hate Japs enough to murder a slant-eyed stranger from Delaware? Could he have borrowed the captain's gear and slipped into the water after Dan? As far as she knew, the two men had never met before. An impromptu prejudice-motivated murder seemed improbable, to say the least, unless Roberson was a serial killer who traveled the world bumping off Asian strangers he met along the way.

The interview continued, with Jerry insisting that he had been napping in Cabin 5 on the day that Dan disappeared. Sandy was snorkeling with the tour group. Neither knew where Dan Kazaki or Summer Westin was at the time.

The mention of her name startled her. Why were the officers asking about *her* whereabouts? She'd already told them that whole story.

Chair legs squeaked against the tile floor inside. Sam decided she'd better disappear before she was discovered eavesdropping. She hustled down the stairs to the main deck, opened the door and passed the tables that were now clear of dinnerware, and then entered the lounge.

The fluorescent lights overhead seemed too bright, the conversation too loud. Constantino manned the tiny bar. The poor guy must work sixteen-hour shifts. She asked him for a Diet Coke just to have something to hold in her hands.

As he poured it, she turned to survey the gathering. Brandon, Ken, both Birskys, and Paige Sanders sat on the L-shaped couch. Their attention was focused on Maxim, who, with marine encyclopedia in hand, endeavored to identify all the fish spotted during the day's snorkel outing. Sam squeezed herself onto the vinyl-covered cushions between Brandon and Ken.

"Goatfish?" Maxim pointed to a photo on the page in front of him.

"I don't think so." Abigail Birsky shook her head. "It

had horizontal black stripes." She flashed Sam a weak smile that might have meant anything.

Various members of the tour group scrutinized her out of the corners of their eyes; she felt their collective gaze on her. She tried to put herself in their shoes. In the beginning, she'd acted aloof because she didn't know what was safe to say and she and Dan were not part of the group. Then they'd observed her in a hysterical state. Next, she got plastered, and now she was acting distant and mysterious again.

What could they be thinking? That she and Dan had ruined their vacations? That she was a psycho who made up a story about a body? That *she'd* killed Dan? Why was nobody talking? She swallowed a sip of her cold drink, and then said, "I didn't kill him."

She regretted the words as soon as they'd escaped. For an awkward moment, silence lay in the room like a dropped condom that nobody wanted to claim. Finally, Paige Sanders held up the book of photos in her lap and asked, "Could Abigail's fish have been a yellowtail surgeonfish?" And the conversation surged into safer marine mysteries.

Sandy and Jerry Roberson returned, accompanied by Officer Schwartz and Eduardo, who told the Birskys that they were needed next. The older couple rose and left with Eduardo, but to her surprise, Schwartz remained in the room, taking a spot on the couch. Maxim ended his lecture and the group's attention turned to refreshing their drinks and chatting with one another. Schwartz sat silently among them, observing. His demeanor reminded Sam of the lurking barracuda.

As usual, Jonathan Sanders was missing from the group. Could that be significant? She watched the tiny bubbles in her glass climb from bottom to top. A whole day had passed, but she had no more clues about what had happened to Dan than she had at this time yesterday.

Maxim leaned toward her. "You work for *Out There*."

She looked up, startled. Had Dan or Eduardo told him that? "You know *Out There*?"

"I love *Out There*." The young guide smiled. "You are Wilderness Westin, reporter and photographer, yes?"

The tourists stared curiously, waiting for her answer. Schwartz was listening intently, too. She squirmed. "That's the byline—the name—they asked me to use."

Maxim's eyebrows lifted in a hopeful expression. "You know Zing?"

She struggled to keep her face impassive. Maxim didn't know she was Zing? She'd assumed that Eduardo was in on the secret. But now that she thought about it, maybe he wasn't. So far, Sam hadn't uploaded a photo as Zing with Dan or anyone else in it. As promised, she hadn't been specific about their dive locations in her posts, and neither Eduardo nor Maxim were divers, so they probably had never seen the underwater landscapes. For all the world knew, Zing was diving from some other boat.

She hedged, "I've met Zing."

"Where does she stay?"

"That's a good question." Sam thought quickly. "We communicate via e-mail and cell phone when we travel." Maybe that would obfuscate the process enough that no one would question the logic. The tourists already looked bored and were turning back to their own conversations.

"You know Vertical Mann?" Maxim persisted, naming a young black mountain climber character that the e-zine had invented for their launch a year ago.

"I never met him." At least half the people listed on *Out There*'s staff page were marketing creations. She'd be happy to expose the virtual reporters if she hadn't signed a nondisclosure agreement promising she wouldn't. And then there was the fact that even she didn't know for sure which reporter was a real person and which wasn't.

Now she worried that Maxim was following her daily posts. He was in the twenty-something age group that *Out There* tended to attract. "What kind of a computer do you have, Maxim?"

The guide made a face. "A very old one. Here, I see Tony's, and I am saving."

So Tony and Maxim were following her daily posts? Who else?

"Will you write about this?" Maxim asked.

She hesitated, acutely aware of Officer Schwartz sitting only a few feet away. But then, he supposedly didn't understand English. "Do you mean about what happened to Dr. Kazaki?"

Maxim nodded.

"Yes, I'll write about it." *It*. Dan's death. Her throat suddenly felt tight.

Maxim nodded soberly. He rubbed his hands on his thighs, then abruptly jumped up, clapped his hands for attention, and launched into a description of the group activities planned for the next day: a visit to Darwin Station and a tour of Puerto Ayora. At the end of his statements, he focused on her again. "Will you come with us, Wilderness?"

Sam winced at Maxim's use of her pseudonym. "I'm coming to Puerto Ayora, but I can't stay with the group. I've got work to do."

She studied the ice cubes in her glass for a second, and then checked her watch. Eight thirty. She had half an hour to post her stories and get ready for her chat sessions. The vinyl cushions squeaked as she rose. "Night, all."

She went outside for a breath of fresh air before descending to her cabin. The wind had picked up. *Papagayo* swung on its anchor. Waves rolled from bow to stern. As she made her way along the metal grating of the exterior walkway, her nostrils picked up the acrid odor of burning tobacco. She glanced up to see a dark silhouette leaning against the deck rail above, the red ember of a cigarette creating a tiny pocket of brightness in the night shadows.

Jonathan Sanders. He and Paige had come on board after she and Dan had. Was that coincidence? Or had she and Dan been followed?

13

IN her cabin, Sam uploaded the posts for Zing and Wilderness and then reviewed her photos and notes, trying to get into the proper frame of mind for talking to her audience at *Out There*. She clicked through the pretty photos from her first Galápagos dive. Sunbeams piercing jade water. Purple sea fan. Sea turtle. It seemed impossible that she'd taken these only three days ago. Her heart lurched at a shot of Dan, holding out the sea cucumber, his almond-shaped hazel eyes clearly visible through his face mask. His gaze was sharp; she'd snapped that photo before the carbon monoxide had dulled his thoughts. It was a very nice photo; she should send it to Elizabeth.

Look after my husband.

"Oh, Dan," Sam murmured. "What happened?"

A loud thump on her door made her jump out of her chair. Sergeant Schwartz and an Ecuadorian Navy officer stepped into her room. Eduardo stood in the doorway.

She could tell by their faces. "You found him."

"Yes." Eduardo looked as if he might start sobbing at any second. "He is floating near Leon Rock."

Schwartz studied her as if he had been tasked with memorizing every freckle on her face.

"Can I see him?" she asked. Not that she really wanted to stare death in the face again, but now she wanted to look at Dan more closely, for marks and injuries. For any hint of what had happened.

"The police take him to Puerto Ayora," Eduardo told her.

Sam took a deep breath. "Has Dan's wife been notified?"

The two men exchanged rapid-fire Spanish sentences, after which Eduardo said miserably, "The American Consulate in Guayaquil is calling."

Sam felt like a coward. Should she have answered Elizabeth Kazaki's call last night, broken the horrible news herself? She rubbed her bare arms and met Schwartz's unwavering blue-eyed gaze. "What will happen now?"

Schwartz said something in Spanish without averting his eyes from her.

Eduardo stammered, "A doctor who studies . . . dead people . . . will check the body. In Puerto Ayora. He is on his way there now. And then he will be sent home."

They had a coroner in Puerto Ayora? Good. She would go there tomorrow. But first, she would visit Darwin Station. She desperately needed someone whose advice she could trust. Surely there'd be a fellow conservationist and English speaker among the scientists there.

"And what about me?" she asked Schwartz.

He replied in Spanish.

Eduardo gave her an apologetic look. "He says what do you have to do with this matter?"

She was fairly certain the police officer meant that to be some sort of trap. "Daniel Kazaki was my colleague and my friend." She stared into Schwartz's icy blue eyes. "And you have my passport."

More Spanish. Eduardo echoed, "It is safe at police headquarters in Puerto Ayora."

"When can I get it back?"

Again Eduardo translated. "We are still investigating. You are not scheduled to leave for three more days."

Her tropical vacation would continue, then, whether she wanted to stay or not. Would she be better off to jump ship and get a hotel room in Puerto Ayora? That is, *if* she could get a room. She remembered the way she and Dan had been thrown out of the hotel there, which reminded her to call Mrs. Vintner, the manager, and ask the woman a few questions about that.

She looked up at Schwartz. "Am I in danger?"

"Why should you be in danger?" Eduardo asked a second after Schwartz replied in Spanish.

Was it standard cop treatment to respond to questions with questions? The technique was annoying. Were the Ecuadorian *fiscalia* serious professionals who would search for the truth, or did they intend to sweep this unpleasantness under the carpet?

She abruptly realized that Eduardo hadn't translated her responses into Spanish. Clearly Schwartz knew enough English to understand her statements. Why, then, did he refuse to speak to her? How many Ecuadorians thought the Natural Planet Foundation was an enemy? Even the woman from the consulate had seemed suspicious of what she and Dan had been up to.

She noticed she was wringing her hands, and forced herself to sit down in front of her computer again and place them quietly on the table. Mercifully, her laptop had gone into screensaver mode, obliterating the image of Dan from the screen.

Finally, Schwartz was done studying her. He turned to Eduardo and made a demand, to which Eduardo replied in Spanish, gesturing toward the stairs. Schwartz and the naval officer followed him out the door, closing it with a thud.

Dan was now officially dead. She stared at the back of the door, trembling, until her computer chimed. The incoming urgent e-mail message from the Seattle office reminded her of the scheduled chat sessions tonight.

She called Seattle and asked for Mike Whitney. He had left for the evening. She had to settle for Tad Wyatt, the last person she wanted to talk to right now.

"I can't do the chats," she explained when he finally came on the line.

"Why not? Have you gone blind?"

"Of course not."

"Can you type?"

He obviously was not going to let her ease into the information. "Dan Kazaki died."

"What?"

"Don't make me say it again."

"He died, just now?"

"Actually, it was yesterday, but it was confirmed just now."

"You've had this story for *two days*? Why didn't you call immediately? Why didn't you mention this in your posts?"

As if he had the right to know first. She tried to swallow her anger. "They just now found his body."

After a second of silence, Wyatt said, "We need the who-what-where-when from you online within a half hour."

"I don't have that."

"Where did they find the body?"

She told him what little she knew. "Look, Wyatt . . . Tad, we should be delicate about this. A good man died here. His family will be in mourning."

"Think the rest of the press will be 'delicate'? At least we can make the man out to be a hero. *Our* hero."

He had a point. The press was rarely diplomatic, and if *Out There* could get a jump on the story, they could at least tilt public opinion in the right direction.

"Send me what you've got ASAP," he ordered. "Then you can discuss details during the chat sessions. Ten o'clock, East Coast time."

Even though the islands were far out in the Pacific, the Galápagos kept the same time as mainland Ecuador, which was on Eastern Standard Time. She checked her watch. It was nearly nine thirty. She quickly typed up the few facts she knew about Dan's death and sent them.

She opened *Out There*'s home page. The articles she'd submitted yesterday were headlined there with thumbnail photos: Wilderness Westin's giant tortoise and iguanas; Zing's sharks. But the main feature was a photo of Dr. Daniel Kazaki in his wetsuit with the NPF logo clearly displayed. The words *Mystery Death* were emblazoned above the photo. Wyatt had already gone public with the story.

One minute to airtime. She clicked the chat room icon and a blue window opened, partitioned into neat rectangles. *Live, from the remote Galápagos Islands: Wilderness Westin!*

She put her mind into wildlife biologist mode. *Hi,* she typed, *it's 74 degrees F here. The air is filled with the calls of black-tailed gulls and barking sea lions. Today I explored Floreana Island, rich in Galápagos history and exotic birds like flamingos. What's up out there?*

She had a few fans from her previous exploits online, and was pleased to see that some of them had found her and joined the conversation. NiniGr8 from Tulsa said they were in the middle of an ice storm. FarmerJane chimed in from rural Kansas, amazed to find Sam in the Galápagos. Sam smiled—Jane, the thirty-three-year-old daughter of Reverend Mark Westin's new wife, was one of Sam's new "sisters" by marriage. It was good to know that some friends were keeping track of her. Her housemate was online, too—BlakeTheBest said Hi and told her that FB man had called and that the roof was leaking over the front hallway. Chase had called her home? Ah, yes, that's how he'd gotten her cell number. She typed *Hi, BlakeTheBest* but otherwise ignored her housemate.

As specified in her contract with *Out There*, she kept the conversation focused on her expedition. MarcGen reported they had two feet of snow in Cincinnati and mentioned how much he loved the dancing bird video. He asked all sorts of technical questions about how she'd filmed it and put it together. She skirted around the details, but took care to specify all the proper names of cameras and software to

keep the sponsors happy. She highly suspected MarcGen
was Tad Wyatt, checking up on her.

EdtheGuy101 suggested that she had to be lonely down
there all by herself, demonstrating how little most readers
knew about where and who she actually was.

SanDman wrote, *As predicted, trouble. Will B a gr8
ride, tho.* She sounded it out—a great ride? What the hell
was he referring to—Dan's death? This guy—at least she
assumed the writer was male—had a lot of nerve. She
ignored him.

MayaHiya wrote, *Hi Sam*, which Sam fervently hoped
would escape notice of all the other readers. *Mst B swt 2 B
n trpcs nw,* Maya wrote, and then asked, *Vlntr @ otwd bnd
cascades 8/13?*

Huh? Something in the Cascades in August? WildWest
replied that she was enjoying the sunshine here in the Galápagos and that August and the Cascade Mountains were
both far away, but she looked forward to discussing it more
with MayaHiya later. Whatever *it* was.

ZenYoga99 from Utah told her he or she was going skiing tomorrow, which made her think about Chase. Where
was he? Desert? Mountains? Was he safe?

She started to reply to ZenYoga99 that she would be
diving tomorrow, then remembered she was WildWest and
changed the message to hiking and hoping to see a flightless cormorant.

JDoe1001 wanted to know why WildWest was spending
her time chasing after stupid animals when Dan was dead
and Zing was getting all these threatening comments—
what kind of a team player was she, anyway? Good question, Sam thought grimly. She typed a painfully cheery
ending to the session: *Get the latest on our Galápagos
Expedition at* Out There *tomorrow!*

The screen redrew, announcing Zing's session. The
model's photo occupied the upper right corner. Sam
straightened her spine and flexed her arms, hardening her
biceps. She pictured herself tall, red-haired, twenty-five.
Afraid of nothing.

The Online rectangle was packed with names of those logged on. She didn't recognize any friends in the list, but then, where would Zing have picked up friends? The character was only a few days old. She'd been down this road before. Just as it had a couple of years ago, her job was devolving from wildlife reporting into writing about the sordid details of a heinous crime. The main difference was that this time Adam Steele was not fueling a media storm from behind a television desk, and she was more or less incognito as Zing.

Because *Out There* made Dan's death sound like a mystery, most of the audience wanted to know the clues. *There's no prize*, she wanted to shout. A real man, a husband, a father, a friend, a scientist, is gone forever. He leaves a hole in the world!

Her head throbbed as she struggled to find the right words. Several people speculated that Dan had been attacked by sharks. Maybe held under by an octopus until he drowned? Died from the bends? Killed by terrorists? And one crackpot thought Dan had been murdered as part of the global corporate conspiracy. A chilling message suggested that Dan had been killed because he was actually an Asian poacher illegally harvesting in the area, which brought Roberson's anti-Japanese rant to mind. She explained that Daniel Kazaki was an ardent conservationist and as American as she was. Well, she *assumed* Zing was American; nobody had told her otherwise.

Another message hinted that Dan deserved to die because he was a foreigner butting into the affairs of another country. She reiterated that he was only an observer doing an underwater survey, and that as yet nobody knew the circumstances of his death.

By the end of the session, tears were streaming down her face. When the digital clock on the laptop flipped to 10:59, she gratefully typed, *Time's up—visit us tomorrow at* Out There*!*

She closed her laptop and tried to sort out the feelings clanging against each other in her head. First and foremost was guilt. For her part in making Dan's death a media event. For not being with Dan when the unthinkable happened. She felt trapped, suspended in time. Stuck here, in the back of beyond. A victim of circumstances over which she had no control. Suddenly, she couldn't breathe. She ran out of her cramped stuffy cabin.

Her footsteps echoed hollowly along the exterior metal walkway and down the stairs as she rushed to *Papagayo*'s stern. Her kayak was lashed to the railing at the side; she unhooked it and let it fall, keeping the bowline in her fist. The boat hit the water with a splash.

As she slid into the cockpit, a crewman leaned over the railing. "No, miss, you cannot—"

"I'll be back in a few minutes," she said to his silhouette.

She swiftly paddled away from *Papagayo*. When she had traveled far enough that she could no longer hear voices or the throb of the generator, she laid the paddle across her lap. The kayak glided to a stop. The ocean swells were small this evening, gently lifting and lowering, rocking her. Overhead, the stars were brilliant. The spangles of light were reflected in the black satin surface of the sea.

She dipped her hand in the water, watched the glow of luminous diatoms stirred up by her fingers. Microscopic comets moving through watery heavens. She flicked the saltwater from her fingertips and watched the splashes sparkle.

Nature had always been her refuge. As a child, while her mother wasted away from Lou Gehrig's disease and her father assuaged his sorrow by ministering to his parishioners, she climbed trees to perch with birds and crouched among her grandmother's currant bushes to commune with butterflies and bees. As an adult, she bought an old house in the woods to be near the deer and the raccoons and the evening grosbeaks. She met Chase while reporting on cougars. She'd taken this crazy assignment to be close to Nature. Nature was at times brutal, but it always kept its dignity, its wonder. Its beauty.

A splash sounded a short distance away. A turtle? Dolphin? Penguin? Ray? She wished she had the eyes of an owl and could see the creatures sharing the night ocean with her. The breeze whispered softly against her face. Planet Earth was breathing.

She had always dreamed of visiting the Galápagos. For conservationists and naturalists, it was a mecca of sorts. The cradle for Darwin's theory of natural selection. A magical living laboratory. These islands were supposed to be a sanctuary for all creatures.

Someone had to tell the truth about what was happening here, and continue to shout it until the world listened. Today she surveyed one of the dive sites on Dan's list. There were only two to go, although the last one was up by Wolf Island, far off *Papagayo*'s route. She had no idea how she was going to arrange a trip up there. But she had to find a way.

"Dan," she whispered to the soft darkness. "Be at peace. I will finish the job we started."

14

THE next morning, *Papagayo*'s second panga, loaded with Sam, Jerry and Sandy Roberson, Tony, and Eduardo, snaked through the boats anchored in crowded Academy Bay. They were following the first panga, which was loaded with the four other tour members, plus Maxim and the Sanderses, who sat in the bow looking like the royalty Sam now knew they were.

During her early morning Internet research, she discovered that Jonathan Sanders was not a typical tourist. Neither was he an aging movie star as she had guessed, but he was a celebrity of sorts, at least in the business world. His full name was Francis Jonathan Sanders III, so he often was mentioned as "Francis Sanders III." His business empire apparently stretched around the world and included all sorts of enterprises, including one called SunSel Tours, which was listed as a yacht rental service with offices in the Caribbean and the Pacific. She hadn't been able to find any specific boat names, but she suspected that *Papagayo* was among his fleet of ships. It made perfect sense that Captain Quiroga and the crew would be deferential to the owner. No wonder he had been curious about why there were two mysterious divers on board his boat. And now one had been killed. He couldn't be happy about the bad press that would bring.

Her panga threaded its way between two new-looking white vessels with *Parque Nacional de Galápagos* painted on their sides. They rested at anchor, their hatches closed and padlocked.

Eduardo noticed Sam studying them. "Ranger boats," he said as if to head off her question.

"Shouldn't they be on patrol out in the reserve?" she asked.

"The Navy must give permission."

He had to be kidding. The Navy chauffeured the Galápagos police around; did they control where *all* the local authorities went? "The park rangers have to get permission from the *Navy* to go on patrol?"

"Go, Navy," murmured Jerry Roberson from her other side. He was probably just trying to rile her; she pretended she didn't hear.

Eduardo shrugged, and then glanced toward the boats again. "Today, no permission. Tomorrow, maybe."

"It must be nice for the park rangers to get a day off," Sandy chirped.

Beside his wife, Jerry rolled his eyes. Both Tony and Eduardo noticed and stifled smiles. Then the dinghy bumped up on the rocky beach, and they climbed out to join the others from the first panga.

"This morning, all are on their own," Eduardo reminded the group. "Those who want to take the additional bus tour, meet at Darwin Station entrance at one P.M. Dinner is also on your own this evening. We will all meet here on the beach tonight at eight to return to *Papagayo*."

The group scattered like cockroaches under a bright light. Most headed for the closest shops. Sam strolled by herself toward the main street.

Free from a diving schedule for a day, Sam finally had the chance to explore Puerto Ayora. The town was a happening place, at least for the Galápagos. A handful of hotels and a smattering of restaurants overlooked Academy Bay, which was wall to wall with boats of all kinds today. People seemed to be stacked on top of one another. It hadn't seemed so bad the first night she'd been here, but after three days in the quiet reserve with only a few other boats on the horizon, the jumble of multistory buildings, paved streets, and billboards seemed glaring and intrusive. Ancient cars deposited clouds of black exhaust in the air, and the low rumble of motorbikes lent a bass track to the overall din.

As she walked along the main street toward Darwin Station, her hand protectively draped over her camera, she passed dozens of T-shirt vendors. *I* ♥ *BOOBIES!* seemed to be the most popular souvenir slogan from the Galápagos.

"Miss!" "Welcome!" "Visit my shop!" Overly cheerful voices beckoned from doorways as she approached, to be replaced by "Later, yes?" and "This afternoon!" as she passed. She spotted Ken and Brandon in one outdoor stall. They seemed more enthusiastic about the selection of beach towels than they had been about the unusual wildlife they had witnessed over the past few days.

She turned down a path toward the Charles Darwin Research Station. Although it was not yet nine o'clock in the morning, at least a hundred tourists crowded the sprawling complex of buildings, tortoise pens, and plots of native plants. From her backpack, her cell phone chimed. Chase? She eagerly pulled it out and answered.

"Way to go, WildWest!" Tad Wyatt shouted.

She jerked the phone away to save her eardrum, and then had to bring it back to say, "What?"

"We're number one in the rankings for the Kazaki story today!" he chortled. "Wilderness has almost four hundred comments and Zing's already over a thousand. And everybody's liking and friending *Out There* everywhere."

Had Wyatt forgotten the reason for the attention? "Nothing like death to bring 'em in," she said bitterly.

"Got that right!" His enthusiasm made her nauseous. "A

San Diego television station picked up the story, too. They showed our website on the late news last night."

San Diego? Sam could guess which station it would be, and which anchorman. She'd been on a television news roller coaster ride once before with Adam Steele.

"The police seem suspicious of me," she told Wyatt.

"What do you mean?"

"They took my passport."

"Why?"

"I suppose they don't want me to leave the area." *You idiot*, she added in her head.

"You weren't thinking about disappearing on us, were you?"

She sighed. "I intend to fulfill my contract to the best of my ability, Tad, although you've got to admit that circumstances have changed. What would you do if I suddenly went missing?" *If I was kidnapped. If I was killed.*

"Good question. I have no clue. There's probably some sort of HR policy for employees, but you're an independent contractor."

"Thanks." Rolling her eyes, she caught a glimpse of the tree branches overhead. Two geckos were stretched out on the lowest bough. "I feel a *lot* more secure now."

"I'm sure we'd think of something. Anyway, good job," Wyatt said. "Try to keep up the momentum when you post tonight."

"Right. Sure thing." She snapped the phone closed. Sam continued toward Darwin Station and tried to forget about the Internet, television news, and the media in general.

She explored the Exhibition Hall with a pack of visitors that included the Birskys. At regular intervals along the wall, huge photos of erupting volcanoes caught her eye. Crimson molten lava spewed through the air, cauldrons of ash-colored mud bubbled, and the sea boiled and steamed. Fernandina and Isabela Islands were the most often featured, with spectacular images of columns of ash and red-hot seams of lava bursting forth. The most recent photo was dated only a few years ago.

"Good heavens," she murmured. She raised her camera and snapped a picture of the image on the wall. A tourist beside her glared and pointed to the sign on the wall. NO PHOTOGRAPHY.

"Oops," she said.

The walls held hundreds of photos of flora and fauna as well as explanations of Darwin's study of finches, from which he developed his theories of evolution of species through natural selection. The finches all looked fairly similar. It must have taken many hours of observation on the naturalist's part to note their slightly different beaks and the different ecological niches they occupied. Charles Darwin clearly possessed more patience than she did. Or maybe he had been plagued by fewer distractions. He probably didn't have to pretend to be two different characters, for one thing. He didn't have to carry a camera everywhere and dredge up exciting stories each day. He probably didn't have to constantly look over his shoulder to be sure that a killer wasn't stalking him, either.

A Station employee rang a bell, startling her out of her speculations. He loudly announced that a slide show would start in five minutes in the theater area toward the back of the hall. Most of the visitors eagerly walked toward the wooden benches there. When the presentation began with a blare of canned music, she headed for the door.

Using the map she received at the gate, she located the Darwin Station headquarters building. There she showed the secretary her most official-looking piece of ID, her press pass from *Out There*. "May I see the director, please?"

The secretary's English was almost as minimal as Sam's Spanish, and the woman soon abandoned her and crossed the foyer to knock on the executive director's door.

The man who emerged was tall for an Ecuadorian, maybe five-ten, middle-aged, and scholarly-looking. Along with gray cotton pants, he wore a white guayabera, the pleated, pocketed, short-sleeved shirt that passed for business attire in the tropics.

"Dr. Ignacio Guerrero." His handshake was firm. His

dark hair was cut into short curls, and his beard was neatly trimmed.

"*Mucho gusto. Me llamo* Sam Westin." She handed him her identification badge from *Out There*.

"Ah." He cocked an eyebrow. "*Usted habla español.*"

"That was the extent of it, I'm afraid," she said.

"Then we speak English." He glanced at the ID. "It says Summer Westin here."

"Sam's a nickname."

"You are a reporter? My secretary will provide you a press kit . . ."

"Thanks, but I write adventure articles, not your standard news or travel stories. I came here on a joint project with Dr. Kazaki . . ."

His expression brightened. "Daniel Kazaki? From the University of Delaware? I have received e-mail from him. I would like to meet him." His gaze expectantly searched the open doorway through which brilliant sun spilled onto the worn tiled floor.

Was Guerrero feigning ignorance? "He died two days ago," Sam said.

"*Dios mío!*" Guerrero lowered his head and made the sign of the cross. He rubbed a knuckle across his bearded chin, then folded his hands together beneath his nose as if praying. After a few seconds in this pose, he looked up again. "I am sorry, Señorita Westin. I heard about a scuba accident, but I had no idea it was Dr. Kazaki."

"I don't believe it was an accident," she confided.

His eyes widened. "Why do you say that? How did this happen?"

"I really don't know. He was here doing a survey for the Natural Planet Foundation, and—"

"NPF?"

"They've worked with you before, haven't they?"

Guerrero grabbed Sam's arm and pulled her into his office, closing the door behind them. His gaze burned with intensity. "Why was the Natural Planet Foundation doing a survey? They didn't coordinate with our office."

"Were they supposed to? I wasn't in on the planning."

He considered for a few seconds, then said, "I'm sure it was . . . what is the word? Routine." He looked at her for confirmation.

"Don't they do this every ten years?"

"Do they? I have only been here for two." He rubbed the back of his neck as he stared, distracted, at the floor. Then he glanced up. "But where are my manners? Would you like a cup of coffee?" He gestured toward his desk, where a steaming cup sat amid stacks of paper.

"No, thank you, but please, go ahead with yours."

He nodded, walked behind his desk, and took a tiny sip from the cup. Sam wondered how anyone could drink coffee when it was at least eighty-five degrees outside.

"Please, sit." Guerrero indicated the upholstered chair in front of his desk.

She pulled off her day pack, placed it on the floor, and sat. He lowered himself into his chair. "How can I be of service to you, Miss Westin?"

Sam cleared her throat. "I need some information about the political climate here."

He leaned forward and clasped his hands together on top of the desk. "Political climate?"

She wasn't quite sure what she wanted to ask. "I think it's likely that Dan was murdered."

Guerrero swallowed nervously, but his gaze held steady on her face.

"I want to know about the local attitudes toward the park and conservation groups and scientists. Especially the fishermen's union. Are they violent?"

He sat back and swept his hand through the air as if to brush the question away. "You are perhaps thinking of the occupation of Darwin Station a long time in the past, in the 1990s. Or maybe you wonder about what happened to the Park Service director years ago?"

That got her attention. "What happened to the Park Service director years ago? Was he murdered?"

"She," Guerrero corrected. "She was urged to leave."

Interesting phrasing. "How was she urged to leave?"

He squirmed and took another sip of his coffee before saying, "Darwin Station and the Galápagos National Park Service are not the same. Darwin Station is a research facility; the Park Service manages the park and the marine reserve and issues permits for fishing and tour boats and such things."

Finally, she had a direction. "I need to talk to the Park Service director, then. You see, a few days ago Dan got bad air and then we were thrown out of our hotel and I'm trying to find out what's going on—"

Guerrero continued as if he hadn't heard her. "We have many new agreements with the government and the fishermen now. We have a new constitution that states the rights of Nature. We are all pledged to work together to protect the Galápagos and to improve the lives of the local people." He picked up his coffee cup again.

She'd heard it all before, but she was no longer buying the company line. "So there's no more illegal fishing?"

He choked in mid-swallow, as if his coffee had unexpectedly thickened between sips. He quickly passed the back of his hand over his mustache. "We have strict regulations now, and the area of the marine sanctuary has been increased. Commercial fishing is prohibited. Local artisan fishers must have permits."

Sam frowned. "I know all that. But is there enforcement? I saw two patrol boats anchored out in the bay."

He gestured toward the window. "Have you seen our marine research facility? It was very damaged in the tsunami of 2011, but it is rebuilt now. We studying how much fishing can be accomplished without destroying the ecosystem."

"That's nice." She forced her lips into a brief smile. "Does Darwin Station believe that the illegal fishing has stopped?"

His coffee seemed to be getting thicker. He examined his cup as he swilled the liquid around in his mouth for a long moment before swallowing. Finally, he set down the cup and focused his gaze on her. "Miss Westin, the local fishing men are simply trying to live. If anyone is—was—to blame, it was the Japanese, the Chinese. You cannot offer so much money to a poor country like Ecuador; of course people will grab for it." He turned toward his office window, which overlooked several research buildings. "Asians," he hissed. "The more rare an animal, the more they want to eat it. The more they *pay* to eat it. I detest Asians."

Shades of Jerry Roberson. She frowned. "Dr. Kazaki was half-Asian."

Guerrero considered that. "Maybe his name was Japanese, but he was American. I know Dr. Kazaki was a true conservationist."

They were getting off-track. "Asians don't control the Galápagos," she pointed out. "Like you said, it's the local Ecuadorians who are selling to the Asians. And wasn't it Ecuadorians who threatened to kill the giant tortoises here? Who held scientists hostage with machetes? Who threatened to sink a tour boat?"

Guerrero rose from his chair and walked around his desk.

"Were any of those Ecuadorians punished?" she persisted.

Taking her hand, he pulled her up from the chair and then continued to hold her hand, clutching it a little too tightly between his broad paws. "Miss Westin, please consider. Puerto Ayora is a small town. Santa Cruz is a small island. Galápagos is a small province. Ecuador is a small country."

She stared at him. "So? That should be even more reason to preserve your natural resources for the future."

He frowned. "The government of Ecuador maintains a position on the board of the Charles Darwin Foundation."

Was he saying that Darwin Station would not do anything that might upset the government of Ecuador? "I guess I need to talk to the National Park director."

His grip on her hand tightened. "The director of the National Park is in Guayaquil at present. He has been in the position only three months. The old one . . . many old ones . . ." He swallowed, and then started again. "Lives were threatened. You understand?" His eyes beseeched her.

She understood that she could expect no assistance from Darwin Station or the Galápagos National Park Service.

Guerrero released his grip on her hand. "We all do the best we can. You will tell the rest of the world that, won't you?"

She turned the doorknob to let herself out of his office. "I wish you the best of luck, Dr. Guerrero."

"My condolences for Dr. Kazaki," he called after her. "He will be missed."

Outside, Sam walked the short distance down the worn pathway to the pen where Lonesome George had once lived. Now there was only a plaque as a reminder. The giant tortoise was easily the most famous reptile in the world. Leaning on the railing, she stared at his replacement—Diego, according to the sign—through tears of frustration. Lonesome George was over ninety years old when he died, a lumbering ancient dinosaur, nearly twice as big as the galápago she'd encountered on the Isabela mountainside.

Lonesome George was the only known member left of his subspecies of island tortoises. None of the eggs he fertilized had ever hatched. She wondered if he had felt a unique loneliness.

She certainly felt alone right now. Her fingers closed around the wire mesh of the fence, squeezing until the links pressed painfully into her hands. Darwin Station was supposedly all about conservation, and the Natural Planet Foundation supplied the data that supported conservation efforts around the world. She'd expected to find allies here.

Guerrero was clearly worried about NPF's survey. Dan would have merely reported his count. That was NPF's mission: to publish the unvarnished truth—good or bad—about the state of the planet.

If the NPF report on Galápagos National Park was filled with bad news about poaching and overfishing, conservation groups would take notice. They'd probably try to apply

pressure; maybe encourage their members to petition the
Ecuadorian government. That could spark a reaction;
maybe the government would impose new crackdowns on
fishing in the islands. But the conservation community had
filed complaints for years about Ecuador allowing too
many immigrants, too many tourists, and too much commercial activity in the islands. UNESCO had once listed
the Galápagos as an area at risk. What would make Dan's
report any different from all the previous ones? Maybe the
issue was all about the timing. This might be the first survey to come out after the new constitution and all the
promises of doing a better job of protecting the area.

Diego pushed himself to his scaly feet. It looked like a
major effort to raise that huge, heavy shell. His toenails
scratched across the packed dirt of his pen as he waddled
pigeon-toed toward his food pile. Stretching his head forward, he snagged a chunk of lettuce with his beak-like
mouth. It was like watching an elephant dine at a salad bar.

She felt outrage that some of these defenseless creatures
had been slaughtered to protest fishing regulations. Galápagos National Park was supposed to be a safe refuge for the
giant tortoises. Conservation groups the world over donated
large sums to protect them.

Then Sam understood yet one more possible angle for
Guerrero's concern. If Dan's report showed that the reserve
was still being damaged by overfishing, would some conservation groups withdraw their funding from Galápagos
National Park and Darwin Station?

She moved to the captive breeding pens and took photos
of the dozens of baby tortoises. When they reached a large
enough size to be safe from predators such as dogs and
hawks, they would be released back into the park to repop-
ulate the islands. Assuming the park still existed.

If conservation groups labeled the Galápagos a lost
cause, Darwin Station might cease to exist. Scientists
would stop coming to study the area if it was no longer
considered a unique living laboratory. Would the Ecuadorian government be content to let Darwin Station vanish

into history, allow settlements and hotel zones to take over the park land, and watch the Galápagos Islands develop into just one more Pacific tourist destination? It was a depressing thought.

Without the park and the unusual animals, the tourists might eventually stop coming, too. There were better climates and more accessible beaches elsewhere. If the tourism trade petered out, then the Ecuadorian commercial fishermen would be completely free to ply their trade.

But there was always the possibility that a negative NPF report could cause the pendulum to swing in the opposite direction. If the Ecuadorian government opted to pacify the conservationists, the Navy would allow park rangers to crack down on poaching, and maybe prohibit even local artisan fishing within the reserve.

There were so many possibilities in play here. It seemed like all parties in the islands had their own reasons to dread an accounting. How the hell could she sort this out? Anyone could be an enemy. A prickle ran down her spine.

She surveyed the crowd. The tourists were easily identified by their cameras and sun hats. Two uniformed Darwin Station employees fed the baby turtles and spoke in English or German to the tourists. Another raked litter from the gravel alongside the paths. Only one person stood out from this picture. A short distance away, a mustachioed man in a black tank top leaned against an ancient gnarled tree, his hands behind his back. His mirrored sunglasses seemed to be focused on her. She quickly turned back to the baby tortoises. When she glanced over her shoulder a minute later, he was still there, his face still turned in her direction. Why did he have his hands behind his back? His tight-fitting jeans couldn't conceal a pistol, but he could easily have a switchblade in a pocket.

Jeez, she was getting paranoid. Black Tank Top was probably waiting for his girlfriend. For all she knew, his eyes were closed behind those mirrored lenses. There were no obvious hit men here. But a hit man wouldn't be obvious, would he? He'd probably carry a camera and wear funky shorts, like that freckled guy over there in a Boston Red Sox T-shirt.

A group of Japanese tourists approached, laughing and chattering. They carried identical green tour bags. With a few loud syllables, their guide brought them to polite attention, pointed to the baby tortoises, and said a few words. The entire group laughed, the women raising their hands to cover their mouths.

Maybe a joke about making the tiny reptiles into soup? Sam found herself scowling. Then she gave herself a mental slap. The Japanese tourists were probably chuckling about how cute the miniature tortoises looked, or about how minuscule the tortoise babies were in comparison to their humongous parents. She needed to examine her own prejudices.

She walked toward the exit, grateful to observe that Black Tank Top stayed at the tree. Stopping at a stand that advertised all profits went to Darwin Station, she selected a turquoise tee with a map of the islands for herself. For Chase, she chose a large burgundy one that sported a pile of iguanas. At least she'd have something to give him when they met in a few days.

If they met in a few days.

She couldn't get on a plane without her passport. And where the hell was Chase, anyway? She'd checked her e-mail and phone messages this morning. She bit her lip. If something had happened to him, would anybody notify her? She wasn't his live-in girlfriend or his wife.

Wife. Elizabeth Kazaki flashed onto her mental screen.

"Help you?" The T-shirt seller stepped close.

She quickly paid for her purchases and backed away from the vendor's stall, then walked out of the Darwin Station grounds into Puerto Ayora, and headed down the side street toward the tiny Hotel Aurora. The stuccoed wall had a small window that opened onto the lobby, and as she passed it, Sam got a glimpse of Mrs. Vintner's distinctive red twist hairstyle behind the check-in desk, along with a black-haired teen. But by the time she had rounded the entryway and stepped through the foyer, only the teen stood there.

"Señora Vintner is not here," the girl said in response to Sam's inquiry. "May I help?"

"That's odd. I could have sworn I saw her through the window."

The girl blinked and smiled politely.

"I wanted to talk to her about Dr. Kazaki. He and I stayed here a few days ago."

The teen's face was completely blank. Either she didn't understand English well or she had no knowledge of the incident or she had an excellent poker face. "Señora Vintner is not available," she said.

Sam walked to the side of the reception desk to peer into the office beyond. A small drawered desk, stacked file cabinets, and a copy machine crowded the space. Unless Vintner was hiding under the desk, she'd escaped through the back door. Clearly Sam was not going to get any information here.

As she exited the building, a tour bus rumbled by, belching a stream of sooty exhaust. Overhead, a plane passed low, taking off from Baltra airport to the north. If only she were on that jet.

Dan was dead. The police had her passport. Clearly the American Consulate was not inclined to intervene. Neither Darwin Station nor the Park Service was going to pull any strings for her. It seemed unlikely that anyone in town would provide information, let alone assistance. She was on her own. She had to get that passport back.

Dusty buildings and scrawny trees surrounded her. On her tourist map of Puerto Ayora was a rectangle labeled *Municipio*. Municipal? It sounded like it should be town hall or something close to it.

After a quick glance over her shoulder to be sure she wasn't followed, she strolled in the direction the map indicated. After a block, it was clear that she had crossed out of the tourist area. Although the businesses prominently displayed the same brightly colored recycle bins she'd seen closer to Darwin Station, here the bins overflowed with unsorted trash. The streets were littered with orange and banana peels, shreds of plastic bags, and soda straws. A line of people spilled out the door and wrapped around the side of a building labeled CLÍNICA. She passed small markets with only a few sad vegetables on display, and stores that offered cheap clothing, plastic sandals, and toys.

Finally she arrived at the *Municipio*. The yellow-stuccoed building was modest, but still the grandest edifice she'd seen so far in the islands. Three shallow marble steps led up to the entrance, which was flanked by cement pillars unconvincingly painted in faux marble to match the steps. Red geraniums bloomed amid fat-leaved sedums in manicured beds on either side of the walkway. As Sam framed the building's entrance in her camera's viewfinder, a man in police uniform walked out. He held up his index finger and wagged his hand back and forth a few times in the international don't-do-that sign.

She nodded, lowered her camera. He passed her without comment. Another blond policeman. Schwartz's brother? Cousin? *Galápagos is a small community. Many are related somehow.*

She returned her camera to her day pack and entered the doorway. To her surprise, it opened onto a manicured courtyard. A tired-looking tree in a huge clay pot served as the focal point of the open space. The surrounding walls featured multiple doorways leading off in all directions. Sam was stopped by an older man in dark pants and white guayabera who guarded a desk near the main entry.

"*Señorita?*"

"Police?" she responded.

He pointed to a doorway above which a huge hand-painted sign proclaimed in black-and-white letters, FISCALIA.

She passed through that portal with some trepidation. Why did walking into a police station make her feel like she was about to be arrested? She'd been fingerprinted at a police station once in college, for a summer job with the Federal Aviation Administration. She'd had to pass through barred electric gates into an enclosed area and wait in line with a group of disheveled men. When it was her turn, the technician was abrupt, inking and rolling her fingers across the paper with motions that seemed more forceful than necessary.

"I'm just getting fingerprinted for a government job," she'd explained.

"Yeah, sure," he'd responded. She'd been more than a little worried that they wouldn't open the gates on the way out.

But there were no electric gates in sight here. Just a scarred wooden desk with a woman in a khaki uniform behind it who watched her curiously.

"You speak English?" Sam asked.

The woman nodded, her black ponytail bobbing at the back of her neck. "I have some English. What can I do for you?"

"My name is Summer Westin, and—"

"Westin?"

"Yes. You have my passport."

"Momento." The woman abruptly rose and disappeared through a doorway to the left.

Sam drummed her fingers on the desk, wondering if she should sit down in one of the chairs that lined the walls. After a few more seconds, she took a seat in the corner.

From her new vantage point, she could see through the doorway into another room. On a stainless steel examination table lay a collection of dive gear. She stood up and walked closer. Shelves, the exam table, and four heavy-duty padlocked locker doors, each big enough to hide one of those rolling drawers that held bodies in morgues on television. There were no corpses in sight. No personnel, either.

On the table was a BCD, an air cylinder, and the top portion of a regulator—the first stage—all still connected with hoses. The section of hose that should have led to the regulator mouthpiece, or second stage, was cut short, and the mouthpiece was missing. A few inches away lay a cracked dive mask. On the strap of the dive mask, the initials DK had been written in indelible marker. This was Dan's gear. The hose attached to the first stage looked as though it had been sliced through, at approximately the same point where she remembered the gash on Dan's neck. This was definitely not the work of a shark or a sea lion.

She glanced toward the locker doors. Was Dan's corpse behind one of them? No labels. Looking back at the table, she noticed that beside the dive mask, inside a plastic zip-lock bag, was a jagged-edge dive knife, identical to the one she carried in the sheath on her BCD. The model was common; Dan carried the same one. Was this Dan's knife? She checked his BCD. No sheath. Then she remembered that Dan kept his knife strapped onto his calf. She walked around the table, looking for the strap-on sheath. It wasn't there, unless it was beneath the BCD. Dan's wetsuit was missing, too; maybe the sheath was still attached. Now she noticed something else disturbing. Inside the plastic bag with the knife was one small silver loop. That was her silver earring, the one she lost on the day she'd found Dan's body.

"No!" The ponytailed receptionist strode into the room, frowning. "You are not allowed." In one hand she carried a glass mug half-full of dark steaming liquid. With her free hand, she gestured back to the lobby. Sam dutifully followed her back to the lobby and stood in front of the woman's desk.

"That earring back there—" she began, but before she could finish or sit down, the receptionist thrust the mug out. *"Café?"*

Sam shook her head, but the woman pressed the mug toward her, causing Sam to grab it with both hands to keep the coffee from spilling down her abdomen. She held the mug uncertainly for a second, then said, "No, thanks. It's too hot for coffee."

The woman blinked at her.

"At least it's hot for me," Sam explained. "I live in the north. Near Canada."

"Yes."

Sam set the cup on the corner of the receptionist's desk, then placed a hand on the desk's surface and leaned forward. "Look, Miss . . ."

"Montero."

"Miss Montero, about that earring I saw back there. And there was a knife, too."

Montero shrugged. "I know nothing about a knife and earring."

I'll just bet. Sam gritted her teeth and went back to her original question. "A couple of days ago Officer Schwartz took my passport, and I—"

"Ah," Montero interrupted, "*Sargente* Schwartz!" Her shout was loud. Schwartz materialized from a doorway to the left.

"Señorita Westin," he said.

"Look here, Officer Schwartz," she started.

His eyes narrowed. She softened her tone. "You have my passport, remember? I have to leave in a few days, and—"

He abruptly swiveled toward the Montero woman, spat out a few words, then turned on his heel and disappeared into the adjoining office.

Well, hell. Sam started after him, but Montero blocked her, holding one hand out. "You cannot pass. Officials only."

"But my passport—"

The woman folded her arms across her chest.

Maybe another tack. "I need to know what the police are doing about Dr. Kazaki's death."

She was rewarded with a glower. She pressed on. "Has an autopsy been done? How are you investigating his murder?"

A spark lit Montero's eyes. "Murder? You believe he is murdered?"

Careful. She swallowed before answering. "His regulator hose and his face were cut. I don't think a shark or a sea lion could do that. I'd say he died under suspicious circumstances. Now, can I speak to—"

Montero interrupted. "Sargente Schwartz says that all will be resolved soon."

What the hell did that mean? Their standoff lasted for another moment, Montero regarding her sternly, Sam glaring back. Finally, Sam decided to leave before she earned herself a personal tour of a Galapagüeño jail cell.

15

"THIS place was originally named Y—you know, the letter—because the highways meet here like in a letter Y." Marshall seemed determined to give Charlie Perini a lesson about the local history. Chase, dressed for the occasion in grubby jeans, a denim shirt, and broken-down cowboy boots, listened to the man with one ear as they wandered around a dusty flea market on the outskirts of Why, Arizona. He was having a hard time wrestling his thoughts away from Summer's phone messages. *Call me when you get this.* Two days had passed since she'd left all those desperate sounding messages. Would she understand that he couldn't call her? Would she think that he was rejecting her because she had rejected his offer? Was she okay?

"Then the politicians say that town names need to have at least three letters, so they changed the name to W-H-Y."

Marshall concluded his local history lesson by rubbing his nose. The guy did it so often that Chase wondered if Marshall had another habit that involved snorting white powder. If the guy was a dopehead, that could come in useful later. Dopeheads were always willing to rat out their buddies to get their next fix.

Randy strolled up in time to add, "Typical, that bureaucrats would make laws about how you can name things. No reason you can't have a town named with the letter Y."

"Yeah," Chase replied. Charlie Perini was a terse kind of guy. The less an undercover agent talked, the less likely he was to slip up. This was the most dangerous time, when nothing was really going down, when he was "in" but just hanging out with new comrades. This was when agents let things slip about their real lives, about their daily habits and family and friends.

The folding tables at the flea market were covered with everything from used tools to leather goods to jewelry. The vendors were mostly Hispanics and Native Americans. As he met the dark-eyed gazes of the sellers, Chase kept reminding himself he was not one of these people. He was not half Latino, half Lakota; he was Charlie Perini, Italian-American. Wife named Nikki.

He looked for Nicole; found her one aisle over and a couple of tables back, pawing through piles of used clothing with Joanne, Randy's wife. The poor woman was so grateful to finally have another woman to talk to that she was proving to be a goldmine of information. Joanne was a true believer in the nobility of the cause. She had eagerly told Nicole the Citizen Army had branches all across the Southern U.S.A., and they were a prime force in stopping the flow of immigrants and drugs coming across the U.S. border.

"Dread's smarter than anyone I ever met," Nicole had drawled in imitation of Joanne last night, "the way he's figured how to beat the mules at their own game. We take their drugs so they can't sell 'em to our kids here."

Either Joanne was too dim to figure out that Dread had his own drug-dealing business, or she was trying to convince Nicole of the righteousness of the group's actions. The men seemed sharper or more suspicious. They were a lot less willing to talk. Chase felt like he was just along for the ride.

"I have a question about Why," he said, turning toward Marshall and Randy. "Or really, it's more about *what*— what the hell are we doing here?"

He and Nicole had joined Dread, Marshall, Randy, and Joanne yesterday afternoon on a road trip, driving south toward the border and then west into ever yet more forsaken desert country. Last night, they set up camp in the desert, barbecued wieners over a fire, and heated beans over Marshall's camp stove. They drank, they blasted away at beer cans and cactuses in the desert. The talk had all been bitching about immigrants and the economy and the need to "take the country back." Once in a long while their new buddies would toss out the name of another member of their group or mention a past event, but he and Nicole needed to lay eyes on more members and witness more activity to build a solid case. They were both getting antsy.

Breakfast this morning had been lukewarm eggs and hash at a greasy spoon along the highway. And now they were here in Why, which seemed like a damn good name for the place. Chase knew that Nicole itched to call her husband, and Chase was dying to talk to Summer, or at least get somewhere with Internet coverage so he could check the latest posts at *Out There*. Nicole had called their office this morning, a call forwarded from her "friend Maureen's" number in Florida, to let their boss know they were both still alive and working. The GPS unit hidden in the pickup bumper constantly reported the location of their vehicle. But that had been the sum of their communication with the outside world for the last couple of days.

"Didn't you guys promise we could make some money out here?" Chase groused to Randy. "I thought we were going to see some action. Where the hell did Dread disappear to?"

"Chill, man," Randy told him. "He's around. Cool your jets and cruise; you never know who's watching. We'll know when Dread's ready."

Chase exhaled impatiently and turned his gaze to the next table. Dread seemed to be the leader of this cell of the

New American Citizen Army. The connections between
cells were so loose they were practically unnoticeable, and
the members were all surprisingly tech-savvy. The FBI
team that had prepped him and Nicole had really blown
this one, giving them older cell phones with no Internet
access.

Instead of meeting in person, NACA passed info back
and forth via cell phones and hashtags on Twitter. The
hashtag changed every day, and sometimes even several
times a day, always some nonsensical combination of
words like #redday or #leafnow. At the diner this morning,
Dread had shown Chase the chatter on his phone. The
hashtag of the moment was #sunshadow and the talk was
all about a big ICE bust of a tire manufacturing plant in
Texas where 90 percent of the employees were illegals.

"Now they'll have to hire real Americans!" Joanne had
chortled.

Chase thought it was more likely that the plant would
simply close down Texas operations and move across the
border to Mexico, but he kept his mouth shut. "How do you
know what tag word to look for?" he'd asked Dread. *What's
the command structure of this army? Who's the general?*

"We got a system," Dread had answered, frustrating
Chase. "I'll clue you in later."

Nicole and Joanne joined the three men in the flea market's jewelry section. Randy fingered a heavy silver belt
buckle and shot sideways glances at the vendor as if he was
considering filching the piece. The wrinkled grandmother
fixed her gaze firmly on him. Among her display of ornate
Navajo squash blossom necklaces and heavy earrings,
Chase spotted a set of silver-framed turquoise squares. The
stones were undulating patterns of sea green instead of the
usual blue. The rectangular pendant hung from a braided
silver chain, and the earrings were simple dangles from silver posts. He could easily picture Summer wearing the set;
they were much more her style than the diamonds Steele
had given her. It was rare that he ran across anything he

thought she would appreciate; she was a hard woman to buy gifts for. But now just wasn't the time or place.

Nicole leaned forward and lightly touched the pendant, saying, "Ooh, that's nice," before moving on down the aisle. Marshall trailed a few steps behind her, his gaze glued to her backside.

Nicole had always been able to read Chase. The green turquoise set was not something she would ever have chosen for herself. Today her earrings were pink crystals, her poufy bleached hair was pulled back into a ponytail, and she wore a stretchy green T-shirt over tight blue jeans and cowboy boots. Marshall's gaze was more often on her bustline than on her face. While Nicole would have backhanded the man inside of five minutes, Nikki seemed to enjoy the attention. Charlie needed to warn the guy about ogling his wife.

The green turquoise set was marked $199. "I'll give you one-twenty-five," he told the grandmother. Navajo? Hopi? He couldn't tell.

She made a clucking noise. "One-sixty." Her dark eyes were sad, and he wondered why she was selling these pieces. In the right place, the squash blossom necklaces would be easily worth three times what she was asking. They were probably family heirlooms.

They settled at one-forty, and Chase dug the bills out of Charlie's worn leather wallet.

"I thought you were flat broke," Randy remarked.

Chase took the small plastic sack the vendor gave him and stuck it carefully in the chest pocket of his shirt, taking care to button the flap down. "I am now," he said. "But if a guy doesn't remember his anniversary, he's dead meat."

Randy snorted. "Yeah, I know what you mean. So it's coming up?"

"Not 'til July fourth." An easy-to-remember date. The Perinis' hypothetical marriage—a second for them both— took place in 2000, an easy-to-remember year.

"You got married on *Independence Day*?" Randy laughed. "Kind of ironic, isn't it?"

"Laugh all you want," Chase told him. "But we never have to pay for the party. And we always get fireworks."

They moved on to a table of leather items. There was even a saddle on the back of a chair. He picked up a belt, uncoiling it to admire the elaborate tooling of flowers and vines. When—if—he ever got married, he'd pick July fourth or December thirty-first for exactly the reasons he had named. He could picture himself as a husband, sharing lazy Sunday coffees with his wife. Somehow he couldn't quite picture Summer lounging around reading the paper or making French toast, though. That bothered him. Seemed more likely that she'd be off traipsing through the wilderness while he sat alone at the kitchen table. But she'd given him that backpack for Christmas—didn't that signal that she wanted him to come with her?

"Charlie!"

A few yards away, Nicole gestured to him. She stood in front of a large old canvas tent with the rest of their little troop, including Dread. Chase put down the belt and joined them. "Sorry. I was thinking about that asshole that fired me down in Tampa."

Nicole reached up and rubbed the back of his neck. "You gotta let that go, sweetie." Her fingers briefly squeezed hard, pinching.

Chase snorted and pulled her arm from his neck. "You're right, hon," he said mildly. But as he turned away, he rolled his eyes and grimaced for the men to show his annoyance with his nagging wife.

Dread pulled aside the tent flap and ducked inside. They all followed, clustering in the center to keep from rubbing their heads on the slanted canvas overhead.

Along the sides of the tent were folding tables. Each featured an array of rifles and pistols and other related paraphernalia: scopes and silencers and night vision goggles. A man with a black goatee and a complicated Celtic tattoo on his right forearm observed them from a chair at the other end of the tent.

Dread moved toward him. The man rose to shake hands and slap shoulders, saying simply, "Dread."

Next Randy stepped forward to shake hands with the stranger, and then Joanne and Marshall. The guy acknowledged each in turn. "Randy, you old skunk." "Joanne, lovely as usual." "Marshall."

Dread introduced Chase and Nicole. "Charlie, Nikki, this here is Ryder, my main man in the desert."

Ryder eyed them, saying nothing.

"Ryder," Dread continued, "Nikki here might look like a sweet flower, but she's one of the best damn shots you've ever seen. And Charlie can match her bullet for bullet."

Chase nodded at Ryder. "Hey." The guy's flat gaze reminded him of a snake waiting for the perfect moment to strike.

"What's up with the tent, man?" Chase asked. "I thought everything was easy in Arizona." The state had practically no laws about purchasing or carrying weapons.

Ryder continued to stare silently at Chase and Nicole, as if trying to remember if he'd seen them before. The hairs on the back of Chase's neck began to prickle.

Marshall stepped close to Ryder. "They're already proven. That little incident couple nights ago? At the old cockroach hotel north of Tucson?"

"He got the light; she got the tire," Randy threw in. "A couple bales of grass went up, but we got away with a big haul—dope, booze, and moola."

Finally, Ryder blinked. "Heard about that. Glad to meet you." He stepped toward them with his hand outstretched. "We got plans to intercept a whole load of *cucarachas* coming across any day now. Or I should say any night. Roaches always travel in the dark."

"That sounds entertaining." Nicole rubbed her hands together. "Is it going to be just us, or is there going to be a big party?"

Nobody said anything for a long moment, and Chase wondered if the question sounded suspicious to the others. To fill the void, he said, "Big, small, I don't give a shit. I'm tired of sitting on my hands; I'm itching for some action."

Ryder nodded. "There will be." He turned to Dread. "How many boxes of ammo you lookin' for?"

Thank God the guy didn't say the big event was going to take place tonight. There was no way in hell he and Nicole were ready for action. They had to maneuver their way to a hotel tonight, someplace with privacy, an Internet connection, and a public phone. Everything was too nebulous; they had to swap info with the SAC and nail down some sort of plan. And he *had* to find out what was going on with Summer.

"Charlie, check out this Kimber." Nikki thrust a pistol in his direction.

He took the weapon from her and turned it over in his hands, feeling the weight, aware of the other men watching him. "Sweet."

"This is even sweeter." Ryder flicked back a beach towel at his elbow to reveal a fully automatic rifle.

SAM walked from the *Municipio* building back to the harbor, her anxiety growing with each step. She understood how a diver might have found her earring near the rocks where she discovered Dan's body, but why was it bagged with that dive knife? Had Dan lost his knife in the same area? Or did the knife belong to Dan's killer? She wanted that earring back, but she was afraid to ask about it. She had a bad, bad feeling about everything that had happened at the police station.

But what the hell could she do about it? Clearly the U.S. Embassy and Consulate were not interested in helping her. Darwin Station and the Park Service? No support there. Some of the tour group might make sympathetic noises, but they had no clout. Even if she managed to talk to Chase tonight, they were thousands of miles apart.

On the corner ahead she spotted the police officer who had finger-wagged her for taking a photo. He watched as she passed, and she felt his gaze burning into her back as she continued down the street. She was a rabbit surrounded by coyotes and a long, long way from her safe hole. She could hardly wait to get back to *Papagayo*.

Her watch told her it was a few minutes past three o'clock. According to the ship's schedule, the passengers were on their own until eight—a night out on the town after several days in the close quarters of *Papagayo*. She'd have to find a water taxi to take her back to the yacht earlier so she'd have time to write and upload posts for Wilderness and Zing.

A rumble erupted from her midsection, embarrassingly loud. She glanced at two Americans standing nearby. They politely looked away. She rubbed her stomach as it gurgled again, reminding her that she'd missed lunch. There'd be no supper on board the yacht tonight, either. At least this was a problem she could solve.

Many of the restaurants had locked doors, and one open-air café was simply vacant. As well as her luck, her timing was lousy today: it was obviously siesta hour. She followed the melody of "Margaritaville" to a small hut surrounded by homemade stools and wooden wire-spool tables. Only one table was occupied, by a couple. A neatly lettered sign advertised *cerveza*, Coca-Cola, and an "especial" called *Pollo Ayora*. She knew that *cerveza* was "beer" and *pollo* meant "chicken," which sounded good after all the fish she'd eaten lately. She slid onto a stool in front of the only table that hosted an umbrella and a circle of shade.

As she pulled out a notepad and pen, a teenage girl appeared beside her, a question on her face. Sam ordered *cerveza* and the *Pollo Ayora*.

She stared at the blank lines on her notepad. Okay, Wilderness: what's your story for tonight? She wanted to keep her two characters separate, but it would be good to tie in something with Zing's quest for the truth about Daniel's death. Her digital camera held photos of Darwin Station,

Diego, baby tortoises, and the Puerto Ayora municipal building. *You are a wildlife biologist,* she reminded herself. The galápagos? Diego or the tiny tortoises. She scribbled a note—*tortoises*. She could write about the captive breeding program at Darwin Station, the threats of tortoise slaughter made during various uprisings by the local fishermen, the tortoises that had been murdered during the protests. After staring at the word for a few seconds, she added, *AGAIN?* She'd already done a post on tortoises; and only two days ago. Puerto Ayora would be a better subject. She pulled out her camera and snapped a photo of the little café, and another of the bay with all the boats. Given everything that had happened to her over the last few days, the pretty scenery was starting to feel like a cheap façade. Could she write about that?

Her beer arrived in an icy glass with a napkin, a small plate of sliced limes, and another with three tortilla chips spread with a pinkish paste. *Ceviche.* She lifted a chip and sniffed the pepper/onion/fish mixture. It smelled fresh enough. She grew up eating perch and catfish out of the river that ran past her grandmother's house in Kansas. She'd cleaned plenty of fish, and after getting a close-up of the parasites that most aquatic creatures carried, she was not inclined to eat uncooked fish. Still, when in Rome or Ecuador . . . She took a bite. Delicious. Sour and oniony and . . . hot! If the lime juice hadn't killed any worms, those peppers surely would. She washed down the rest with a swallow of beer and picked up a second chip.

Out in the harbor, sea lions had taken over a number of small boats, using the craft as personal sunbathing platforms. Maybe Wilderness Westin should film these bullies on the way back to *Papagayo.* As Eduardo said, the sea lions—or sea wolves, as they were called in Spanish—were the true rulers of the Galápagos. Sam closed her eyes for a moment, giving them a rest from the blinding reflections off the water. Think. Could she tie in sea lions with Dan's death? Frolicking sea lions had led her to his body.

The tooth marks on his thigh, the sea lions tugging off his flipper . . .

Was it possible that Dan's death was an accident? Could a beachmaster have killed Dan? She pictured a huge bull seizing a diver by the leg, dragging him through the water until he lost his mouthpiece and . . . No. Dan's regulator hose had been sliced through, and he had a gash on his neck and face. That wasn't the work of a sea lion. The officers had acted surprised by her suggestion of murder, but she was reasonably certain that they *were* acting.

"*Pollo Ayora*." A heavy ceramic plate thunked down onto the table in front of her. Sam opened her eyes. From her apron pocket, the girl pulled a knife and fork rolled into another paper napkin, and placed them beside the plate.

Steam rose from a chicken quarter stewed in tomatoes, cilantro, pineapple, and onions. A pile of brown rice occupied the other side of the plate. Sam ordered another beer and dug in. "*Delicioso*," she announced when the child brought the second beer. She was pretty sure that was a Spanish word. It must have been, because the girl repeated it loudly to her mother behind the stove.

As she ate, Sam mulled over her ideas for her blog posts. Wilderness Westin hadn't written anything about Dan yet—that had been Zing. Zing had reported on shark finning and other illegal fishing, then on longline fishing and the dead albatross, and Zing did the chat session about Dan's death. So Wilderness had better write about Puerto Ayora and leave Dan's death for Zing.

Did Wilderness dare write about the Navy and the Ecuadorian government and Darwin Station and the Park Service; the way the whole system worked? That might be interesting as a blog post, but it would hardly persuade the authorities to help her. She couldn't forget that knife with her earring at the police station. What were the *fiscalia* doing? Who were they listening to? *Crap*. She'd fallen into a snake pit. How was she supposed to tell the vipers from the harmless look-alikes?

A stool scraped the concrete floor as the tourist couple left their table. They left behind a newspaper, and Sam jumped up to grab it. What she wouldn't give for the *New York Times* right now.

No such luck—the headlines were in Spanish. *Gazeta Galápagos*. The local rag. The front page featured a photo of two men in Galápagos Park Service uniforms; they looked as if they might be father and son. She couldn't make out the story. Another photo of a brushfire eating up the vegetation around a beach was also intriguing. And a headline that contained the words *cientista* and *muerto*. A dead scientist—that had to be about Dan. She tucked the paper into her day pack so she could study it later with dictionary in hand.

A shadow fell across her arm. She swiveled to look at the young man who had taken the stool at the table beside hers. She felt the blood drain out of her face as she recognized Black Tank Top from Darwin Station. Her own twin reflections stared back at her from his sunglasses.

He raised his beer glass in a salute, his neatly trimmed mustache parting to reveal white teeth. A tiny designer label—PCB—was etched in gold on his sunglasses where the earpiece joined the right lens. Just like the glasses worn by the hostile boat driver, Ricardo Diaz.

"Wilderness Westin?" Black Tank Top stood up and walked close, looming over her, blocking her view of the harbor.

A thrill of fear spilled down her backbone. Should she grab her pack and leave? But where would she go?

He stuck out his right hand and said, "Carlos Santos. I'm glad to meet you."

She exhaled with relief. He wasn't a killer stalking her. But she wasn't accustomed to meeting fans in person. And she certainly wasn't used to strangers identifying her on sight. Somewhat reluctantly, she said hello and placed her fingers in his. His grip was hard and dry. Calluses roughened his palm. That hand didn't spend all its time at a desk or at a computer keyboard. When he released her fingers, she resisted the urge to massage out the cramp he'd squeezed in.

Using his index finger, he snagged the nosepiece of his sunglasses and slid them down his nose. The irises of his eyes were such a dark brown that she had to look hard to distinguish his pupils. He smiled, and a few crinkles appeared at the corners of his eyes. Carlos Santos was a very handsome man.

"May I join you?" He slid onto the stool across from her, plunking his beer onto the table. "You *are* Wilderness Westin, aren't you?" His accent was heavy, but his use of contractions and inflection proved he'd spoken English for a while.

"I'm Westin," she confirmed.

"I'm sorry for the loss of your colleague, Dr. Kazaki," he said.

Her throat tightened. "Thank you." That always struck her as an odd way to respond, but she was well trained from her youth as a pastor's daughter.

His gaze flitted around the café. "Where's Zing?"

"Zing isn't here."

"You were together at the hotel."

Hotel? She stared at him in confusion. She'd only been in one hotel today, and she'd been the only visitor there at the time. "You mean Hotel Aurora?"

He nodded.

He had to be referring to when she and Dan had stayed there. But she hadn't even known what Zing looked like then. When she first heard the name of her alter ego, Sam had pictured Zing as an Asian anime type, not a brazen red-haired dive diva.

Abruptly, the scenario clicked into place in her head. Santos had seen the red-haired Scandinavian tourist return Sam's sunglasses. That woman had long red hair and was pretty. Maybe she had looked like Zing. Santos must have been the newspaper guy in the lobby. This was creepy. How long had he been tracking her?

She shook her head. "You're mistaken. I haven't seen Zing since I arrived."

Santos peered over his sunglasses, narrowing his eyes. "Where is Zing now?"

Sam tried diversion. "I'm surprised that people here read *Out There*."

He pulled off his sunglasses, placed them on the table, and smiled again. "We're not all hicks. There are many computers here in the Galápagos. It's one world now with the Internet."

Great. Just what she needed. Another Galapagüeño keeping track of her. "You speak English well," she told him.

"I worked in L.A. for three years. I have a brother there."

"Ah." *Snap out of it,* she chided herself. *You're a reporter: here's your chance to get the straight scoop from a local.* She leaned forward. "So, you live here in Puerto Ayora?"

"Villamil. There is a ferry."

Her throat tightened. Villamil? Was he a fisherman who followed *Out There*? Then he had no doubt seen her stories about illegal fishing. Correction: Zing's stories. *Shit.* She wasn't cut out for this undercover crap. Her expression would give her away any second now. She took another swallow of beer and decided that Wilderness should play dumb. "I didn't know there was a ferry."

"It runs every day." He wiped down his mustache with a finger. "Where is Zing staying?"

Thank God *Out There* made her write under that stupid pseudonym. "I don't know where she is right now," she told him. *Actually, I've never laid eyes on her.* She suddenly felt like giggling and pressed her lips together to stop the urge.

He put his elbows on the spool table. "Can you give Zing a message?"

"A message from Carlos Santos?"

"From the fishermen of Galápagos."

Her stomach did a flip-flop. "You represent all the fishermen?"

"Yes." He flashed her another handsome smile. "When will you see her?"

She used her fingertip to draw a zigzag design down the side of her beer glass. "I don't know. I can send her an e-mail message," she offered. She looked up and returned his smile. "But then, so can you. Just use the link on *Out There*." Maybe he'd already sent one of those threatening comments.

"No e-mail," he said enigmatically.

What did that mean? That he didn't have e-mail or that he didn't want to leave a computer trail? She was afraid for Wilderness Westin to seem too curious. "What's the message?"

"Tell her she's got it wrong." As he turned his head, sunlight glinted from a large diamond stud in his left earlobe. Fishing must pay well here.

"I don't understand." Sam swirled the remaining beer in her glass. "What does Zing have wrong?"

"Tell her there's nothing illegal about fishing in the reserve. Fishing boats are licensed; we are allowed to fish for our families. I eat shark, and so do many Galapagüeños."

So he was upset at Zing's post about shark finning. "But the quantities are strictly limited, right? And—according to Zing—there were so many remains, and most of them were missing only the fins—"

He picked up her spare napkin and began to shred it into confetti. "How would Americans like it if someone wanted to kill their jobs?"

The word *kill* brought Dan to mind. Maybe it was her second beer or the fact that Santos had produced no weapon, but she was feeling braver by the minute. Not to mention angrier. "If my job was destroying an ecosystem, it would be right to end it."

He stopped shredding for a minute to meet her eyes. "Americans do not have the right to control the rest of the world." His voice was low and calm. He sounded eminently reasonable.

"Americans have nothing to do with it. The Galápagos

were declared a World Heritage Site in 1978. This area has been protected for decades."

He picked his sunglasses up from the table and slid them back onto his nose, obscuring his eyes. "The sea wasn't off-limits until people like Zing started butting in."

His dark eyes had at least seemed human. The mirrored sunglasses seemed hostile. "Zing is simply describing the current state of affairs," she said. "I wish she was here, because I'm sure she would like to learn more about the local fishing issues."

"Issues?" His tone was taunting.

"We've heard about problems here. Didn't fishermen take over Darwin Station, threaten to kill scientists and tourists? Didn't they hack up some tortoises with machetes? Didn't they threaten the director of Galápagos National Park?"

He crossed his arms over his chest. "Who tells you this?"

In his mirrored lenses, she watched herself shrug. "Zing heard stories from some people around here."

He stood up, raised his beer glass to his mouth, and drained it.

"Zing would like to know if the fishermen here still sell sea cucumbers and lobsters and shark fins to Asian ships. Do you still threaten scientists?"

"We never killed anyone." He wiped a finger over his mustache again.

"Until now?" She knew she shouldn't have said it, but she was so damned tired of these games. Zing wasn't here to grill the man. Sam Westin needed answers.

Santos slammed his empty beer glass on the table. "Maybe some people deserve to die," he hissed.

A prickle of fear crawled its way up from her ankles toward her throat. *Way to go, Westin.* She'd pushed him too far. The guy could have a switchblade in his pocket. The tables around them were vacant. The cook and the child waitress watched from inside the kitchen. Would they intervene if Santos decided to stab her?

Over Santos's shoulder, Sam saw a familiar stocky figure passing in the street. "Eduardo!" she shouted.

Eduardo didn't hear her. He wore jeans and a T-shirt and held the hand of a tiny dark-haired girl. With the tour group from *Papagayo* exploring the town, it was a free day for the naturalist guides. Eduardo lived here.

Santos grabbed her forearm. "You tell Zing what I said," he growled. "You tell Zing that fishermen had nothing to do with that *cientista*'s death."

Eduardo was almost past. She half rose from her seat. "Eduardo!"

His head swiveled in her direction. She waved frantically. Eduardo pulled the child in the direction of the café. The two of them stepped up onto the cement patio beside Sam's table. When Eduardo caught sight of Santos's face, he stopped, swallowed, ran his fingers through his unruly hair. Then he knelt at the child's level, tilted his head toward Sam, and said, "This is Señorita Westin, Marisela."

Sam smiled. "*Mucho gusto*, Marisela."

The girl removed a finger from her mouth long enough to chirp, "*Mucho gusto*," and the finger went right back in. Then the little girl's face turned toward Carlos Santos, and her eyes darkened with uncertainty.

Eduardo straightened. "Marisela is my granddaughter. We are on our way for *helado*—ice cream."

"*Helado!*" the little girl chirped.

"See you in a few hours, okay?" Eduardo said to Sam. The little girl tugged on his pant leg. He picked her up and, turning to leave, finally acknowledged the presence of the other man with a curt nod. "Santos."

Carlos Santos bumped Eduardo's shoulder with a fist. "Duarte."

Eduardo gave the fisherman a strained look, then turned to go.

Don't leave, she wanted to shout at Eduardo's retreating back. Santos continued to glare at her, standing with his feet and hands tensely held outward. Sam tucked more than enough money to cover the bill under her beer glass. "Well, I should be going."

"You be careful." He smiled and displayed his perfect teeth. "We love our visitors. We have already lost one. We wouldn't want anything to happen to you."

As she passed, he whispered softly, "Enjoy the rest of your tour on *Papagayo*, WildWest."

16

SAM hired a speedboat that sported a TAXI sign to ferry her back to *Papagayo*, paying the driver extra to zigzag among the craft in the bay so she could film the sea lions using dinghies as personal rafts.

When the water taxi bumped up against *Papagayo*'s stern platform, a crew member materialized on the upper deck. She waved. He returned the gesture and then disappeared back to whatever he had been doing. The ship was silent and mostly vacant, with only a few hands on board. Instead of feeling claustrophobic now, her cabin seemed peaceful and almost cozy.

The day had not gone anything like she had hoped. She hadn't retrieved her passport. She hadn't recruited a single ally. Instead, she'd met an enemy. But at least she could now match a face to a threat: Carlos Santos.

Maybe some people deserve to die. Had Dan known that he was in danger from the fishermen's union? Had NPF known about the threat? She booted up her laptop, then retrieved Dan's flash drive from its hiding spot and plugged it into the USB port.

She sorted through Dan's e-mail to and from NPF. The messages were mainly business details about travel arrangements and dive sites to survey, but one from Karl@npf.org was intriguingly labeled "Rumor Confirmed."

Just recd confirmation of rumor re planned resort project in Villamil: Chinese delegation scheduled to arrive Puerto Ayora on March 16, will attend parade & celebration on March 17. Local government eager to impress. It's crucial to make study results public well before so Chinese will factor them into their decision, but do NOT reveal prior knowledge of visit or our source could be endangered. Numbers will speak for themselves. Let Out There provide commentary.

The Chinese planned to invest in Villamil? The word *resort* was ominous in itself. Food and drinking water were shipped into the Galápagos towns from the mainland each week; how much would a resort require? More ships, more tourists, more flights . . . Dan had mentioned unpunished encroachments into the park around the town of Villamil. Did the developers plan to build this resort on protected land? Would the resort include a waste treatment plant, or would it, like many existing Galápagos enterprises, dump raw sewage into the marine reserve? She experienced a brief ugly mental image of sea turtles swimming through unspeakable muck.

No wonder Dan had felt this survey was urgent to complete. No wonder Santos was so alarmed about Zing's reports. Had Dan been killed because of a planned resort?

Her conversation with Santos had made one thing clear: she needed to keep Wilderness Westin completely separate from Zing. But now that she was pissed off, Wilderness was no longer content to be the blithely happy tourist she had been up to this point.

Sam decided her post would compare the growing human population in the islands with the sea lions in the harbor. She wrote about the thuggish beachmaster sea lions and threw in her video clips of sea lions on sinking dinghies, as well as a photo of crowded Academy Bay. Neither the people nor the pinnipeds intended to sink the perch on which they had chosen to land, but that was likely to be the ultimate result.

To keep *Out There* from completely freaking about her anti-tourist slant, she ended by saying that if readers wanted to see anything close to the original Galápagos environment, they had better book a trip soon. The editors would happily link that comment to Key's travel site. She proofread and sent the text and visuals, then turned to the more complex problem of Zing's post.

Carlos Santos's smirk danced in front of her eyes as she stared at the blank word processor window.

The hell with him. She typed, *I came here to publish the truth, factual observations, and statistics. For that, I have received threats from a local fisherman who accosted my colleague, Wilderness Westin. Was Daniel Kazaki killed simply because he was collecting data on the state of the Galápagos?*

She decided to include the first underwater photo she'd taken of Dan with the sea cucumber, as well as the photo of him topside. Let the readers see that he had been a kind, valuable person.

I will continue to report everything I observe here, she wrote. *Today, Wilderness went to Darwin Station and the headquarters of the Galápagos National Park Service, in hopes of finding support for our team.*

Speaking of the Park Service, hadn't there been a photo of park rangers on the page of the local paper? She pulled the *Gazeta Galápagos* out of her day pack and unrolled it. Naturally, the text was Spanish. She scanned the front page, found a website URL listed in the upper-right corner, connected to the Internet, and brought up the paper's website. Luckily, it contained the same article and photos. She copied the article address and pasted it into an online translator, then clicked Spanish to English.

And presto, the article reappeared, now in the mangled

English that the Internet translation program provided. The two rangers were father and son, as she had guessed; the son was just entering the service. The father had served for nearly a decade and was famous for having been shot three years ago when he had stopped to investigate a fire on a remote island. There was a confusing paragraph about illegal camping and hunters and giant tortoises that burned to death.

These might not be current events, but the article was proof that the islands had a troubled history. Even Carlos Santos couldn't blame her for reporting a story that had already appeared in the *Gazeta Galápagos*. Well, of course he would, but he'd be blaming Zing.

She added links to the *Gazeta*'s web page to Zing's article, along with brief explanations of the events. Park guards shot. Burned islands, dead galápagos. The trouble in paradise had started long ago and continued to this day. She added a tranquil-looking photo of the sunset from Puerto Ayora. A PRETTY FAÇADE DISGUISES TROUBLE, she labeled it. She bit her lip, remembering Dr. Guerrero's request, and then added some wording about how the Darwin Station personnel and park rangers were doing the best they could under extremely difficult conditions, but that they weren't in control.

Which begged the question—who *was* in control? And where did the *fiscalia* stand in this mess? With the conservation community? With the locals? Hell, the police *were* locals, weren't they?

She was scheduled to depart in three days. Would they let her? In five days, she was supposed to meet Chase at the ski lodge in Utah, no matter what. Would either of them show up for their rendezvous? Or would they still be stuck thousands of miles apart, playing their endless game of voice mail tag?

She sent Zing's post, hoping *Out There* would not notice Zing had no dive footage this time. Then she downloaded all her e-mail. Wilderness's folder held a few messages.

One from the elusive SanDman said, "Tell Zing sometimes the better part of valor is discretion."

"Tell her yourself, asshole." What was that supposed to mean, anyway? In Zing's e-mail folder, detractors were nearly as numerous as supporters. Several messages were in Spanish, all with a lot of upside-down exclamation points in the subject line, and there was a nasty one in English—*Butt out, bitch!* She didn't bother to read any of them.

There was no e-mail from Chase in any folder. She checked her phone for the hundredth time. Nothing from Chase. She punched in his home phone number just to hear his voice mail message. *Hi, you've reached you know who and you know what to do.*

The beep screeched in her ear. *"Hola, querido,"* she said. "I know I can't call you, Chase, but I really want to talk to you." She hesitated a second, then forged ahead. "By now you probably know that things aren't going so well down here. Dan Kazaki is dead; I think he was murdered." Her throat constricted, and she had to swallow before continuing. "The police took my passport, and now they have my earring found at the site where Dan's body was located. I don't know what that means, but I don't think it's good. I'm not going to let them win, though; I can't allow Dan to have died for nothing. I'm going to finish the job we started." There wasn't anything more to report. "I wanted to say that I love you and I'm thinking about you and I still hope to meet you on the twenty-second. Stay safe, *mi salsa picante.*"

She ended the call, wiped her brimming eyes, and stood up to stretch. Outside her door, she heard footsteps and the voices of Brandon and Ken, then the Robersons. Various clanks and thumps. The tourists were back on board.

Her phone bleated from its resting place on the desk. Finally! She picked it up and flipped it open. "Chase!"

"Sam." It was more of a statement than a greeting. The voice belonged to a woman. Dan's wife.

Guilt overwhelmed Sam. "Elizabeth, I'm so, so sorry. I should have called you the instant that I knew—"

"Are you okay?"

Oh jeez, how could this poor widow be worrying about *her* when her own husband had just died? "I'm all right," she said, swallowing around the lump in her throat. "How are you and Sean?"

"Shocked."

"Of course. We all are." The vision of Dan's dead eyes behind his flooded face mask wavered in front of her gaze. Sam shut her eyes to make it go away.

"What happened?"

Should she tell Elizabeth the story of finding Dan's body two days before the consulate informed her of his death? Should she tell her about the bad air at the beginning of the trip? No. She needed to make some kind of sense out of the whole chain of events first.

She said, "We're still trying to figure that out, Elizabeth." Who the heck were the others in this mysterious "we" she kept mouthing? As far as she knew, no one else in the Galápagos was even looking for answers. "What did they tell you?"

"Just that there was a terrible accident and he drowned. He's on a plane now. I mean, his—" She sniffed and then Sam heard a muffled sound as if Elizabeth had pressed the phone against her body. After a second, she was back. "You weren't with him?"

Why did that question make her feel so guilty? "I was out hiking, Elizabeth. It looks like Dan decided to go diving alone. I had no idea he might do that."

The other end of the connection was quiet except for a few sniffs. Elizabeth was either crying or trying not to. Did Dan's wife have any other information? "Did Dan say anything to you about the way the trip was going, or what he thought about the survey he was doing?"

"Dan rarely told me much about his work."

A long, uncomfortable silence followed. As it dragged on, Sam pondered several expressions of sympathy, but they all sounded insincere in her imagination. Nothing was adequate for Elizabeth's loss. Nothing was equal to her own guilt. Finally she began, "If there's any—"

"I want you to know that I don't blame you," Dan's wife interrupted. "He knew that underwater research was dangerous; but he loved it. He always told me"—Sam heard a soft sob at this point, but then Elizabeth continued—"that if he died on a trip like this . . . he died a good death . . . doing important work . . . in a place he wanted to be."

Hot tears blurred Sam's vision. She found it hard to talk, but she choked out, "Dan loved you, Elizabeth. He loved Sean." God, this was awful. Nobody should have to talk this way over thousands of miles, over a telephone. This sort of conversation should be face to face, crying onto each other's shoulder. Although Sam had known Dan only a few days, she and Elizabeth would be forever connected by this horrible event.

If only she had her father's faith and easy assurances that Dan's death was justified by some heavenly blueprint. *Dan's in heaven. God called him; it's part of a grand plan. You'll see him again someday.* She couldn't bring herself to say any of that.

"You take care, Sam," Elizabeth said softly.

"I'll do my best," Sam said. "And I'll let you know everything I find out."

A soft click ended the call from Elizabeth's end. Sam sat on the bunk staring out the porthole for a moment, seeing Dan raising a beer, seeing him showing the Birskys his photo of Elizabeth and Sean, seeing him smiling as he said, "I refuse to have a peon for a partner."

She took a deep breath and wiped the wetness from her cheeks. "I *will* find out what happened, Dan."

As she brushed her teeth, she heard the anchor chain rolling up from the depths. She stepped up on her lower bunk, preparing to crawl into the top one, and then she heard footsteps descending the stairs. They stopped right outside her door.

Sam froze, both feet on the bottom bunk, hands

clutching the top bunk frame. Did she hear breathing, or was that her imagination? After a minute, the steps backed away, and she would have sworn she heard the door to Cabin 4, Dan's cabin, open and then close. Who the hell— were the *fiscalia* back on board? Or was that a crew member? Tony or the captain? Maybe Jon Sanders, the owner? It couldn't be Santos. But it could be someone who worked for Santos. Why the hell didn't these rooms have an interior lock? She stepped down and jammed the desk chair under her doorknob.

Feeling shaky now, she climbed into her bunk. As *Papagayo* plowed through the water, she saw the waves lapping below the porthole. No good-omen dolphin appeared this time. There was just endless dark water.

17

THE next morning, Sam awoke determined to finish the job as quickly as possible. She wanted to find Eduardo before breakfast and make a plan about how to survey the last two sites on Dan's list.

She stepped out into the hallway. As she pulled shut her door, she heard the door to Cabin 4, Dan's room, open behind her. Sam gasped and turned around.

"You've got to be Summer Westin." An African-American woman, dressed in a red T-shirt and navy cotton shorts, stood in the open doorway. Tiny black braids flowed from her strong square face to an elaborate knot at the back of her head.

Sam closed her open mouth. She'd always wanted hair like that: hair that made a statement; not a limp, pale mane like hers. Who the heck was this? Had the captain given Dan's cabin away? "Uh," Sam stuttered. "Who—"

"I'm J.J." The woman extended a hand. "From NPF. I'm here to take Dr. Kazaki's place. Summer, right?"

"Call me Sam." She held out her hand uncertainly.

"And you can call me *Dr.* Bradley." The woman held her

gaze for a long moment, then her eyes crinkled and she laughed. "Couldn't resist. I just got my Ph.D. last summer. No, seriously, you can call me J.J."

"Okay, J.J."

"It stands for Juanita Jane." J.J. dramatically rolled her brown eyes. "I know, I know. It's two versions of the same name. My mama was not what you'd call intellectual. More the poetic type. She liked the sound of Juanita Jane. And she loved me."

"Good for you." It was the only thing Sam could think of to say. J.J. still held her hand. Sam wondered how to free it gracefully. "When—"

"I got in late last night, right before the boat moved out. I thought about knocking on your door, but it was late and I couldn't hear any movement inside."

"That was you." Sam breathed a sigh of relief.

"Come on in." J.J. pulled her across the threshold, propelling her toward the lower bunk. "Sit down."

Sam tripped over a BCD and tumbled onto the lower bunk mattress. The floor was strewn with clothes and dive gear, a wetsuit, reference books. Sam righted herself, then peered at the woman between curtains of clothing that hung down from the bunk above.

"I was so sorry to hear about Dr. Kazaki. That must have been awful. Tell me about him."

Sam pushed the sleeve of a windbreaker aside and leaned forward. "You didn't know him?"

J.J. folded her arms across her chest. "He was a prof at the U. of Delaware, wasn't he? NPF likes to use subcontractors. They wanted another independent to replace him, but they couldn't find one on such short notice. I normally work in D.C. at the Natural Planet Foundation headquarters, but I just concluded a survey around Cocos Island off Costa Rica, so they sent me to finish up here. They say they're missing four reports. Is that right, four spots remaining on the survey list?"

"We missed one on the south side of Isabela on the day Dan . . ." Sam stopped there and took a breath. "I did one of the areas yesterday by myself—Ola Rock." It felt good to say that. "I can give you that report."

J.J. stared at her. "You went by yourself, after what happened to Kazaki? You got balls, girl."

Sam shrugged. "I was not completely alone; I was with Eduardo Duarte. He's the conservationist guide that Dan made the deal with."

"Yes, I called him in town and made sure he knew that the deal was still on."

Sam was startled. Eduardo hadn't mentioned it at the café, but then, with Santos there, it was probably wise of him not to.

J.J. continued, "I dive alone when I have to, but it can be eerie, can't it? Say, you know what happened to Dan's computer?"

"Do you know what happened to *him*?"

That stopped the flood of words. For a second. "I know he died in a diving accident," J.J. said.

Sam swallowed. "You heard it was an accident?"

"You think it was something else?" J.J. crossed her arms and waited.

J.J.'s appearance was a godsend; finally Sam had someone she could talk to. She told J.J. about the carbon monoxide and the hotel incident and then about the slashes on Dan's body and equipment. She concluded, "I never thought NPF was at all controversial; all you do is conduct studies and publish the data."

J.J. solemnly gazed at her. "And then that data gets used by various organizations to make decisions on all sorts of issues. That's why we usually try to fly under the radar when we operate outside of the States. Kazaki knew that."

"But I was hired by Key Corporation to make NPF's findings public on *Out There*. Isn't that"—she struggled for the right word—"counterproductive?"

J.J. gave her a curious look. "What's the use of collecting data if nobody knows about it? We always try to find a third party to broadcast the results, especially if they're time sensitive for some reason. What's *Out There*?"

"You don't know about *Out There*? Key's 'news' "—Sam crooked her fingers in air quotes—"website? I'm one of their reporters."

"I spend a lot of time underwater," J.J. explained. "And usually in Third World countries. I'm not exactly part of the wired set." Then she crooked an eyebrow. "You mean you've already been posting reports on the *Internet*?"

Sam nodded grimly. "Daily. I write about geography and land animals as Wilderness Westin; and I've been writing about diving under the name of Zing."

"Zing? Sounds like a breath mint."

"I guessed mouthwash. I'll show you." Sam dragged J.J. across the hall to her room, booted up her laptop, connected to *Out There*'s website, and brought up Zing's latest post about trouble in paradise.

J.J. studied the screen with her arms crossed. "Guess that snake's already out of the bag."

"And everyone's out hunting it with machetes. The only bright spot is that the locals don't seem to realize that I'm Zing."

J.J. sighed. "We've just got two more dives, so three more days and we're outa here, right?"

"Easy for you to say." Sam told her about the *fiscalia* and her passport.

"Whoa." J.J. rubbed at a frown line on her forehead. "Let's hope that's just a formality."

"Yeah, let's hope." No way was she about to tell J.J. about her earring. J.J. might run screaming for the nearest plane, and then she'd be all alone again.

"You might want to lighten up on the criticism until we're out of here," J.J. suggested.

"Too late." Sam clicked back through Zing's posts, showed J.J. the gory shark video and the photo of the long-lined albatross, told her about the chat session and about how Zing had suggested that Dan's death might be tied to the overfishing issues. "*Out There* is thrilled with the controversy. There have been hundreds of thousands of hits on the website. If they didn't know about problems down here before, the Chinese will certainly be aware of the situation now."

J.J. rolled her eyes. "Well, alrighty, then. Mission accomplished. Just don't use *my* photo or mention my name or my connection with NPF. Deal?" She stuck out her hand again.

"Deal." Sam shook the extended hand. "But I never used Dan's name, either."

They looked at each other. Sam knew her expression was as grim as J.J.'s.

"We will stick together like glue, right, Sam? Nobody's going to pick us off one at a time. Eduardo's taking us to Flores Reef this morning."

Back into the dangerous depths. But at least she wouldn't have to do it alone this time.

"I was told Dan had a notebook computer?" J.J. asked.

"The police took it." Abruptly remembering the paper-thin walls, Sam leaned close and murmured, "But I managed to copy most of his files first. They're on a flash drive. And I snagged his handheld, too."

She dug them out and handed them over. J.J. turned toward the door. "Only Eduardo knows who I am. As far as anyone else on this boat is concerned, we're just friends diving together, right? I came to support you in this trying time."

Sam touched J.J.'s forearm. "I'm glad you're here, Dr. Bradley."

J.J. pulled open the door. Her nostrils flared. "Is that bacon I smell? Let's get breakfast, girlfriend."

Sam introduced J.J. around the tour group as her friend from the States. The tourists seemed more surprised to see Sam back on board than to meet a new passenger, and she realized that they didn't know about her passport. "I can't go home yet," she told them. "I have a job to finish."

SAM watched with envy as the tour group departed after breakfast to hike on Tower Island, aka Genovesa. Clouds of birds swirled over the island. On the shore were some small furry rust-colored blobs with shapes similar to the harbor seals back home.

"Galápagos fur seals," Eduardo verified. "They are making a comeback."

He ferried J.J. and Sam in their scuba gear a short distance to a U-shaped inlet. There was a buoy in the middle of the bay, to which Eduardo tied the panga. The wind blew from the mouth of the inlet, chopping the surface water into foot-high pyramids as waves rebounded from the shores on all sides to bang against one another in the center of the bay. Sam was glad that she was not in her kayak, where she would be slapped from all sides.

For once she was relieved to slip under the surface, where the rise and fall of water immediately lessened to a gentle rocking motion. At sixty feet down, there was virtually no water movement. Yellow-tailed snappers, king angelfish, creolefish, and dozens of species Sam couldn't identify flitted in and out among orange cup corals, yellow anemones, and spiky white-tipped sea urchins. J.J., using Dan's handheld computer, immediately went to work counting.

Sam shot a few minutes of video, then switched to still mode and captured a few of the most colorful scenes. To her eyes, this location looked healthy. As she swam over a patch of sand, rows of garden eels retracted into their holes. Cup corals, curly pale green seaweed, and pink encrusting sponges spread like vibrant flower beds over the reef, attended by swirling clouds of rainbow-colored fish. This scene was such a relief after the butchered sharks and the longlined albatross. There were the usual hovering barracudas, but now she was used to their flat black predatory gaze and they didn't seem so ominous. Lying on the bottom was a small whitetip reef shark. Sam kept a wary eye on it, but it seemed to be napping. In the distance, she saw the kite-like shapes of eagle rays and clouds of silvery jacks.

This was probably how all Galápagos reefs looked decades ago. When J.J.'s gaze met hers, Sam made a clapping motion, applauding the beautiful sight. If only Dan could have seen this and known that all was not yet lost. J.J. nodded and continued her counts. Sam focused on taking a wide-angle photo of a cloud of tiny blue fish hovering around a massive violet-tipped anemone, and then a close-up of a delicate basket star, a pumpkin-colored creature with so many curlicue arms it seemed impossible that it didn't get tangled up in its own appendages. The eagle rays swam closer, their triangle shapes evenly spaced like jets flying in formation. She switched to video and captured a few seconds of the squadron's sleek motion.

Now *this* was what Sam had hoped for from scuba diving. When she glanced at her computer, she saw that nearly thirty minutes had passed, along with half her air supply. She wanted to grow gills and stay forever.

A shadow crossed overhead. Sam looked up, expecting to see a boat's hull. Against the glittering surface she saw a snorkeler spread-eagled. The woman's long red hair floated in the water, and she wore a black-and-white dive skin, similar to the one that Zing wore in her photo on *Out There*. Sam had the weird sensation that her cyber-ego had assumed solid form to join her for this exploration.

Other dark shapes bobbed at the surface, bouncing in the waves not far away. A snorkeling tour. Their boat was probably tethered to the same buoy as Eduardo's panga was. What bad luck for the tourists, or maybe bad planning on the part of the tour guide; she certainly wouldn't enjoy snorkeling under such rough conditions.

Where was J.J.? Sam sat upright in the water, turned the camera back on in video mode, and slowly twirled, looking for her dive buddy. It was amazing how, when suspended in liquid, movement in any direction was easy. Mermaid magic. She spotted J.J. quite a distance away, nearly cloaked by a school of king angelfish as she carefully inspected the reef surface.

The reverberation of a boat engine overhead broke the spell. The female snorkeler still lay on the surface, but the hull of a speedboat was cutting through the water, closing fast on her. Sam rolled over on her back, afraid that she was about to see the snorkeler run over by the boat. She pulled up the camera to get the incident on film. But at the last minute, the boat swerved, coming to rest beside the snorkeler, pushing a wave in her direction. The woman's face mask left the water and her feet dropped as she looked up toward the boat. The wave washed over her and she kicked in place for a moment. Must be talking to the boaters.

Then the woman's mask dropped back to the surface of the water and she was floating spread-eagled again, next to the boat. The boat engine revved, the woman's body bounced, and two projectiles streaked out beneath her. Tiny silver fish? Sam couldn't make sense of the image.

The speedboat roared away. A red cloud blossomed around the snorkeler, who was thrashing now in the water, her face no longer pressed against the surface. A wave bounced the snorkeler, and Sam heard faint noises that sounded like distant screams.

Oh sweet Jesus! Sam streaked for the surface. She came up under the snorkeler and pushed the woman over on her back. The snorkeler's dark eyes were panicked, she was making unintelligible noises, and no wonder. She was having problems staying afloat as she pressed both hands to her right leg, where blood poured out of a bullet hole in her calf. She flailed, reached out a bloody hand for Sam's shoulder, and then went under.

Sam let go of her camera and grabbed the woman's hand, spat out her regulator, and pumped extra air into her BCD so she could float without kicking. The snorkeler surfaced again, sputtering and coughing, and shouting in a foreign language.

"Calm down," Sam said loudly. "I've got you."

The woman clawed at Sam's arm and would have pushed her under if her BCD hadn't been inflated. With some difficulty, Sam managed to turn the other woman around and hug her from behind. "I've got you," she murmured again into the woman's ear. "You're going to be okay. You're safe now."

She certainly hoped that was true. She couldn't help

envisioning what the two of them, flailing legs surrounded by a haze of blood, would look like from below to the reef shark or even to the barracuda she'd seen just a few minutes ago.

"Hey! Help!" Sam shouted in the direction of the buoy, where a small cabin cruiser was tied next to their inflatable panga. A wave slapped against her right ear and then moved over her head.

The boats seemed impossibly distant. She couldn't see anyone moving. The other dark neoprene shapes in the water were oblivious. Had they all been shot?

Sam kicked, towing the woman's body toward the boats. J.J. surfaced on the other side of the woman and spat out her regulator, then clamped her hands over the woman's leg wound. She kicked from behind as Sam towed the victim. "What the hell happened?"

"She was right above me. A boat swerved in, then blam, blam!" Damn, it was hard to swim on the surface in an inflated BCD and heavy scuba tank.

The waves continually broke over them from all sides. Sam's camera dangled from its safety strap, banging against her back and side as she kicked through the water. Swimming was a little easier with J.J. pushing as Sam pulled. The poor woman seemed resigned to whatever would happen next. Or maybe she was already in shock. As they neared the boats, a few of the surrounding snorkelers raised their heads, and then started swimming toward them. A radio blasted hip-hop music from the cabin cruiser.

"Hey!" J.J. shouted.

"Help!" Sam yelled as loudly as she could. They were only a couple of feet away from the cabin cruiser when Eduardo and the other boat pilot emerged from the cabin. The cruiser pilot wore a blue baseball cap with the name KYLE emblazoned across the front.

"Shit!" Kyle yelped. "What happened?" The men grabbed the snorkeler by the arms and hauled her over the side of the boat, then they all vanished into the cockpit of the cabin cruiser.

Sam and J.J. removed their fins and struggled up the boat ladder, J.J. going first and taking Sam's camera as she handed it up. The woman lay on the floor of the boat as Eduardo pressed a folded towel on top of her leg wound. She moaned and asked questions in her language, which Sam now recognized as Norwegian. This was the same tourist she'd met in the Hotel Aurora.

Eduardo looked at the stranger and shook his head to indicate he couldn't understand. "*Español?* English?" he asked.

The woman choked out a few heavily accented words in English. "Why? They shoot—why?"

Sam and J.J. unbuckled their BCDs and let the vests and tanks slide to the rear bench of the boat, then turned back to watch the first aid effort. The towel under Eduardo's hands dripped blood into the floor of the boat.

Sam knelt beside the woman. Unfortunately, this was not the first time she'd encountered a bullet wound in the middle of nowhere. She grabbed two clean towels from Kyle, folded them, placed one beneath the woman's leg, then slid Eduardo's hands aside and pressed the new towel down hard on the top wound. The woman groaned.

J.J. sat down on the bench on the other side. To Kyle, she said, "Got some straps of some kind? Or a belt?"

The guy nodded and ducked into his boat cabin again.

"Why?" the woman moaned.

Kyle returned with two yellow nylon straps grimy with mildew and rust spots, but they would do the job. J.J. took one and pulled it tight above the bullet wound, sticking a finger between the strap and the woman's leg to make sure the tourniquet would not completely shut off circulation. Then she took the other and wrapped it around the towel pads, pressing them tightly against the bullet hole.

"Hey!" a snorkeler shouted from the back of the boat. A swim fin waved in the air.

"You need to get the snorkelers out of the water right away," Sam told Eduardo.

Eduardo looked at his bloody hands, flashed on her

meaning, and then both he and Kyle moved to the stern, tossing snorkel equipment into the bottom of the boat and quickly hauling tourists up the ladder.

The victim moaned again as Sam pushed a life preserver under her head and J.J. positioned another under her wounded leg, but now the woman had her eyes closed. Even with a grimace wrinkling her face and her eyes closed, she bore a startling resemblance to Zing. Maybe she was the model who'd posed for Zing's photo. "What's your name?" Sam asked.

"Bergit," the woman croaked.

Having hauled all the snorkelers on board, Kyle returned to his wounded passenger's side. With tousled sun-bleached blond hair curling from beneath his baseball cap and dressed in a yellow T-shirt and cutoffs, he looked all of twenty. What sort of fly-by-night company thought it was a good idea to send a kid out alone in rough water with a boat full of snorkeling tourists?

He reached for a list attached to a clipboard on a nearby seat. He ran a damp finger down the list. "Bergit Moller." He looked at the victim in the cockpit and made a face. "I guess I should call the head office."

"You need to get her to the hospital," Sam said. Surely the run-down, overcrowded clinic she'd seen was not the only medical facility in the islands. "And you need to call the police."

Eduardo and Kyle discussed something in Spanish, probably who should do what next.

The other five foreign tourists talked excitedly among themselves. One of the women knelt beside Bergit and took her hand, murmuring words of encouragement. The dorsal fin of a shark briefly surfaced not far away in the water, and the others turned to look at it, pointing to other sharks visible through the clear water.

The sunlight was way too bright. Everything seemed to slow to a crawl. Sam's head ached. Darting zigzags of twinkling lights stabbed into her field of vision. She'd been drifting with all those amazing creatures, feeling as if she was one with the reef world, and the next minute, she'd witnessed an attempted murder?

She squinted her eyes against the pain. "Who saw that other boat?"

Blank looks all around. "The other boat—the one with the red hull—that zoomed up to Bergit?" she clarified. *The one with a killer aboard who shot Zing.*

The matched pair—clearly mother and daughter—shook their heads, and after a quick translation by the portly woman, so did the other foreign tourists. Sam checked the faces of Eduardo and Kyle. No and no.

J.J. shrugged. "I saw the wake of a boat moving away."

That was just *great*. She was the only one who'd seen it? And all she could describe was a red hull? She sat down, rubbing her forehead. The cabin cruiser bounced in the waves. Her headache segued into massive throbbing. Lightning slashed across her field of vision, bright stars bursting within the zigzag shapes. She closed her eyes for a minute. It didn't help. She opened them again; staggered toward the other side of the boat, fighting waves of nausea.

"Eduardo, let's go back to *Papagayo*," she said, crawling back into their inflatable panga. "This boat needs to hightail it back to Puerto Ayora so Bergit can get to the hospital."

J.J. followed her and pulled her down to the bench. "You okay?"

"Why wouldn't I be? Just because I saw someone get shot?"

"You're holding your elbow like it hurts."

"It does." That was a little weird, now that she thought about it. She didn't remember banging it on anything. Her right arm felt prickly, too, like it had fallen asleep.

"And you're staggering."

"Did you not hear the part about witnessing an attempted murder? You'd be staggering, too. And my head hurts like you wouldn't believe." She lowered her head into her hands, blotting out the painful sunlight.

She felt J.J. rise and jump to the cabin cruiser, but she was back a minute later, jiggling Sam's arm. "Here."

She lifted her head. J.J. waved a plastic mask in front of her face. It was attached via a plastic tube to a tank labeled OXIGENO. Sam waved it away. "I don't need oxygen."

"I think you do. We need to move you back to the other boat. You need to go to Puerto Ayora, too. I just checked your dive computer. You came up awfully fast."

J.J. was criticizing her dive skills now? That was the last thing she needed on top of this blinding headache. "You would, too, if you saw someone bleeding out above you."

J.J. pressed the plastic mask against Sam's face. "Ever heard of the bends?"

The bends—DCS—decompression sickness. Nitrogen bubbles in the blood going places they weren't supposed to. Potential for strokes, heart attacks, paralysis. Pure oxygen helped, but the only cure for serious decompression sickness was time in a decompression chamber.

"Eduardo!" Sam gestured him to come over from the other boat.

He crawled into the panga. "But Sam—"

"We'll keep the oxygen," she yelled to Kyle. "You go, now!"

The cabin cruiser's powerful engine roared to life beside them and a cloud of blue exhaust wafted their way.

"Sam!" J.J. tugged at her arm. "Don't be an idiot."

The snorkel tour boat pulled away, leaving their inflatable rocking in its wake.

"There's only one decompression chamber here," she told J.J.

"But she is—" Eduardo started.

"Out of commission," Sam finished the sentence.

At the same time, Eduardo said, "Broke."

J.J. looked horrified.

Sam took a deep breath of the cold oxygen. The shooter had hit the wrong target, but he may have finished Zing just the same. Sam slid off the bench onto the floor of the dinghy.

18

WHEN she bounced off the floor, Sam came to. It took a few seconds to register the meaning of the clouds zooming dizzily past overhead. She saw plastic in front of her nose and reached up to pull it off.

A dark-skinned hand swatted hers away. "Just relax and breathe," J.J. said. Strong fingers lifted her head and slid a boat cushion beneath it.

She was body-slammed from below again. She was on the floor of the panga, still in her wetsuit, speeding back to *Papagayo*. The banging of the bow slamming into the waves was making her headache worse. The bends, she had the bends. And there was no decompression chamber. She closed her eyes and concentrated on breathing the cool, pure oxygen.

Was she going to die in the Galápagos? That would really piss her off. This was supposed to be her tropical holiday, her well-paid contribution to the conservation cause. How the hell could everything have gone so wrong? First Dan, and now Bergit—God, had that poor woman been shot because she looked like a fictional character?

"Bullets!" She tried to sit up. "We've got to go find the bullets."

"No, we don't." J.J. pressed her back down on the floor. "We are not exactly in CSI territory."

It'll be like a vacation, Wyatt had said. A horror movie vacation, where the innocent tourists stumble into a hotel run by demons and then get murdered one by one. Zing's writing caused an innocent stranger to get shot, and now it looked like her alter-ego WildWest, aka plain old Summer Westin, was going to end up as collateral damage. She had the bends in the middle of nowhere. Her hands felt like pins and needles. Every dive magazine she'd read reported someone dying from the bends or ending up in a wheelchair.

She didn't feel like she was going to die. But then maybe every diver with the bends thought that in her last moments on earth. Why hadn't she moved in with Chase and learned to cook and lived happily ever after?

J.J. leaned close. "How're you doing?"

Sam pulled down her mask to say, "That woman got shot because of me. And for the record, I'd rather die than end up paralyzed."

"I hear you," J.J. murmured. "Welcome to the war."

That response irritated Sam. She'd expected something along the lines of, *This isn't your fault, everyone is going to be fine.* What kind of friend said, *Welcome to the war*?

Another body slam levitated her. The hell with this. She pushed herself into a sitting position and leaned against the bench next to J.J.'s knees, facing the stern. Eduardo alternately glanced at her and the waves ahead as he manned the tiller, his forehead knotted with worry lines. She ordered her right hand to rise and gave him a weak thumbs-up, which made him smile a little. She wiggled both feet. They felt a bit numb, but all her appendages worked on command. "Look," she said to J.J. "I am not paralyzed."

"Good to know. Keep the mask on," J.J. said.

By the time they bumped up against *Papagayo*'s stern,

her headache had lessened a bit, and the zigzag flashes of light twinkled only at the periphery of her vision. Her elbow still hurt, but maybe she *had* actually banged it on something.

She ripped off the oxygen mask and climbed from the dinghy to *Papagayo*'s platform under her own power, carrying her camera.

J.J. followed her down the stairway to their cabins. She carried the oxygen tank and mask and pressed it into Sam's arms as she opened the cabin door.

"I'm fine," Sam told her.

"You're pigheaded." White salt crystals dotted J.J.'s mahogany skin and black hair.

"I've got to get that video on the Net before anything else happens."

"Not yet." J.J. stepped behind her and unzipped Sam's wetsuit. "Does anything hurt?"

"Not too much."

J.J. frowned. "Do you see any visual anomalies, like flashes?"

"How'd you know?"

J.J. gave her an exasperated look and tugged on the neck of Sam's wetsuit. "Take this off, lay down, and put that mask back on. I'm coming back to check on you in a while and you better be horizontal."

"Can you find out how Zing—I mean Bergit—is?"

"I'll try." J.J. turned toward her cabin.

Sam shucked off her clammy wetsuit and lay on her bunk in her bathing suit, sucking on the cool oxygen for a few more minutes. It really did help her headache. Could anyone buy a tank of oxygen? Maybe she'd get a little one for home use. Blake might appreciate a toke when he stumbled out of bed after a late party.

J.J. came back to check on her. She made Sam sit up, raise both arms, and then hold them in the air with her eyes closed. It was a test that she must have passed, because J.J. said, "Looks like you're going to be okay. But lie back down and do ten more minutes, just to be safe. Oh, and it looks like Bergit's going to be fine," she added. "She'll have quite the story to tell the folks back home." Sam heard the door close behind her as she left.

Back home. It felt like years since she'd been home. It was still winter back in Washington State. Had Blake mentioned something about snow?

In a few days, she was supposed to be enjoying snow with Chase. She grabbed the phone from her desk to check the missed calls. The screen was blank. *Damn it.* She'd forgotten to plug it into the charger last night.

She set the dead phone on the desk and lay back down. She couldn't wait to introduce Chase to cross-country skiing. He was a downhill skier, so he'd have the snowplow down; that was the hardest part. Of course he'd be klutzy at first. But Chase was fit, and soon he'd be sidestepping up hills and crossing streams on snow bridges.

She'd show him why cross-country was superior to downhill skiing. She'd point out prints left by hares and birds, listen to the hoots of owls hidden among the snow-laden branches of the evergreens. When they stopped for lunch, they'd be visited by gray jays—birds that would perch on their hands, featherlight, their clawed toes wrapped around human fingers as they ate crumbs out of human palms. The jays, also called "whiskey jacks" or "camp robbers," were brazen wild creatures. Once a fluffy gray bandit had swooped down from a branch and sheared off a chunk of the peanut butter sandwich Sam held. Remembering that incident brought a smile to her lips. But wait—the gray jays were in the Cascades. Did they live in Utah, too?

A soft knock sounded at her door. She pulled off the oxygen mask and turned off the flow. Just as she recalled the word *Pase*, Eduardo slipped in, accompanied by Captain Quiroga. Yeesh, was there no privacy on this boat? She assured the two men she was fine, raising her arms and waggling her fingers to prove it.

"Lunch will be served in a few minutes," the captain told her.

The thought of food made her feel nauseous. She must have looked a little green, because then he said, "I will have someone bring soup?"

She nodded. "Thanks."

They left without saying a word about the woman who had been shot.

Sam pulled herself out of bed, plugged the phone into the charger, then trudged to the shower and rinsed off the salt that gummed up her hair and made her skin itch. She exchanged her bathing suit for shorts and a T-shirt.

When she emerged from the tiny bathroom, a tray containing a bowl of steaming soup and a chunk of bread was on the desk next to her laptop. Her bed had been straightened. The traffic in and out of her personal space was downright creepy.

Muffled noises from the adjoining room told her the tour group had returned. She heard Ken say, "You idiot!" followed by a loud thump hitting the wall, then mutual laughter.

Each day in the Galápagos felt more surreal. The sun was shining, the scenery was stunning. Only hours ago, she and J.J. had explored a magnificent reef. They were sharing a yacht with a bunch of happy-go-lucky tourists. But Dan was dead and someone had just tried to kill Zing. She had slipped into a twisted parallel universe.

For a change, the Internet seemed like an ally instead of an enemy. She booted up her computer, attached the camera, and brought up her video of the attack on Bergit. The footage started off distant and blue, but when she watched closely, she spotted the bullets as they streaked through the water. She didn't remember doing it, but she had obviously kept the camera focused on Bergit as she swam upward, bringing the bloody scene into startling close-up. Then the video became all dizzying motion as she dropped the camera and let it trail, twisting on its tether while she swam with Bergit and J.J. to the boat. At some point the camera had shut down to preserve battery power.

Sam deleted all the blurred footage and saved the

remaining video on her laptop, along with the colorful stills of the fish and the basket star.

She connected the phone and computer and brought up *Out There*'s home page. At the right side of the screen remained Dan's photo and the words *Mystery Death*, but above that, surrounded by flashing markers, was the message: ZING ATTACKED AND SHOT!

What? She clicked on the headline, which brought up another short notice.

An anonymous source in the Galápagos Islands has reported via e-mail that our correspondent Zing was attacked and shot this morning. Stay tuned to Out There *for updates.*

She checked the missed calls on her phone. Sure enough, there was a message from Wyatt, marked with a red exclamation point. She played it. "Is it true? Were you shot? Are you all right? If you're not dead, you need to report in right away."

She briefly considered *not* calling him, to find out what he would do next. While she was pondering the professionalism of that move, he called again.

"Hi, Tad," she answered.

"Zing, is that actually you?"

"No."

"What? Who is this?"

"My name is Sam, remember?"

"Whatever," he growled impatiently. "Did you get shot this morning?"

"Nope."

"Bogus," he said to someone else. "Totally bogus. Someone's playing us."

"Tad!" she said loudly to get his attention back. "*I* didn't get shot, but a woman who looks like Zing did. I'm writing the story now. Can you forward me the e-mail message you received about the shooting?"

"I'm posting it now on the website. When will your story be done?"

"Half an hour?"

"Try for fifteen minutes." There was a pause, and then Wyatt said, "Glad you're still alive, WildWest." She heard him talking to someone—probably the editor—before the connection ended.

She wrote a brief account of the dive and the attack—the video pretty much spoke for itself. *Will the police arrest the attackers?* Zing asked at the end of the post. It was a damn good question. She uploaded the story and video, savoring the thought of Carlos Santos reading this post and realizing his thugs had missed his real target. They'd been tracking the wrong woman.

When she received *Out There*'s acknowledgment— *Great video!*—she sat staring at the words for a second. Shit! Had she just blown her cover? There had been no other boat in the bay when she and J.J. had entered the water, but the thugs who had tracked "Zing" might have been observing the area from the island. Her video clearly showed her position at the time of the attack, so if any of the snorkelers or tour guide Kyle thought about it, they'd realize she had shot the film. She had posted as Zing but anyone watching would know that she was Summer Westin.

She slurped the soup—seafood bisque—as she thought about the scenario for a moment longer. Oh hell, this had been true all along. Either her enemies were already after her or they weren't that analytical.

She checked *Out There*'s home page again. A link had been added to the notice. It led to the e-mail message received from the Galápagos:

This morning two strangers in a speedboat shot Zing as she snorkeled in a tranquil bay. Galápagos was a peace-full paradice before foreign influences brought vio-lence. In less than one week, we have one death, and now a shooting—more violence than was seen here in five years past. Zing and friends Wilderness Westin and Daniel Kazaki entered our islands posing as tourists, but clearly they came to make trouble for reasons we can not understand. We pray that our government will protect our peacefull citizens and our tourists from foreign agitators like these.

Sam snorted in disgust. *Peacefull!* Whoever wrote that clearly didn't know the meaning of the word or how to spell it. The phrase *foreign agitators* brought to mind her conversation with the woman at the consulate. Did the police now consider her a foreign agitator? Were they amassing evidence to use against her? Carlos Santos, Ricardo Diaz, and perhaps Tony, too, wanted to get rid of her. If she appealed to them, could they persuade the police to give her passport back? She squirmed in her chair, thinking about trusting any of them to help. It seemed more likely that they'd kill her and dump her body overboard.

If only Chase weren't in the wind. She looked at the newspaper headlines in Arizona. No new reports of bodies in the desert. No mention of the FBI. She decided to believe that no news was good news, at least in the United States. In the Galápagos, it seemed likely that no news meant a story had been swept under the rug.

It was only a little after four thirty, so she dialed the American Embassy in Quito, and connected with an English speaker there by the name of John Dixon. After she explained who she was, Dixon said, "We are aware of the situation with the death of Dr. Kazaki."

"There's been another attack." She explained the shooting incident she'd witnessed this morning. Dixon interrupted in midstream.

"This Bergit . . . is she an American citizen?"

She hadn't anticipated that question. "I don't think so, but she was mistaken for one."

There was a long pause as they both considered the implications of that statement. Then Dixon said, "Explain how you know this."

Was she about to step on a land mine? "Are *you* an American citizen?" she asked.

When Dixon responded that he was, she felt slightly more secure, so she explained the whole crazy business of the Zing pseudonym and the redheaded avatar. All Americans under the age of sixty knew about social media and screen names and images by now, didn't they?

At the end of her account, she heard only the distant clacks of computer keys. "Hello?"

"I'm looking at your blog posts now," he said.

"Check out the comments on Zing's post. There are threats."

"So . . . you believe that your blog posts led to this attack on the Norwegian tourist?"

Put that way, *she* sounded like the criminal. She swallowed her annoyance and confirmed, "They thought they were attacking Zing."

"Are you aware that in Ecuador you can be arrested for participating in a political protest, Miss Westin?"

Not that again. "I'm not engaged in a political protest."

"The government of Ecuador may not see it that way. There have been no attacks on *you*, correct?"

"Yet."

She hoped she only imagined the scoffing noise before he said, "I advise you to cease the critical posts. And you might want to leave the country as soon as you can."

She explained that the police had her passport. Another prolonged silence followed by a faint click. Had he invited someone else to listen in?

"You referred to this shooting of the Norwegian woman as 'another attack.' Are you saying that Dr. Kazaki was attacked? According to our information, his death was accidental drowning."

"His air hose was severed and his neck and face were slashed. Does that sound accidental to you?"

A beat. "Do the *fiscalia* consider *you* a suspect in Dr. Kazaki's death?"

The image of that dive knife and earring in the police station leapt into her head. "You'd have to ask them. They haven't detained me."

Another beat. "So, in summary, nobody has threatened you, Summer Westin, or indicated that you will be mal-treated in any way?"

Damn it. Dan had been killed and Bergit had been shot. How had Dixon succeeded in making her feel like a neu-rotic wimp? "That's correct," she responded quietly.

"I'm sure the *fiscalia* will return your passport as soon as they finish their investigation."

"Uh-huh." *And when might that be?*

"We will continue to monitor the situation, Miss Wes-tin. Thank you for contacting your U.S. Embassy." The dial tone announced the end of their conversation.

"That went well," she said to her computer.

She was tired of thinking about the whole sordid mess. She was sick of her tiny cabin. If she was going to get a bul-let through the head, she'd rather die outdoors than in her bunk. And since she hadn't actually died yet, *Out There* would expect her to do a post today for Wilderness as well as Zing. She slung her binoculars and camera around her neck and walked topside. Her head still ached, but the fresh air felt good.

Papagayo was anchored in Darwin Bay, nestled in the crescent of Genovesa Island, also known as Tower for its looming eighty-foot-high cliff. The tour group had explored the island this morning as she and J.J. were diving. Hun-dreds, or maybe thousands, of birds still swirled over the island. According to her guidebook, the island was home to red-footed boobies, frigate birds, swallow-tailed gulls, red-billed tropicbirds, storm petrels, masked boobies, and a wide variety of gulls and terns. If she was lucky, she might spot short-eared owls. She would head for Prince Philip's Steps—a trail that lead to the top of the cliff.

When her kayak hit the water with a splash, a crewman leaned over the railing, then shouted something over his shoulder. Constantino rushed out, waving. "Miss, we eat dinner in one hour!"

"Save me some," she yelled. She slid into the kayak cockpit and paddled away before anyone could stop her.

The wind had died down and the water was calm, lapping gently at the white sand beach. She landed the kayak there, pulled the boat up out of the reach of rogue waves, and then climbed the trail. Birds dipped and swirled overhead, soaring in a circular pattern around the island, so thick she felt like she was climbing into a cloud of giant gnats. The only sounds were the breeze and myriad birdcalls. It seemed impossible that this morning she'd gone scuba diving and witnessed attempted murder. She was probably the only tourist to whom each day in these islands felt like a month.

She shot a video of hundreds of birds wheeling against the orange sunset, then quickly captured several stills of the small gray storm petrels ducking into narrow rock crevices that hid their nests. As she zoomed in on an arriving petrel with a fish in its mouth, she spotted an owl sitting motionless only a few yards away. The petrel parent disappeared into a narrow crevice, and Sam heard the cheeping of a chick inside. After a few minutes, the adult petrel oozed back out of the crevice, flapped its wings, and was airborne. The owl leapt into the air and came down hard on the petrel with its talons. With a piercing cry, the petrel slammed into the rock and fluttered there, dazed. Before it could regain its feet, the owl pounced again, digging its talons into the unfortunate seabird. With a flurry of feathers, the owl took off with the still-shrieking petrel squirming in its deadly grasp.

Sam continued to film its flight, but if she'd had a rifle at that moment, she would have shot that owl. It was a crazy thought for a naturalist. This was the natural order of things. The petrel chick had lost its parent, but the owl had found food for its babies tonight. As she listened to the soft cheeping of the hidden and now orphaned chick, she couldn't stop thinking about Dan's toddler son Sean.

He would grow up wondering why his daddy never came home. Why had Dan been killed? Her imagination moved on to Bergit, an innocent tourist shot to scare off Zing. She was sick of predators.

A wave of birds took off a short distance away. As their wingbeats and raucous calls subsided, Sam heard a footstep behind her.

19

BEFORE she could turn, a hand landed on her shoulder. "Relax," said J.J. "It's only me."

Sam dropped the rock she'd grabbed. "How'd you get here?"

"Panga."

"They let you take one?"

"I didn't ask." J.J. smiled. "Are you one hundred percent again?"

"Maybe eighty. My head still aches, and my hands and feet still tingle."

"And you're still rattled by what happened this morning."

Sam studied the other woman's face. "You're not?"

J.J. plopped down on a stone step. Sam sat down beside her. After unzipping the black nylon waist pouch she wore, J.J. rummaged for a second, and then held out a photo.

The dog-eared snapshot showed a thirtyish man, with unruly long dark hair and a rakish smile. He raised a champagne glass toward the camera.

"Carl Bascom. My lover, I guess you'd say now. We

were engaged." J.J. made a wry face. "That was before his right foot was torn off by a land mine."

Good Lord. "Is . . . was he a soldier?" Sam asked.

J.J. shook her head. "He's an NPF biologist, just like me. He was checking reports of poaching in a tiger preserve in Thailand."

Sam resisted the urge to clamp her hands over her ears. She handed the photo back.

J.J. gently traced a fingertip around her lover's paper image. "The poachers got tired of trying to track the tigers. The cats were too unpredictable," she said sadly. "So they set land mines around the watering hole."

Sam tried hard not to envision the resulting damage to man or tiger. "I'm sorry, J.J."

"Carl broke off our engagement. Said he didn't want to saddle me with a man who wasn't whole." J.J. stuffed the photo back into her pouch, brushed the back of her hand across her eyes, and then looked out at the sunset. "Right now NPF has fifty teams in the field, combing this planet, counting plants, animals, insects. The world needs a wakeup call, and we're going to give them one." She pursed her lips, thinking for a moment, then turned to Sam. "Are the locals trying to scare us? Of course they are. They desperately want that Chinese company to build that new resort."

Her expression was grim as she turned her face back toward the sea. "But the thugs are not going to succeed. Someone has stand up for the animals, for the planet. Even if they kill us—make us martyrs, like Kazaki—we'll be continuing the fight that way, and NPF will send someone else. So it doesn't really matter what they do to us."

Doesn't matter? Sam felt a chill that had nothing to do with the breeze wafting up the hill.

J.J. continued. "You didn't die, and Zing—"

"Bergit," Sam corrected. Bergit had no hint she was part of this battle. The phrases *innocent bystander* and *collateral damage* trotted across Sam's brain.

"—didn't die. So it's a win for our side. The enemy has

shown their hand, and they made themselves look stupid."
J.J. stood up and stretched. "Let's go have dinner. Do you
think you might be up to the last dive at Wolf tomorrow?"

Sam nodded. She wanted to get this job over with.

J.J. squinted at her. "You sure? It's not a great idea after
a DCS episode. We could put the dive off for a day."

"I'm fine. I want to finish tomorrow." Her plane reservation home was two days away. She still wanted to believe
she was going to be able to use it. One more dive, two more
posts. Her contract would be done, the world would be
wiser, and she'd be out of here.

"Okay, then," J.J. said. "We need to get to bed early
because we have to get up before dawn tomorrow. It's a
long trip up to Wolf."

"Who's taking us?"

"Some guys I met in town," J.J. said over her shoulder.
"I picked the fastest boat; otherwise it would take all day."

"Who are these guys?"

J.J.'s shoulders rose and fell in a shrug. "Could be drug
runners, for all I know. It's a pain in the butt to get to, but
Wolf is especially important. It's remote and it's jam-
packed with sharks and other fish, so if any area is getting
strip-mined, it will be there." She glanced at Sam. "Stop
looking so worried. The boat owner has a sideline business
running a high-speed shuttle service between island towns,
so he can't be too sleazy. Plus, my deal with him was under
the table, with only half up front. Half on safe return to
Papagayo. So we'll probably be okay."

Probably? Sam was beginning to hate that word. She
followed J.J. down the steps in the growing darkness, no
longer feeling quite so reassured by the other woman's
presence. J.J. was fearless because she had a death wish.

Summer Westin, on the other hand, didn't have the
makings of a true eco-warrior. Sam didn't want to end up
like Dan. She wanted to feel Chase's lips on hers, help
Maya make a quilt, hear Simon's husky purr as he curled in
her lap, eat Blake's latest concoction, and even watch the

inevitable endless slide show from her father's honeymoon trip.

It doesn't really matter what they do to us? Of course it mattered what happened to Dan. To Bergit. To Carl. To J.J. To her. It all mattered. She wanted to save the planet, but she also wanted to live.

AFTER dinner in her cabin, she wrote Wilderness's post, focusing on the owl killing the petrel and the need to always be on the lookout for predators. It would not make her Seattle editors happy, but she'd sworn she was going to write about the real world of the Galápagos.

Wilderness's e-mail folder held a message from Elizabeth Kazaki. *Dan came home this morning*, she had written. *This little tag was in the pocket of his wetsuit. Is it important?*

That explained why Sam hadn't seen Dan's wetsuit at the police station. Attached to the message was a photo of a small metal tag. It looked to be brass. The beginning encrustations of coral or barnacles obscured much of the engraving, but between blotches, she could make out a J, followed by either an F or a P and the numbers 4 and 3. The end pieces were broken through and it was bent in the middle, looking as if it had been pried off a larger piece it had been screwed or nailed into. The image seemed vaguely familiar, but she didn't know why.

She sent a note of thanks to Elizabeth and said she would report any connections she made.

An e-mail from Tad Wyatt told her to keep the murder clues coming. *Readers are intrigued. At least this is something positive from Dr. Kazaki's death.* Wyatt had no doubt added the last sentence as an attempt to console her. Only an asshole marketer would consider increased readership a trade-off for a man's death.

There were still no messages from Chase in her e-mail or voice mail. He was just unable to contact her, she told herself; it didn't mean he'd rejected her. It didn't mean anything terrible had happened to him. Did it?

She crawled into her bunk feeling such a mix of emotions that she wasn't sure she could ever get to sleep. Grief over Dan's death. Anger and guilt for Bergit's shooting. Frustration from her failure to discover who had killed Dan and her inability to contact Chase. Anxiety because the *fiscalia* had her passport and earring. Worry that thugs like Carlos Santos knew where she was. Armed thugs.

But as J.J. had pointed out, she had *survived* a near-death experience today. Zing and WildWest—and poor Bergit—lived to fight another day. The trouble was, her team was getting awfully tired of the battle.

CHASE wished he'd worn a down vest under his windbreaker. The Arizona desert was surprisingly cold after dark. He and Nicole were hunkered down in a makeshift blind along with Dread, Randy, Joanne, Marshall, and Ryder. Between the seven of them they had an arsenal—six long-range semiautomatic rifles, the full automatic Ryder brought, a pistol apiece, and heavy backpacks loaded with ammunition.

Each of them wore a pair of night vision goggles strapped to their heads. Only Marshall's were in place at the moment as he peered into the dark desert. Without the goggles, Chase saw only dim silhouettes of saguaro cactus. They looked like an army of alien beings surrendering, spiky arms held high.

The stars were magnificent. Summer had given him back the stars—had he ever told her that? He'd tell her when they met up in a few days. He'd also tell her that while he wanted more time with her, he'd take whatever time she would give him. Whether that was a few days, a year, or forever.

Undercover work was proving to be simultaneously tedious and stressful. Every day felt like he was hiding out in a foreign country. That thought made him wonder continuously what was happening to Summer on those god-damn Ecuadorian islands.

"Any minute now," Dread said, interrupting Chase's thoughts. The glow from his cell phone lit up the planes of his face. "They're supposed to be coming through any minute now."

"Says who?" Nicole asked.

Dread held up his cell. "We got eyes at the border."

"If you can see illegals coming through, how come Border Patrol can't?"

Ryder snorted. "Border Patrol sees 'em just fine."

The muscles in Chase's neck tightened. Homeland Security's constant worry was that the ranks of the Border Patrol were being infiltrated by cartel members or corrupted by massive bribes to overlook the flow of people or drugs across the border. "You telling us Border Patrol notifies you when they're coming?" he asked.

Ryder spat into the dust. It was hard to tell in the dark, but Chase thought the slimeball might have nailed the toe of his boot. "Let's just say that the *official* Border Patrol can't deal, right? All they're allowed to do is net the wetbacks, give 'em a nice chauffeured ride back across the line, and then do it all over again in a few days."

"That's the government for you," Joanne said.

"But there's those inside Border Patrol that know there's only one way to get rid of the problem." Randy pulled a flask from the chest pocket of his jacket, unscrewed the lid, and took a swallow. He held the flask out and glanced around their little circle.

Chase knew he was still on probation, so he reached for the flask, threw back his head, and took a gulp. Whiskey. It tasted like Jack Daniel's. Good, burned all the way down his throat. "Thanks." He handed the flask back.

"So the Border Patrol knows we're here?" Nikki pressed. "I don't want to get shot by an officer thinkin' I'm a wetback."

Chase apologized for Charlie's wife. "Nik's a worrywart."

Ryder put his hand on Nikki's forearm. "Don't sweat.

They know all about this. Hell, they support us, 'cause the man doesn't let them do what needs to be done."

"Don't touch my wife." Charlie frowned at Ryder and Nikki shook off the man's hand. Ryder held up both hands in mock surrender.

Was what Ryder said true? Chase's gaze connected briefly with Nicole's, and then he quickly looked away. Was she as worried as he was? This was supposed to be a joint operation between Customs and Border Patrol and the FBI. But if the CBP connection was corrupt, anything might be happening right now.

Last night, Nicole had managed to find an Internet café and send an e-mail message to her old friend *Rhonda@ freeflorida.net*, which was the actual e-mail address of their FBI superiors. The encrypted message, labeled *Nikki's Vacation Report*, was full of details about their traveling companions and plans and, most importantly, Dread's cell phone number. That cell phone was gold; it was the portal they'd been seeking into the New American Citizen Army network.

The response that came back from *Rhonda@freeFlorida.net* was *Glad you're enjoying your trip. Expect you wear your new jewelry these days. You wearing it Right Now?*

Which meant "Continue, wear your GPS transmitters and microphones from now on, and that the come-rescue-us phrase was 'right now.'" But Chase had no way of knowing if they had any friends out there monitoring their transmissions.

Dread was staring at him and Nicole. Ryder frowned in their direction, too. Chase forced a laugh. "You're not telling me that *you guys* are Border Patrol?"

Dread answered in a cold voice, "I'm tellin' you not to ask."

Chase gave him a look. "I'm here, aren't I? Just trying to pass the time."

Dread pulled his night vision goggles over his face and turned back to the desert.

Chase hoped the tiny mike in his jacket collar was

picking up all their conversation. Or that Nicole's was. And that their backup was within receiving range. The code "right now" was supposed to unleash a team of local and federal law enforcement, who would rush in and arrest the lot of them. But was their backup actually out there?

"Damn, it's getting cold. I thought you said they were coming any minute now." Nicole pulled a pack of gum out of her pocket, helped herself to a stick, and then offered the pack around. Nobody took her up on it. She stuffed the stick into her mouth and chewed a couple of times. "I read about those cockroaches that turned up dead close to here last week. Nice work, guys."

Randy turned to look at Marshall and Ryder. Chase couldn't be sure, but he suspected they were smiling.

"Shut up!" Dread hissed over his shoulder. "Didn't I just tell ya not to ask?"

"I wasn't asking," Nikki retorted, tossing her hair. "I was compliment—"

"I see something," Dread interrupted.

They all crowded to the lookout, pulling their night vision goggles down into place.

The first guy Chase spotted was big and burly and headless. Then he realized he was looking at a kid, maybe fourteen or so, buckled into a backpack twice his size.

"Drug mule," Marshall snarled.

That looked like a possibility. The backpack could hold a bale of marijuana. The man that followed a few paces behind carried two bulging black plastic garbage bags, which could also contain drugs. But trailing behind him was a woman with a baby carrier strapped to her chest and a small bag over her shoulder. A dozen more forms walked in the distance, flashing in and out of the cactus forest. A mixed group, maybe; drug carriers and illegal immigrants, coyotes making as much money as possible per trip.

"Why the hell are they going that way?" Marshall grumbled.

"They're too far away," Ryder whispered. "Fan out." He

moved toward the opening, with Joanne and Randy in his wake.

"You mean right now?" Nicole murmured in a low voice.

Dread threw her an annoyed look over his shoulder. At least Chase figured that was what the guy was doing; it was hard to read anyone's expression with night vision goggles obscuring half their faces.

"Of course, he means right now!" Chase whispered angrily. "Let's go!" He shoved Nicole out into the darkness.

Their group scattered, ducking and weaving from cactus to cactus. Chase almost leaned against a saguaro before remembering the thorns. This outing was going to hell. Where was their backup? Neither he nor Nicole wore Kevlar vests because that would have instantly tipped off their group. The best they could do was their matching red Southern Sting Shootout Champion windbreakers, which, if seen and recognized, might help identify them as good guys. But in the dark, that was a gigantic *if.*

Ryder moved quickly, crouching low, approaching the hikers. He stopped, raised his rifle, and sighted down the barrel. There was a *fftt* sound like a bottle rocket launching and then the biggest hiker grunted and flopped into the dirt. The woman with the baby screamed and started to run. Ryder aimed his rifle in her direction.

Shit! These nutcases were going to *murder* all these people. Where the hell was their backup? Another *fftt* vaporized the arm of a saguaro. The woman kept running, the baby screaming along with its mother now. Ryder tracked them with his scope.

Chase heard a man's shout cut short. Someone else had been hit. Nicole was off to his right. He had to keep her in sight. *Fftt. Fftt.* Footsteps. Shouts for help in Spanish. *Ayúdame!*

Chase jogged to keep up with the fleeing immigrants and their pursuers. Why didn't he hear a helicopter or ATVs? All he heard was screams and shouts in Spanish. The hiss and thunk of bullets flying. He couldn't just watch this slaughter. He aimed at Ryder's foot while bellowing at the illegals to hit the dirt. *"A la tierra! Bajense!"*

His shot kicked up the gravel beside Ryder's boot, and Ryder swiveled. Dread appeared out of the dark at Ryder's side.

The bullet caught Chase in the shoulder. The impact knocked him to his knees. He barely managed to keep his rifle raised. Ryder had him in his sights. Chase squeezed his trigger first. Ryder fell with only a faint grunt.

"Motherfucker!" Dread bellowed. "Charlie's a god-damn rat!"

Nicole fired squarely into Dread's back. The big man dropped facedown to the ground. Then suddenly there were more people running through the cactus and everyone was shooting and swearing and screaming in English and Spanish. New voices boomed over megaphones. Spotlights and headlights flashed through the cactus. The flickering light illuminated the mother crouched over her baby, hunched against a rock and half-hidden behind a bush. Chase staggered to his feet and walked in her direction.

Randy burst into view ten yards away, his night goggles pulled up onto his head. His face was a mask of fury. The pistol in his hand was aimed at Chase.

Chase felt another burning kick, this time in the middle of his chest. He landed on his back, stunned. The fall knocked the breath from his chest and the night vision goggles from his head. He stared at a sky strewn with incredible stars, suddenly deaf to the firefight blazing in the desert around him.

He hoped the Mexican family would live. He hoped Nicole had escaped. He hoped their undercover work would keep this from happening again.

The bullet wounds didn't hurt as much as he'd expected. More uncomfortable was the ground he lay on; he could feel a rock under his right hip and another jacking his bleeding shoulder off the ground. God, he was cold. Thirsty. Exhausted. He could barely keep his eyes open. How could he be running and shooting and screaming, adrenaline pumping one minute, and so completely content to lie motionless the next? He should try to get up. But he was so tired.

The desert sky was so big. This wasn't such a bad way to die. The stars were truly beautiful out here, away from city lights. Summer would really appreciate this view.

20

J.J. was already in the dining area when Sam dragged herself upstairs at 5 A.M. the next morning. Somehow J.J. had coerced Constantino into giving her breakfast early. Her plate was half empty when Sam slid into place across from her.

"Aha," she said. "I was giving you two minutes more, then I was going to knock on your door."

Sam blinked sleepily as Constantino placed a plate of scrambled eggs and fruit in front of her. "How did you say you found this guy who's taking us?"

J.J. shrugged. "I asked Eduardo who had the fastest boat in town, and then I looked the guy up at the harbor before I got on this boat."

"Is he a licensed dive guide? To take divers, boats are supposed to have a special license."

J.J. looked up from buttering her toast. "You're trying to tell me that you always follow the rules?"

Sam pondered Dan's special arrangement with Eduardo, their illegal lack of displaying dive flags, her solo wanderings on the islands. How many regulations had she violated here?

"That's what I thought." J.J. said. "I've always found that in small towns—and although the population here is spread between a few islands, it still all adds up to a small town—everyone finds a way to fit into the system, even if that means looking the other way at times." She pointed her fork in the direction of Sam's plate. "Better eat up. Our boat's coming in twenty minutes."

Sam quickly downed her breakfast and packed her diving duffel—wetsuit, regulators, weights, buoyancy vest, face mask, fins, camera, and waterproof case. It weighed a ton.

She found J.J. waiting for her on the stern platform. Her diving gear was zipped into a black duffel at her feet, and a white plastic-wrapped package lay on top of it. "Lunch," said J.J.

The approaching boat was a pale scab on the blue plane of the horizon. The buzz of its engine arrived long before the craft did. It was a huge flashy go-fast boat with giant twin outboards, the kind that drug runners favored to outrun patrol boats. The owner, a baby-faced young man with smooth olive skin, introduced himself as Domingo Guerrero.

"Guerrero?" Sam repeated. "At Darwin Station, I met—"

"Dr. Ignacio Guerrero," Domingo supplied. "My uncle."

"And I"—the other man held out his hand—"am Nicolas Ayala." Although he was heavyset and middle-aged, Nicolas reminded her for some reason of Carlos Santos.

It was the sunglasses, she realized: on top of his head were perched the same PCB frames and mirrored lenses as Carlos Santos and Ricardo Diaz. *Relax*, she told herself as she sat down on the padded stern bench. Wearing the same sunglasses probably didn't indicate an alliance of any kind.

As they pushed off from *Papagayo*'s stern, Eduardo stepped out from the engine room, yawning.

Ayala waved. "*Buenos*, Eduardo."

"*Primo*," Eduardo responded in a low voice. As they

pulled away, he watched, frowning, his arms folded across his chest.

Wolf Island was nearly four hours away, even at full throttle with powerful twin engines. The noise of the engines made it impossible to talk, so Sam and J.J. reclined against the seat cushions in silence. The sea was nearly flat, and they zoomed through the dark like a racing hydrofoil. Was the driver watching out for whales? Floating debris? If they hit anything at this speed, they'd be airborne and then, most likely, dead. But nothing happened. After half an hour of watching the two men at the front of the boat, Sam lay her head on her arm at the side of the boat, and dozed off.

She awoke hours later with a stiff neck. J.J. was slouched beside her, her eyes still shut. The day was bright, the sunlight rebounding from the mirror surface of the Pacific. Those rays would be scorching when the boat stopped, but for now, with the wind flowing over her skin, the temperature was perfect. The water surface rippled and flying fish launched themselves into the air alongside the boat, sailing on transparent outstretched fins. What flashed through their tiny fish brains? Did they think the speedboat was a fiberglass-covered predator? Or maybe they jetted out of the water at any sudden movement, operating on pure instinct. Did larger fish race ahead to swallow them when they touched down?

Ahead, the dark cliffs of Wolf Island loomed out of the Pacific, rising more than seven hundred feet from the water's surface. Guerrero guided the boat around the south end of the hook-shaped island. As they neared the shoreline, the cacophony of thousands of birdcalls overtook the noise of surf and engine. Tropic birds and swallowtail gulls swooped in and out of clefts in the vertical walls; white horsetails of guano marked their nest sites. Layers upon layers of birds circled overhead. In the topmost air traffic layer, Sam spotted the unmistakable silhouettes of great frigate birds.

"Por allá!" Ayala pointed at the water. "Look!"

Sam and J.J. leaned over the starboard side. Two bottle-nose dolphins raced alongside the bow, their sleek skins breaking the surface between crystal sprays of water.

J.J. moved to the port side. "There's another one over here."

"There are always dolphins at Wolf and Darwin Islands." Guerrero smiled.

Ayala added, "They are the park guards here."

Oh good, thought Sam. Just what she needed: another reminder that she and J.J. were in a remote area with perfect strangers and no official authorities. Not that she trusted the official Ecuadorian authorities to come to her aid. Look at Director Guerrero's speak-no-evil attitude; the suspicious demeanor of Sergeant Schwartz and his cohorts. Eduardo and Maxim were the only local officials she had met who seemed genuinely interested in protecting the park and the visitors.

Guerrero throttled the engine back to idle. The dolphins vanished. Some guards.

"The best diving, it is right here." Ayala pointed to the space between his feet. "There are lava pillars and tunnels, lots of hammerheads."

"Sweet," commented J.J.

Sam blanched.

Guerrero must have noticed her tense expression. "Friendly hammerheads," he said. "All the sharks in the Galápagos are friendly."

Sam had heard the "friendly sharks" bit a number of times since arriving in the islands. She still couldn't decide if it was meant to be a genuine reassurance for visiting divers or some sort of local joke.

She and J.J. stripped to their swimsuits and then pulled on their neoprene layers. J.J. was speedier in her preparations, and was double-checking her tank and regulator while Sam was still fumbling with her weights.

"Lost your knife?"

Sam looked up. J.J. pointed to the empty sheath on

Sam's belt. "I noticed it was missing yesterday when you were lying in the bottom of the boat."

"Really? I had it only a couple of days ago." She'd used it at Ola Rock to cut free the longlined albatross. She searched through the remaining gear in her duffel. No knife.

The image of the dive knife at the police station swept into her mind. *No way.*

"Probably got dislodged when we were towing that poor woman back to the boat," J.J. suggested.

That seemed like a logical explanation; there'd been a lot of thrashing around. But too many disturbing coincidences kept cropping up: the knife in the police station, half brothers Ricardo and Tony Diaz, their guide Guerrero being the nephew of the director of Darwin Station, the way that Carlos Santos had fist-bumped Eduardo's arm in Puerto Ayora, and for that matter, the way that Eduardo had reacted on seeing Ayala, their other guide today. "J.J., you know some Spanish. Do you know what *primo* means?"

"*Primo*?" J.J. frowned. "It means 'cousin.' "

Sam flashed a glance at Ayala. Was this Eduardo's cousin who had been fishing at Buoy 3942? Was he a poacher? Did he know who she was? His gaze met hers; he smiled at her.

"What's the holdup?" J.J. stood with arms crossed, looking as if she would be tapping her toe if she hadn't been wearing swim fins.

"Uh . . ." Should she say something? Or was she simply being paranoid?

"I already double-checked everything." J.J. hefted the tank with attached hoses, slung it in Sam's direction. Sam caught it and slipped the BCD straps over her shoulders.

J.J. turned to Guerrero. "You'll follow?"

"It is necessary. There is always a strong current. You must stay close to the rocks."

"We will. If you see our bubbles getting too far away, please catch up."

He snapped off a little salute. "You are the boss."

"Let's do it, Sam." J.J. sat on the starboard edge of the boat, hanging her tanks out over the water, and then flipped backward with a splash.

Last dive on the list, Sam reminded herself. Ayala looked harmless enough at the helm. Eduardo could have many cousins. These two guys had ferried her and J.J. over miles of water; they could have dumped them anywhere if they'd wanted. Eduardo knew where they had gone. She'd get through this final dive, write her last two blog posts tonight, and be done with *Out There* and the Galápagos. She turned and handed her camera to Guerrero.

"Good luck," he said.

Sam took a last lungful of the fresh air, snugged her mask over her face, took an experimental puff on the mouthpiece, closed her eyes, and leaned backward. The water slapped her on the back hard, then wrapped around her like a cool cloak.

She rolled to the surface, took the camera and clipped it to her BCD, then exhaled and descended. The sequence was starting to feel routine. Despite her anxiety about what might happen, she was still awed every time she sank beneath the ocean surface. Each dive was like a trip to another planet. Sunlight brightened the blue-green liquid to a verdant pastel near the surface. Brighter shafts of light stabbed the depths like searchlights in an evening sky. A school of yellow jacks circled to the right, just a few yards away.

Silvery bubbles streamed upward in the distance. J.J. was already hard at work, thirty feet below and at least forty feet east of her, punching buttons on the little hand-held computer as she swam over a long shelf of black rock. The scene was familiar; Sam couldn't help thinking of Dan. *Focus*, she reminded herself.

J.J. looked up, her face mask reflecting the surface sunlight. She raised a neoprene-clad arm. *C'mon down.* As Sam watched, the current pulled her over and then right past J.J. *Crap.* She was flying fast. She turned into the force and kicked her way down, grabbing a rock a few feet away from J.J. to hold herself in place. She'd been taught not to touch anything underwater, but if the alternative was being swept out to sea, she was going to clamp herself to the rocks like a limpet.

As long as they stayed no more than a foot or so above the ragged lava bottom, the current was manageable. Red starfish clung to the rocks. They swam over a canyon. Sam would have been content to glide over the top, but J.J. swam into the depression, and so she followed. Hundreds of tiny striped soldierfish darted out. Two were immediately sucked up by a hovering trumpet fish. Life was cheap down here.

J.J. twisted toward Sam, beckoning her, pointing toward a dark hole. Sam swam closer. A lava tube, a small cave formed by superheated lava flowing into cold seawater. Lava tubes might extend for hundreds of yards or only a few feet, like the one near which she had found Dan's body. She realized that she was biting into the rubber of her mouthpiece, and tried to relax her jaw. J.J. didn't expect her to explore that dark tunnel, did she? Then her eyes focused on a vaguely sharklike shape inside the dim cave. It was a strange pig-nosed fish, with spiky brown skin and white polka dots and a white-tipped spur on its back as well as a floppy-looking dorsal fin. A horn shark. Wow. She hadn't even known they inhabited the Galápagos. She framed it in the viewfinder and took a photo.

Next, J.J. shook her head and pointed to what first looked like a lump of rock. Then it breathed through its gills and morphed into an amazingly camouflaged scorpionfish. Sam nodded and held her free hand up to show she understood the danger. So much for grabbing on to rocks.

A shadow drifted overhead, and they both looked up to see the white hull of the boat suspended forty-five feet above them. A feathery insect dipped and zigzagged off the port side like a wounded squid. Sam squinted, but still couldn't quite bring the unusual creature into view. On the starboard side, the surface plane of the water shattered briefly, and a similar creature floated down to join the first. Now Sam could identify the nearly transparent threads that joined the waterbugs to the world above. Ayala and Guerrero were fishing.

A scalloped hammerhead swam into view below the boat. A prickle ran down Sam's spine. A friendly hammerhead, she reminded herself. She framed its pickaxe shape in her viewfinder. The white undersides of both shark and boat nicely complemented the shafts of light beaming through the jade water. Then she noticed the distinctive silhouettes of more of the goggle-eyed sharks as they surrounded the boat. Oh, swell. Schools of circling sharks. Wolf was famous for them. So far, the sharks didn't seem interested in the two divers exploring the bottom. Or maybe they hadn't spotted them yet.

As she and J.J. rose up from the canyon, a striped snout shot out from the outcropping below them, jaws agape to display jagged teeth. Sam recoiled as if hit in the stomach, realizing a second later that those teeth belonged to a zebra moray. The eel had to be nearly as long as she was tall. J.J.'s eyes crinkled behind her face mask, and Sam was pretty sure she was laughing. The moray glided backward into its lair as easily as it had surged forward, and hovered there, watching them, its jaws rhythmically opening and closing.

They spent fifteen minutes swimming over the miniature mountain ranges and canyons of the bottom. J.J. constantly tapped on her computer, noting the abundant wildlife. Sam recognized several species from her guidebook. She photographed yellowtail grunts and amberjacks, a couple of rainbow-colored redtail triggerfish, a plaid longnose hawkfish among strands of black coral. Goatfishes, surgeonfishes, cushion stars, brittle stars, parrotfish, blue-and-gold snappers, a spotted puffer. A tiny blue-striped nudibranch. Two green sea turtles, a lone spotted eagle ray that slid past like a spaceship touring planet Earth. The variety was incredible. J.J.'s fingers must be ready to drop off. Dan would have loved this. She liked to think he could see it now.

Another shadow passed overhead. This time, instead of spotting the boat, Sam saw a giant shark. Her heartbeat doubled. The leviathan had to be at least thirty feet long. The fish's dark skin was speckled with white spots, and it swam leisurely, propelling itself with slow swishes of its huge tail. It turned in her direction, and she saw its mouth gaping open. Thank God. A whale shark. While that maw could easily have swallowed her, she knew whale sharks were filter feeders that ate only plankton and small fish.

Mesmerized, she parked herself in the lee of a rock and was filming video of the magnificent monster when J.J. tapped her arm. The other woman pointed to her watch, then to the surface. Sam was almost sorry that their time was up.

As they rose, the whale shark disappeared into the distance with a couple of quick tail swishes. Two hammerheads swam between them and the surface in a slow spiral. As they slowly neared the glittering surface, Sam realized that the boat was no longer above them. She searched the surface plane for the familiar shape of the hull.

The hammerheads swam away as Sam and J.J. reached their level. On breaking the surface, Sam immediately spat out her mouthpiece and sucked in a mouthful of real air, squinting against the piercing brilliance of the sunlight. J.J.'s eyes narrowed as she pushed her mask onto her forehead. They slowly treaded water as they surveyed the area. The abandoned lighthouse at the top of Wolf Island was visible from their position. They were at least a quarter mile from the rocky shore, and the current was pulling them out.

The go-fast boat was nowhere in sight.

21

"THOSE goddamn shitheads!" J.J. hissed.

Sam panted. Was this shortness of breath due to the tension that was squeezing her chest, or to the effort of treading water in full scuba gear? She added a bit more air to her BCD and stopped moving her legs. Where were those sharks? She flipped onto her stomach, putting her face into the water to survey the blue-green depths. Was it her imagination, or did the water feel colder now? A stingray flapped toward the canyon they had explored, dipped gracefully over the lip of rock, and disappeared from sight. The only hammerhead in view was quite a distance to the south, barely visible in the cobalt dimness. Unfortunately, she spotted several sharp-finned silhouettes that seemed to be swimming in their direction.

She pulled her face out of the water, gulping in the fresh air, studying the rocky shoreline. The current had moved them a few yards farther away from Wolf's shoreline. Would it drag them out to sea? She swallowed hard, trying to keep panic at bay.

"Hammerheads?" J.J. asked.

"Only one now. A long way off. But there are other sharks moving this way. Smaller. Sharp noses."

J.J.'s eyes widened. "Galápagos sharks. Let's keep an eye on them. They have a rep."

A wave of dizziness swept through Sam's head. A frigate bird swooped low overhead to get a better look at the strange apparitions in the water. She felt a ridiculous longing to reach out for it.

J.J. groaned. "Looks like we have to swim for it."

"Can we buck this current?"

"Not all the way to the island, we can't. We might be able to go under, but I've only got a few minutes of air left. You've probably got even less, the way you were huffing down there. That rock." J.J. thrust out her chin in a southward direction. "It's our best bet."

"That rock" was a jagged spear of basalt the go-fast boat had rounded when delivering them to the bay. A black sentinel, rising perhaps thirty feet above the waterline, bordered by ragged chunks of smoother lava. It was difficult to estimate distances from sea level, but Sam guessed the rock might be as much as a thousand feet away. "That's the same direction as the sharks," she said grimly.

"And it's not getting any closer." J.J. pulled her face mask and snorkel into place and set off toward the spear, her fins breaking the surface now and then with silvery splashes.

Sam folded her arms against her sides and followed, kicking for all she was worth. The current pushed at her left side, and she tried to fin harder with her right foot to counteract it.

There was way too much time to think. She debated dropping her tanks to make the going easier. Would *Out There* deduct the cost of lost equipment from her check? First her partner died, and then the police confiscated her passport. Next, she was threatened by a disgruntled Third World fisherman, and then duped and dumped by a couple more. And she'd have to pay the expenses to boot?

The absurdity of this line of thought suddenly hit her.

Why was she worrying about lost equipment? Hell, she probably wouldn't survive this particular adventure. Even if they made it to the rock, Wolf was a long way from anywhere. It could be days before a boat happened by. Damn it, she should never have jumped in the water from a boat manned by Eduardo's poacher cousin.

She imagined the staff at *Out There* fuming in frustration tonight as they waited for her dispatches. Would they sound the alarm and mount a search? Would Eduardo?

She raised her head to check her course. J.J.'s flippers churned thirty feet away. It didn't look as if they'd made much progress toward the sentinel rock. She lowered her face back to the jade-colored world below. The Galápagos sharks—she counted five—were keeping pace with them, paralleling them. *Focus on swimming.* She tried to imagine her legs as pistons, fueled by solar energy from the bright sun overhead. Stroke, stroke, stroke, long slow breath in, stroke, stroke, stroke, long slow breath out.

A large silvery shape rose rapidly toward her. Flared pectoral fins, dorsal triangle. She lost count of strokes and breaths. Her stomach muscles clenched in anticipation of the shark's rush, the vise grip of powerful jaws. *If attacked, kick, hit, make sure the shark feels pain,* she remembered her instructor saying. *Make the shark think you're not worth messing with.* She felt the push of water as the creature veered away at the last minute. It had a racing stripe down each side. It took another few seconds for her brain to register the spaniel-like eyes, the horizontal tail fluke. A dolphin.

When the second one came, she was prepared. As it neared, she stretched out a hand, but it flashed away, disappearing in the silvery fog of bubbles churned up by J.J. After Sam had doggedly done a couple dozen more strokes, the two silver bullets streaked back again, turning when they were within a few yards, as if deflected by a force field. They spiraled into underwater barrel rolls and loop-the-loops.

Were the dolphins mocking the clumsy humans churning

through the water overhead? Clearly, these creatures had never heard the legends of dolphins rescuing swimmers in trouble. Or maybe they didn't do their lifesaving routines until the humans were actually drowning. Sam felt only minutes away from sinking lifelessly toward the bottom.

A Galápagos shark zipped into position directly below her now, thirty feet down. The creature had a dead-looking white eye. Were all the sharks coming closer? The dolphins playfully zipped through the space between her and the shark, paying no more attention to the shark than they did to the school of yellow jacks they jetted through. Sam just kept moving her arms and legs through the water.

The waves began to slap her from all sides, bouncing her like a Ping-Pong ball. The surf was rebounding from the standing rock ahead, as well as from the line of rocks that stretched between them and the island's shoreline. She'd surge forward with a couple of strong kicks, then be bounced backward. Every muscle in her body burned. She glanced up. The rock spear was still so far away.

The heck with this. She'd drop her tank. She was fumbling for the harness buckle, holding her breath as she floated a foot beneath the surface, when she spotted J.J. with regulator mouthpiece in place, swimming a couple of yards beneath the churning waves. The other woman made a *c'mon* motion with her hand, then turned and disappeared behind a ridge of lava. Sam pulled her own mouthpiece into position. Even a few minutes of canned air might get her to the rock. She followed J.J., swimming ten feet down, making much better time as she avoided the chop at the surface. The dolphins zoomed close, slowing for a curious gaze as they passed. As their shadows passed overhead, a small spotted ray burst forth from its hiding spot beneath the fine sand on the bottom. One of the dolphins dove down to nip at it.

Suddenly her mouthpiece vacuumed the oxygen out of her lungs. Out of air. She clawed her way to the surface.

Gasping between ragged coughs, she struggled to keep her mouth clear of the waves that buffeted her from all sides. She was in a washing machine. Rebound chop repeated endlessly around her in foot-high triangles of water as far as she could see. She was treading water between rounded boulders and sharp points of rock just under the surface here, at the edge of the outcropping from which the rock stack arose, still hundreds of feet away. Impossibly far. Shivering with cold and exhaustion, she fumbled for the buckle to release the tank. Her fingers felt as useless as waterlogged sausages.

Her leg scraped against a rock below the water's surface. Or maybe it was a shark, bumping her in a test nudge before it took a real bite. She rolled over onto her back, too tired to care. A wave sloshed over her face, followed by another. She coughed. Among the slapping of the waves and the bird cries, she heard scraping as her tank banged against something. The sun overhead was merciless in its brightness. Another beautiful day in the Galápagos. A wave pounded her head under the water, then bounced her back to the glittering surface. First she'd go blind. Then she'd drown.

Her left arm was abruptly pinched in a vise grip. She'd thought a shark's teeth would just slice neatly, not mash and bruise like that.

J.J.'s bronze face appeared, and fierce brown eyes peered into hers. "You're not dying on me, are you?"

"I might," Sam mumbled. *Dan, I'm coming to join you.*

J.J. released Sam's harness buckle and stripped off her tank, dragging her underwater for a moment before hauling her back up. Then J.J. shucked off her own tank and BCD. Sam summoned enough energy to help her hook the equipment over a sharp fin of rock that barely broke the surface. They bobbed in the waves for a few seconds, catching their breath. The clanking of the air cylinders added to the cacophony of the slapping waves and raucous seabirds.

"There's no place to haul out here," J.J. yelled in Sam's ear. "We've got to make it to the stack."

Sam put her face in the water again. *Damn.* J.J. was

right, that black fin of rock was straight up and down. And
there were more slender spears, thrusting up from the bottom like dragon's teeth. They might be able to cling to
them, but not for long. The larger rock they were headed
for was still at least two hundred feet away. A two-hundred-
foot maze of churning waves, bone-breaking boulders, and
flesh-piercing spears of lava. In spite of being surrounded
by liquid, her throat was desert-dry. "Shit," she croaked.

"Swim!" J.J. yelled.

Sam's arm dragged over rough lava. Felt like being
scoured with heavy grade sandpaper. A wave slapped her
face, hard. At least she thought it was a wave. This was not
a peaceful place to die.

Zing wouldn't put up with this crap. Zing would survive. Sam struggled to push herself away from the rocks.
She lifted leaden arms in an excruciatingly slow crawl.
One hundred strokes, she promised herself. Then she could
rest. One. Two. Three. Disconnected visions of all the men
in her life floated through her thoughts. Her roommate
Blake. The guy worked at a greenhouse for twelve dollars
an hour. She'd given him the house in her will before her
last stupid escapade, so at least he'd have a place to live.
Would he take care of her cat Simon? Would he be kind to
Maya? Twenty-five, twenty-six . . . Chase. What would he
do with that hot pink ski suit? Thirty-two . . . Who was she
kidding? He probably had any number of women he could
give it to. Maybe he was with one of them now. If he was
still alive.

She inhaled water instead of air, thrashed blindly as she
coughed it out. Forty-five, forty-six . . . Adam Steele. Former lover, handsome jerk, charming ambitious pseudo-
friend. As a Christmas gift, he'd sent her a coffee mug
featuring a woman howling with wolves. What did he
want? Sixty, sixty-one . . . Her father. She could hear his
deep Reverend Westin voice delivering her eulogy. *She
died in the back of beyond, out someplace nobody ever
heard of. But that was Summer. Always running after birds
and lizards and mountain lions.* He'd be so disappointed

that she'd never married, never had children. Had never returned to the church.

The neoprene over her elbow snagged on one of the dragon's teeth. She ripped it loose, slammed her knee against the rock in an attempt to shove off. Seventy-four . . . seventy-five . . . Dan. Oh, damn it, Dan, I did my best.

You really think so? her conscience asked sarcastically. *You're going to let them win?*

She was a complete and utter failure. Her limbs felt like petrified wood. The air she breathed through her snorkel seemed too thick to suck in.

J.J. was yelling again, somewhere up ahead. Sam followed the sound, unable to raise her head. She was away from the dragon's teeth now, but she could no longer lift her arms. She settled for a modified breaststroke. Eighty-seven . . . eighty-eight . . . Pretty soon she would really have done her best. Then she could just stop and settle to the bottom, wriggle into the sand like a stingray. Ninety-four . . . ninety-seven . . .

J.J.'s screaming increased in volume. The woman was practically roaring. Probably because Sam slowed down. She let herself drift, sinking below the surface for long moments of peace and quiet. She opened her eyes to blue-green. Diamonds of sunlight glittered above.

The roar grew louder. She floated up next to J.J. Between waves, Sam saw the triangular shape of a boat's hull heading in her direction, the long white comet tail from the engine streaking out behind. Two silver torpedoes raced alongside, leaping and then diving back into the jade liquid. Those same damn dolphins.

Maybe she wouldn't die today after all. The pointed hull swung in their direction, approaching at alarming speed. Could the driver see them swimming in the water? The boat bore down on them. Should she dive to safety? She couldn't summon the energy. Her limbs were numb. Where were those infuriating dolphins? Were they hovering nearby, waiting with the sharks to see how Guerrero and Ayala finished her and J.J. off?

22

THE boat coasted for a long moment. It looked like its path would cross directly over her belly. She'd be cut in half. Sam flailed, trying to swim out of the way. Then there was a strong surge of water as the twin engines rammed into reverse. She struggled to keep her face above water.

J.J., beside her, was still yelling. "You goddamn shitheads!"

Ayala's head appeared above the curve of white fiberglass, and for a moment Sam saw the whole scene reflected in his mirrored lenses. His face was curved into a frown around the designer sunglasses.

Guerrero's visage swam into focus beside his partner's. He, too, wore an anxious expression. Or maybe an angry one—it was hard to tell through the film of salt water that sloshed against her mask.

J.J. switched to Spanish. *"Idiotas!"* Was it wise to be calling them names right now?

Guerrero hefted a long metal pole to shoulder level. It made a hissing sound as it split the air, descending toward J.J.'s head. The black woman dodged sideways, and the

pole wedged against a hump of black rock behind her.
Guerrero pushed, shoving the boat away from the lava outcropping. He barked an order in Spanish to Ayala. The
other man disappeared. A second later his dark curls reappeared, struggling with something he carried. A rifle?
Speargun? Sam waited for the barrel of a weapon to slide
over the side of the boat.

A boat ladder splashed into the water in front of her.
One of those horrible cheap things, metal chains and plastic steps. It immediately floated sideways. Ayala struggled
to keep it in place. Sam grabbed one of the chains. At least
it was something to hold on to. J.J.'s fingers clenched on to
a yellow plastic step. The boat bounced into them. Sam's
legs drifted under the hull. She fought to pull herself
upright again.

Ayala shouted something in Spanish. "Fins!" J.J.'s voice
was loud in her ear.

Sam let go of the ladder, sank beneath the surface, and
laboriously peeled off her swim fins. She cracked her head
on the hull as she fought her way through the current and
back into the world of air-breathers, surfacing in time to
see J.J's muscular calves and slender feet disappear over
the side of the boat.

Ayala took her swim fins, and Sam curled her fingers
around the chains at the sides of the ladder. She forced her
feet onto a step, which swam under the curve of the boat.
Just a few more inches, she told herself. You can do it. It
may take a while, but . . . Then her forearms were enclosed
in a bruising grip and Ayala hauled her over the side. She
tried to find her legs, but instead collapsed onto the floor of
the boat. Her shoulders and head lolled against the rear
seat. She abruptly realized that as well as her BCD and
tank, she'd ditched her camera. *Out There* would not take
that news well.

The ride was not any smoother topside. With a horrible
scraping sound, the boat jolted off a rock. Sam bit her
tongue, and the taste of blood filled her mouth with a metallic tang. There was a lot of shouting and jumping from side

to side in the cockpit. More bouncing, rocking. J.J.'s air cylinder and attached BCD swung over the side of the boat, suspended on a boat hook, and then thunked into the cockpit in front of her. Sam's gear followed. She watched as the camera crash-landed on top of J.J.'s BCD.

Her head hurt. Her tongue hurt. Bile burned her stomach and throat, but throwing up would require crawling to the side of the boat. She closed her eyes and focused on breathing slowly.

The bouncing changed to rocking. The swells still made her stomach lurch from side to side, but the rolling was better than the pounding. She felt the motor's vibrations beneath her back as Guerrero switched from reverse to forward. When she was sure she was not going to vomit, Sam opened her eyes and studied the sodden heap at her side. Juanita Jane Bradley lay sprawled on the floor, her head propped up on a life vest. It was satisfying to see that J.J. looked done in, too.

One brown eye opened. "God Almighty," J.J. groaned.

"Amen," said Sam.

Guerrero manned the wheel. Ayala clutched the back of a seat, holding a satellite phone to his ear. *"Las llevamos ahora."* He snorted, then added, *"Claro, vivas."*

J.J. translated in a hoarse whisper. "We're bringing them now. Of course, alive."

Sam couldn't decide if that was ominous or reassuring. She was so tired of not knowing what was going on, of feeling like a very small rodent in an endless cat and mouse game.

"Guess we're not going to die today," J.J. said.

Ayala stuck the phone into his pocket and then stepped between them, opened the compartment beneath the rear seat cushions to extract rough wool blankets, which he then flung over Sam and J.J. He pressed a thermos top full of brown liquid into Sam's hand, and when she didn't put it to her lips, he held it there for her. Why was everyone always forcing coffee on her? She tried to form the words to say that she didn't want it, but he poured it down her throat

anyway. Not so bad. Lukewarm coffee, but it burned. Some
kind of liquor in there, too.

"Who were you talking to?" Sam gasped.

"Papagayo." Ayala poured another cupful and pressed
it into J.J.'s hands. After another minute, Sam's teeth
stopped chattering and she was in control of her own jaws
again. It was a reassuring feeling.

Where her leg pressed against J.J.'s, Sam felt waves of
shivering as they passed through the other woman's flesh.
J.J.'s perfect teeth chattered against the steel thermos top as
she drank down the contents. Ayala returned to the front of
the boat. J.J.'s gaze followed him. "Shitheads," she growled.

She apparently said it loud enough for the two men to
hear. They erupted into a flurry of apologies in both English and Spanish. Most of their words were lost in the engine noise and wind, but *sorry* was echoed at least twenty
times, and Sam caught the word *fishing* as well. Then she
noticed that the solid heap over which her legs were
stretched was not a rolled-up tarp but a huge mackerel. Its
sleek silver scales were already losing their luster in this
alien world.

". . . hooked, but he swim fast," Ayala yelled. "We follow him, just a little way far from the rocks."

"So the line would not break," Guerrero chimed in.

J.J. was not appeased. Through clenched teeth, she
hissed, "You damn near killed us."

"Yeah." Sam could hardly believe such an inane addition had come from her lips. She pressed them firmly
together to keep it from happening again.

"But everything ends happily, no?" Ayala yelled, beaming. "You are safe, we are here, we have this excellent fish."

Sam pushed her feet against the excellent fish, using its
weight to lever herself into a more upright position. She
rubbed her hand over her aching forehead and leaned
against the rear seat cushion. They were headed back east
to *Papagayo*'s moorage. The lighthouse on Wolf was
already a tiny blur at the top of the island silhouette, difficult to make out in all the burning brightness. Where had

her sunglasses gotten to? A second later she wondered if she'd voiced the question, because Ayala handed them to her, along with a paper sack and a can of soda. "Enjoy your lunch."

Ayala helped J.J. onto the padded bench, tucking the blanket carefully around her legs. He placed a similar sack in her lap and returned to the bow. Sam stayed on the floor, chewing carefully, determined not to bite her tongue again as they hydroplaned over the tops of swells.

"Let's toss their excellent fish overboard, J.J.," she suggested.

"Maybe when we get to *Papagayo*."

Oh, yeah, they were not quite safe yet. But they were getting there fast. Had these two guys intended to kill them? Had they been saved only by that call from *Papagayo*? Was that Eduardo's doing? She was grateful to be alive. She turned to her dive partner. "We did it, J.J. That was the last site on Dan's list."

J.J. held up her right hand. Sam clapped it in a weak high five.

She'd write her posts for the day, and then she'd be done with this crazy job. She'd accomplished her mission. Hard to believe that she'd been drowning fifteen minutes ago. She should be thinking profound thoughts after such an experience, shouldn't she? Instead, her mind was a complete blank. She rested her head on the seat cushion.

Maybe it was the sudden drop in speed as they approached *Papagayo* that awakened her, or maybe it was J.J.'s muttered "Oh, shit. Not now."

Sam kept her eyes closed for a minute longer. What else *could* happen? Surely the law of averages was on her side now. Her neck was excruciatingly stiff from lolling backward against the seat cushion. Could she even hold her head upright? Maybe she'd pretend she was unconscious; let the crew carry her from this boat to her bunk.

J.J. nudged her with an elbow, forcing her to sit up. The vertebrae between her shoulders popped as she raised her head.

It was just past sundown. A strip of orange still marked the transition between the inky blue ocean and the night sky, but that would disappear within minutes. The islands in the background were unfamiliar. *Papagayo* had moved to the next stop on its itinerary so the tour group could explore James (Santiago) Island on their last day. Tomorrow, the boat was scheduled to deliver the passengers to the Baltra airport to catch their flight home.

The Navy boat was rafted up alongside *Papagayo* again, a couple of officers standing attentively in its bow. For a brief moment, Sam had hope that they'd stopped by to drop off her passport. But then she saw Officers Schwartz and Aguirre, and Montero, the ponytailed woman from the police station, on the walkway surrounding *Papagayo*'s main deck, observing the arrival of the go-fast boat.

Above the *fiscalia* officers, the tour group and Jon and Paige Sanders lined the railing on the uppermost deck. Clearly everyone was waiting for the main event to begin. It didn't seem likely that returning her passport would be such a big attraction.

The go-fast boat slid into position on the other side of *Papagayo*. Sam stood up to step aboard. Sergeant Schwartz descended the steps, pulled his pistol out of his holster, and pointed it at her.

23

NOW Sam knew how a perp walk felt. Except that instead of being paraded from jail to court down an alley lined with reporters, her perp walk involved being awkwardly transferred from one bouncing boat to another. Did the presence of the woman officer mean they intended to strip-search her or something equally awful?

J.J. leaned close. "They won't get away with this."

Sam wasn't so sure about that. Nobody was protesting at the moment. Guerrero and Ayala stuck to the far side of their boat as she climbed over their excellent mackerel and onto *Papagayo*'s stern platform. She was painfully aware of the two male *fiscalia* officers' pistol barrels tracking her movements. Officer Montero stepped onto the platform and took hold of Sam's arm in a firm grip. "You are under arrest," she said in English.

No shit, Sam thought. "What the hell for?" she said aloud.

Surprise flashed across Montero's face. "For murder of Daniel Kazaki."

Sam held her breath, expecting them to read her rights.

They didn't. *Oh crap.* She was far, far from home. And in big, big trouble. "What?" she squeaked.

"Dr. Kazaki was cut." Montero made a slashing motion from her cheek down her neck. "We have your dive knife with your fingerprints, your earring, all found where he died."

"No," Sam said. "That's not possible." When she'd found Dan's body, she hadn't even had her dive knife with her.

Did she have the right to an attorney in Ecuador? How the hell would she find one? Would she even get a phone call? Damn it, how could Chase be incommunicado when she needed him most?

Eduardo squeezed past J.J. on the stern platform and bent close to Sam's ear. "I will come see you tomorrow night." Was that supposed to be reassuring? Then Eduardo climbed back up to the main deck to join the tourists and crew.

The officers didn't bother to handcuff her, but merely shoved her aboard the Navy boat. Her two duffel bags and her computer and camera cases sat on the deck, bulging with what Sam supposed was gear and clothing from her cabin. The sight gave her a glimmer of hope. Maybe they'd simply deport her; put her on the next flight home.

As the Navy boat pulled away, the tourists and staff watched the spectacle. Abigail Birsky kept one hand curled against her chest as if fighting off a heart attack. "God bless you, Sandy," she shouted in a wavery voice.

Sandy Roberson gave the older woman a sideways glance. Ron Birsky leaned down to whisper in his wife's ear, no doubt telling Abigail that she'd called Sam the wrong name. Ken raised a clenched fist in the air. Which meant what? *Fight? Stay strong?* Sandy Roberson smiled and waved tentatively. *Bon voyage?*

As soon as the Navy captain maneuvered the patrol boat out of sight of *Papagayo*, the police holstered their pistols. They didn't bother to handcuff her on the way back to Puerto Ayora. A sailor helped her stow her camera and dive gear. She lifted the computer case and was relieved to feel the weight of her laptop inside. "My phone?" she asked.

Schwartz pulled it out of his shirt pocket, turned it on, and held it out toward her. She could see a long list of voice mail messages, but she didn't have the chance to read the names before he turned it off and slipped it back into his pocket.

"Don't I get a phone call?"

"Mas tarde," Schwartz growled.

Montero translated, "More later."

She changed into dry khakis and a T-shirt in a tiny interior cabin as Officer Montero watched and Schwartz and Aguirre waited outside the door. Then they all trooped up to the bridge to join the two Navy officers there.

As the boat plowed through the inky water, the police and Navy officers shared sandwiches and conversed in Spanish, laughing now and then. Clearly they all knew one another.

Except for an occasional over-the-shoulder glance, nobody paid much attention to her. She could dash though the door and jump overboard before they would even notice. And then what? Tread water in the midst of miles of dark ocean with lots of friendly sharks? That might be what the officers were hoping for.

She consumed a sandwich and an orange drink that Schwartz handed her, then stretched out on a bench inside the cabin. She'd save her strength for whatever was coming next.

After docking in Puerto Ayora, Aguirre said *adiós* and strolled off, leaving Schwartz and Montero to handcuff Sam and escort her through the town. It seemed odd that they had no police vehicle waiting. But then, as more and more interested faces appeared at windows and peeked from beneath the lamps in outdoor cafés, the light dawned. She was the main attraction in a piece of Galapagueño performance art. She straightened her spine and tried to assume an appearance of outrage and innocence.

The Puerto Ayora jail was about two blocks away, a small cement-block building set back from the street. In passing, Sam would have mistaken it for a water district or electric utility hut. As they entered, Schwartz switched on the lights. The building housed a small, bare front room with a desk and, behind a cement-block divider, a narrow hallway fronting only two cells. Apparently the government wasn't expecting a lot of criminal activity. A pungent odor—equal parts urine, old beer, and ammonia—filled the jail area. If she'd had a free hand, Sam would have pinched her nostrils shut.

The first cell they passed held two men in tattered clothing. Both lay on their bunks, each with an arm thrown across his eyes.

Montero pushed Sam against the bars of the second cell as Schwartz unlocked the door. The front wall was barred, and a bed extended from each of the three cement walls that enclosed the cell. A metal toilet with no seat occupied one corner. A mottled brown gecko had glued itself to the wall a few inches above the toilet tank; it swiveled its head as Schwartz opened the door.

A young man looked up from his position on the center bed. Early twenties, Sam guessed. His khaki shorts hung to his knees and exposed a good two inches of jockey shorts above the waistline. He wore no shirt and his face and chest were sunburned. No socks with his Nikes. Pale hair hung to his shoulders and matching stubble dotted his chin. Was he going to be her cellmate?

Schwartz jerked his chin in the direction of the open door. The youth rose and scuttled sideways past the officers.

"No more trouble," Schwartz growled as he passed. The kid flashed an uncertain smile, then fled the building.

Sam stared at Schwartz as he pulled her through the doorway. "I knew you spoke English."

He shrugged, then stepped behind her to unlock the cuffs. They slipped off her wrists. The door clanged shut behind her. Her heart leapt to her throat.

"Wait a minute!" she yelled at their retreating backs. She wrapped her fingers around the bars. The door was solid; it didn't even rattle when she tested it. "Where's my phone call? What's going to happen now?"

In answer, there was only a muffled epithet from the other cell. No doubt the Spanish equivalent of "Shut up."

The lights abruptly went out and she heard the building door shut with a thud, followed by the sound of a lock clicking into place. Clearly there would be no answers tonight. Sam fumbled her way to the opposite wall in the dim light that spilled from the single window overhead. She sat down hard on the thin mattress the kid had vacated, wincing at the shock that traveled up her spine. The pad rested directly on a poured concrete bench. No springs. No pillows. She collected one of the other two mattresses and layered it on top of the first, then rolled the remaining pad into a semblance of a pillow. Tolerable, she judged after stretching out on it. But there was only one thin gray cotton blanket, and it was already chilly in the cement building after dark. The high window had no glass, only a heavy wire grid.

Could she signal for help? She stood up on the concrete bench and twined her fingers through the window mesh. Standing on tiptoe and leaning against the block wall, she stretched until she could see over the lip of rough concrete. The cell looked out on a field of rocks and sparse grass, weakly illuminated by a bare yellow bulb on the back wall of the building. A spotted horse occupied the lean pasture.

"Help?" she murmured. The pinto raised its head and pricked its ears in her direction, chewing thoughtfully. Was this going to be her view of the outside world from now on?

She let herself drop back down to the mattress, where she sat, legs crossed, her face in her hands.

What was she going to do now? What *could* she do now? At least the team at *Out There* would notice that something had gone wrong. They would already be upset that her posts for the day had not arrived on time. J.J. would yell at someone, or more likely at everyone.

She stretched out on the bare mattress and pulled up the blanket. Something scuttled across the floor beneath her bunk, and then there was a crunching sound. The gecko had no doubt scored a meal, probably a cockroach. The saga of predator and prey continued, even in a jail cell. She felt a flash of sympathy for the roach.

Snoring ensued from the cell next door, stopped, and then started again. Sam closed her eyes and tried to envision herself home on the couch, with Simon purring in her lap, Blake cooking in the kitchen, and Chase by her side.

24

THE clang of the steel door startled Sam awake. Her tongue and throat were dry. She opened her eyes just in time to catch Montero's legs walking away under a khaki uniform skirt. The exterior building door thudded shut. One of the guys in the cell next door yelled something in Spanish. This time the words sounded more like a plea than a curse.

She pushed herself up on her bunk. A large cockroach fell off the blanket down near her ankles, landing upside down on the floor with a tiny click. Ugh. She itched all over. Her hair was stiff with salt from yesterday's adventure; she couldn't even work her fingers through it. Good thing there was no mirror in the cell.

But her depressing accommodations now held interesting items: sitting on the floor just inside her cell door was her clothes duffel, a paper sack and covered cup, and most startling of all, her computer case. They gave back her laptop?

She quickly searched through her belongings. Her cameras were stuffed inside her clothing bag; that was a relief. But there was no phone. Was Schwartz exploring the numbers on the satellite phone? She hoped he was calling all of them.

She opened the paper bag. Two stale cinnamon buns. They were better than nothing, and she was especially grateful for the coffee in the cup. It was lukewarm but strong. And she definitely needed strength this morning.

Why had they given her back the laptop? That would never happen in a U.S. jail. Maybe they worried about accusations of stealing it? The case was clearly marked, PROPERTY OF KEY CORPORATION.

Maybe they didn't think she could communicate without the phone connection to the Internet. The loaner from Key Corp had a built-in Wi-Fi receiver. But would there be a wireless network in range? It didn't seem likely that the Galápagos jail was a hot spot.

There was no electrical outlet in her cell, which she guessed shouldn't have been surprising. Sam booted up the laptop, praying the officers hadn't wiped the hard drive or run the battery down to zero.

Her normal password screen appeared. She entered her code and was rewarded with the appearance of the browser home screen. The battery power was 89 percent. She immediately opened the network list. *Searching . . .* the program reported. The battery power drained down to 81 percent as she watched. *C'mon, come on!*

Finally, the computer coughed up three nearby wireless networks. Cafenovo was secured so she couldn't get in without a passcode; but Casa de García and Hotel Milagro were not. She selected the one with the strongest signal: Casa de García. After connecting, her laptop reported the signal as "poor." Hell, she was grateful to find any connection.

The laptop had probably been used by a Key Corp employee before she got it. She didn't want to rely on e-mail; who knew how long that might take to get delivered? What were the odds . . . she searched through the programs. *Yes!* Skype was installed. She launched it and typed in Tad Wyatt's number at *Out There*. There were geeks at Key who actually slept in their offices. It was not yet 6 A.M. on the U.S. West Coast, but after her failure to report last night, he might be sitting at his desk, fuming at her, and trying to concoct posts for Zing and Wilderness.

She was right. "What the hell is going on? I called you at least ten times," he answered. "Did someone else die?"

She snorted. "Well, J.J. and I almost died yesterday, if that counts for anything."

"I can barely hear you," he shouted. "Who's J.J.?"

She leaned closer to the laptop's built-in microphone. "I'm using Skype; they took my phone. J.J.'s the gal who replaced Dan Kazaki. But don't mention her name anywhere."

"Westin, what the hell—"

"I'm in jail in Puerto Ayora, Tad." She cut him off. "I got arrested last night."

"What?"

"I've been charged with Dan Kazaki's murder."

There was a long pause. "Wyatt? Did you hear me?"

"I heard you. Murder. Jail. Using Skype to call from your laptop."

"Yes, but I can't do it for long. I only have battery power, there's no outlet in my cell, and a guard could show up at any minute."

"Then you better start writing now."

"Wyatt! Tad! You've got to help me."

"Don't sweat, we'll think of something. But posting your predicament is your best defense. Do it *now*." He broke the connection.

Unbelievable! *Don't sweat?* Easy for him to say.

She called the U.S. Embassy in Quito. When she told the clerk she'd been arrested, the woman said, "Yes, we have been informed. We are studying the situation."

"Oh, that's fantastic. I feel *so* much better. Thanks for your support." She was about to click End when the network app reported a lost connection, saving her the trouble.

Tad Wyatt could be right; maybe posting her story online would be the most useful thing she could do at this point. While the laptop searched for a wireless connection, she typed as fast as she could, describing yesterday's events and explaining she was being framed.

Still searching . . . the network app reported. She located her camera cable and downloaded her photos from yesterday so Wyatt could see she'd done her job, even though it seemed slightly lunatic to be worrying about her status as an Internet reporter right now.

Finally, the laptop reported it had connected to Casa de García again. She uploaded the article and photos.

What next? She chewed her thumbnail for a few seconds, took another swallow of cold coffee, and then called her home phone number. Blake didn't answer—he was no doubt still sleeping—but she left him a message. She had no idea what her housemate might do with the information, but she wanted him to know that she might not be back for a while. At least he could feed Simon and pay the utility bills.

There was still no e-mail from Chase. She checked the headlines for Arizona and the national news. Record snowfall in the Rockies. Multicar collision in fog on the East Coast. Congress deadlocked over budget again. Then—oh God, there it was: SHOOTOUT IN ARIZONA DESERT LEAVES TWO DEAD AND SEVEN WOUNDED. A gun battle between government agents and illegal immigrants and some group called the New American Citizen Army. Two government agents killed, two wounded, one illegal immigrant dead, and five others—unnamed as to what group they belonged to—wounded.

Two government agents killed. Had Chase been dead all the while she'd been cursing him? Maybe Nicole was dead, too. Or maybe they were only among the wounded? She called Chase's home number. No answer.

"Chase," she began. Her throat closed up as she choked out the only words she needed to say: *"Te quiero."* I love you.

Next, she looked up the number for the FBI office in Salt Lake. "Special Agent Chase Perez, please."

"He's in the field, ma'am. Would you like his voice mail?"

"No. I'm a personal friend. I really need to know if he's . . . all right."

"I'm connecting you to HR."

Human Resources? Was she being handed over to some grief counselor? It was true then, Chase was dead.

But the woman didn't seem sympathetic enough to be a counselor. "Which agent are you inquiring about?"

"Chase—well, Starchaser Perez."

"And you are?"

"Sam Westin. Summer Westin," she quickly corrected. "He always calls me Summer."

"Your voice is fading in and out. Did you say Rae?"

Who the hell was Rae? "Summer! Summer Westin!" she yelled.

"Oh, sorry. You're not on Agent Perez's list of approved personal contacts. I can't give you any information." The woman ended the call.

Battery power was down to 62 percent. She wiped the tears from her cheeks and searched the Internet for any news containing the words *Summer Westin*, *Zing*, or *Daniel Kazaki*, and turned up an article from the *Gazeta Galápagos*. In Spanish, of course. She turned the Google translator loose on it.

The mangled result was hard to parse, but the basic story was that Summer Westin had been arrested for Dr. Daniel Kazaki's murder, because—*what the hell?*—Westin was "jealous in attentions of Kazaki to Zing." There was absolutely no mention of NPF or illegal fishing.

Crap! She had not only murdered Daniel, but killed him because of a sordid love triangle! And the third person didn't even exist.

The situation might be funny if it wasn't so terrifying. The *fiscalia* had her knife. They had her earring. And now she realized that the weird coffee ceremony she'd been subjected to in the station had been designed to collect her fingerprints for the match.

She'd been the first person to report finding Daniel's body. Here, in the local newspaper, was at least one person spreading a story about her. People were convicted every day on less evidence.

She was imprisoned in a foreign country. Her own consulate and embassy were suspicious of what she was up to. For all she knew, there were thousands of Americans incarcerated in foreign countries for crimes they didn't commit.

She didn't have time to fume. She stood up, smacking her hand against her forehead. *Think, think, think—Summer, you idiot, who thought this was going to be a grand vacation—who else might be able to help you?* Wyatt already knew. Her father was unreachable in Europe, and what the heck would he do, anyway—pray for her release? She might be able to contact one of her new sisters by marriage—Jane or Julie—but the thought of explaining her predicament was unbearable, and how could they possibly help?

Finally her mind zeroed in on one acquaintance who might have some clout: Adam Steele, now a big-deal news anchor in California. No doubt he had resources she couldn't even imagine. Did she dare? Two seconds of staring at the jail cell bars answered that question. Thank God he had never changed his number. She punched it into the Skype on-screen keypad.

Of course she got his voice mail. *Yep, this is the number you called. Tell me who you are and what you want, and I'll call you back if I want to.* She checked her watch—9:40 A.M. here, which meant it was only 6:40 A.M. in California. Surely Adam hadn't already taken off for work.

"Adam," she began, "it's Sam. I really need your help—"

"Hi, babe," Adam broke in. "Do you have any idea what time it is?"

"Sorry." She laughed weakly. "You'll never guess where I am, Adam."

"Let me give it a shot—in jail in Puerto Ayora, Galápagos?"

"Great guess." She blew out a nervous breath. "How'd you know?"

"Since you never call me first, I've got a Google alert set for you. Did you really kill that guy? I mean, I've known you to do some crazy shit. Look at that last stunt onstage with the knife and all. But this—well, this kinda takes the proverbial cake. Still, you should have called me."

Why had she expected him to be sympathetic? "First—I've been sort of busy, Adam. Second—no, I didn't kill anyone. How could you even think that? Dan Kazaki was my friend. I am being framed."

"Interesting," he said. She could tell he was scribbling notes. "Who's framing you?"

She snorted. "There are so many parties in this mix, you wouldn't believe it. Can you help?"

"Can you get me an interview with Zing?"

She laughed bitterly. "Get me out of here, and I'll get you an exclusive with both of us—you can interview the whole damn team. We'll tell you everything."

"You're fading. Did you say exclusive?"

"Yes! Zing! Exclusive!" she shouted at the laptop. "After you get me out of here."

"Interesting," he said again. She heard a female voice in the background. Clearly Adam was not sleeping alone.

"Adam? Can you help? Do you have any pull in Ecuador?" He didn't respond. "Adam?"

"*Cállate!*" yelled one of the men in the next cell. She was shouting, so that no doubt meant "shut up."

"I'm thinking, babe. Nothing comes to mind right now. How come Mr. FBI isn't riding to your rescue?"

An arrow straight to her heart. Hot tears welled up, blurring her vision. "I can't find him."

Something terrible had happened to Chase, she knew it; otherwise he *would* be helping. *You're not on his list.* "The FBI won't tell me anything," she said through clenched teeth. Damn it, she was not going to sob on the phone like a child. *You owe me*, she wanted to wail. "I really am in jail," she told him, her voice cracking a little. "They're accusing me of murder."

"I believe you."

Battery power was down to 40 percent. "I have to go, Adam. I'm almost out of battery power. Please help me." She was prepared to grovel if she had to.

"I'll follow the story. I'll do whatever I can. I'll promise the execs an exclusive with you and Zing. But no matter what happens, you're going to see me again. Believe it. Ciao!" And then the computer reported the signal was lost.

I'll follow the story? No matter what happens?

The clunk of a key turning in the exterior door signaled that she was about to have visitors. She quickly shut down the laptop, slammed the lid closed, and shoved it back into its case. By the time Aguirre and two middle-aged women appeared through the doorway, she was sitting on her bunk.

The two women carried aluminum foil–wrapped plates. The trio entered the hallway, but then disappeared from Sam's sight as they moved to the cell next door. The scent of garlic and baked chicken wafted into her space. There was a clang of a door opening and shutting and quiet conversation in Spanish, and then Aguirre and the two women walked back, empty-handed now. Aguirre didn't look at Sam, but the women glanced at her over their shoulders before vanishing out of sight. Sam waved at them and swallowed the saliva pooling in her mouth. When was her lunch coming?

The answer turned out to be "never." Around one thirty she gave up hoping, pawed through her duffel until she found an energy bar she'd packed over a week ago in Bellingham. That was it; that was all the food she had. Maybe her imprisonment would be short; only however long it took to starve to death. At least—assuming that heaven actually existed—she'd get to see her mother and grandmother again. Dan. And maybe . . . Chase.

She gave in to self-pity and let the tears stream down her face. One of the geckos ran down the wall and across the edge of her bunk, stopping as it neared her leg. The little reptile opened its mouth and bounced its head in typical lizard threat fashion.

"You better be scared," she told it. "I might have to eat you."

25

BY midafternoon she was terribly thirsty. There was an odd sink arrangement welded to the top of the metal toilet tank. It seemed unsanitary to get drinking water from a faucet attached to a toilet, but clearly that was its intent, so she gingerly filled the paper coffee cup with lukewarm water and drank that.

The only benefit of being locked up was that she had nothing to do but think about everything that had happened since she'd arrived in the Galápagos. The bad air. The hotel. Eduardo and *Papagayo* to the rescue. The tourists—forgetful Abigail Birsky with her kind husband Ronald, dour Jerry Roberson, sunny Sandy, grad students Ken and Brandon. The regal Sanderses. The beauty of the islands and the reefs. The horror of what was happening behind the scenes. The gruesome shark dive at the buoy, Dan's dead face, the longlined albatross, the threats from Carlos Santos, the shooting of Bergit, the photo of the familiar-seeming brass tag that Elizabeth sent.

The brass tag! She turned on the laptop to confirm her

suspicion about where she'd seen it. And as she stared at the photo she'd taken when she and Dan had discovered the shark massacre at the seamount, Sam suddenly realized where Dan had been killed. And by whom. The truth was worse than anything she had imagined.

Just around sunset, she heard a low voice outside her window. "Sam! Sam!"

She stood on her bunk and looked out. Eduardo was at the side of her window, holding a cloth bag and looking hesitantly up, glancing from one cell window to the next. The horse stood behind him, watching curiously.

"Eduardo!"

He walked over. "Are you okay?"

Stupid question. "I'm in jail, Eduardo. How could I be okay?"

He bent and rummaged in the bag. "I bring food." He passed a thin foil-wrapped package through the window grid. She eagerly grabbed it and pulled it in, sniffing. A warm tortilla. She unwrapped the foil. There was a thin layer of brown paste inside the coiled tortilla. She bit into it. Beans, onions, and peppers. "Oh jeez, so good. Thank you," she mumbled through the mouthful.

Eduardo shoved four more foil cylinders toward her. They just fit within the grid openings, which were around three-quarters of an inch square. He held out a paper-wrapped candy bar, used his fingers to squeeze it into a longer, narrower shape, and passed it in, too.

"You've obviously done this before," she observed.

He shrugged. "In Galápagos, there is no food service in jail."

That confirmed one of her fears. She'd read about people having to buy food in foreign jails. "Then what happens to the prisoners?"

"Their families feed them."

That explained the women visiting the men next door.

"Sometimes the *fiscalia* let out the prisoners to buy food."

"Sometimes?" she asked.

Eduardo shrugged. "People get out, or they are take to Guayaquil."

"Are *taken*," she said sternly.

"Taken," he repeated. "Thank you."

She didn't want to think about being taken anywhere. She bit off another piece of tortilla and bean paste. "Did the all the people on the tour leave today?"

"We say good-bye this morning."

"J.J., too?"

"She get—got—on the airport bus with the others."

So much for her expectation that J.J. would do battle with the local authorities. Sam didn't blame the woman for getting the hell out of Dodge, but she prayed that J.J. hadn't already crossed Summer Westin off as another martyr to the cause. Surely J.J. was in Guayaquil or Quito, pressuring the authorities to release Sam. She had to believe that, or she'd go crazy.

"You know I've been charged with Daniel's murder?" she asked.

The horse nuzzled Eduardo's arm. He turned and stroked its nose. "I know."

"How can this be happening, Eduardo?"

He focused on the horse, rubbing its forehead.

"Did you notice that Abigail Sanders was losing her memory?"

Eduardo momentarily looked startled, but then recovered and said, "She have the Alzheimer's. Ronald tells me."

"She called Constantino Maxim, and she called me Sandy."

"Poor lady."

"And when I asked where you were the morning that Dan disappeared, she told me you were with the group. She called you 'such a nice young man.'"

The daylight was almost gone, but she saw the shiny trail of a tear as it slid down his face.

She had nothing left to lose. "You know, don't you?"

For a second, their eyes met. His expression was stunned,

as if she'd slapped him. Then he quickly looked away. "Know?" he asked.

"You know how Dan died." He only swallowed in response. "You took him back to Buoy 3942."

Eduardo refused to look at her.

"They shipped his body home in his wetsuit. In a pocket in that wetsuit was an identification tag from a lost fishing gaff that we saw there."

He scratched the horse between its ears.

"Authorities might be able to trace that tag back to a specific boat. Maybe a poacher's boat? Maybe your cousin's boat?"

Eduardo met her gaze for a few seconds. His eyes beseeched her to stop.

"Dan's wife has that tag, Eduardo."

He folded his hands in front of his chest and stared at the ground.

"I have a photo of that tag, a photo I took that day Dan and I went diving at Buoy 3942."

The horse butted Eduardo's back, wanting more scratching, and Eduardo stumbled forward a step.

"I believed Abigail when she said you were with the tourists, but Abigail could never keep names straight, could she? The 'nice young man' she referred to was actually Maxim, wasn't it? You might have dropped the tour group off on Isabela, but then you took Dan back to the buoy. He wouldn't have asked anyone but you."

He closed his eyes and made the sign of the cross.

"Did you murder Dan?"

"No! He was my friend!" Eduardo opened his eyes, which now brimmed with tears. "He was a good man. He would not want . . ." His words trailed off without ending the sentence.

"Did you deliver him to a killer? Did you watch someone else murder him?"

He flinched. "No."

She waited for the rest.

He looked away as he said, "It was an accident."

"An accident?" She'd seen the cut regulator hose, the slash on Dan's face and neck.

"I . . ." He choked for a second, then swallowed and began again. "I take Dan to the buoy, like you say."

"I knew it."

"He says he will be quick. He only wants to get something there. He says the current is too strong for you."

Oh God. That's why he'd gone diving alone; he thought she wasn't up to it. Dan had been trying to protect her.

"When he is diving, I see my cousin's boat coming. He should not be here."

"Was he fishing illegally?" she asked. "Was he meeting another boat there?"

Eduardo sagged. His face reflected all of his sixty years now. "I do not know. I do not ask. I only know that he should not be here when I and Daniel are here; it is *peligroso* for all. I untie the panga, I go out to tell him to leave. I am only gone for a minute. Then I turn and go quickly back to the buoy."

Sam suddenly felt sick as she guessed what was coming.

Eduardo wiped away a tear from his cheek, and he swallowed hard before continuing. "I am driving the boat very fast to hurry. I am almost there."

"And then . . ." she prompted.

"And then . . ." He looked at the ground. "And then I feel a . . . a bang. I have hit something. I stop the motor. I see bubbles. And then I see blood."

Eduardo looked so miserable that for a second she felt sorry for him. Then she remembered that she was sitting in a jail cell while he stood outside.

He put his face in his hands and sobbed. "I run over my friend!" He stood clutching his head for a long moment, and then he seemed to pull himself together. Wiping his hands on the front of his shirt, he continued. "I tie up the panga. I dive. My cousin comes, too. But we have no masks. And the current is too strong."

Sweet Jesus, she could see it all now. Dan surfacing, Eduardo racing over him with the panga, hitting him with the propeller. The impact must have knocked Dan out and pushed him below the surface, where the current took him. With his regulator hose cut, Dan had probably breathed in water and drowned before he ever became fully conscious again. She hoped he never knew he was going to die.

Her chest hurt, and she could barely speak for the lump in her throat. "Your cousin told Carlos Santos, didn't he?" Santos had been friendly toward Eduardo that day at the restaurant.

"I guess so."

"So now you're a hero among the fishermen."

Eduardo shook his head in horror. "Never."

"So if it was an accident, Eduardo, why didn't you tell?"

He took a shaky breath. "It is trouble for so many, Sam. Capitán Quiroga could lose his job; he does not have a permit for a dive boat. If Mr. Sanders lose his tour permit for *Papagayo*, then also the crew lose their jobs. Maxim maybe lose his job because I, a park guide, make this deal with Dan. The director. My family. My pension . . ." He shook his head and made a gesture as if throwing everything into the air. She was reminded of a mother saying to a toddler, *Poof. All gone.*

She got it; the list of collateral damage was long. But she was angry. "So you took my dive knife and you framed me!"

He held up his hands. "No! That is not me."

"The captain?"

Eduardo shook his head.

"The police?"

"No."

She knew then who it had to have been. The diver who had gone with the search parties. "Tony."

Eduardo sighed. "*Papagayo* must continue; the park cannot give the permit to another boat. The captain must continue. Tony must keep his job. He have a son with— how you say?" Eduardo used his index finger to draw a line from a nostril to his upper lip.

What? "A cleft palate?" she guessed. This was all so irrelevant.

Eduardo nodded. "And he have two more babies coming—twins."

Yeah, it was a sad story. A real tearjerker. But *she* was the one in jail. "So it's okay to sacrifice one tourist? Is that what you call justice in Ecuador? It's all right with everyone if I spend the rest of my life rotting in prison?" She gripped the wire mesh between them with her fingers.

Eduardo wiped his eyes. "This will not happen."

"Why the hell not?"

He shrugged. "You have many friend in the world. You are on the Internet. Somehow it will get fix."

"The same way it 'got fix' so I wouldn't be arrested? And what about that poor tourist who was shot—Bergit? Those were real bullets, Eduardo. Who tried to kill her?"

Discomfort, or maybe embarrassment, flitted across his weathered face. "Yes, real bullets, but a warning for Zing, not for that woman." He shook his head. "Young boys. They have too little to do here; they want jobs but there are none. So they get into trouble. The boat bounces; they didn't mean to *hit* her. They have no"—he searched for a word, came up with—"wisdom." He swallowed. "Their parents will punish them."

"And you think that's enough?" she yelped, outraged. What would those parents do? She pictured the lecture: *You shot an innocent woman, son: no video games for a week.*

The yellow night light abruptly flicked on, illuminating the exterior of the building. Eduardo nervously glanced at it, and then turned back to her. "I must go now. Do not worry. I am always your friend." He slipped away down the side of the building out of her sight.

"Eduardo! You can't leave me here!" The horse lifted its nose in her direction, its ears laid back against its neck. Shit. Obviously Eduardo *could* leave her here. Obviously everyone in the Galápagos was fine with leaving her here.

She slid down onto her bunk and stared at the wall

beyond her feet. One of the geckos had positioned itself at the same level as her face. Its eyes swiveled backward in her direction and they matched stares for a moment before the spotted lizard's eyes pivoted away to search for insects. The other gecko was still on the ceiling, miraculously able to cling upside down, nearly invisible against the camou-flage of mildew patches there.

"Go outside, guys," she told them. "There are plenty of cockroaches out there."

26

THE next morning, when the exterior door opened, Aguirre came into the building with the same two women from yesterday. Sam pressed herself against the bars at the front of her cell to watch. To her disappointment, none of them carried food or drink. She heard a brief incomprehensible conversation in Spanish, and then the two men in the adjoining cell were released. One of them carried a rumpled, stained paper sack under his arm, and when he noticed her clinging to the bars of her cell, he walked over and handed her the sack before exiting with the others, leaving her alone in the building.

Inside the sack was a bun slathered with margarine, and a handful of raisins. She eagerly crammed the bun into her mouth. She followed the bun with a chaser of lukewarm water from the toilet faucet, and then savored the raisins one by one. If this wasn't pitiful. How quickly she'd been reduced to being oh so grateful that a stranger gave her the remains of his dinner.

If she didn't die of starvation, she'd die of boredom. She

made herself do fifty push-ups, then fifty sit-ups, then a few yoga stretches. That took less than an hour.

Hoping for a visitor, she checked the vacant lot outside her window. Even the horse was ignoring her now. She pulled out the laptop. The power readout was down to 35 percent, and she watched it dwindle to 31 percent as the computer searched for a network. Finally it determined that Casa de García would work again, and Sam searched for news on the shootout in Arizona. The only new addition was that one of the injured had died in the hospital, upping the death count. Had that been Chase? She had no tears left; the cold numbness of sorrow was already setting in.

She opened *Out There*'s home page. Her story was the main feature. *Intrepid Reporter Jailed in Galápagos*. She quickly scanned the comments. There was a bit of outrage, but most readers wanted to know if Wilderness Westin had really murdered Dan. Others wanted to know why Zing had dropped off the face of the earth.

The wireless connection dropped out and she lost the Internet connection. The computer reported 25 percent battery power, and it was down to 22 percent when it found a usable connection, this time with Hotel Milagro.

Returning to the *Out There* site, she posted a message from Wilderness—*Release me! I am innocent!* She thought about posting one from Zing, saying, *I am in jail, too.* But the discovery of her subterfuge might cause more outrage from the locals. She decided not to risk it.

There were messages from Blake, sent yesterday—*What's happening down there?*—and Maya—*WTF? R u OK?* Later, the girl had added, *Jail's not so hard, hang in,* reminding her that the teen had spent time behind bars. But Maya's cell had central heating and meals delivered three times a day, not to mention a likelihood of release in the near future. Sam didn't respond—what could she tell them?

There were no messages from Chase or Nicole or Adam or anyone at Key or *Out There*.

"*Puta americana!*" a male voice yelled from outside.

"Dónde está Zing?" Two thuds hit the side of the building a short distance from her window. A small clod of dirt sailed through the wire grid. Two more voices joined in, chanting, *"Zing es un cobarde. Cobarde! Cobarde!"*

She heard Zing's name, but understood nothing else except for the hostility of their tone, which was unmistakable. How many were out there? Did they know which cell she was in? It sounded like they were on the street to the side of the building, not in the vacant lot, but she was afraid to look out the window. After a few more shouts in Spanish, an authoritative voice interrupted the hecklers and everything went quiet again.

Nineteen percent power. She navigated to the website for Adam's television station. Yes, her story had been repeated there yesterday; that was a good thing. But there was no mention of any negotiations with Ecuador or plans to rescue her.

Had the locals discovered she was Zing? If the *fiscalia* called her employers at Key or tried to track down this Zing character, they'd figure it out. Sam was terrified the hecklers' next tactic might be a Molotov cocktail through her window.

The little power icon was almost empty. Ten percent. She sent an e-mail to her father. *Just wanted you to know that I love you.* Reverend Mark Westin wasn't even back in the country yet. He wouldn't read her message for a while, but if she suddenly disappeared, at least he'd know his daughter had thought of him. He was the only blood relative she had left.

The screen flashed, *WARNING! Low battery! Shutting down . . .*

Then the laptop shut itself off.

For years, she'd wished she could get away from computers. Now she felt like she'd lost a friend. She even missed the previously annoying sound of the fan. She stood up on the bed and looked out the window. The horse had company now. A speckled dog sprawled in the grass, basking in the sun. Could she get more pathetic than envying a dog's life?

Thoreau had said that most people led lives of quiet desperation. That phrase definitely described the atmosphere in her cell; she felt like screaming inside, but the silence of her cell was deafening. She lay down and closed her eyes and tried to envision her tranquil home life and a happy future with Chase. She was supposed to meet him tomorrow. Would he be at that ski resort expecting her to show up? Was he still alive?

Her mind kept taking her down dark roads that ended with trials and bloodshed. She heard voices on the street outside, but no more angry shouts. C'mon, J.J., Adam, Wyatt—anyone! Surely they were trying to spring her, weren't they? Before his admission, she would have added Eduardo to the list, but now it seemed like he'd simply wait for whatever came next.

A few minutes after sunset, she heard someone enter the building and then a greasy paper sack was thrust through the bars of her cell. She was surprised to see that the hand holding it belonged to Schwartz. He stared at her as if trying to come to a decision, and then turned on his heel and left without saying a word. She wondered if the chicken sandwich and cookie came from him or his wife, or some other benefactor in town.

SAM was awakened the next morning by a tickle on her forehead. Ugh! Damn cockroach! She swept her hand over her brow. Something light fluttered away. She scooted to the edge of the mattress and inspected the floor, then retrieved the curly scrap of paper she saw there. Someone had rolled it up and pushed it through the window screen during the night. Handwritten in blue ink, the note read:

Sandman says meet u @ Villamil Airpt today

She laughed bitterly. Right. As though she could walk out of here whenever she wanted. And even if she could, Puerto Villamil, the stronghold of the fishermen, was the last place on earth she would head. What kind of new threat was this?

If she strolled into Puerto Villamil, she'd be like that poor finless shark she'd filmed, surrounded by others of her species ready to rip her to shreds. Who the hell was this Sandman who kept invading her e-mail and now her jail cell? This note indicated he might be local. Could Sandman be Carlos Santos?

She lowered herself to the floor and did push-ups, toying with two-syllable words in her head instead of counting one-two. Sand-man. San-dos. San-tos. Sand-y. Sand beach. Sand-storm. Sand-ers.

She stopped and sat up. Sanders! Jonathan Sanders owned *Papagayo* and other ships. Dan's death and her current notoriety had to be awkward for business. He'd love it if she simply vanished from the country, wouldn't he? And he had the means to make it happen. He could easily have a personal jet waiting on the tarmac at the Villamil airport. Maybe Sandman was an ally, not an enemy. Sanders might be arranging her release right now. The note had to have been stuffed through her window by someone local, someone allied with Sandman. Eduardo? A girl could hope.

She did twenty more push-ups, fifty sit-ups, and twenty jumping jacks, then decided it was time for a break. She lay on her back for twenty minutes, listening to her stomach growl. God, this was boring. No computer, no books, no television, not even the conversation of other prisoners to listen to. She had a sudden unwelcome vision of withering to a skeleton all alone on this bunk. Mothers would drag in their juvie kids, point to her bones, and say, "That's what will happen to you if you don't straighten out."

She rummaged through her duffel bag, extracted a hairclip, and tried to pick the door lock with the metal end. The metal was too soft and merely twisted in the lock. She twisted it back into position and pulled it out. If only she had her dive knife, or any sort of real tool. It didn't seem likely she'd be able to chisel her way out of here with a pen.

She pulled a notebook from her duffel and wrote notes.

I am innocent; help me—Summer Westin. I am being framed; help me—Summer Westin. I am hungry, feed me—Summer Westin. She toyed with the idea of writing, *I am bored; entertain me*, but that seemed frivolous. Maybe later. She folded each note in half and pushed them through the window grid. The horse came over to investigate the paper fluttering to the ground. He lipped a note, spat it out, and then sneezed green specks over the others.

Sam lay down on her bunk again, closed her eyes, and thought about whether lifers welcomed death just to alleviate the tedium of imprisonment. Maybe she could tear her clothes into strips, weave them together into a long rope, wind it through the bars of the door like a pulley and yank out the wire grid in the window. Maybe she could use the concrete walls to sharpen her pen into a blade and attack the next officer who came in. Or slice her own wrists and get this over with. There was a word for that sort of weapon: A shiv? A shank?

Yeesh. This was only her second full day in jail and she was already thinking like an inmate. She worked on various other suicide scenarios—swallowing buttons, hanging herself with her homemade rope or the handles of her duffel bag. *Jail's not so hard, Maya?* You try solitary with no food for a few days and you'll change that song.

Only two days had passed, she reminded herself. Blake, Wyatt, Adam, J.J., and Eduardo knew where she was. Sandman's note gave her some hope of rescue today. She eagerly awaited one of Jon Sanders's minions. She hoped he'd bring a cheeseburger with him.

Instead, at midafternoon, the exterior door opened to admit Sergeant Schwartz and the female officer, Montero. The woman stood outside Sam's cell while Sergeant Schwartz unlocked the door. Their expressions were unreadable.

"What's happening?" Sam asked. Was this her release? It was about time.

"Transfer to Guayaquil." Montero's gaze met Sam's briefly, and then jerked back to the floor. "Stand up. Put your hands behind the back."

Guayaquil? That couldn't be good. How would anyone locate her in Guayaquil? No—she was supposed to be rescued today. Where the hell was Sandman's team? "I didn't kill anyone. Eduardo Duarte killed Dr. Kazaki. You've got to talk to him! Eduardo Duarte!"

Montero glanced at Schwartz, a quizzical expression on her face. He said something to her in Spanish. It must have been along the lines of *ignore her,* because they both did after that. Schwartz clamped his hand around her bicep.

"Please," she begged. "Let me call someone; surely I have the right to do that."

Schwartz said something in Spanish. "No time," Montero translated.

Schwartz jerked Sam's hands behind her back. This couldn't really be happening, could it? *Get real, Westin.* How many times had she had this stupid debate with herself in the last week? Of course it was happening. Dan had been killed, she had been arrested for his murder, and now she was being shipped off to some antiquated Third World prison, where she'd die before anyone found her. She was going to spend the rest of her short life in Ecuador. Bad things happened to good people every day, and now they were happening to her.

As Montero bound her hands together behind her back with a plastic zip-tie, Sam noticed the blue cover of an American passport peeking out of Schwartz's front pocket. Hers? After slinging the straps of the computer case and duffel bag over his shoulder, he grabbed her arm and towed her out of her cell and down the hallway. They exited through a metal side door into a small dusty parking lot.

She was trembling as Schwartz shoved her toward the police vehicles parked back there. Her heartbeat was so loud in her ears that it drowned out the city noises around them. Goose bumps erupted on her arms even as she felt a trickle of sweat slide down her backbone.

What would happen in Guayaquil? Would there be a trial? A new, even more horrible idea crossed her mind—would there be an execution? Did Ecuador have the death penalty for murder? Two women carrying grocery bags stopped at the entrance to the alley to watch. One pointed a manicured fingernail at Sam.

"I'm innocent!" she yelled. "It was Eduardo Duarte!"

Schwartz shoved her duffel and computer case into the backseat of a small SUV with a light bar on the roof and an official-looking insignia on its flanks. He tucked her passport into the front pocket of her bag, and then shoved her in beside them. After climbing into the driver's seat, he pulled out of the parking lot. There was no barrier between her and Schwartz, as there would be in an American police cruiser. The back doors had regular latches. Could she bang her forehead into the back of his head and knock him out? Hardly. There was a padded headrest between his head and hers, and it wasn't as if she could get a running start. Could she unlatch a door and roll out?

The SUV picked up speed, making that plan seem like a bad one—with her hands bound, she had little control. If she didn't get run over by a following car, she'd likely land on her head, break her neck, and end up a quadriplegic lying at the side of the road.

As they headed out of Puerto Ayora, the scenery changed from crowded town to scrub brush. A few bike riders dotted the sides of the paved road. A loaded airport shuttle passed them going toward town. A few more fingers pointed in her direction from the open windows. Nausea rose, burning her throat, and she swallowed frequently. She was going to throw up on herself and then have to ride on a plane soaked in her own vomit and then—Oh God, was she really going to prison?

Schwartz abruptly took a ninety-degree right turn onto a gravel side road. Sam bounced hard as the wheels dropped off the pavement, and then she nearly fell over sideways in the backseat. *What the hell?* She braced her feet far apart on the floor. "Where are you going?"

His cool blue eyes glanced at her in the rearview mirror, but Schwartz clenched his jaw and said nothing, and then turned his focus back to the rough gravel road ahead.

Fear seized her in its jaws. *This will not happen,* Eduardo had said. Damn him, it *was* happening. Schwartz had no intention of delivering her to Guayaquil. On the horizon, she spotted the blue of the Pacific to the southeast. Shit, he was going to execute her and dump her body in the ocean. She'd never see her log cabin again. She'd never hold Simon and feel his soothing purr; she'd never get the chance to form a real bond with her father; she'd never again tell Chase she loved him. *Oh please, oh please, oh please, God—I was just doing my job; I was trying to save the animals, I was trying to do good—if you're really there, if you're listening—*

Schwartz slowed the SUV to a crawl as the road joined another in a T intersection near the rocky shore. Schwartz turned left onto the coastal road. Ahead Sam saw what looked like a rough airstrip, but there were no planes in sight. A windsock flapped listlessly on the light breeze. There were no planes, cars, or people in sight. The airstrip wasn't big enough for a plane to Guayaquil. It looked like a great lonely place for a murder. To the right, on the rocky beach, was a small inflatable dinghy, resting next to a crude wooden sign leaning against a boulder: FAST BOAT TO PTO VILLAMIL. $120. Out from the shore, a long low speedboat rested at anchor. Sam stared. It was the same go-fast boat J.J. had hired to take them to Wolf.

There was nobody in sight at the sign to take the money, unless a couple of seagulls had been drafted for that duty. The birds were busy squabbling over fish guts left out on a wooden plank balanced on top of another rock. The remains of another excellent fish, no doubt. Maybe Guerrero and Ayala were off selling their catch somewhere nearby.

That boat might be her only hope. Sam twisted in her seat until her fingers touched the passport extruding from the pocket of her bag. She slid it out and, on the second try, managed to slide it into a back pocket.

The coast road was full of potholes. Swerving around the worst, Schwartz slowly drove past the inflatable. She twisted toward the door latch. She pulled up her feet and abruptly shot them out with all her might, hitting the back of Schwartz's seat. The seat collapsed. Schwartz's head hit the windshield with an audible crack. She pulled the door latch and then flung her shoulder against the door, rolling out of the slowing vehicle. She hit the ground hard, scraping her right arm from shoulder to elbow. Her hip banged into the rough black lava. A loud screeching crunch erupted ahead of her. She focused on wriggling to her feet and then she ran toward the water.

She glanced back over her shoulder. The SUV had come to rest with a wheel halfway up one large rock and the front smashed into another. There was no movement except for steam curling up from the radiator. Had she killed Schwartz?

Whether he was dead or unconscious, it seemed like a bad idea to hang out in plain sight. Crap. If she took the inflatable, it would be obvious where she had gone. And there was no way she could untie it or paddle with her hands behind her back. Shit, shit, shit. This always worked in the movies. She stumbled a couple more steps toward the signboard and the boulders. Could she hide behind them?

The bickering gulls launched themselves into the air as she neared, knocking the fish cleaning board askew. One of the birds dropped the large fish head it was trying to lift. The head bounced the cleaning board off the rock, tossing a metal object onto the ground. A shower of fish scales dripped down onto gleaming metal. Sam blinked. A knife. Covered in blood and guts and fish scales, but a knife! The tip was broken off but the remaining blade looked sharp enough, serrated on one side and smooth on the other. She threw herself down onto her knees and awkwardly twisted around to grab it, nearly losing her balance backward and slicing her thumb in the process. After she had the knife in hand, she rolled into the cover of the boulders to shield herself from Schwartz's sight. Clearly she was not superspy or master criminal material; it seemed to take forever to maneuver the knife into proper position and saw through the plastic zip-tie.

Finally free, she wiggled her fingers for a second—she was bleeding from multiple cuts—and then, afraid to stand up, she stuffed the plastic tie into her pocket so as not to leave evidence behind, tossed the knife close to the fish head, and slithered on her belly into the water.

Damn, it was cold. She took a deep breath and dove as far as she could, pulling herself forward with strong breast-stroke motions. Her feet were next to useless in her sandals, but she kicked as hard as she could. Her eyes burned in the salt water. Her surroundings were one big blur, but she kept going until the blur above seemed more white than blue, her lungs were exploding, and she was seconds away from sucking down a mouthful of water. Flipping over onto her back, she floated upward, mouth first so she could grab a breath of air without exposing too much flesh to Schwartz waiting on shore with a gun.

She recognized the white plane of fiberglass a second before she cracked her forehead against it. Shit again. Rebounding, she slid up the boat's flank and surfaced on the far side, gulping a welcome lungful of oxygen-laden air. If there was any good thing she'd gained from this trip, it was a new appreciation for the breathable atmosphere on the planet.

Trying not to gasp too loudly, she peeked around the stern of the boat. She saw no one on the beach. She worked her way back to the side of the boat, stretched her hands up over the edge and grasped a metal cleat, then heaved with all her might. She failed on the first try, swung back under the boat. Cursing silently, she let go, then took a deep breath, kicked as hard as she could on her second attempt, and finally managed to get her arms over the side. She didn't risk any time looking at the shore, but flipped herself down inside the cockpit.

Lifting up the seat cover on the stern storage bin, she slithered inside, for once glad to be a small woman. She arranged her feet on either side of the anchor there, her head on the biggest coil of rope, and tried to ignore the section of chain and rough rope in between that dug into her backside and shoulders. Harder to ignore was the strong smell of fish and the heavy vapors from the diesel fuel.

The only up side of her hiding spot was that it was relatively warm. She was out of the breeze and on top of the motor, which, judging from the rising warmth, had been running not long ago.

Meet u @ Villamil Airport. Was Sandman really waiting there? Was she running from or to certain death? Villamil seemed like the lesser evil at this point. In Guayaquil, there could be nothing but more police and another jail cell waiting for her. On the island of Isabela, she might be able to hide out or hitch a ride with a sympathetic cruiser passing through. Things couldn't get much worse, could they? She had attacked—and maybe killed—a police officer. And probably her escape would not endear her to Ecuadorian authorities, either. Whatever might be coming next, she was committed to Puerto Villamil now.

It seemed to be standard operating procedure here to make problems go away, so she hoped that Jonathan Sanders planned to help her disappear from these islands and escape back to the States.

The possibility that Sandman was Santos was a little more worrisome. But maybe the fishermen's union would be glad to assist her imminent departure, too. We never *killed* anyone, Santos had told her. Now those words seemed slightly, perhaps insanely, reassuring.

The rope dug into her backbone. As she squirmed to shift the irritating line down beneath her buttocks, there was a thump from the side of the boat. Muffled voices in Spanish; one with an American accent. Various thuds all around, and then the squeak of the boat cushions overhead.

The engine rumbled to life beneath and behind her, drowning out all other sounds with a head-pounding decibel level, and then they were off. The fumes from the diesel combined with the surging motion as they passed over waves, and she fought to control the bile that rose in her throat. She couldn't throw up in here. Her nose was less than two inches away from the lid; there was no way she could even roll over.

No. She. Would. Not. Throw. Up. She could outlast the nausea. How long could it take for this fast boat to reach Puerto Villamil? An hour? Ninety minutes? She slid a hand across her stomach, pinched the knob on her watch to light up the dial, and looked down her side to note the time. The tiny light also illuminated the blood drying on her hands and wrists. That sight made her knife slashes start hurting again, but at least the pain took the edge off her roiling stomach.

Closing her eyes, she tried to think about sleep, but taking a nap wasn't an option with her head periodically bouncing off the rope coil and the chain and anchor clanking between her legs. Please let us actually be going to Villamil, she prayed. And not headed out to sea to land another excellent mackerel.

That thought reminded her of J.J. Had the woman even tried to get her out of jail? Well, she obviously hadn't tried fast enough or hard enough. Neither had Eduardo. Adam Steele hadn't been involved in this particular caper, so she really shouldn't be blaming him, but he hadn't come to her rescue, either. Tad Wyatt and the folks at Key were the ones who should have pulled every damn string they could unravel to get her back to the States.

By the time the boat stopped, she had worked herself into a fine fury at nearly everyone she knew, including Chase. How could he have asked her to give up her life in Bellingham to assume his in Salt Lake? Why did *she* have to give up her home? Why did everything have to be *his* way? And if he was dead, she was even more upset at him for making her love him and then leaving her alone.

She checked her watch—seventy-five minutes had passed. After the noises of disembarking were gone, she made herself lie still for another half hour, trying not to inhale the diesel fumes too deeply. All she could hear was lapping water and the occasional squeak of a boat cushion or a foam bumper. Just as she was reaching for the lid, she felt the boat tilt and a weight come on board. Shit. She waited another five minutes, but sensed no more movement. Maybe someone had stepped on, and then off?

She pushed gently on the compartment cover. It didn't budge. She put both hands up and pushed. It didn't move. Oh sweet Jesus, had they locked her in? No! She was not going to spend another minute crammed inside this bin! There wasn't enough room to get her feet beneath the lid, so she bent her legs and placed her feet as flat on the floor as she could for leverage, and then she placed both hands flat on the lid. Taking a deep breath, she contracted her abdominal muscles and shoved up with all her strength. The lid moved up an inch, the weight slid off with a loud thunk, and then the lid abruptly banged open.

Someone was sleeping on top of her hiding place? She shoved herself to her feet, swaying slightly on cramped leg muscles, her heart hammering, her hands thrust out to defend herself.

A female sea lion stared at her from the floor of the boat, snorted, and then backed up with a bounce of her flippers. Sam made a strangled snorting sound herself, then leaned over and grasped the edge of the compartment, weak with relief.

The go-fast boat was anchored to a buoy in a harbor, surrounded by other boats. Judging from the red of the western horizon, the setting sun would be visible to the west of Isabela, but the harbor, in the shadow of the closest volcano, was nearly dark. The village beyond the water's edge had to be Villamil.

The sea lion sniffed loudly and moved a front flipper, her claws making a scratching sound on the boat floor.

"Be scared. Be very scared," she murmured to the crouching sea lion. "I am a dangerous escaped criminal."

She lowered the lid of her compartment, repositioned the seat cushions, and sat for a moment, letting the blood flow back into her legs. The sea lion stretched her neck, twitched her whiskers forward, and sniffed Sam, her snout wrinkling delicately.

"I've been in jail," she said by way of excuse. "And rolling around in fish guts on the beach, and then in a locker used for storing fish. You wouldn't smell like a rose, either."

The sea lion shuffled forward, looking as if she might lay her big brown-furred head in Sam's lap. Clearly the animal lusted after the cushioned bench Sam sat on.

She studied the town on the horizon. More rustic and much smaller than Puerto Ayora, although the lights of a few bars fronted the harbor. The owners had taken the dinghy to shore. There was no remedy except to swim for it.

"Wish me luck," she said to the sea lion. And then she slipped overboard and swam toward the shadows under the long dock.

The water seemed even colder in this harbor, but maybe that was because it was dark now. She didn't attempt to swim underwater, but paddled awkwardly at the surface. Why hadn't she removed her shoes and hung them around her neck? She wasn't thinking clearly. But then, what escaped criminal was thinking clearly?

Something splashed nearby. She tried not to think about how sharks frequented harbors at night, searching for food scraps thrown from boats. Then of course she couldn't think of anything else. Every swish of water around her was a predator only inches away. She expected to feel slashing teeth at any second. When her knees and hands collided with the sand bank beneath her, she was supremely grateful.

Pulling herself out of the water, she sat shivering for a moment under the dock. Faint music played in the distance. Two people passed by overhead, chatting. Then nothing. Puerto Villamil was a quiet town. That would change, if the Chinese invested in the huge resort the residents wanted.

She strolled through the dark streets, trying not to squish. The airport would be on the outskirts of town, but which direction? She guessed north because it would be the biggest flat area, and headed that way.

She passed a group of storefronts, their lights out and

doors locked. The first window held fishing gear. The second, T-shirts and ball caps. The half-torso mannequin wore both, as well as a pair of familiar-looking sunglasses, and all items bore a distinctive logo—PCB. The word *SALE!* was scrawled across the window in white paint. She almost laughed. Maybe all the sunglasses didn't indicate anything more than the latest deal.

As she passed by a house, the front door opened, spilling a square of light directly onto Sam. A cat strolled out, and the woman who'd opened the door jumped back, startled at finding Sam in the street. *"Dios mío!"* She pulled her sweater closed over her chest as if for protection.

"Airporto?" Sam asked her.

The woman gave her a strange look, but pointed in the direction in which Sam was already headed, and then closed the door. Sam took a moment to pet the friendly cat. Then she headed off again, trudging down the dirt road. On the outskirts of town, two roads met at right angles and then disappeared into the distance. But there was, blessedly, a sign: AEROPUERTO.

She really could have used a *restaurante* at this point, or at least a bottle of *agua*, but she kept walking. Her exertions had warmed her and dried her clothes to a soft dampness that promised the onset of jungle rot if left in place for too long.

If she ignored her hunger and thirst, not to mention her headache and cuts, it was a pleasant night for a walk. The half-moon and stars were bright enough to distinguish road from grass. She remembered the magical times she and Chase had roamed the Utah plateaus in moonlight and made love under starry skies in the thick forests of the Olympic Peninsula. Was he still alive?

A few dark shapes darted across the road—lizards, at least one snake, and what looked like a rat, which wasn't supposed to exist in the islands at all. But then again, neither were the cats and dogs she'd seen here. She stumbled only twice, once tripping over a loose rock, and once when an iguana darted between her feet instead of out of her way.

A cluster of dim lights shone in the distance. She followed them to a couple of metal buildings and a runway. The first building she passed was dark and padlocked, but lights spilled from the open door of the second one. She heard voices. A small jet was parked close to the building, with its folding stairway leading down from an open door. She scurried in that direction, keeping to the shadows.

Was this Jonathan Sanders's—Sandman's—private jet? She skirted the side of the building. Standing in the shadows, she strained to see the logo on the jet. A giant S-something-something swoopy and more somethings. Sand—? No. SkyCo ExecuJets. Not helpful.

She sidled closer to the open building doorway to listen, and heard multiple male voices she didn't recognize, but they were all speaking American English, which seemed like a good sign. Then she heard a deep, familiar voice say, "Keep looking. We'll be here." She'd know that voice anywhere. She'd woken up next to that man more than once.

Stepping forward into the square of brightness, feeling a bit like the proverbial dead person going to the light, she put up a hand to block out the glare from the unshielded bulb above. Adam Steele stood on the concrete floor with his back to her, blond hair gleaming in the light, beer in hand, chatting with three other men. Two wore white uniform shirts and pressed khaki pants. The third, like Adam, wore an expensive lightweight travel shirt and pants with more pockets than anyone would ever need. They all stood around a folding table laden with—food! Her stomach growled at the sight of sandwiches and cookies.

"Adam," she said softly.

They all turned to stare at her.

"Sam!" Adam, looking movie-star-handsome as usual, swooped down to fold her in his arms. She briefly felt the cool dampness of the sweating beer bottle against her shoulder blade. Then he backed off almost immediately, waving a hand in the air. "Whew! Everyone's looking for you on that other island . . ."

"Santa Cruz," the man in the plainer uniform shirt supplied. Copilot, Sam guessed.

The guy with the black ponytail was grinning like some sort of simpleton. The man with gold braid and epaulets—obviously the pilot—flipped open his cell phone.

"Looking for you on Santa Cruz," Adam repeated. "For hours." He pointed the neck of his beer bottle at her. "Where the hell have you been?"

"It was too hot in that jail. I decided to go for a swim." She grabbed the bottle out of Adam's hand. The cold brew tasted wonderful. She moved to the table, snagged a sandwich, and wolfed it down, chugging beer between swallows. The men stared. She couldn't have cared less. Finally she wiped her mouth, burped, and elaborated, "The police were taking me to Guayaquil, but then I escaped and stowed away on a go-fast boat."

"We've got her," Epaulets said into his cell.

"Who are you talking to?" she demanded. The pilot glanced at her out of the corner of his eye but didn't answer. Her pulse jumped into double-time. She turned to Adam. "Who is he talking to?" Were the police going to descend with flashing lights and handcuffs any second?

Adam shrugged, seemingly unconcerned.

Black Ponytail said, "You gave poor Sergeant Schwartz a concussion. He needed eight stitches."

She quirked an eyebrow at the stranger. "*Poor* Schwartz?"

The stranger nodded. "He risks his career to help you escape and you K-O the poor schlub before our Piper can land."

She blinked at him. Black Ponytail was starting to feel familiar, though she would swear she had never laid eyes on him before. "Schwartz is one of the good guys?"

"He is today. Tomorrow, who knows? When that woman from NPF, Dr. Brady—"

"Bradley," Sam corrected. So J.J. hadn't boarded a plane after all. Some word from her would have been nice, though.

"Anyhow, when Dr. Bradley tried to strong-arm the authorities into letting you go, Schwartz made some back alley deal with her."

Epaulets chimed in. "The rest of the police are still searching for a murderer on the loose, though, so we'd better take off while we can. I'll prep the jet. C'mon, Lyle." The two uniforms took off in the direction of the runway.

Ponytail spoke again. "Yeah, let's boogie. Schwartz didn't volunteer for WildWest to clock him like that, although it certainly adds credibility to his tale of a vicious escaped criminal."

"Wyatt?" Sam asked, suddenly realizing that Ponytail wasn't precisely a stranger. "Tad Wyatt?"

He grinned. "You didn't really think I'd leave you and Zing here, did you, WildWest?"

Hell yes, she did think exactly that. "Why didn't you tell me the plan?"

"Too risky. Plus, we had no way of knowing it would work out." He shrugged. "And you made it; you're here. Besides, it makes a better story this way, don't you think?"

"It's a hell of a story," Adam agreed enthusiastically. "Why didn't we bring a photographer? Sam, where's your camera equipment?"

"Uh. Back in the police transport?" Along with the laptop and her duffel bag with all her personal effects in it. She was happy nobody was taking a photo of her right now; she no doubt looked as bad as she smelled.

Then Adam held out his cell phone between them, raised it half an inch, and pressed a key.

Drat. There was no privacy anymore.

Adam grabbed her arm. "Where's Zing? You guaranteed an exclusive."

"I guarantee that Zing will be on the plane," she told him. "She'll tell you everything. Can we go now?" She wouldn't feel secure until they touched down in the U.S.A. "Sanders isn't coming?"

Adam's forehead wrinkled. "Who?"

"Jonathan Sanders. Sandman. The guy who sent the note telling me to come here."

Adam laughed. "I think you mean San—dee—man. As in San-capital D for Diego-man."

"What?" Suddenly it all made sense. "You're SanDman?"

"Of course. You know Jonathan Sanders?" Adam's eyes gleamed. "*The* Jonathan Sanders?"

Headlights abruptly zoomed into view. The police? No! The crunch of tires stopping too fast on gravel made Sam turn for the shadows. Adam grabbed her arm again. "Wait."

The car door opened and slammed shut again, and as Sam tried to shake Adam off to make her escape, a lone figure dashed toward the building, grumbling, "That town is just plain creepy after dark. This dried-up old troll in the bar said—Sam!" A spiky-haired girl sprinted forward and threw her arms around her.

"Maya?" Sam hugged her and then stepped back. "*Maya?* What are *you* doing here?" She turned toward Adam. "What is Maya doing here? How do you even know each other?"

Adam shook his head. "This girl has called nonstop for two days. Not to mention Blake."

"But mostly me," Maya bragged. Sam noted that the girl's short spiky hair was midnight black now, not the maroon it had been the last time she'd seen her, a few months ago.

"But what is she doing *here*?" she asked Adam.

Maya rolled her eyes. "*Hablo español.* These turkeys can barely order a taco."

Sam stared at the girl.

The teenager put her hands on her hips. "My name's not Maya Velasquez 'cause Grandma came over on the freakin' *Mayflower*, you know."

"But I've never heard you speak a word of Spanish."

"Why would I speak Spanish around you?"

Good point. But how could Maya board a plane for South America? "I'm surprised you have a passport."

"I asked for one so I could take school trips to Canada."

The kid had a passport for school trips? Maya's teen years were a far cry from what Sam's had been like, growing up in rural Kansas. Sam had had no need for a passport until well into adulthood. Which reminded her. She reached for her back pocket, surprised to discover that her own passport was still inside. She pulled it out and began to peel apart the sodden pages. "Where does your foster mother think you are right now?" she asked.

"Foster mother?" Adam squeaked, taking an involuntary step forward.

"Oops." Wyatt fingered his earring nervously.

Ignoring both men, Maya told her, "Overnight at the Seattle Aquarium?"

Adam stepped between them. "You have a *foster mother*?" he asked Maya.

"She's seventeen," Sam told his back.

"Seventeen?" He stared at the girl in horror.

Sam put her hand on Adam's arm and turned him around. "And you tell me *I* should be more careful."

"Cripes," he groaned. "This is *not* going in any news story." He turned back to Maya. "As far as I'm concerned, young lady, you are not here at all."

Maya rolled her eyes again. "Whatever."

The pilot stuck his head in the door. "Anyone else planning to take off with me?"

Sam tried to put her arm around Maya as they walked toward the plane, but the teen shrugged it off. "I'd love to get all teddy bear with you, Sam," she said, "except, I mean, like, you're a little rank."

Sam laughed. "I forgive you. Maybe you could loan me a clean shirt?"

"Good idea."

"How did you know about me and Adam, anyway?" They'd split up long before she'd met Maya.

"I Google, you know. I looked up all that old cougar stuff and saw that he was the reporter. Then the way it all went together, Blake said you used to date a television reporter, so . . . duh! Adam Steele."

"Duh," Sam repeated, grinning at Adam.

They entered the jet, the pilot coming up the stairway last, and then pulling it up after himself.

Sam plopped down into a seat. Maya sat down next to her and began pawing through her backpack.

"Wait!" Adam turned to Sam. "Where's Zing?"

"Sorry, I'm bound by nondisclosure." She intended to run her fingers through her hair in a nonchalant gesture, but the salty tangles thwarted that goal, and all she ended up accomplishing was to open up the cut in the web of her right hand. She rubbed her bleeding hand on the front of her T-shirt, noting for the first time that the fabric was already splotched with bloodstains. So were the khaki pants she had on. She'd have to wrestle Adam's phone away from him and delete that photo he'd taken.

From his seat across the tiny aisle, Tad Wyatt grinned at Adam. "You're staring at Zing right now."

"What?" Adam glanced from Sam to Maya and then back to Wyatt. Then Wyatt and Maya opened their mouths at the same time and chorused, "Duh!"

Sam looked at Maya. The girl widened her eyes at Sam's unspoken question and shook her head in teen disgust. "You told me all about the scuba diving lessons?"

It took Adam almost a minute to clue in. As they began to taxi down the runway, he dropped into the seat across from Sam. "I of all people should have known."

He buckled his seat belt and looked deep in thought as the jet gathered speed. Then as it left the ground, he shouted over the roar of the engine, "This is even better!" When they'd leveled off, he extracted a tiny notepad and pen from his shirt pocket. "Murrow Award, here I come!"

Sam managed to stay awake long enough to tell him almost the whole story of her week in the Galápagos. As she pulled up a blanket and reclined her seat, Adam frowned and said, "Wait a minute! Who killed Daniel Kazaki?"

During her long solitary walk, she'd come to a conclusion about what she'd say if she was still alive at this point.

"His death has been reported as an accident. But as far as I'm concerned, the shark poachers killed him. Dan would never have died if he hadn't been risking his life to collect evidence against them." *Take that, Carlos Santos. Ricardo Diaz. Gun-toting idiot kids who shot Bergit. And all the rest of you thugs that I never met.*

They stopped twice to refuel before reaching San Diego, where a television camera crew met them. Adam had allowed her to comb her tangled tresses back into a braid and wash the worst crud from her face, but she had no makeup to cover the bruise on her brow from banging her head against the boat and the scratches across her cheek she'd picked up diving out of the police car. He insisted she put her bloody T-shirt back on for the short interview.

After agreeing that she would return for a longer session with the station's talk show in a few days and that she would write the full story for *Out There*, Sam borrowed money and a cell phone from Tad Wyatt and made him promise to see that Maya got safely home to Tacoma. Then Sam boarded a flight to Salt Lake City.

27

WHILE sitting on the runway in San Diego, Sam called the ski resort where she and Chase were supposed to be staying right now. Chase had never arrived.

She showed up at the FBI Building in Salt Lake City, determined to get the truth about Chase out of them. With six inches of snow on the streets, she must have looked deranged dressed in Wyatt's extra large blue *Out There* windbreaker, Maya's fuchsia-colored I LOVE BOOBIES souvenir T-shirt, her bloody tropical weight khakis, and sandals. When she told the front desk guard what she was after, the guy immediately pointed at a row of chairs lining the wall, then picked up the phone.

As the elevator door opened, she was afraid that a couple of federal thugs might appear and take her away. Instead, Nicole Boudreaux, Chase's partner, stepped into the lobby. Her right arm was in a black sling and her face was lined with fatigue, but her light gray pantsuit was expensive and spotless, and every hair in her chin-length auburn bob was in place. So much for the jeans-clad Dolly Parton look-alike that Chase had described; Nicole was back to her usual immaculate self. Sam stood up to meet her.

"What are you doing here?" Nicole lightly touched Sam's arm. "I thought you were in Ecuador. You look like hell."

"I . . ." Sam started. "It's a long story." She felt the tears overcoming her, so she stopped there to ask, "What happened to Chase?" She braced herself for the worst. *Tortured. Shot. Blown to bits.*

"Nobody told you?" Nicole studied her, one eyebrow raised. When a tear escaped Sam's left eye and ran down her cheek, Nicole's expression softened and she quickly said, "The agents who died were Border Patrol."

Did that mean what she thought it meant? "And Chase?"

"Mercy Hospital, Room 309."

Sam dashed out of the building and almost fell down on the ice in her rush to flag down a taxi. But after reaching the hushed corridors of Mercy Hospital, she approached Room 309 with trepidation. Was she prepared for what she would find? Why hadn't she asked Nicole about Chase's condition? Would he be conscious, would he have all his parts? She should have asked what it meant that she wasn't on Chase's list. Would he even want to see her?

She edged toward the open door. Even with his back to her and his shiny black hair reduced to dark stubble over his shaved head, she recognized the lean muscles of Chase's back and shoulders. The hospital bed was raised halfway, his legs were beneath the sheets, but he was shirtless and half turned toward an attractive young woman with smooth olive skin and raven black hair swept back into a low clip.

The woman held out a water glass to him, crooking the straw so it would be easy for Chase to drink from. She smiled at something he'd said. Her face was a perfect oval, drop-dead gorgeous. Her movements told Sam she had an easy familiarity with the man in the bed. That woman was exactly Chase's type. Somehow Sam knew that *she* was on Chase's magic list at FBI headquarters. That woman had been informed every step of the way about what was happening, and *she* had been the one to fly to Chase's side when he'd been injured, whereas Sam had been left to twist in the wind. Or rather, rot in a South American jail.

Sam was poised to walk away when the woman looked up and caught her eye. Then Chase turned, too. His expression of astonishment was quickly replaced by a broad grin.

"Summer!" He thrust out a hand in her direction.

She walked into the room, hesitating at the doorway. "I don't want to interrupt."

"You're alive!" Chase exclaimed. This had been his greeting to her on more than one occasion.

"No matter what," she said. She took his hand. "That's what we promised, right? Sorry to arrive a day late."

His chest was swathed in bandages. Red scratches like road rash decorated his right cheek, like he had slid facedown along a gravel road. He also seemed thinner than she remembered. It was unsettling to see him looking so damaged, but maybe part of the concentration camp effect was due to his lack of hair.

"I beat you back," he told her. "But *I'm* sorry to say, I've been a little out of it."

"He was unconscious for nearly forty hours," the woman added.

Chase ignored her, and ran a hand over the stubble on his head. "See?" he said to Sam. "It's already growing back."

"And the tattoo?" Sam asked, trying to keep the conversation light in front of the other woman.

He raised his right arm, wincing a little as he twisted toward her. Then he flexed his right bicep. Sure enough, there was a faint indigo *Don't Tread on Me* image there. He rubbed a finger over the snake's open mouth. "It's harder to get these things off than they say."

His eyes met hers, and they studied each other for a minute longer. His left ear was pierced, but now a small silver loop was threaded through it, not a dangling skull.

His right eyebrow rose, giving him a quizzical expression. "You really thought I was dead?"

He always had a knack for knowing exactly what she was thinking. A lump formed in her throat and choked off her speech. She nodded.

"Come here." He reeled her in with surprising strength, and she leaned toward him. He gave her a long bruising kiss, holding her tightly to him with his left arm. When he finally released her, he said, "You look like you just returned from the tropics, *querida*. You even taste like salt water."

Behind them, the other woman pointedly cleared her throat.

Chase gestured from one woman to the other. "Raven, this is the amazing, intrepid woman I've been telling you about—Summer Westin. And Summer, this is my sister, Raven."

"Call me Rae, please," the woman said.

Rae. Sister. No wonder she and Chase looked like a matched set. Sam smiled weakly. It was official now, she *was* socially retarded. She was an idiot when it came to relationships.

Chase squeezed her fingers. "I would have called you if I could."

Clearly, he hadn't been surfing the Internet or listening to his voice mail in recent days. There would be time enough for explanations later. She squeezed his hand in return. "I can see that you've been a little preoccupied, Chase."

"I'm getting out tomorrow morning." He gave her a sly look. "That cabin's still ours for the next three days."

She looked at him doubtfully. She was not a nurse, or even a natural caretaker.

"*You* could ski or snowshoe," he said. "I could cook."

And they would no doubt talk about their relationship. She never wanted to lose him again, and yet even the possibility of being permanently attached to any man was still a little terrifying. What would he expect from her? She wiggled her bare toes. "I need to go shopping first." Tad Wyatt's corporate credit card was in her jacket pocket.

"The airline lost your luggage?" Rae asked.

"Something like that," Sam said. "It might show up later." According to J.J., Schwartz had promised to ship back all the belongings she'd left in his vehicle.

"I've always wanted to see the Galápagos," Rae said. "Were Darwin's enchanted islands everything you expected?"

Chase winked at her. Obviously, he hadn't told his sister about Dan's death.

"The Galápagos Islands were everything I expected," she told them. "And so much more."

EPILOGUE

"IF I hadn't been a novice diver, maybe Dan would not have gone alone to that site." Sam mashed the phone against her ear to block the sound of the breeze sweeping in from the south. Out in Chuckanut Bay, an osprey snagged a fish, and Sam pointed to direct Chase's attention to the sight while continuing her conversation. "If I'd gone with him, maybe Dan would still be alive."

Back in Delaware, Elizabeth Kazaki sighed. "Or you both would have died." She hesitated briefly, and then added, "Thank you for the photos and the article."

Sam had sent Elizabeth enlargements of the best photos she'd taken of Dan on their trip. Dan smiling on the deck of *Coqueta* before their first dive, Dan in his dive gear underwater, holding out the sea cucumber. She'd also sent Elizabeth a copy of a photo and an article that had arrived from Charles Darwin Research Station in the Galápagos. The photo showed Eduardo Duarte onstage accepting a plaque from the director of the Park Service for his thirty years of service. The director of Darwin Station, Dr. Ignacio Guerrero, was on the platform, too, along with several unidentified dignitaries.

The banner behind them was in English—PROTECTING THE GALÁPAGOS FOREVER.

The article from the *Gazeta Galápagos*, translated by Chase, reported that the Chinese delegation had not shown up for the big celebration. They had withdrawn from discussions of a resort in Villamil, citing "concerns about potential impacts on the unique environment of the Galápagos."

Right now it seemed like a small victory, but at least her work with Dan and J.J. had accomplished NPF's immediate goal. The count was done, the word was out, and the resort would not be built anytime soon.

"It's your call, Elizabeth," Sam said into the phone. "I will name names if you want me to." *Out There* would welcome another post from Zing or even Wilderness Westin if it was salacious enough.

"Dan talked about Eduardo many times. I know he considered him one of the good guys. You believe him, that it was an accident?"

Sam recalled the tears in Eduardo's eyes as he had confessed, and her own eyes welled up. "I believe him."

"Then let's just remember that Dan died doing work he thought was important, in a place that he loved."

"I wish I were half as gracious as you are, Elizabeth."

"And I wish I were half the fighter you are, Sam. Let's both resolve to live joyful lives from here on."

Sam took a breath to steady her voice. "I'll do my best."

She ended the call and tucked the phone into her pocket. Chase wiped a tear from her cheek with a gentle finger, and curled his arm around her. She welcomed the warmth; the rock on which they sat was draining her body heat.

"You already did your best, *querida*," he said.

Sam doubted that. She could never go back to Ecuador, and she'd be looking over her shoulder for the likes of Carlos Santos for a long while. She'd never be able to sort out the good guys from the bad in the Galápagos. At least for the moment, she'd lost her desire to explore other countries.

She knew that Chase had psychological injuries, too, along with his physical ones. As usual, he hadn't told her the details, but the media reported that certain leaders of the New American Citizen Army were brutal thieves preying on illegal immigrants and that a corrupt Border Patrol officer had fed them information for a percentage of the profits.

Chase had done his job, but she knew all the deaths weighed heavily on his conscience. She laid a hand on his denim-covered thigh. "I'm sure you did your best, too, Chase."

He made a scoffing sound and turned away for a second, then handed her a plastic cup of red wine, and held up his own. "To happier days ahead."

"Amen to that." Sam clicked her cup against his. "Although I'm pretty happy right now."

"Thanks for letting me recuperate here."

She'd had him to herself for three weeks now. Well, not precisely all to herself, especially in this last week. At this moment, Maya was at her house helping Blake and his daughter Hannah cook chicken enchiladas and something called *empanadas*. Blake called it an "Adiós Family Fiesta." Spring break was over. Tomorrow the girls were leaving to go back to school, and Chase would board a plane and return to work.

Sam and Chase sipped wine and watched the sun sink behind the San Juan Islands to the west. On the small outcroppings near Chuckanut Island, basking harbor seals raised their tails and heads above the cold water to catch the last of the warm rays, curling their bodies into lopsided smiles. The incoming tide had risen to their bellies; the seals looked as if they rested on top of the shining plane of water. Sam wished she had a camera to record the sight.

"Ready to go?" Chase held out his hand for her empty cup. He stood up, pulled Sam to her feet. "You know, we should call this dinner party 'Hasta Luego,' not 'Adiós.' 'Hasta luego' means see you later, and we'll see each other again in six weeks, right?"

Sam had set a rendezvous date with Chase a month and a half from now, in Boise. It was halfway between her home and his, and Boise was the town where Chase had grown up. What were credit cards for, anyway?

"I'll be there," she said. "No matter what."

Don't miss any of the
Professor Gideon Oliver novels, with
"a likable, down-to-earth, cerebral sleuth"
(*Chicago Tribune*).

From Edgar® Award–winning author
Aaron Elkins

"Aaron Elkins is a gifted storyteller."
—*Midwest Book Review*

"Elkins has established himself
as a master craftsman."
—*Booklist*

SKULL DUGGERY

UNEASY RELATIONS

LITTLE TINY TEETH

UNNATURAL SELECTION

WHERE THERE'S A WILL

GOOD BLOOD